THIS MAN'S CHOICES

By Kathleen Whitney Rohr

THIS MAN'S CHOICES

This is a work of fiction. Names, characters, businesses, places, events, locales, and incidents are either the products of the author's imagination or used in a fictitious manner. Any resemblance to actual persons, living or dead, places or actual events is purely coincidental.

Printed in the United States of America. No part of this book may be used or reproduced in any manner whatsoever without written permission except in the case of brief quotations embodied in critical articles and reviews.

Library of Congress Cataloguing-in-Publication Data is available.

Dedication

to
Bill, who keeps me alive.
And Kristie, who makes life worth living.

Acknowledgements

I love the people who took part in writing and publishing THIS MAN'S CHOICES. They either understood the significance of the material to me or appreciated it independently.

My Antioch University Los Angeles teachers: Alistair McCartney, who told me this story needed to be a novel, worked with me on the first iteration, and who taught me to walk; Christine Hale, who worked with me two semesters on the second iteration and who taught me to run.

My UCLA teacher and writing goddess: Lynn Hightower, who gave me critiques of the plot and characters, offered significant suggestions for improvement, gave me her wisdom on publishing, and who taught me to fly.

I have three sisters, each awesome for different reasons. I lament my inability to acknowledge all three of them first. So, in no particular order of awesomeness: Kelly, who sat with me one day for hours and hours while I told her the entire plot. Jessica, who read everything I put in front of her through several iterations, told me the story's strengths, and listened to my complaints. Kris, who taught me the importance of nurturing one's family, especially if 1,200 miles and three time zones apart.

Lorenz, my great brother, who flew across the country to play the Theremin for me while I was in the hospital. How did he explain it to the TSA agent?

Kristie, my wonderful daughter who is generous with her time, gave me "atta girls" as I completed various steps to complete the manuscript, and was intent on getting the book published.

Susan, my friend from Antioch and the world, who believed in my characters and gave me unfaltering support. (She has become my book whisperer.)

Brian, who translated my vision of the cover, even though my vision seemed to change weekly.

Aileen, who shared her views of the characters and encouraged me to put the manuscript in front of other people.

Margaret, who gave me a doctor's perspective as it relates to child adoptions and the psychological impact of a man worshipping his father.

My Antioch writers' group: Tom, Lise, Rachael, Michelle, and Sara, who shredded my early version of Nichol, while listening to my defense of her then passive personality. They taught me she was actually a strong woman.

The Women's Fiction Writers Association community for help with various writing ills.

Carl, who listened patiently to my descriptions of the story during our many, long car rides.

Bill, who loves me and keeps me going even if he doesn't understand my writing.

Epigraph

Who are you going to believe, me or your own eyes?

Groucho Marx

There are two ways to be fooled.
One is to believe what isn't true;
the other is to refuse to believe what is true.

Søren Kierkegaard

Table of Contents

PART ONE

Chapter One

The best Royce could hope for was that Tamra would keep her clothes on. One evening in January of 1994 as he nervously waited at the curb outside Musso & Frank Grill for the limo that carried both his mother and Tamra, Royce imagined Tamra swearing, telling scandalous stories about her acting life, and putting her topless torso through the limousine's moon roof. He envisioned irreparable emotional harm to his shy, discreet mother by his spontaneous, passionate fiancée. Royce waited on the sidewalk with his hands in his suit pants pockets and looked down Hollywood Boulevard. He stood beneath the green billboard-sized sign that was mounted on the roof of the restaurant that announced in neon lights that the Musso & Frank Grill was the "oldest in Hollywood."

The stretch limousine, looking as though it had been dipped in liquid black patent leather, pulled up to the curb. Royce opened the door and drew back for a second because he was hit with a club atmosphere coming from inside the car: it reeked of alcohol. He had not even considered that Tamra might get drunk in front of his mother.

As he helped Tamra get out of the limo, she belched, a sound that was both joyous to release and painful to hear. He wasn't aware that a person as compact as Tamra could produce such a sound.

Royce said, "You have to hold it together tonight. Please."

And then he gave his mother his hand. She gracefully exited the limousine. She smelled like she had been drinking, too, but did not appear to be drunk. She was her customary elegant self in eggplant wool pants and silk sweater and gray flats. She wore a single strand of pearls that Royce's father had given to her.

"Don't give her a bad time, dear," his mother Evelyn said and giggled. "I'm the one who got her tipsy."

Tamra was straightening her conservative dress. The dress, navy blue, had a plain white collar, had actual sleeves, instead of spaghetti straps or no straps at all. The dress came to her knees. He had never seen her in such a dress. She was wearing dark shoes with a one-inch heel, not her six-inch gold sequin "fuck me" stilettos. The positively matronly outfit constricted her energy and looked like it would choke the life right out of her. Royce wondered if Tamra had borrowed clothes from her mother. Or someone's costume closet. She wore a single strand of pearls, identical to Evelyn's, that Royce had given to her. Tamra followed Royce and Evelyn into the restaurant.

Waiters in red jackets with black lapels glided from table to table. The polished wood-paneled walls held sconces, and the lights made everyone in the room look as though they had had facelifts. Beautifully dressed women laughed as if they were wind chimes. Men in custom suits with short haircuts dominated the room. George H. W. Bush country. There were also multi-millionaires with long hair wearing hippy uniforms from the Dolce & Gabbana Spring-Summer collection, preparing for Woodstock 1994. To get the waiters' attention, the entitled patrons simply raised their chins and turned their heads fifteen degrees. Tourists in the room could not compete.

As Royce and the women approached their designated table, his father Reginald stood and buttoned his suit jacket. He wore a gray bespoke suit made by a tailor in London who had been making his suits for forty years. Reginald was about the same height as Royce, about six feet tall, but he had a good sixty pounds on Royce. The good life had fed Reginald well. He had a full head of white hair, light brown Mediterranean complexion. If he had smiled, he would have been a handsome man. He greeted Evelyn with a chaste kiss and a warm, "Hello, Evie," but he was looking at Tamra.

Royce rested his hand on the small of his fiancée's back and gave her a tiny push. "Tamra, this is my father, Reginald Kallas."

Reginald extended his hand. "Welcome to my favorite restaurant. Good meat and potatoes."

Royce hoped his father would say *Congratulations on your engagement* or *I'm looking forward to your being my daughter-in-law* or *It is about time Royce married since he is almost forty.* Instead, Reginald said, "The au gratin potatoes are darned good."

Tamra was mute, as though she were an actor with no dialogue in this scene.

Royce settled his mother and Tamra into a red leather banquette. The men sat next to their respective partner. A waiter, who had been with the restaurant for thirty-three years, left a plate of sourdough bread on the white linen-covered table.

"Famous celebrities have eaten here, Tamra," Royce said. "The restaurant named some of the tables. This is Charlie Chaplin's booth." He unfolded his napkin.

"You mean Charlie Sheen, don't you?" Tamra giggled, a sweet sound he had come to love. She had no idea who Charlie Chaplin was, and he was likewise clueless about Charlie Sheen.

"Royce, are you going to get involved in the wedding planning?" Evelyn asked.

"We won't talk about that tonight," Reginald said. "Let us enjoy ourselves."

He put both elbows on the table and took a generous quaff of his martini, the restaurant's specialty, prepared by Manny. He looked over his shoulder, but the waiter was already on his way to the table. Reginald sat back against the banquette and motioned slightly with his head. He made a circular motion with his index finger indicating the rest of the group who, Royce knew were already at least one drink ahead of him. He ordered champagne for the table.

"Father, tell Tamra how great-grandfather started Kallas, Inc.," Royce said.

Reginald was off and running. Tamra appeared to listen. She nodded and smiled or assumed a serious visage. She had one wrist on the table and the other in her lap. Tamra was affectionate with Royce—but not *too* affectionate. She touched his arm when Reginald segued into a long story about nine-year-old Royce going to the office with him and reciting prices and market conditions for his ten favorite stocks to the Kallas, Inc. employees.

While Reginald gave Tamra the long version of his family's history, Royce's mind drifted. Three days after he proposed to Tamra, he had lunch with his father. Although Royce was the CEO of Kallas, Inc.-International, one of the companies under the Kallas, Inc. umbrella, he acted and sounded like a schoolboy in his father's presence. His general deference to Reginald was fueled by love and respect, and he was blinded with unexamined hero worship. He had been reluctant to tell his father he was marrying Tamra, with good reason.

"Do I know her people? Is she connected to anyone we know?" Reginald had asked.

"I do not imagine so," Royce had said.

"How extraordinary. You proposed to this person?

Yes, it is past time for you to marry, yet you tell me you are marrying a person of whom I have no knowledge."

Reginald became enraged that Royce hadn't discussed a prenup with Tamra. Royce assured his father that he and Tamra did not need a prenup.

"We are going to be married until we die, like you and Mother."

Royce was not naïve. He was vigilant against people who wanted to separate him from his money. But, simply, Tamra was not one of those people.

Reginald did not embark on a disquisition, but, rather, rationed his vitriolic imperatives as though he were being charged by the word: "I demand that you take care of this now."

And that was the end of that conversation.

As Reginald talked with another martini in front of him, Evelyn assumed a posture with her quiet, serene face like a wife whose politician husband was giving a stump speech she had heard a hundred and nineteen times or confessing to having had sex with his intern. Looking at his mother and Tamra sitting on the banquette, Royce noticed similarities between them: both blonde, green-eyed, both in the five two to five four range. And then he remembered that his mother was twenty years younger than his father, just like Tamra and he.

Tamra's steak sizzled in butter when presented to her. She looked traumatized. Royce knew she would fear gaining five pounds. She originally ordered a chiffonade salad for dinner, dressing on the side, but Reginald said, "When you come to Musso & Frank, you have to have a slab of beef," and so he ordered for the table. She declined bread, potatoes, and sautéed mushrooms. When Royce told Tamra where they were going to be having dinner, she said that if she was going to eat food that contained fat, she might as well eat directly from a can of Crisco. Royce himself usually watched his triglycerides, but not when his father ordered his dinner.

Reginald concluded his forty-five-minute discourse on Kallas, Inc. and the Kallas family. "Tamra," he said and paused for thirty seconds, a technique with which Royce was familiar. His father would wait a couple of beats until the person to whom he was speaking looked at him, their eyes locked onto his face.

Reginald's fork and knife were poised over his burned cow. Royce thought there was something primitive about the way his father devoured meat.

On cue, Tamra looked at Reginald—calmly, Royce noted.

"We have to get something settled tonight," Reginald said. He attacked his steak and gave Tamra a malevolent look meant to intimidate her.

God, here it comes, thought Royce. He looked at his prime rib, an island in a puddle of béarnaise sauce, and put his utensils down. He did not speak.

Reginald let his fork drift into his au gratin potatoes. As he lifted the fork to his mouth, thin strings of cheese clung to it and left entrails on his bottom lip. "You need to sign a prenuptial agreement," he said, chewing and drumming his hand on the table. Pause. "Or this wedding is not going forward," he said, swallowing.

Royce looked at his father in his peripheral vision. "Father, as you said, let us—"

Reginald held up one hand in Royce's general direction. Both men looked at Tamra. Evelyn shook her head. "Darling—" she started, looking at her husband.

"Of course, we're getting married, Reginald," Tamra said, as she leaned into the table and smiled at him. She took a bite of her strip steak, avoiding the slick butter that covered most of it. "Mmm."

Reginald sniffed the air and did not look pleased at the smell. "If you want to get married, that's up to you and Royce…except there will be a prenup in place before…the happy event," he said. His fork attacked the creamed spinach that resembled Louisiana swampland.

"Don't you think that's between me and Royce?" Tamra said, her voice cold steel, tempered with warm oil. She dabbed with her napkin at the corners of her mouth.

Short of leaving the table and taking Tamra with him, Royce did not know how to stop Reginald from eviscerating Tamra.

"I am not going to engage you in an argument, young lady." Reginald sucked his teeth. "This is not negotiable. I would demand a prenup for anyone Royce was marrying, but especially in this situation—"

"What do you mean, 'especially in this situation'?" Royce asked, looking up from his ratatouille.

"Darling," Evelyn said, reaching for Reginald's hand, "let's have this conversation on another night."

"Absolutely not, Evie. Royce, I mean that especially considering Tamra's financial situation."

"How would you know… Wait, did you do a background check on her?" Royce asked, a fist on each side of his plate.

"Of course I did. The detective I hired found that she has maxed out four credit cards, has defaulted on her student loan—and, by the way she dropped out of college in her first year—is three months behind on her car payments, and has several matters in collections." He looked hard at Royce.

Tamra smiled at Royce and squeezed his hand. Royce did not squeeze back.

"I cannot believe you, Father." Royce's voice rose. He was not using his indoor voice.

Their waiter scurried over to ask if they wanted something. Reginald waved him off.

"Reginald, in your investigation of me, I'm sure you learned I am an actress. It is an industry that is not well paying," Tamra said, her well-modulated voice taking on the character of a high school principal. "I have been out of high school for two years and have like worked hard, but…" Wet, salty tears leaked out her eyes. She put her napkin up to her face and her shoulders shook.

Royce looked around the restaurant to see if anyone was watching this tableau unfold. He shot his father menacing looks, he hoped. He did not like hearing the details of his father's inquiry into Tamra's financial condition.

"Now look, dear, you've made her cry," Evelyn said. She put an arm around Tamra, who leaned into her shoulder.

"There's no need for histrionics," Reginald said, a large piece of well-done rib eye speared on his fork, dripping with Musso & Frank steak sauce. "It's very simple. Sign the prenup and we give you the wedding of your dreams, just what every girl wants. Right? I am aware your parents cannot afford a big wedding."

"What, you had them investigated, too?" Royce said. He had given up on his dinner and laid his napkin on the table.

Tamra straightened her spine, which pushed her small breasts against the fabric of her dress. Royce thought it was polyester. Her face was surprisingly composed and she got a bead on Reginald. "Me and my parents like don't have a lot of money, that's true." She folded her hands in her lap.

"If you think you're going to marry my son for his money, you better finish your steak and leave." Reginald pointed his index finger at Tamra's face.

Royce needed an exit strategy.

"You're correct. I am going to marry your son because of his money."

Royce was stunned. He looked at her, but she was focusing on his father like a heat-seeking missile. He thought Tamra loved him. She said she did. He felt sick. The rest of the room faded to a blur, and it was just the four of them, twirling around the room like the teacup ride at Disneyland. How could he have been so wrong about her? What his father did was reprehensible, but the litany of Tamra's financial transgressions shocked him. He concluded she had three possible choices to respond to Reginald: one, she was marrying him because she loved him or, two, she was after him for his money. Or the third possibility: telling his father to fuck off. Apparently, she had chosen option two.

In the six months since they had met, they had never discussed her finances. He assumed she did not have much money since she was living at home with her parents and drove a 1987 Ford Escort. She seemed to enjoy the perks of his money: driving Royce's Porsche and Maserati, spending time in his houses in Beverly Hills, Telluride, and Rancho Mirage and apartment in Manhattan, vacationing on his yacht which was docked in Marina del Rey, using the company jet, having private parties at the Ahmanson. But to marry him because she wanted his money? Of course, women in Royce's past had been seduced by his money, but he had thought Tamra was different.

He thought she was only taken with his Maserati

because it was fast, not because it was expensive. He thought that having Tamra as his wife gave him a lock on happiness. And the sex was amazing, too. He wondered whether he should leave her there at the table to fend for herself. No, that would be rude.

"Your son is who he is because of his money," Tamra said. She sat up tall in the banquette, leaned in and trained those green eyes like hundred dollar bills on Reginald's mouth, which was changing from a broad grin to a grimace. "He is intelligent, strong, confident, and brave because of his money. He is protective of me. Does he need money to be all those things? No, but take the money away from him, and he would be a different Royce. I love this Royce."

A full minute passed. Reginald nodded, pursed his lips, and dropped his fork onto his empty plate. He smiled, a small tight smile as though his lips had been sewn together with concertina wire. He sniffed the air again and looked in the direction of their hovering waiter.

"We're going to have dessert," he said to the waiter. To his dinner companions, he said, "One of my favorite desserts here is boysenberry pie. I sometimes get the little seeds stuck in my teeth, but it's worth it, the pie is that good. The chocolate cake with ice cream and chocolate sauce is good, too, but tonight I want you to have the boysenberry pie."

The waiter rushed off to bring them all pieces of pie. Royce disliked boysenberries. He looked in the general direction of Tamra and his father. He did not know what to say or do. There were words on the roof of his mouth, but he couldn't coax them out. Was his father yielding that round to Tamra? Royce had never seen his father capitulate on an issue, a point, an argument. Yet it seemed that he had found Tamra's answer acceptable.

Tamra giggled, like tinkling glass. "Boysenberry is like my favorite. I love boysenberry jam, boysenberry pie, boysenberry ice cream."

"I did not know that," Royce said, cautious, not feeling on firm ground with either his father or fiancée.

"I don't know. I guess it never came up, you know. For my birthday I get boysenberry pie instead of cake."

"Then we shall make sure you get one for your birthday," Evelyn said, taking Tamra's hand in hers.

The tension at the table was cut by a small piece of fruit.

They ate their desserts as though nothing untoward had happened, although Royce's pie stuck in his throat as though he had swallowed the champagne cork, and Evelyn gave him and Tamra apologetic looks.

When they left the restaurant, Evelyn hugged her. "Call me to set up a time to plan the wedding, dear. We'll have a grand time. Invite your mother, of course."

Reginald had a toothpick in his mouth. He waggled his index finger in her general direction until Evelyn grabbed it, kissed it, and encircled it with both of her hands.

"I'm glad you got to eat in a darned fine restaurant," Reginald said. He shook hands with Tamra and Royce and turned toward Evelyn who was being assisted into the limo by the driver.

After Tamra and Royce got into his car, he leaned over and gave her a kiss, the console of his Maserati blocking an embrace. "The boysenberry pie was a nice touch. Thank you."

"I really like the stuff," Tamra said.

He took her hands in his. "How did you have the presence of mind to talk to him like that? By the way, thank you for the nice compliments."

"My improvisation classes have taught me to be prepared, because you like never know what you're going to get hit with. But, shit, I meant what I said. You're like an amazing man, and I love you, you know." She put her hands on his shoulders.

"The private detective's report. That was the only time you cried. My father can make grown men cry."

"I hadn't used some of the crying techniques our teacher told us about, so thought I'd like try out a couple. Did I do a good job?"

"Tamra, I am sorry I have to ask you. Was my father telling the truth about your finances? Are you delinquent on your accounts?"

"Oh, my God. Do we have to talk about that?" she said, as she sat back against the passenger window, sniffled, covered her face with her hands, and began sobbing.

"Oh, I have upset you. I am so sorry." Royce reached his arms toward her.

"See, like that," she said and smiled, wiggling in her seat as though she were sitting on a vibrator.

Her cheeks were wet. He thought she was very clever and smart. But he did not for a minute think that the prenup issue had been settled.

Chapter Two

When Royce originally proposed to Tamra on Halloween 1993 at Denny's, Tamra tried to hide her disappointment. After he gave her an eight-carat Asscher cut diamond with ninety-six tiny diamonds going completely around the platinum band valued at $519,000 (She later had it appraised. Of course she did), she had asked him if she could have another gift. He asked her if she wanted matching earrings—which she admitted later would have been divine—but what she really wanted was for him to propose somewhere exotic.

"Why did you propose here?" she had asked. She had hoped the tone of her voice did not give away her frustration. She had fantasized about his taking her to Paris or Hawaii for the proposal, although she would have accepted a proposal at the No. 3 pump of the Gas-'n-Go.

"Anyone can propose at the top of the Eiffel Tower," he said.

Royce was troubled. He could not get his father's Musso & Frank intervention out of his head, and he had promised Tamra he would take her to the Seychelles to re-propose.

On Valentine's Day 1994 they took one of the Kallas, Inc. jets to Desroches Island. He was preoccupied on the flights. He did not watch movies with Tamra and did not hug her close to his chest as had become their custom. He decided to discuss the prenup while in the Seychelles, and he hoped the romantic atmosphere would prevent a bad reaction.

They came to about noon local time the day after

their arrival in their 5,000 square-foot villa, complete with butler, chef, massage therapist, and housekeepers. He slid the wood and glass doors into the walls, so they had a fifty-foot wide view of the Indian Ocean. They enjoyed the frangipani and salt smell of the sea, the view of the private gardens, tropical beach, and the sounds of the waves. As Royce fed his caffeine habit and surreptitiously checked his computer to see if there were any emergencies at the office, Tamra went swimming in their private pool. He went outside to join her and found her standing in the shallow end pouring water over her bare breasts.

"Hi, sweetie," she said in her fake Marilyn Monroe whisper.

As she turned onto her back and floated with her head back and arms stretched out, her breasts and cleft of Venus rose above the water line. Satisfied that the privacy of the pool was sheltered by bougainvillea and bamboo, he dove in.

After Tamra seduced Royce in the pool, she slithered into a caftan. They wandered out to the beach and walked through the surf, Tamra holding the bottom of the caftan so it did not get wet. He did not say much. They held hands and walked back to the villa where trays of cheeses, regional fruits, shrimp, lobster, and crab sat on the rattan table by the doorless vista. A bottle of champagne accompanied the food.

Royce read the card. "They think we are on our honeymoon. Funny."

"Maybe we should just get married here."

"Uh-huh."

"Really?" She actually squealed.

He shook his head no.

They sat down at the table and grazed.

"Honey, we need to talk about something serious,"

he said, making a sandwich of a piece of crab and two shrimps. His heart felt sweaty.

"Anything, sweetie," she said, her eyes on her ring.

"You know I have a bit of money."

"A bit. That's like saying Bill Clinton likes girls." She ate a piece of cheese, so un-Tamra like.

"It is not just my father who wants me to have you sign the prenup. The trustees of my trust requested that I have you sign—"

He let the words settle amid the bubbles of the champagne. They chewed for a moment.

"You're talking about the prenup. Now? Here? You're kidding, right? Are we back to that boring topic? How can I be a good wife to you if I'm not a part of your whole life?" She took her eyes off the ring, stood up, stomped her feet, held her arms out toward him. Her lower lip stuck out and quivered. "I love you." Her voice changed, plaintive and tender.

He put down his flute and paused. He did not want to be swayed by her coquettish demeanor. "Of course you will be a part of my entire life. We will make a life together. I will tell you about my business, to the extent you are interested."

"Royce, baby. You know we're going to be married like forever. It won't be an issue."

"The prenup protects my assets," he said.

"We're going to live in a big house and have children," she said. "I'm going to wait on you hand and foot." She dangled a piece of lobster as though it were a metronome, marking each of her words.

"They are standard practice in families that have substantial…funds."

"I'll have as many babies as you want. I'll be a good

—

wife and mother. Let's not do this." She sat down, put her elbows on the table. "If a problem comes up later, then I'll sign it. But not now, sweetie." She paused. "You know, it might be right for me to sign it if I know what money we have."

He shook his head. "With a prenup, any assets—any money—that I have before the day we marry will be my property, not our property." His shoulders were hunched. His benignant comportment belied the formidable tone of his voice and his words.

She dropped the lobster onto the platter, licked her fingers, stared at him and got up onto her rattan chair and then onto the table in the matter of seconds. Royce swiftly moved the platter away from her feet with red-polished toenails. She stood with her back to the beach. In rhythm to the sea she began to gyrate, gyrate a little faster, then slower, while she slid the fabric of her caftan up to her calves. She hummed something that sounded like "Bali Hai."

Royce looked at her, both irritated and intrigued. She slid the caftan up to her knees. She did not hurry with the unveiling. Her hips moved a little faster, but not too fast, and the caftan was raised to her thighs. Royce sat in his chair with a shrimp up to his mouth, but he was not eating it. Tamra had his attention and his rising interest. The caftan inched up past her bikini wax job.

He gulped, unable to focus for a few seconds. "Tamra, Tamra, stop! The entire wall is exposed! The staff is here!" He dropped the shrimp on the table and stretched his arms out toward her, but she moved back on the table. He lowered his gravelly voice. "You are exposed."

Up to the diamond-clad belly button. Royce jumped up, knocked over his chair, reached over, and pulled so hard on the bottom of Tamra's caftan that she lost her footing. She let out a little yelp as though she had discovered a Chanel bag at a vintage store. She jumped into his arms.

She kept him occupied, so the prenup was not mentioned again that day or any other day of their vacation.

On the plane trip home, Royce pondered how he would get the prenup signed. He wondered how long he had before his father jumped on him—again.

Chapter Three

When Tamra and Royce returned to California, she told her parents, who were eating breakfast, sitting on bar stools at the kitchen island, that he had proposed. Belle and Laramie knew at some level that Royce would propose, and they were armed for a Come to Jesus talk with Tamra. The sun-filled latticed patio created patterns of morning light on the kitchen floor. The Wooden home was a yellow ranch-style house that sprawled across a neat lawn. The yellow theme carried into the kitchen on the walls, on the wrought iron chair seats. Two bar stools nuzzled up to the island.

"Where's Sophie?" Tamra said.

Tamra had told Royce that back when she was in boarding school in Arizona, her parents had taken Sophie in as a foster child. "I was an only child. My mother expected me to be perfect. She was always pushing me to do well in math and science, because those had been her favorite classes in school. Well, they weren't my favorites, and my mother was always disappointed in me. Like when I brought home my report cards, even if I got good grades in English or dance, she acted like *she* had failed. Then she would get really pissy, like for the next week she would yell at me and constantly ask me about my homework. My dad had to get her off my back. When I was fifteen my parents, like my mother really, unloaded me in boarding school. Then my parents got Sophie from foster care."

Later they adopted her. Tamra believed that Sophie was the daughter Tamra's mother had always wanted. Tamra and Belle had an ongoing contentious relationship because Belle wanted Tamra to be like Sophie, and Tamra wanted Belle to be like a '50s TV mom. The only thing Tamra and

Belle shared was their appearance, although Belle was taller.

"A sleepover at Janine's house," Belle said and turned around on her stool to look at Tamra. And coming to the subject she wanted to discuss, said, "Royce is twenty years older than you."

"He's nineteen years older. Yeah, so?" Tamra stood by the sink, leaning against the tan Corian counter.

The kitchen smelled like grease that is exclusive to mornings.

"So," Belle said. "He's more mature than you are. He clearly has seen more of the world than you have."

"Well, he can take me places and teach me about them, like he just took me to the Seychelles."

"Are you sure about this, Tamra Belle?" her father Laramie asked. "Royce is a serious, responsible man. He lives differently than you." He finished his eggs and sausage. He looked like he was debating whether to cook more food or continue with the current discussion.

Tamra looked at her father, who was tall, about six three. He had fair hair, not quite covering his scalp, and a full beard, beginning to gray. He was usually smiling, except when he refereed Belle and Tamra's brawls. His disappointment was hidden by his facial hair.

"You're not going to take advantage of him, are you?" asked Belle, who knew Tamra's history in more detail than Tamra liked.

"No, I'm not," Tamra said with finality.

Tamra was furious. She felt as though both her parents and Royce's father were sticking their noses in where they didn't belong. Tamra wanted to be with Royce, but on her terms.

She remembered her initial contact with Royce, which was not propitious for a future together. She met him after he put her in the hospital. On a hot Saturday night in June 1993 she walked into the club Gramercy Welders Society to have a drink. The club was packed. Music pulsed against the walls, floor and ceiling, causing permanent hearing loss for thirty percent of the yuppies in the club. Steam from alcohol and sexual juices rose from the dance floor.

Royce was sitting on a stool at the bar, with his back straight, his long legs clad in black wool slacks, his black Italian loafers on a rung of the stool. His broad shoulders and muscled arms could be seen through a wool salt and pepper jacket. He was overdressed for the club, but in an outstanding way. He looked like he had a great tan.

Confronting Tamra the morning she gave them the happy news of her engagement, her parents pressed on.

"Have you told him about boarding school?" Belle said. She threw her breakfast in the garbage disposal and turned it and the water on. The disposal pulverized the food, like a good juicer.

"Sure," Tamra hollered over the sound.

"Did you give him a sanitized version or the truth?" Laramie asked. He watched his wife throw away two eggs sunny side up with four small sausages. "Honey, why did you throw those perfectly good eggs and sausages away? I would have eaten them. Well, Tamra?"

"God, it's so tough to talk. You've got the disposal running, and you're talking about food. Can we just get through this, please, so I don't have to have this conversation again?" She paused until they were both looking at her. "I just told him I went to boarding school. What do you want me to do? I am going to marry him. Don't screw this up for me." She poured herself a cup of coffee and put the cup down on the counter so energetically that coffee spilled onto her hand. "Oh, shit."

"Tamra, listen to us. You have to tell him about boarding school, about the baby, everything," Belle said.

A shadow passed over Tamra's face. "No. And don't you guys tell him. I can't talk about this anymore. I wanted to tell you Royce asked me to marry him while we were on a fantastic vacation, and all you want to do is dump on me." She grabbed her keys and purse and ran out the front door.

Chapter Four

Reginald called Royce into his office one day at 3:00 p.m., two weeks after Royce re-proposed to Tamra in the Seychelles. Sitting at a conference room table roughly the size of a landing strip and made with eight kinds of wood, were the trustees of the Kallas Family Trust and the Royce Hamilton Kallas Trust and a handful of suits with whom he was not familiar.

"What is this about?" Royce asked.

Reginald was standing in front of his chair at the head of the table. He reached down to the bowl of Hershey's Miniatures that always rested by his left hand. He tossed one back on his tongue, balled up the yellow and red foil between his thumb and index finger and dropped it on the table.

"You have refused to have the girl sign a prenup, and we're going to make sure it happens," Reginald said, as he crunched on a Mr. Goodbar, which resulted in him spitting tiny peanut pieces on the gentleman seated to his left. "These gentlemen—and ladies—are experts in preparing prenups and trust provisions for people with substantial assets. They will educate you on the reasons why going forward with this wedding without a prenuptial agreement is financial suicide."

Royce listened to his father make roughly the same comments as at the Musso & Frank dinner and asked no questions. Then, "Was Mother hesitant to sign your prenup?" he asked.

Silence. All eyes, except Royce's, looked down at the table, rather than on Reginald.

"That is an impudent question and hardly appropriate for this forum," Reginald said.

Royce leaned forward in his chair, putting his arms

on the table. "Did Mother sign a prenup?"

"Circumstances were different," Reginald said, popping two chocolate miniatures in his mouth.

"Why? You had family money."

"It is irrelevant to the present time." Reginald smiled a small, insincere smile.

"I think it is relevant. You are asking me, demanding me to have a prenup, but, apparently you do not have one with Mother." He looked at the beginning of the sunset that glowed yellow, pink, and orange in the floor to ceiling windows that looked onto Wilshire Boulevard.

"When I met your Mother she was a model woman. Perfection."

Several men nodded.

"And Tamra is not, in your view," Royce said. "You have only met her once, where you spent the evening pontificating about Kallas, Inc. and attacking her character." He wanted to ask about the qualities that deemed his mother perfect, but did not. In other circumstances, he would have agreed that his mother was the consummate wife and mother.

"Son, this is outrageous." Reginald pounded his fist on the table top, causing his pen to fall on the floor. Royce was waiting for him to pound his shoe on the table like a Soviet premier from decades past.

Royce got up and paced the width of the room, his hands behind his back. He thought about his father blindsiding Tamra at dinner, calling this meeting, and now he learned his father and mother did not have a prenup.

On Royce's eighth birthday, after friends handpicked by his parents based on their pedigree played the games, after the guests ate the hamburgers prepared by the Kallases' chef, and after Royce blew out the candles, his father directed Royce—who was on a sugar high—to his study. Reginald gave him the first installment of lectures engineered to teach Royce about his position in the cosmos. By the age of eight, Royce believed every word from his father's mouth was written on a tablet or uttered from a burning bush. Royce was a nimbus to Reginald's authority and power.

Royce was not a stupid man. He knew he was embarking on a cliché: wealthy man marries much younger woman, one who is an actress wannabe and could likely be after his money and who uses sex to get what she wants from him. He understood all the arguments against such a union. He had dated women who, he quickly discerned, wanted to get into his wallet. It was a familiar scenario. But he knew that his relationship with Tamra did not fit into the stereotype. Theirs would be a successful marriage. However, other than saying she was feisty, he could not articulate reasons for his conclusion. Was Tamra someone he made up?

No, she wasn't. He remembered seeing her at Gramercy Welders Society the previous summer.

He had just sat down at the bar and ordered a Maker's Mark and basket of decontaminated peanuts from Jerry the bartender.

Jerry yelled to be heard. "Hey, how's it hangin', dude?"

Royce hated slang and the epidemic use of contractions. "I am fine, good. I have been working." Aromatic perfume, hairspray, lust, and bullshit blended into a gas that filled his nostrils, the rising atmospheric pressure exciting his endorphins.

—

Facing away from the crush of bodies, he watched the scene in the mirrored wall behind the bar. A 1970s era disco ball lit the space. Patterns of blue, pink, and yellow light flew around the otherwise dark room like butterflies on magic mushrooms. On the dance floor pairs, threesomes, and singles bobbed, weaved, clomped, and jumped, looking like a syncopated Maori dance of welcome.

Looking in the mirror through the shelves of liquor, Royce saw the reflection of a girl with custard yellow hair, and he swiveled on his stool and looked at her. She wore a silver mini sheath and six-inch gold sequined "fuck me" heels. What sort of girl looked like that? Certainly not lady material for Royce. The women he dated did not wear hooker heels; they wore thousand-dollar Jimmy Choo's. And beneath that glittery dress, if she raised her arms, he could probably determine the carat weight of the diamond she wore in her belly button. If it was a diamond. The girl looked like someone he knew, but he could not figure out whom she resembled. She was cute, like a Labrador puppy. He scowled and concentrated. Who did she look like?

"Whatcha up to?" Jerry asked.

"I went deep sea fishing in Costa Rica recently," he said. He described the country's beaches and nightlife and then turned sideways on the stool.

"I caught a sailfish. It was this big."

Lost in the memories of fishing, Royce threw his arms wide to show the size of the fish—and truth be told the fish wasn't *that* big—and whacked the girl with the custard yellow hair with the back of his right hand. The impact was so energetic and powerful that she fell to the floor and hit her head. He had coldcocked her. Clubgoers gasped as if they had learned a tab for the house was going on their credit cards. The crowd formed a circle around her inert body. She lay before them, a toy on the twenty-sixth of December.

The music stopped and the lights came up.

Paramedics arrived a few minutes later with a backboard and gurney. Royce watched them attach a blood pressure cuff and cervical collar, start an IV and check the girl's pupils. While he knew it was an accident, he also knew he was responsible. He thought of all possible outcomes. Like a boy scout, he was always prepared. His father would respond negatively if he learned what had happened. How would the incident impact Kallas, Inc.? He watched the paramedics put her on the backboard, and he winced in sympathy.

Jerry walked through the crowd and stood next to Royce. He gave one of the paramedics a driver's license he had found in the girl's purse.

"What is her name, Jerry? I am going to the hospital," Royce said.

"Tamra Wooden." Jerry handed Royce Tamra's glittery silver clutch, small, yet too big to fit in his pocket. Royce held the clutch like a football, perhaps subconsciously attempting to render the spangled object masculine.

Royce's head got back in his present state of affairs, sitting in the conference room with a cenacle of attorneys citing case law and discussing prenup provisions that benefitted Royce and, secondarily, Tamra. Reginald stopped talking. He continued to shove candy in his mouth. The other participants spent eight hours using their best persuasive skills to convince Royce of the proper course of action. At some point Royce perceived his only function at the meeting was to say "yes, sir," acquiesce to the provisions of the prenup, and drink the Kool-Aid. Which he did. At 11:03 p.m.

—

29

Chapter Five

A week after Reginald's ambush at the office, the affianced couple drove to Royce's house and went into the great room.

"I thought we were going to the movies. I want to see *True Romance*. It's like us." She twirled around the room, thoroughly enjoying herself.

"I do not think a Quentin Tarentino movie is a romantic comedy. Maybe we can go to the movies later. I have to settle with you about the prenup and—"

"Not again, Royce. Come on, sweetie. Let's go to the movies."

"I plan to entice you with this." He held a Tiffany box in his hand.

"Oh, sweetie. Let me see." She stood in front of him and grabbed for the box.

"Not so fast," he said, he hoped playfully, as he put his hand that held the box behind his back. "Let us get this prenup settled, and then I will give you the box."

"You are such a sweetie. I love you."

"I love you, too. Here are the proposed provisions." He attempted to hand her a document as thick as a phonebook for a large metropolitan city.

She stood with her hands on her hips. "We're going to have such a good life together."

"Please read these pages. Here, sit down." He patted his tan leather couch, as soft as a puppy's belly.

She started to sit on his lap facing him.

"No, no, you do not. Sit down," he said with authority, impatience, and regret. "Okay, simmer down."

She sat next to him, put her hands in her lap, and looked up at him. He handed the document to her. She sighed and looked at him as though she knew she was in control, which tactic had always worked well for her.

"You have to read these proposed provisions. You need to retain an attorney."

For the first time she looked at the pages. Six hundred and forty-seven pages, of which 112 were definitions.

"You want me to read this whole thing?" He saw a flash of anger accelerate and then quickly diffuse as though she were braking the Maserati from ninety to zero.

He stood up and paced the length of the great room with his arms crossed over his chest. He looked out the French doors to the patio. The lights to the pool and yard, on timers, were off. All he saw was black. He realized there were shades of black.

"You don't need to be mean." She began to read and stopped at the second page. "You know I don't understand 'whereas' and 'supra' and 'heretofore' and 'aforementioned.' How am I supposed to read this?"

"You need an attorney." He stood before her, arms still crossed.

"Tonight? Now?" She burst into tears. If one approach didn't work, she tried another. She was silent for about five minutes as she breezed through the pages. She held her arms out to hand them back to him.

"Keep it, dammit," He said. "And, no, I do not expect you to find an attorney tonight."

"Do you see what this is doing to us? You're going to have an attorney, and I'll have an attorney. How horrible!"

"Do not interrupt me again," Royce said. "Here, let me have those pages." He held out his hand.

She gave him the document and smiled as though she had won a prize. "Now do I get my present?" she asked as she sat on the couch on her knees. An automatic smile, no feeling behind it. He knew that smile.

"No, I am going to read parts of this document to you, without the definitions, and explain words you do not understand. Then you are going to get an attorney and have him or her discuss the provisions with you so you understand them." He began to read. He spoke in his daytime voice, as though to a prospective client. He emphasized particular phrases and sentences: 'The Party of the First Part'—that is I—" He read legalese drafted by four transactional attorneys, "'…Royce Hamilton Kallas Trust and all money it generates is separate property of the Party of the First Part.'"

She gasped and put her hand to her mouth.

He plunged ahead and did not look at her. "'Any acquisitions made by the Royce Hamilton Kallas Trust are separate property of the trust. Any inheritance I receive from any source is my separate property. Any income or other financial benefits I receive or is accrued before the marriage is my separate property. Any houses, apartments, boats, vehicles…'" He droned on and on. "'…are *my* separate property. Upon *my* death, the Party of the Second Part—that is you—will receive $50,000,000 with the remainder to any children born of the marriage and/or adopted by the Party of the First Part and the Party of the Second Part." He hurried over the last bit because he was embarrassed by the relatively small amount she would inherit upon his death. Fifty million might sound like a substantial amount of money, but not when talking about Royce Kallas's wealth.

"That's it?" she asked.

"I skipped over the 'wherefores' you did not want to hear. And you can tell that this goes into excruciating detail." He made a movement as though he were dropping the document, trying to bring levity into the room.

—

"That's really it? I live in poverty."

"You will hardly live in poverty. What a strange comment to make," Royce said.

She stood up, walked to the bar, poured herself a twelve-ounce tumbler of scotch and walked back to the couch.

"That seems a bit excessive," he said.

"I think so, too, but apparently you don't."

"That much liquor is not a good idea while we discuss this."

She put the glass to her mouth, winked, while she took a hearty gulp. "I get nothing. Nothing."

"We need to keep clear heads tonight," he said looking up at her.

She threw the contents of the glass at him. "Here, this is probably your separate property."

He jumped up from the couch, looked down at his drenched shirt and jeans and then at the couch. "Oh, shit." He ran to the kitchen, grabbed several towels out of a drawer and ran back to the couch, which he wiped down, sopping up the amber liquid. "Oh shit, oh shit."

"It's nice to see you care about something. Was that paid for by the trust? Is it your separate property? Of course it is. It exists now before our wedding. It ain't mine, folks. I don't even get this much." She dipped an index finger in the remaining puddle of scotch in a couch cushion and drew a line dividing the couch in two.

"Stop it. You are completely out of control." He wiped away the line.

"What happened to my present?"

"It is magic, sleight of hand."

"Just like that fucking document."

"Tamra! That is outrageous."

"Oh, fuck you and your opinions about how I talk."

He finished cleaning the couch and went into the pantry for leather conditioner. Her imprecations stunned him. He returned and wiped the conditioner into the leather.

"I have an idea." His voice was shaky. "I will talk to my attorney and add more provisions to the prenup that will benefit you. You will discuss them with the attorney you are going to get."

While he talked, she lay on the loveseat and took a small pink bottle out of her purse. "What kind of benefits?" She fit into the loveseat like a coffin.

"Money for each year of marriage and every child we have. Do you understand?" He lifted his head from the couch, his exegesis complete, and looked over at her.

Tamra blew pink bubbles through a soapy wand. "Can I have my present now?" Her eyes tested him, and she sucked in her bottom lip.

"Now it is soap bubbles on the leather?"

Chapter Six

For the month that followed the winner-take-all event that occurred at Royce's house, the couple did not address the prenup. The word was not spoken between them. They talked about any issues raised by the prenup only through their respective attorneys, pretty much like Tamra said it would happen, except Royce had an entire stable of attorneys representing him. Time together was awkward for Royce, while Tamra seemed to be in total control. She rationed sex. Royce rationalized that she was stressed planning the wedding, which now might not go forward. Royce's friend Steven, the only person he told about the difficulty in getting Tamra on board, said the odds were three to one that Tamra would not sign the document.

A month after the drink-throwing, Royce and Tamra met at Royce's attorney John Phelan's office in a conference room with plush carpeting, plank and glass walls, and honey-colored deep leather chairs. Royce had chosen Phelan because he seemed to be a confident, objective, forthright, sympathetic man, and he and his wife had been married twenty-three years. With a prenup. Phelan had successfully worked with Tamra's attorney to include provisions each of the parties could accept.

Royce arrived at Phelan's office before Tamra. He wore a $2,500 bespoke suit from Henry Herbert in England, a $400 Boss tie, and $1,800 Martin Dinoman leather crocodile shoes, clothes that were only labels until he dressed in them and gave them substance. The air-conditioned room felt heavy to him. Although he was not prone to sweating except when he was working out, he felt sweat on the back of his neck as he stood in the conference

---

room, waiting for Tamra to arrive. He reached his hand to his neck. Nothing. He had emotional sweat. He heard sounds of employees making money for the firm like bookies taking bets.

Royce watched Tamra walk into the conference room. She had dressed in the smart Chanel suit, one he bought for her on his mother's recommendation. Jacket, pencil skirt, silk blouse, muted colors of mint and baby blue. However, he noted, she apparently could not resist wearing her "fuck me" stilettos. He looked at her body, her face for hints as to whether she would sign the prenup and how much of a conflagration would accompany the signing. She smiled at the attorneys as she shook their hands. She looked at Royce in a coquettish, shy manner. As she walked to the table, her head was bowed and her shoulders were hunched. That posture was unlike her because she generally walked lifting her chest to show off her small, perky breasts. He wondered if she was playing the victim role.

Royce noted his own body, every muscle coiled like a burlap bag of hungry cobras. He mitigated the tension when he took in a breath. He held his hands quietly on the table. They did not reflect the emotions he felt. He wanted to pound the table and demand that she sign the document. He willed her not to make a spectacle, specifically not to take her clothes off.

Phelan passed a copy of the contract to Tamra's attorney, Vi Pelant. Pelant flipped to specific pages and nodded her head, having already spent the entire past month doing nothing but negotiating the Kallas prenup to benefit Tamra and taking pee breaks. Tamra had her own copy; she knew the contents of the contract and turned to the pages with financial incentives. Royce had agreed Tamra would receive $5,000,000 for each child born of the marriage that survived twelve months (taking into account adopted children). She would receive $2,000,000 at the end of each year of marriage, unless circumstances reflected her abandonment of the marriage, failure to parent the children of the marriage or her involvement in extra-marital relations. After twenty years of marriage, Tamra would receive a one-time gift of $25,000,000. If the marriage terminated, except due to the listed exceptions, Tamra would receive the Beverly Hills house and a stock portfolio with a 1994 value of $25,000,000. Royce watched her read the pages as though she were reading a *People* magazine article about herself.

A notary slipped into the room. Phelan motioned for her to witness Royce's signature on the original prenup. Then Phelan slid the blue-covered document toward Pelant—its heft gave it the appearance of a barge as it slowly moved across the table—who flipped through it and gave it to Tamra. She rubbed her fingers over the cover made of coarse blue paper. She looked at the pages with the incentives one more time. She looked as though she was reading the provisions to memorize them. Perhaps she was.

While Tamra added up all the zeros, Royce thought about the night they met in the emergency room of St. John's Medical Center in Santa Monica after he smacked her at Gramercy Welders Society. He told the receptionist he was Tamra's brother, and a nurse's aide took him to her examination bay. "Your brother's here," the aide said to Tamra.

Royce stopped a few inches into the cubicle. Tamra resembled a child attacked by kitchen appliances. His stomach flipped like a stack of blueberry pancakes. Her arms lay at her sides. She wore a blue blood pressure cuff on her left arm and an IV on her left hand. A plastic thing attached itself to the index finger of her right hand. She wore a cervical collar. Blue ice bags covered her eyes and the top of her head. While Royce was tenacious in business and urbane in social settings, he felt awkward standing in an emergency room close to her, a girl he did not know.

"I know I got hit on the head, but I'm pretty sure I don't have a brother. Who are you?" she said, lifting one of the ice bags and peeking out at him.

"I'm the man who hit you. Accidently," he said.

"Look at your handiwork," she said.

"You made a pun," he said.

"Yeah, well—" Tamra took the ice bags off her head and eyes.

She was bruised, her forehead, eyes and cheekbones a Christmas ham. Under her eyes, blotchy mascara. She had a cut on the bridge of her nose. He replayed the fish scene and then looked at his right hand. His Harvard ring. Skin was embedded under a claw that held a black onyx stone in place. The girl's flesh. Red lipstick was smeared on her chin. The overall effect was of a clown left out in the rain.

"Like what you see? Wanna go for the whole face next time?"

Tamra, Royce realized, did not know how she looked. He already had injured her entire face.

Tamra grimaced. "I'm getting a major league headache, and I didn't drink that much." She put her hands to her head. She paused for a moment. "Why are you holding my purse?" She started to giggle, then gasped. "Oh my God, there's an echo in my head."

Royce cleared his throat and put the clutch softly onto the foot of her bed, as though he were handling a live fashion forward grenade. "Again, I am sorry," he said. "I will pay for your hospitalization. And for any time you miss from work." He attempted to regain his footing as if he were a window washer on the sixty-seventh floor.

She tried to laugh, but then groaned. She whacked the bed with her hand. "Oh, my head."

"I will leave. May I come back to see you? Tomorrow?" He rationalized that he was responsible for her injuries and should check on her progress, and—if he understood his attraction to the girl—he could ask her out. But that would be ridiculous. He just met her and under such bizarre circumstances. And she was a child. She looked about twenty. And she might suc him. The scene both nauseated and baffled him, understandably since he had never hit a woman before.

"Call me the day after tomorrow," Tamra said. "Do you have a pen?"

Royce took a pen from an inside pocket of his jacket. He took out one of his business cards.

She recited her phone number and then replaced the ice bags. "And say hello to mom."

Royce sat with Phelan, Pelant and the notary and waited. His personal life was either going to begin or end that day. He saw her put her hands in her lap. He did not know if they were balled up in fists, which was a clear indication of her displeasure and—as he had learned—was a precursor to rampant ugliness. She did not raise her head, but appeared to be transfixed by the document as though she were staring into a mirror, looking for evidence of any imperfection.

"I'm done here," she said, stood, and picked up her handbag.

Four sets of eyes came to their own conclusions as to the final judgment.

She began rooting around in her bag, leaned over the table with her butt in the air and her blouse falling open slightly, and asked if anyone had a pen. Instantly, four people produced four pens. She took the one proffered by her attorney. She sighed and then signed the document. The energy changed across the table.

Tamra blew Royce a kiss. "For you, sweetie."

Chapter Seven

A week later, in the spirit of goodwill after Tamra signed the document that shall not be named, Royce invited Tamra's parents to dinner. And bring the little girl, he offered. While talking to her mother on the phone, Tamra learned that he had extended the invitation. She told her mother they couldn't have dinner with Royce.

Tamra remembered the first time her parents met Royce. Two weeks after he sent her to the hospital, he invited her to go running with him. He picked her up at her parents' home. She introduced him to them. Her father Laramie shook Royce's hand firmly the way men do, while her mother Belle gave him a restrained hug because she was holding a wine glass.

"Please sit down," Belle said. "Can I get you some wine?" She held a glass by its stem, filled with a dark red liquid.

Royce demurred, saying he needed a clear head for running. And it was just eight o'clock in the morning. Laramie sat in the living room, drinking a cup of coffee. At the kitchen table sat a girl of four or five years. Royce did not feel qualified to decide. She wore pajamas with princesses and ate scrambled eggs with boysenberry jam toast. Blotches of the jam stuck to her face.

Belle, still standing by Royce, called into the kitchen, "Sophie, say hello to Mr. Kallas."

"Oh, please. Royce is fine. Hello, uh, Sophie."

Tamra cleaned off Sophie's face.

With a mouthful of toast, Sophie said, "Ha-whoa."

Tamra said, "Okay, all the introductions have been made. Mom, we have to go. We want to run before it gets too hot."

Weeks later Tamra invited Royce to her house to have dinner. She promised him an authentic Welsh dinner that she learned how to make from her grandmother: Welsh rarebit and shepherd's pie. The house was quiet when Royce arrived. Belle and Laramie were out bowling. Royce was surprised because he thought they would be having dinner with him. In fact, he had brought Belle a bouquet of tulips.

Tamra set the table in the dining room, lit candles, dimmed the lights, and showed him where to sit. She told him he had to drink beer with his dinner, and she served the rarebit. She fed him mouthfuls of cheese, and he wondered what his cholesterol level would be at the end of the evening.

While Royce and Tamra ate Patagonia cream tarts with coffee, Laramie and Belle returned home, followed by Sophie, who ran to her bedroom. Belle, after filling a tumbler with beer, turned the dining room light on and sat down at the table next to Royce. She told Tamra she was getting wax on the table from the candles.

"Mom, we're still having our dinner. Please, okay?"

"Do you mind if I sit here?" Belle asked Royce. She sounded petulant.

What could he say? He looked to Tamra for help.

"Dad, would you please come in here and get your wife?"

Laramie obediently stood behind Belle's chair and said, "Let's put Sophie to bed."

Belle got up, topped off her beer. "Come back soon. I can make Welsh dinners, too. It's my mam that Tamra learned from."

After her parents left the room, Royce asked Tamra about the foster child.

"What do you want to know?" she asked. He wanted to know how it came about that her parents took in a foster child. Tamra said she didn't know the process her parents had to go through. She reminded him she was away at boarding school when her parents got Sophie. One day a call came from a social worker that a baby born at Westside Hospital had been abandoned by its mother and there was no father of record. Not having names of relatives of the mother, the county immediately put the baby into the foster care system. The social worker asked if the Woodens would like to take a newborn.

"Well, like my parents went for it big time. I was already packed away at boarding school, and so they got a fresh new baby to replace the bad old daughter. I came home at the end of the school year, and it's like they're playing dolls with the kid. I remember her crying every night. I got no sleep that summer. And, of course, they wanted to go out to get a, a, what's the word—rep, reprive."

"Reprieve," Royce said.

"Yeah, so they wanted a reprieve, and so I had to like babysit. She was pretty cute when she was little." She paused. "And, so, I have a little sister."

Since the night of the Welsh rarebit, Tamra had made it her mission to keep her parents away from Royce except for perfunctory "hello" and "how are you?" She never left Royce alone in a room with them. Belle told Tamra they had already accepted his invitation to dinner, and, furthermore, if they called to cancel, she, Belle, would tell him why they were flaking on him.

"Come on, Mom. What are you doing here? I've

—

45

signed the Goddamned prenup. I'm planning a big wedding. Are you going to ruin it all for me?"

"No, you can do that all by yourself. You have to tell him before the wedding. I'm telling you, Tamra Belle, he has a right to know. You can tell him, or I will. *Before* the wedding."

They met for dinner at Patina, a French restaurant in Los Angeles. Royce greeted the Woodens and got a half hug from Laramie and full court press from Belle. He forgot the little girl was coming. He wondered if the restaurant would have anything for her to eat. The chef greeted Royce and suggested that he prepare a tasting menu and choose wines. And he could make spaghetti for Sophie. After the chef left the table, Royce noticed that Belle, Laramie, and Tamra seemed to be locked in a silent battle, their faces grim and focused, Laramie less so. The silence was too big for Royce to pierce. As he scooped Petrossian caviar onto a blini, Royce decided to talk to the child.

"Sophie, that is a pretty name."

"Uh huh." Apparently disgusted by the look of the caviar, Sophie played with her flatware, hiding it under the maroon linen napkin. She wore a pink dress with lots of ruffles and lavender high tops. He assumed that was the uniform of choice for five-year-old girls. Her blonde hair fell down her back.

"Are you in school?"

"Of course."

"Where do you go to school?"

"Fern Elementary kindergarten school, Hollywood, California."

What else could he ask her?

"Where did you get those green eyes?" Green eyes that were curious, probing, waiting.

"I was borned with them. Don't you know that?"

"I probably should have known."

The silence of everyone else at the table and the non-conversation he was having with the girl confounded him. He watched Laramie eat a prawn as though it were his last meal and, Belle spear scallops. He didn't want an explosive argument—he had been with Tamra long enough to know that was possible—but also did not want to sit in silence. "Everyone, why so quiet?" he asked and looked at Tamra.

She blushed all the way to her tawny roots. She moved beef tenderloin around on her plate. When she did not make eye contact with him, he looked at Belle and Laramie for some sign. Laramie looked away, seemingly fascinated with the decor of the restaurant. Belle looked right at him, her eyes locked onto Royce's face. He made a slight shrug of his shoulders. He prided himself on his communication skills, but whatever message she was attempting to send, he was not receiving it.

"Sophie, tell Royce about your teacher," Belle said.

"My teacher is Miss England, like the country. I don't know what that means." She sighed. "She's very pretty." She looked at Royce for the first time that night and smiled. "I can read," she said. "Mama, can I have my book?"

Tamra shuddered and Laramie smiled.

While the other adults played "Who is going to blink first?" Royce listened to Sophie read about children who live in Kenya. He commented to anyone who would speak to him that the material seemed sophisticated for a five-year-old.

"This one," Belle nodded her head toward Sophie, "started reading when she was four and she loves reading, unlike Tamra here, who is averse to reading unless it's a script."

Tamra shot her mother a professional grade hate look and then nervously looked at Royce. The remainder of the evening consisted of terse questions, followed by one-word answers, with Royce playing host to a five-year-old.

That dinner was unlike Royce and Tamra's early dates. Three weeks after Royce and Tamra met at the hospital, he took her to dinner where she wore a black pillbox hat with veil to her chin to hide her bruises, and the waiters served her a meal of French words. The next week they had dinner at Yamashiro, 250 feet above Hollywood Boulevard, where she wore a pink cloche. She smelled like strawberries. He didn't usually like faux fruit scents on women, but strawberry suited Tamra.

"You smell like strawberries." Royce said, spearing a piece of sashimi. "I had a strawberry dessert at The Arnaud's restaurant in New Orleans," he said. "The strawberries were soaked in $25,000 wine and served with whipped cream and mint. And for those in the market for a little jewelry, for $1.4 million dollars it included a 4.7 carat purple diamond, 18-carat rose gold ring."

She looked at him as though he were speaking Urdu. "My cologne reminded you of a strawberry dessert that came with a million-dollar ring?"

He changed the subject and brought up the accident at Gramercy.

"Do you know how long you will be off work?" he asked her.

"No-o-o-o. Why?"

"It is probably too early, but I wanted to get a good idea of your damages."

"Why? What's damaged?" She touched her hat. He

paid attention to her green eyes. She wore little makeup, just mascara and lip gloss. Perhaps she thought the bruises were enough color on her face.

"Your damages. That means your expenses, like the hospital and ambulance bills. Your time off work." He left out pain and suffering. He had a feeling she could probably come up with major pain and suffering on her own. But that assumption did not dissuade him from wanting to be with that girl. In fact, he was interested in everything about her. He wanted to know why she wore those hats and "fuck me" heels.

And yet as he drove away from her house at the end of the second date, Royce asked himself why he was remotely thinking about dating Tamra. He had told his best friend Steven reasons why he should not date her, with the first reason her age, the second that she was not marriage material. He made a commitment to himself that he would end the silliness with Tamra before she got hurt.

However, she found a myriad of ways to make him forget to have the conversation, and she never brought up the accident again.

On their fourth date, after he picked her up at her parents' house, they went on a hike. Tamra wore a baseball cap, and her bruises looked like dirt. After they had hiked together for an hour—with him shortening his strides so she could keep up with him—she removed her hoodie, peeling it off as though he had put a hundred-dollar bill in her thong. Then she walked off the path and took off her sports bra. When he told her to put on her clothes before someone came by, she giggled and told him to cover her up, which he did. So much for that.

—

The first time they had sex in a bed, Royce took Tamra to his house in Beverly Hills. It was in the flats, so would not slide down a hill in a southern California rainstorm. The house was on a cul-de-sac with other tasteful homes with mature landscaping of tall palms, birch trees, lavender, and green lawns manicured to within an inch of their dark roots.

Tamra paid attention to the cars they passed on the way to his house. If there was a car in a driveway—and there was not much need to leave a car out because most of the houses had three-car garages at least—it was a sensible Mercedes sedan or a delicious Ferrari.

Royce's house was English country with four bedrooms—one of which had been turned into a weight room—stone fireplaces in the living room, master bedroom, and great room, hardwood floors throughout. He offered to give her a tour, but Tamra said she wanted to explore. She walked through the entire house, asking him questions as though she were a real estate appraiser. Why didn't he have curtains? Was the stove electric or gas? Did he put in the bar? Who kept the house so clean?

French doors from the master bedroom and great room led to a brick-paved patio and a rectangular pool. When Tamra saw the pool, she shrieked like an adolescent girl with a ticket to a Pearl Jam concert. She ripped off her clothes and dove in before Royce had walked outside.

He sputtered like an old tea kettle. "Tamra, wait. We are going to the movies."

She stood in the shallow end and poured handfuls of water onto her breasts. "Sweetie."

"Tamra, outside, in the yard? In daylight?"

"Yes, sweetie."

She slithered down into the water, lay on her back and floated with her head back and arms stretched out. The poor man did not know what to do. He had entertained any number of ladies in his home, and they had availed themselves of the pool and spa, but at night, with the lights off. Tamra chuckled, got out of the pool, and lay on her stomach on a wooden chaise with a navy-blue cushion. She listened to the birds and other quiet tasteful sounds. She did not hear Royce walk up behind her.

He picked her up with his arms around her waist. "Okay, you want to play, we will play. But in the house."

He dropped her unceremoniously onto his bed. As he walked away, she heard him mumble, "Ach! You got me all wet."

Tamra felt the ridges of the corduroy bedspread exfoliating her skin. Royce was back in the room.

"Now you are getting the bedspread wet."

"You left me here."

She turned over onto her back, and he pulled her off the bed by her feet. She laughed and grabbed onto the bedspread, but she did not stand a chance against a two-hundred-pound man who ate weights for breakfast. Tamra landed on a soft rug at the foot of his bed and hoisted herself up on her elbows. Royce stood above her.

"Baby, you have no clothes on," she said.

"Apparently, this house has become clothing optional."

"How about we christen this bed?"

"News flash, I have slept in this bed already."

"You have. And probably a good bunch of the females in LA County have. No, don't shake your head 'no.' Uh uh." She waved her index finger in his general direction. "But we haven't. We're going to fix that."

—

51

"I have not slept with a good portion of the female population of Los Angeles in this or any other bed. End of that discussion. FYI, I will never ask you about your past relationships. They have nothing whatsoever to do with us. Now, under your rules, let us christen this bed."

"I'm going to make you so happy, you'll put a plaque up above the headboard with my name and the date," Tamra said.

While they might have appeared to be a strange couple, they made sense. Royce appreciated Tamra's wildness, a personality trait he coveted yet could not afford to have himself. Rather, he absorbed other people's personalities and feelings, hiding them within his well-sculpted structure. He carried other souls, while Tamra deflected them. She did not allow other people to touch her emotionally. Those competing attributes were leveled by a ballast of their growing passion for each other.

If Royce had sought Reginald's counsel about the wisdom of dating, much less marrying Tamra, that is to say, not just fucking her, but actually taking her out among their people—and Royce decidedly did not consult his father—Reginald would first have exploded. When the tremors stopped and the Earth's tectonic plates settled, he would have reminded Royce, as he did through prep school and college, that he needed to be concentrating on building his social infrastructure for the future, not wasting his time and reputation with an unsuitable girl. That lecture would have been followed by a homily related to people who wanted to separate him from his money, which would lead nicely into a question whether Royce was focused on the end goals: raise capital, locate joint ventures, and research investments, which was when the contacts were handy. Royce's energy should have been focused on accumulating wealth, generating money through ideas that solved problems. Reginald's bottom line, one he practiced every day of his life, was to direct one's focus on being wealthy.

When Royce and Tamra were together, she talked about her acting classes and told him she played Emily in *Our Town,* the graveyard scene. She did some of the dialogue for him, standing up and looking wistfully down toward Grover's Corners. He told her about some of his acquisitions, a textile manufacturer in Uruguay and coconut oil plant in the Philippines. Tamra was interested in coconut oil. She used it as a moisturizer. She asked him if he could get her a couple bottles. He chuckled and said he would see what he could do. He described beaches in Costa Rica and Maui, where he surfed. They fell into an easy relationship as soon as Royce gave up on the plan to stop seeing her.

A month after they met, he took her on his yacht, along with Steven and his flavor of the month, Jessica. The Fourth of July was a beautiful day with puffy clouds on a cerulean sky. The Pacific, dark blue, produced seagulls, never-ending seagulls. Royce had not told Tamra exactly the size of his boat. In fact, he referred to it as a little boat. When Royce and Tamra got to the Dolphin Marina at Marina del Rey, she looked at the sailboats, cats, and other boats in assorted sizes and tried to guess which boat was his. He stopped in front of a yacht christened Gre*ek Seas.* Tamra squeaked. "That's not a little boat."

"In the world of yachts, it is."

A crew of eight, wearing cobalt blue golf shirts and khaki shorts, waited for them to board.

—

53

"How big is it," she whispered to him.

"One hundred fifty feet," he whispered back.

As they went aboard, Tamra looked back at him. "Why do you act like what you own is nothing, but then you kind of—I don't mean to be nasty here—you show it off."

Royce, startled, opened his mouth to respond—although he had no idea what he would say—and wanted to get Tamra out of earshot of the crew, yet not look as though he was rushing her. In that second Steven and Jessica joined them, giving him a respite. He hoped. Introductions were made all around. Tamra acted cool, as though she spent every day on a yacht—most likely larger ones. She appeared differently to Royce, her clothing and behavior. If Royce had known her better, he would have realized she was acting, playing a part: the rich girl. She wore white capris, a rugby shirt and Topsiders. When Tamra saw their suite, she said, "Very nice, Royce."

Royce, with her words on the dock in his head, watched her open a Louis Vuitton bag (*Where did she get that?*) on the queen bed and go into the en suite head. Mechanically, he moved up to the pilothouse, ostensibly to have a conversation with the captain, but it was to get out of Dodge before Tamra's new personality emerged. He reversed course when he realized he had left Tamra with his other guests. He found her sitting with Steven and Jessica in the forward salon on grey linen barrel chairs, munching on cheeses and deciding which wine to open. Royce pointed to one on the bar, and the other three talked at once: "Of course," "That's the best," and "Excellent choice," the last comment coming from Tamra.

Steven turned to Royce. "So, what's the plan?"

"We are sailing to Two Harbors at Catalina today. We will stay on board tonight."

"This yacht (Steven pronounced it "yach-it") is about as far as we can get after a couple yards at the Saloon."

"Tomorrow we will sail down to Newport Harbor, get sunburned on the way, and then maybe play some poker, because I will need money to pay for gas."

"My man, you better choose some other money-producing vocation, because your poker skills suck. Your face gives away your cards. Your ears get red when you try to bluff," Steven said.

Apparently to demonstrate, Royce's ears reddened. Royce and Steven bantered back and forth like they were seven years old. Since they were so engrossed, Tamra stood up and walked to the galley where she bumped into two of the crew members who were stowing the groceries.

Tamra, just scoping out the boat, fumbled. "I, oh, I guess, I mean, I would like a glass of water."

"Certainly, miss," the female said as she poured the water into a cobalt stemmed glass. "There will always be fresh water in a carafe on the bar."

When she returned to the salon, Royce put out his arm, indicating either he wanted her to join him or he was hailing a taxi. "Let me take you and Jessica on a tour."

And so they did. Jessica was cordial to Tamra and teased Royce about finding someone to care for him in his dotage. They started with the pilothouse and worked their way down: jet skis, kayaks, sunbathing deck, diving board, forward suite, forward salon, mid-ships suites, galley, mid-ships salon, Royce's suite. The high-polished woods, linen chairs and couches, mother-of-pearl top of the dining table that sat eight, original paintings above the bar and in the suites, stationery in Tamra's name aboard the *Greek Seas*.

After they had lunch, they played board games Clue and Pictionary, with Tamra being flirtatious, the Tamra with whom Royce was familiar.

The engines cut, and Royce stood up. "Jet skis, anyone?"

Tamra got into a bikini, and when they met the other couple on deck, Steven turned to Royce, and over the heads of the women mouthed to Royce, "Sweet."

Tamra, who had never jet skied before, took to it like a fish to water. They raced in circles around the boat.

After they docked at Two Harbors, the foursome ambled with the slow gait of the truly relaxed. They looked like they were walking in slow motion or toking in sync.

They went to the Harbor Reef Saloon, where, although they had talked big about getting a yard, ordered four Buffalo Milks. Although she didn't want to ask and appear unworldly—even if they were only on Catalina Island—curiosity forced Tamra to ask, "Is this milk from a buffalo?" She squinched up her nose and held out the glass in front of her as though she didn't like the way the contents smelled.

"Nope," Steven said, and listed the ingredients as though he were their bartender. "Much better. It's crème de cocoa, kalua, crème de banana, vodka, half and half, whipped cream and nutmeg."

"Why is the drink called Buffalo Milk?" she asked.

"Bison were brought to the island in 1924 for a Zane Grey movie, 'The Vanishing American.' It cost too much to take them off the island," Royce said.

"And they left their swimmies at home," Steven said.

"But you said bison. What does that have to do with buffalo milk?" Tamra asked.

The other three laughed as though she was making a joke. Royce noticed that the more she drank, the more her personality reverted to the "real"—in Royce's mind—Tamra. And they did drink. They had shots while eating a bucket of clams, drank beer with their appropriately named buffalo wings and onion rings. To initiate Tamra, the guys decided to get a yard and gave her the first gulp of beer. She needed help holding up the yard-long flute, heavy with liquor. In turn, they passed the flute around. Tamra didn't understand what all the fuss was about until the flute was about half full. That is when things got interesting—and wet. The foamy amber liquid rushed through its glass funnel toward the mouth of the victim. By the time they finished, all four of them had wet chests, and, as Steven and Royce noticed, Tamra was not wearing a bra.

The alcohol turned three functioning able-bodied citizens of the upper class into almost falling down drunks as they walked back to the yacht. The fourth person, decidedly a member of the middle class, walked fine and had broken into song, although she didn't have a singing voice.

"But I would walk 500 miles and … ta da ta da ta da…who walked 1,000 miles … ta da ta da … down at your door." She accompanied herself on an invisible drum and guided Royce, who appeared to be both drunk and blind.

Holding securely onto the bow, they watched fireworks from Avalon.

When they got into their cabin, with the door closed, Tamra and Royce faced each other, standing on opposite sides of the bed. Royce swayed, but not in rhythm with the boat. To that point in their dating life Tamra had not seen Royce drunk or out of control. She kind of liked it. Royce was silent for a moment, his head moving from side to side as though his neck were not strong enough to hold up his skull.

"What were you doing earlier?" he asked, "When you were not yourself. Who were you trying to be?"

She was caught off guard, but thought with Royce's degree of drunkenness, she could say almost anything.

"I was being Crystal Carrington from 'Dynasty.'"

"But why, babe?"

"It's obvious, isn't it?"

Royce sat on his side of the bed to remove his shoes and pants. He had trouble unbuttoning his shirt, so she walked over to him and unbuttoned it for him. "I think I need to lie down," Royce said, lowering himself to a pillow. "I love you, Tamra," he said as he settled into drunken sleep.

She closed her eyes and pumped her fists in the air like Rocky. Then she let Royce sleep even though she had a fierce need to be fucked.

The next morning, late, late morning, they were served coffee, croissants and fruit in bed. *Royce is a class act all the way*, she thought. His own yacht, a crew of eight, boat docking fees, gas. *How much is this guy worth?* She made getting the answer to that question her priority. True she had bagged the guy, but she wanted to know more about the bounty.

That afternoon Jessica and Tamra lay on the aft deck to par broil themselves. When Royce went on deck, he found them both topless. He sputtered. He looked back at Steven, who shrugged his shoulders.

"When in Paris," Steven said.

Royce's ears turned red like a cranberry at Thanksgiving dinner.

Jessica read a book. Tamra had her eyes closed and

let her head droop to one side so it appeared she was sleeping. Royce and Steven sat on two chairs designed for fishing for large catches off the deck. She listened to them talk baseball, golf, and wines, straight out of *GQ*. Then she heard what she had been waiting for.

"Did you go in the tank on Rambus?" Steven asked.

"No, I had already bailed. I am sticking with Microsoft and Apple."

"When did you get into Microsoft? Have you been in since the beginning?"

"Yes, I bought it during the initial IPO. A hundred thousand shares. The stock has split four times, so I now own 900,000."

"Christ, almighty. Are you shitting me? Where do you stand now?"

With the exception of his father, Royce discussed the particulars of his asset portfolio only with Steven. Royce pointed at Tamra and shook his head no. Steven nodded.

"As of three days ago a bit over seventy-eight," Royce said.

Steven mouthed "million."

Royce nodded.

"And Apple?"

"That was one of the first stocks I bought. It is doing well."

"Hell, I was going to go in fifty-fifty with you on the gas for this buggy. Doesn't sound like you need my contribution." Of course, Steven had no intention of offering to pay for the gas or anything else related to the trip. It was a given among their set that the host always paid.

Tamra attempted to translate what she had heard into regular English. She listened to the names of stocks. She didn't know what an IPO was. She would ask her dad. He might understand it. Royce said he owned 900,000. Dollars? Seventy-eight?

Having gotten permission to dock the yacht in Balboa Marina, the foursome skulked around Balboa Island, looking at overpriced t-shirts and hats. Tamra asked Royce to buy her a t-shirt that said, "Small busted women have big hearts."

"Is it true?" he asked her.

"You will just have to stick around to find out." She wasn't ready to reel him in just yet. She wasn't going to get sentimental with that one. Royce was a big fish. Monstro-sized. She intended to apply emotional acrobatic flexibility and her body to cement the deal.

On August 29, 1993 they went to the Ahmanson Theater to see "Phantom of the Opera" on its last day in Los Angeles. Afterward he took her to a private party for the cast. She was enraptured talking to the actors. She told them about her acting classes, and they talked about themselves. Then Royce and Tamra found a quiet corner.

"My family has had season tickets to the Ahmanson since it opened in 1967," Royce said. "I would like to continue the tradition and bring my wife and children here." He kissed her forehead. Her hair tasted like her signature smell: strawberries.

"I want a family," she said. "I want children to love and take care of and a husband who will protect me. When I think of a husband, I picture someone who will wrap his arms around me," and she demonstrated.

She looked blissful. He wanted to be married. He had shown her the fountain of youth under the money tree. He wanted a family, and she had keys to the baby maker.

At Patina after the valet brought up Belle and Laramie's car and they drove off with Sophie waving from the backseat, Royce and Tamra left in his car.

"You want to tell me what that was all about?" Royce asked. "I planned a nice evening for your parents at an excellent restaurant. You know I am not stingy with my money, but that dinner handpicked by the chef cost $2,800, and other than nods of the head from you and your parents, the only person I had to talk to was your sister."

Tamra swallowed, her head bowed. Approaching headlights streaked across the black leather interior of the Maserati, and he saw her cheeks were wet. She made no effort to wipe her face.

"Are you crying?" he asked, looking between her and the road in front of him.

"Not so much. She sighed dramatically. "My mom says there's something I have to tell you. It's not my idea."

"Okay, go."

"Let's wait until we get to your house." She sighed again.

—

Chapter Eight

They walked into the great room. Royce opened the French doors, and a slice of a languid moon lay against a black sky. The trees and bushes were in silhouette, as though they were a painted set for a play. He brought out wine and glasses, and they sat on the zebra-pattern rug. She leaned back against the couch and hugged her knees. She looked at him and then away when he returned her gaze and she spontaneously burst into tears, real, honest, naked tears, he thought. He was not sure anymore. He put his arms around her.

"It is all right, whatever it is, everything is all right," he said. He caressed her hair and brushed it away from her face. He did not like to see her cry.

She shook her head and cried louder. "I didn't tell you the whole truth about something." She shrugged away from him. Her face was red, her green eyes beyond sad. "You can't interrupt me. When I'm through, you can ask questions. If you want to, you know. God, I don't want to do this!"

Royce put his hand to his heart and started to say something. Tamra would never know what he was going to say, because he stopped himself. He nodded his head and sat facing her. He heard crickets in the bushes and looked out onto the patio. The pool was lit, creating a turquoise oasis.

"I told you my parents sent me to boarding school when I was fifteen, right?" she said.

Wanting to respect her edict against his interrupting, Royce did not move to acknowledge her question. He held his wine glass to his mouth, but did not drink from it.

"So, okay, I did go to boarding school." Still crying. "I was sent away to a school in Arizona because I was pregnant." Tamra said the words quickly, as though she was on a timer. She looked at him for any sign, any sign at all.

His eyes widened and he took in a breath.

"So, yeah, I was fifteen years old and having a baby." She paused.

"Are you finished?" he asked. "May I respond now?"

"No, not yet. I'm going to get through this now." She stopped crying and inhaled deep into her lungs. She settled herself and talked as if she were reading an eye chart. "Most girls get abortions or give their babies up for adoption. I mean, like what fifteen, sixteen-year-old kid can take care of a baby? Right?" She shrugged her shoulders. He could understand that. "My mom didn't want me to get an abortion. Me, I was in shock. I hardly knew the guy, you know." She put her hand over her mouth and quickly took it away. "I mean, he was a friend, but I didn't love him. The boy, the guy who I was pregnant by, he signed away his rights to the baby. He couldn't sign fast enough. You guys have it so easy. No, no, I don't mean you. Just guys in general.

"Through a private organization I met a couple who wanted to adopt the baby. They were pretty cool. Me and them and my parents went to lunch together. My mom grilled them. I guess they passed her test, because my mom told them they could be in the delivery room. No one asked me if I wanted them there. I felt like they thought I was just the baby carrier. Hmm, I guess I was." Her voice was bruised.

"So, I'm in the delivery room and I'm breathing and pushing and doing everything I was supposed to do." Back to crying. Hands over her face. She began speaking again and Royce could not understand her, so he gently moved her hands. "There was a problem, so the doctor decided to do a Caesarean." Her voice was husky and raw, as though she was playing Katherina in *Taming of the Shrew*. "They put me on happy juice because they were going to cut into my gut. It all went by so fast."

Royce grimaced and tightened his hands around his glass.

"I like heard my baby cry for the first time, and then a nurse handed me a wrapped-up papoose. When they cleaned me up, the couple came in. They were so happy, taking pictures with her holding the baby, then him holding the baby, and then they asked my dad to take a picture of the three of them. I didn't want them to touch the baby, but I didn't think I had any say."

Royce had a feeling of sponginess where his heart should be.

"All the attention was on the baby, and I lay in bed with my stomach cut up." She lifted her blouse and touched the scar. "I told you that was from an appendectomy. It wasn't."

He looked at the scar and sniffed as though his nose was congested.

"After the couple left to call family or something, I asked my dad to take a picture of me holding the baby. My mom said, 'Are you sure that's a good idea? Do you want that memory?' Well, damned straight I did. So I got my picture." She looked in her handbag and pulled out a photograph that was dog-eared. It looked like it had been handled often.

Royce saw a photo of teenage Tamra. She looked at the photo, too. She sighed. She had become an award-winning sigher. In the photo Tamra had straight blonde hair, some of it on her face, and a sweet look about her. Big smile. She lay in a hospital bed and held a baby swaddled in a blanket. A pink head with wisps of light hair peeked out from the blanket.

"That was my baby. I had forty-eight hours from when the baby was born to give up my rights."

Royce suddenly stood up and paced the room; he indicated he was listening by dipping his head toward her, as though he were bidding on a piece of art at Sotheby's. Tamra moved up to the couch where she tucked her feet under her.

"I was alone that first night, crying because I was by myself and because my stomach hurt. A nurse rolled the baby into my room and gave me a hot water bottle for my stomach. Then she left. I talked to the baby and unwrapped her blanket so I could look at her toes and legs, her hands. She gripped my finger. I swear." Tamra held out her hand extending the index finger as she was doing show and tell.

Royce nodded his head, a slow nod as though he were a toy with a dying battery.

"And she kept turning her head toward my chest, her little mouth open," Tamra said. "I untied my gown and let her take my breast, and she sucked. Oh, I had a sensation in my belly—" She put her hands on her stomach.

Royce stopped pacing as he listened. What she said sounded sexual, probably not what she meant.

"I can still remember it. I didn't have any milk yet, but she sucked for the pure pleasure of it, I guess. The nurse came back, and I thought I was going to get in trouble, but she said, 'Look at you, little mama.'" Tamra blinked tears on her eyelashes, her lips red from biting them.

Royce shoved his hands in his pockets and paced again.

"Two days later, my parents were with me. It was the day to sign the papers saying I was giving away baby girl Wooden. But I told them I was going to keep her."

Royce felt like his legs would give out on him.

"You should have heard my mother. She went off like a rocket. She said no way the baby was going home with us. And she gave me ninety-nine reasons why I couldn't keep her. My dad said we sounded like we were talking about reasons to not get a puppy. He was serious, but then he said, 'But there is a couple ready to adopt her. You should see how excited they are. Their parents are here.'

"My mom took the baby from my dad and said silly things to her, pretty much like she *was* talking to a puppy. She put her cheek on the baby's cheek. I started to cry, from deep inside me like happiness and loneliness together. Then my mom told my dad to take a picture of her and the baby. And she said, 'Take another picture.' And she told him to take another one and another one. After a few minutes, she said, 'Maybe this little princess can come home with us.' Before she could change her mind, I said, 'I have the name for this baby girl: Sophie Grace Wooden.' I think Sophie is a name for pretty girls, Sophies are always beautiful, get a lot of attention, are usually the girls that every boy wants."

Royce sat down next to Tamra. He looked at her in profile, because she did not make eye contact with him. Even though the room was air conditioned, he could feel heat coming off her, especially when she said the baby's name. He attempted to control his breathing. For the first time that night he had an actual expression on his face, dissimilar to the waxwork of his face the rest of the evening. Her face was red and bloated. Mascara had migrated under her eyes like black half-moons. She appeared to think about what she would say and what was the truth, not that those two would necessarily correlate.

"My dad told us again that Sophie had adopted parents. I said I was Sophie's mother. My mother said again the baby girl could come home with us. I didn't register at that moment that my mother wasn't talking about the baby as being mine. Before she could change her mind, I called the adoption agency and told the social worker I was keeping the baby. 'Think about the couple,' the social worker said, and I was like 'But what about me?'"

For Royce, the rest of the world was silent except for the crickets, the icemaker, and the grandfather clock, the sounds of the world with which he was familiar.

"We broke the news to the couple that was going to adopt Sophie," Tamra said. "They both started crying right away. I apologized nine ways to Sunday. The next day, my dad shows up with a car seat. How cute was that. So we drove home.

"My mom said I couldn't say the baby was mine, because I would be like a freak at school." Tamra chewed on her lips for a moment to stop the sobs that were in her mouth. "My mother made up the foster parent story, and now Sophie calls my mom 'mama,' and I'm just Tamra. When I take her somewhere like to the mall, someone will stop me and say how cute she is, and I tell the truth. I say I am Sophie's mother. Then I tell Sophie we're playing pretend." She touched his arm. He neither flinched nor leaned into the caress. "I love you, sweetie. Royce, I love you so much. I wanted to tell you the truth, but I just couldn't. I was afraid you wouldn't understand. And then we got engaged, and my mom's been on my back nonstop. Please, believe me now." She gripped his arm. She sounded like she was going for a big finish. "I don't know how we can tell her I'm her real mom, but we'll figure it out. It can be the three of us, our little family. Except I want more children, too, sure. Okay, I'm done."

Her body slumped over as though she were a large balloon leaking air. She turned to look at Royce, gave him a coquettish smile, and his eyes revealed nothing.

"Well?" she said.

"I would like to take you home, think about everything you have told me, and formulate my comments," he said. Royce's mechanical tone probably insulted her. He knew he sounded like he did not care and like he was being a lawyer.

They drove to her house in silence, with, of all things, a Sirius re-broadcast of a baseball game from the previous season that Royce had turned on, a buffer. She cried part of the way, but that did not move him. She sat leaning up against the door and looked at Royce. He stopped at the curb, and when she asked him if he would like to come in, he said it was late—it was three o'clock in the morning—and he would talk with her soon.

Chapter Nine

How did Royce feel after listening to Tamra's admission? No time for feelings. As he drove home, he attempted to organize the issues into manageable compartments. There was the issue of the child, her very existence. Then the question was whether Tamra—after five years—would claim Sophie as her own. If she did, what did that mean for him? Would he be expected to raise her as his daughter? And, secondly, the question of Tamra's lying. Would she have told him about Sophie if her parents had not pressured her?

He was awake the rest of that night, not staring at the ceiling, but sitting on his bed, leaning against the headboard, working with yellow legal pads. He had a pad for each of the two issues: SOPHIE, with subcategories of Adoption, Psychological Fallout, and Social Ramifications. The second issue: LIES.

Royce was extraordinarily lucid after the confession. And angry. They had successfully maneuvered through the prenup and now there was Tamra's disinformation about the child. Through ruses created and perpetuated by Tamra and her parents, Sophie called Belle mama, but Tamra wanted to claim her.

The second issue was the more difficult to process. Was Tamra an opportunist? Was her mendacity limited to this child or did it encompass their entire relationship? Was his father right that she wanted to marry him just for his money? Was Tamra a rapacious, immature child? He decided to speak to attorney John Phelan, who would have answers to some of his questions, before he talked to Tamra. His heart was beating strong in his chest and as long as he focused on the first issue, he was clear headed. When he strayed to Tamra's lies, his eyes welled up as he attempted to digest the possibility that Tamra's capricious conduct had a sole purpose: taking advantage of him. Could he forgive her? He wrote on the LIES pad: "Boarding school-lie, pregnancy-lie of omission, appendectomy-lie, Sophie-lie." A reticulation of lies. Her credibility had been vitiated by her perfidious behavior. When Tamra lied to him, she forfeited his trust. That thought rooted in his mind and grew. Royce started to feel sad, but the sensation flickered by him, too quickly for him to notice.

Chapter Ten

After Tamra's revelation, she didn't call Royce. Although she had twisted herself into a Gordian knot, part of her believed Royce would not only forgive her for her lies, but would also "fix" any issues related to Sophie. Whether delusional or smart like a fox, her thinking emboldened her. Royce loved her, he had proposed to her, his parents wanted him to be married, he wanted to be married, she had already started planning the wedding, he wanted a family, the stuff she said that wasn't true shouldn't make a difference to him really. Lots of girls get pregnant in high school. She didn't have an abortion, so that should get her points. She let her parents raise Sophie so that Tamra could finish her education and ensure that Sophie had a good life. That was good, right? She was on a roll now.

Royce met with Phelan, who contacted the Woodens. Phelan told Royce the Woodens were surprised and irritated that Royce didn't ask them the questions himself. Royce was surprised to learn that the Woodens had not adopted Sophie. Tamra had told him they had. Tamra and the boy were on the birth certificate as mother and father, and the boy had relinquished his rights.

On Phelan's recommendation Royce talked to two child psychologists about the potential ramifications of Tamra telling Sophie that she was her mother. After Royce talked to the psychologists, he called Tamra and asked her and her parents to meet him on neutral territory, the Denny's where he had proposed. He also asked her not to bring Sophie. He heard hesitation in her voice, probably because he had invited her parents to join them. Was Tamra concerned her parents would divulge more secrets?

He was waiting for them in a booth. As though leading a meeting of the acquisitions department of Kallas, Inc.-International, Royce began to tell them the opinions of the psychologists.

Belle interrupted him. "What's going on? Do you think you're deciding how we raise Sophie?"

Laramie gave Royce what he thought was an "I'm on your side" look.

"Of course not, Belle, but Tamra, evidently at your request, told me about Sophie's, uh, history and basically laid the issue at my feet. I believe I am stating Tamra's position accurately. She wants to acknowledge Sophie as her own and wants her to be a part of our new life."

He raised an eyebrow and looked at Tamra. She had been quiet. When he looked at her she was engrossed squeezing the contents of a red plastic ketchup dispenser onto her plate of fries and then put her hands in her lap.

Belle nodded. "Okay, I get it. Go ahead, please." She put one hand on the table. "I'm sorry for jumping the gun."

Coffee came for the four of them, and they busied themselves with cream and sugar.

Royce soldiered on. "The psychologists agree that if Sophie is to be told Tamra is her biological mother, she is at an age where the news will not be shocking if handled correctly, as opposed to say waiting until she is twelve or thirteen. The revelation now would just be information to her." Royce put his arms on the table and took a packet of NutraSweet from Tamra that she was pushing around the tabletop in circles. "They recommend that Tamra sit with Sophie and tell her that she was Tamra's baby, but she was very young and could not take care of her."

Belle bristled and put her hands up as if to say,

"stop."

Royce continued. "Now Tamra could be her mommy. Belle and Laramie," he nodded to them, "will always, always be her mama and daddy, but Tamra is her mommy. Are we solid so far?"

Uncharacteristically, Laramie shot his wife a look that was anger personified. "Belle, I told you that it was a mistake to tell the girl we were her parents. I told you it would come back to bite us in the butt. No, don't say anything. Let Royce talk," apparently not recognizing he had been the one to interrupt.

Royce spoke louder to cut Belle off at the pass. "The psychologists agreed there would be steps to undertake." He ticked them off on his fingers. "One, Tamra bond with Sophie as her mommy."

Tamra and Belle gave each other sideways glances, but neither made a sound. Quiet, mumbled conversations and the clinking of dishes could be heard from other booths. A waitress made two passes to see if they wanted anything.

"Two, introduce me into her life, sometimes at my home. Three, build a relationship with me over time. This process assumes you will not be antagonistic to the process," he said nodding toward Belle and Laramie. "Also, the wedding should be put off a year."

"*A year*," Tamra said. She sat up suddenly, looking like a meerkat sensing danger. "I don't want to wait a year, Royce." She looked at him with those killer green eyes that said "Please." She put a hand on his thigh.

He steeled himself against the spell she usually expertly put on him. "My role in the second and third steps presupposes my continued relationship with Tamra." He looked right into her eyes, daring her to say something.

With a small voice, Tamra said, "I don't know what

presupposes means."

"It means assumes, as in I assume I will stay with you. But at this point I do not know if I will be with you."

"But, please. Oh, okay." She drew in a breath and stretched her back against the tan Naugahyde seat. "Thank you for talking to the doctors. I, I…will talk to Sophie. I want to talk to her." A weak smile. "I just have to figure out the words to say." Tamra was being conciliatory, and Royce noted that usually preceded a forward assault from her.

"Maybe your maternal instinct will kick in," Belle said, looking straight ahead.

"That is a mean thing to say. You should be ashamed," Laramie said. He reached across the table and grabbed Tamra's hand and squeezed it.

Royce watched the three of them unraveling and wondered how Sophie would fare in their midst. He stood up. "Tamra, I will speak to you soon."

"Can't I go with you?" Tamra asked, starting to stand up.

"Not now," he said and left. As he walked out the door, he heard Belle ripping into Laramie.

Initially reluctant, Royce talked to Steven about Tamra's revelation and desire that the child would automatically become part of their new family. They had the conversation while playing golf at the Vintage Club course in Indian Wells. They were staying at Royce's Rancho Mirage home. They wore Bermuda shorts and golf shirts on a crisp spring day. Royce laid the entire story out, including the recommendations of the psychologists.

Steven shook his head and leaned on his club. "Do you want out?"

Royce sighed and looked up toward the jubilant blue

sky and the San Jacinto Mountains dusted with snow like someone had sprinkled powdered sugar on them. "The idea—and it is just an idea at this point—that I could become an instant father bothers me on several levels. Added to that is Tamra's lies, and I just do not know—"

"So I ask again, do you want out?"

Royce continued to look at the mountain. "No, no, I do not. For ill or good, I love Tamra. After taking time to think about this situation, I understand why she thought she had to lie to me. She was afraid of my reaction. She was fifteen years old and was forced by her mother to perpetuate a lie." Royce took his shot. He was not pleased with it.

They drove the cart on the fairway to Steven's ball. They were stuck behind a group on the green so they stayed in the cart to wait for them to clear.

"She wasn't fifteen when she lied to you. She was twenty. Can you trust her?" Steven picked up a fluorescent orange golf ball.

Royce said nothing.

"You're going to do it, then? You're going to marry Tamra and adopt, what's her name? Sophie?" Steven swung.

They rode in the cart to Royce's ball. He swung, and his ball went into a sand trap. "Perfect," he said. But he got on the green in two strokes, putting for par.

Royce deferred answering Steven's questions until they were back in the clubhouse. They settled into barrel chairs at a table with windows that framed palm trees and the blue-gray mountains.

"I do not...oh, God, this is difficult. It would be so much easier if it were a situation where I have to approve or deny an acquisition in Saigon. That I can deal with."

A server took their drink and lunch orders. While they waited for their scotch rocks, they talked about any topic except the one at hand. Royce leaned back in his chair and shook a couple yellow tees out of his pocket. Steven looked out the window. With their drinks securely in front of them and a promise of two cheeseburgers medium with steak fries on the way, they munched on dill pickle spears.

"So, how about those Chargers," Steven said.

"Nice try, but it is April. Not football season. Okay. Yes, I am going to marry Tamra and adopt Sophie. But not according to Tamra's timetable. I want us to walk Sophie through the steps the psychologists suggested."

"Do you understand the dynamics of your plan, or are you functioning only with the brain in your pants?" Steven said.

Royce coughed down a piece of pickle. Steven's question was the reason he was Royce's best friend. At that propitious moment, the burgers arrived.

"I have never considered this question." Of course he had. "Oh, I have dated women with children, and a few attempted to throw them at me. One or two conveniently forgot they had children. Nothing similar to this situation and never with anyone like Tamra. And I say that keeping in mind there has never been anyone like Tamra."

Steven took a big bite of the burger and then attempted to talk. "I'm sorry but I've got to ask the question. With all the drama between the two of you, why do you stay? Besides the physical attraction, what's going on with your relationship?"

"She's inquisitive, she wants to learn about the world, travel, history, cultures, foods. When I have had a particularly rough day, she holds my hand and either listens to me vent, or, if I do not talk, we sit quietly together. Yes, I agree that there are negatives to the relationship, but I hope the *drama*," he emphasized the word, "will end when we get married.”

“If you go forward, you won’t get a mulligan. One chance, guy.”

Royce waited another week before calling Tamra. She sounded happy to hear from him, but not desperate. She had evidently recovered from her earlier pleas to him. On the one hand he enjoyed seeing her unsure of her footing, needy, without her unwavering confidence. He chastised himself for having such a thought and was pleased he heard her spirit revived.

He picked her up at her house. They drove around Los Angeles with no destination in mind. He stopped at Philippe’s for French dip sandwiches. She got roast beef, and he got lamb. The sandwiches dripped with au jus. And his had cheese. They sat across from each other at a black wooden table.

Royce gave her a bullet point response. “Number one, I want to marry you.”

Her sandwich sat on waxed paper uneaten. She nibbled her potato salad.

“Number two, I would be honored to adopt Sophie.” He took a large bite of the sandwich and waited until he had cleaned up the juice that ran down his hand before proceeding. “Number three, I want to go forward according to the psychologists’ recommendations.”

Tamra took a bite of her sandwich using a fork, not her fingers. “I love you for having faith in me,” she said. “I love my daughter. There, I can say it, ‘my daughter.’ The thought that I can like have both of you to make a family fills my heart.”

Royce thought she laid it on kind of thick. “Have you thought of how you will tell Sophie?”

—

79

"Oh, I already told her."

Royce had taken a healthy bite of his sandwich, too large to interrupt Tamra. He had to speak with facial expressions, giving her the pinched eyebrows look.

"I took her out to play miniature golf. It was really easy. Easy peasy. I even let her beat me." She chewed on ice cubes.

"Why did you tell her already?" Royce choked out. "Suppose I said I was not going forward with the wedding? The psychologists said to wait until you and I had worked out our, for lack of a better word, situation." He attempted to push the lamb down his esophagus by taking a large swallow of his iced tea.

She pushed an ice cube into one cheek.

"Does she know we are planning to get married?" he asked.

"No, I figured I should wait to talk to you. You haven't exactly been sounding like you wanted to."

He was alarmed by her impetuousness while also surprised by her discretion, even though it was half-ass. "As to how to initiate my getting to know Sophie and vice versa—"

"I already told her she's coming to your house to go swimming tomorrow," she said as she took a small bite of potato salad.

"...going slowly..." He was getting a knot in his stomach.

"Nah, this is going to be a piece of cake. We don't have to put off the wedding."

"Tamra, the psychologists said—"

"Yeah, yeah, I know. But what's the difference whether she's with you now or later? There is no difference." She emphasized her point by slurping the dregs of her coke with a straw.

"No, I will not go forward until that child—"

"Her name is Sophie. If you're going to be her dad, you have to know her name," she said with what could only be described as cheerfulness.

"Exactly, I barely know her name."

They went back and forth, and Royce felt he lost ground every time Tamra spoke. He loved Tamra, more than was safe for him.

Chapter Eleven

Tamra did indeed take Sophie to Royce's to go swimming. The girl was shy around him, while quite animated when Tamra talked to her. Without fear, Sophie jumped into the pool to Tamra again and again. Royce realized Sophie was the first child to be in his pool.

The three of them went to the San Diego Zoo, to the beach, to LEGOLAND, and Disneyland. He took them to see the Dodgers play. Sophie was not interested in the game, and she got sick eating an entire bag of peanuts. Other than some of his frat brothers, Royce had not seen anyone vomit, certainly not in the stands in Dodger Stadium. Royce cooked spaghetti for Sophie, and they went to G-rated animated movies.

He bought her Mickey Mouse ears, balloons, and snow cones. When she wanted a Shamu plush toy and Barbie I Can Be a Sea World Trainer at Aquatica, Tamra told Sophie to ask Royce. He had no experience telling a child she could not have anything she wanted, so he simply—as with her mother—gave her what she asked for. She loved to read, so he took her to Barnes and Noble and let her buy as many books as she wanted. He waited patiently while she chose thirty-five books. In the meantime, Tamra looked at bridal magazines.

Like Tamra, Sophie loved clothes, and, left to her own devices, would choose interesting combinations of dresses, shirts, pants, and shoes. He chose restaurants, not for their Michelin stars any longer, but for child-friendly menus. Sophie did seem to accept Tamra as her mommy. When he took Tamra's parents to dinner, Sophie called Tamra "mommy," and Belle "grandmamma" and there was tension between the two women, nothing new on that front.

Royce saw something else emerging when he read to Sophie or when he watched her model new clothes. Tamra seemed slightly irritated, actually jealous of her daughter. Tamra asked Royce to watch TV with her or modeled some of *her* clothes, attempting to upstage the girl. Sophie, who certainly was her mother's daughter, said, "It's my turn."

He had, for the most part, approached the issue of getting to know Sophie like a project, just as he would in his professional life. He stated the issue and solution with all available resources.

He saw one of the psychologists. He met with her several times until it seemed to him that she was asking him questions about himself, not the child.

"How do you feel about becoming a father to a five year old? She's five, right?" Dr. Redland said.

Royce thought for a moment. "I think her birthday is in July. I need to learn that. She is a polite, apparently happy little girl."

Royce sat in a hardback chair, bypassing the red and blue floral couch. He pressed his shoulder blades into the chair's back. The doctor sat opposite him in a rocking chair.

"Yes," Dr. Redland said. "But how does that make you feel seeing her happy?" She adjusted her glasses.

"I do not understand how my feelings come into play." He folded his arms over his chest.

"You are about to be a parent, not to your biological baby, but to an almost six-year-old girl you basically do not know. Don't you have feelings about that? Are you angry, happy, fearful, confused?"

"I had not thought about any of those feelings. I guess I would say...if I have to choose one...probably happy."

"Do you believe you have had good role models for you to be a father?" Dr. Redland said.

"My father, of course," Royce said, a little too emphatically.

Dr. Redland said nothing. She waited.

"My father is an excellent role model." He crossed his legs, right over left.

"Why is that?" She gently rocked in the chair. Sunlight that arched into the room from windows close to the ceiling touched her red hair, and it looked like it was on fire.

"He works hard, provides for his family, loves his wife, and is well respected in the community." His right foot shook slightly.

"Those are admirable qualities in a person. Do you think these words define a father: hard worker, good provider, loving husband, pillar of the community?"

"It seems, doctor, that there are particular answers you are looking for. What is it you would like me to say? I am asking so that we can move the interview along. I am consulting with you about Sophie, not me." He gestured with his hands as though kneading pizza dough.

"I don't want you to say anything in particular," the doctor said and rested her notepad on her lap. "It seems that you are unfamiliar with identifying feelings, so I want to see if you can process how you feel if I ask specific questions related to your experience with parenthood, namely, your father. Are you comfortable with that approach?"

"Doctor, honestly, I am not comfortable with any of this, but to be a good parent, I need to know what I can do for Sophie." He put his elbows on his thighs and hunched over, a very un-Royce like posture.

"For Sophie's sake, I commend you for making this

effort. Meetings like this one can go a long way in taking on, not only a ready-made family, but one in which the child was raised to believe that her mother was, in fact, her sister." She paused.

Royce opened his mouth.

"That's all the time we have for today." Dr. Redland stood. "Would you like to schedule another appointment?"

"Do we have to discuss feelings?" He hoped he sounded as though he was making a joke.

The only obvious kink in the burgeoning family's tether was Reginald. Royce took his parents to Mastro's, believing—optimistically and probably naively—Reginald would be an easier sell if he had a piece of bloody meat in front of him. Royce was not concerned about his mother. She would love Sophie on sight.

After his father had three fingers of scotch, Royce forged ahead. "Father, Mother, I want to tell you about something wonderful that has happened to me. It is a gift, really." Steven's girlfriend Jessica had coached him. He did not use Tamra's suggestion: "Dad, I have a daughter. Now chew your steak before you choke." He handed his father a photo of himself, Tamra and Sophie at Disneyland.

"What is this?" Reginald growled. "Did you buy a theme park?"

"That is Tamra's daughter."

"Tamra's daughter?" Evelyn said, leaning over to look at the photo. "Look how cute she is."

Yes, Royce thought, she is cute. Like her mother.

Reginald gave the photo to Evelyn and went back to cutting, chewing, cutting, chewing.

"Sir, I am adopting Sophie after the wedding." He had not touched his dinner.

"Royce, I am so happy you are going to set a date," Evelyn said, not knowing the drama of the past months.

"How old is that child?" Reginald asked.

"She is five, six in July." He had learned her birthdate.

"My heavens, darling. How old was Tamra when she had her?" Evelyn said.

"Fifteen, Mother, a teenage indiscretion."

"How long have you known about her?" Reginald asked. Looking directly at his son, knife poised in one hand, fork in the other, and a steak begging for its life on the plate.

"A few months. I have been spending time with her and—"

"Where was Tamra hiding her?" Reginald said.

"She was not hiding her. I met her a few times before I learned she was Tamra's daughter."

"Who was raising her, darling?" Evelyn asked, acting as the buffer between her husband and son.

"Tamra's parents were raising her."

"My, how nice," she said.

Reginald used all of his resources—except a rifle—to beat his steak into submission. Evelyn asked when she could meet Sophie, asked if Tamra and Sophie could visit her. Yes, Evelyn would love Sophie. Reginald's pronouncement regarding the green-eyed, blonde child would wait for another day.

Two days later Reginald did the unimaginable. He walked into Royce's office and sat down on Royce's lemon-colored linen sofa. That was only the second time Reginald went to Royce's office instead of the other way around, the first time was when his mother got pneumonia and was hospitalized.

—

Royce sat down in a club chair facing the sofa. Reginald gave Royce an unnecessary discourse on the Kallas name and its predecessor Papadakallas. He emphasized and re-emphasized the ancestors who carried the name. "Now," Reginald asked, sitting forward on the sofa, slapping his hands on his knees, "a girl who is not blood to the family will carry the Kallas name? Moreover, she will be the first— am I supposed to call her my granddaughter?"

Royce saw a way in. He also sat forward and put his elbows on the tufted arm of the chair. "Yes, she will be the first granddaughter. Mother will make quite a fuss over her. She will be thrilled to be a grandmother."

"Yes, yes, she will, I suppose. And your wedding is when? Next year. Long way away. Things can change in a year."

So much for a way in. "We are not going to tell Sophie about the adoption until after the wedding."

"That is smart, son." Reginald stood up.

Royce stood up.

They shook hands.

Royce could not be budged on postponing the wedding. The psychologists said one year, so they would wait one year. In exchange, Royce told Tamra she had a limitless budget for the wedding.

Wendy Weinstein, the wedding planner to the stars, handled the entire event: caterers, furniture, hand-written invitations, tent, flowers, food, music, and chandeliers. They decided not to have a parade of attendants, Royce because he had too many friends from whom to choose, and Tamra because she did not want competition at the altar. She didn't tell Royce that, of course, but he intuited that was her motivation. He chose his best friend Steven. Tamra asked her bar crawling, wingman Monica to be her maid of honor. Monica and Tamra had met in an acting class several years before. Sophie would be the flower girl.

Chapter Twelve

The year moved forward. When Sophie started first grade in the fall, Tamra and Belle got into a bit of a tussle because Tamra said she should take Sophie to school on the first day, and Belle said that she should. Laramie came up with the outrageous idea—to Tamra and Belle—to let Sophie choose.

Sophie chose Royce, who, although scheduled to be in New York for a week, postponed his trip for a few hours. He was nervous, a ridiculous sensation he decided, when all he was doing was driving a little girl to school. Royce noticed her outfit: purple tennies and socks, white long shirt. *Is it a dress or a shirt?* He wondered. White did not seem practical. She wore white pants with a pink paisley pattern. He introduced himself to Sophie's teacher. He wanted to clarify his relationship to Sophie, yet he was uncomfortable with telling the teacher. He introduced himself as a family friend. He reported to Tamra and Laramie, Belle was too miffed to get on the phone, that Sophie had been safely delivered to school.

"How did it feel?" Tamra asked him.

Again with the feelings.

Tamra, in a quiet moment in the midst of wedding planning 24/7, thought about being married to Royce. She sat in the bedroom she would soon be vacating, sitting cross-legged on her bed with wedding magazines covering the white chenille bedspread. Married. Being faithful to one man for the rest of her life. She had never been faithful in her past relationships.

The man she would miss was her "fuck buddy," Morgan Breedlove, a fellow acting student. They hooked up from time to time, generally during fallow periods in their lives. Tamra was actually fond of Morgan. She didn't love him, but they were kindred spirits, passionate about their craft, cunning manipulators. Morgan somehow subsisted on income from acting gigs, and Tamra emulated him. She thought about cutting Morgan out of her life. Could she do that?

Royce. The ticket out of her parents' orbit and the struggle to pay her credit card bills. A life of travel and excessive spending. But Tamra didn't want to be with Royce simply for his money. She wasn't a gold digger. No. She cared about the man. He made her feel safe and protected. She liked that he was tall, and she fit into his hugs. He loved her and treated her like a princess. Except for that prenup nonsense. But that was over. Even though she signed it, she thought she could get around it somehow. He would be generous and give her whatever she wanted. The stores on Rodeo Drive would get to know her quite well. Did she love him? Well, sure. She was turned on every time she saw him. He was gorgeous. He had the disciplined body of a triathlete or a maximum-security prisoner. His golden skin and deep brown eyes knocked her out. That was love. He would be Sophie's father and father to other children they had.

He took away her loneliness, although she never told him she was lonely. Before Royce, even though she went out every night she didn't have an evening acting class, the friends she went out with were just bar crawl buddies. They drank together like drinking was an Olympic sport. In the light of day, her hookups left her feeling hollow, as though her insides had been scooped out and tossed to the side of the road, all pink. Uck! What an image!

Was she really going to be faithful to Royce? Wow, she hadn't thought about it before now. The sex with him was major, but she didn't want to give up Morgan. Royce didn't know about him. She only told him about her female friends. Maybe having sex with Morgan wouldn't count, because she already knew him and had sex with him before Royce. Fucked her silly, Morgan did. Well, she'd play it by ear.

Chapter Thirteen

On sunny May 6th in 1995, the wedding took place at Royce's friend's estate in Malibu in his backyard garden—in the same way that St. James Park is the backyard garden for Buckingham Palace—with ivy-covered walls on three sides. Reginald had been frosted when Royce told him the location of the wedding. His father said they should be married in the church. However, Royce, that is, Tamra prevailed. Reginald also weighed in on the proposed guest list: business associates and clients. Tamra said she didn't mind; she expected they would buy outrageously expensive wedding gifts.

Guests entered the wedding site under a trellis covered with baby pink and salmon English roses, white stephanotis, and ivy. Orange and lemon trees gave off a delicious smell: happiness, innocence, trust. The smell of the Pacific Ocean, salty and cold, blended, rather than competed, with the trees. Two hundred fifty white chairs were arranged in rows of half circles facing the altar bisected by an aisle.

As a harpist played and a soloist sang, "Love is a Many Splendored Thing," a bishop of the Episcopal Church led Royce and Steven from a side gate to the covered floral canopy. Royce stood at the left side of the bishop. The guests applauded.

Royce had a big smile on his red face until he heard the beginning notes of Canon in D Major on violins and harp. He saw Sophie walk down the aisle in a calf length white gown and white Mary Janes. Her hair had a small crown of roses. She carried a basket with orchids that she presented to Belle and Evelyn. She curtsied as she handed them their flowers. Royce's heart did loop-deloops, his pride was that great. That was his daughter, his first child. Tamra's friend

Monica walked down the aisle in a pale pink floor-length strapless gown.

Royce was more nervous than he had ever been before and wanted to pace, but he could not. He had to stand still, and he looked as though he were waiting for the last lifeboat off the Titanic. That is, until he saw delirious Laramie begin the walk with Tamra's hand resting in the crook of his arm. Tamra was tiny in her wedding dress, a soft white Vera Wang ball gown with pink pearls, crystals, and yellow sapphires encrusted on the strapless bodice. Royce knew that because he had heard Tamra on the phone with his mother pretty much constantly as the wedding date got close. Tamra looked at Royce, a schoolgirl with a crush, through a wispy veil that reached to her chin. The veil was attached to a white silk pillbox hat. Tamra and her box hats. Royce got tears in his eyes that threatened to fall down his cheeks. He took in a breath and exhaled. He smiled and watched her walk down the rose petal aisle by Laramie's side. She held a bouquet of pink, salmon, and yellow roses and greens. The only reason he knew the names of the flowers was because roses came up quite a bit in Tamra's monologues.

When Tamra and Laramie were a few feet from him, Royce held out his right hand to her. She did not let go of her dad's arm or the bouquet. They closed the gap, and Laramie gave him Tamra's right hand. She clasped Royce's hand and did not release the pressure. She handed her bouquet to Monica and held his left hand, too.

The bishop looked at them. "Tamra, he's not going anywhere."

Laughter from the congregation.

Royce whispered "Whew."

The bishop addressed the congregation. Royce's brain drifted in and out as he continued to check Tamra out like a fine Ferrari. "…the union of husband and wife in heart, body, and mind…for the help and comfort given one another in prosperity and adversity…for the procreation of children and their nurture…Into this holy union Royce Hamilton Kallas and Tamra Belle Wooden now come to be joined. If any of you can show just cause why they may not lawfully be married, speak now; or else forever hold your peace."

Silence.

"I require and charge you both, here in the presence of God, that if either of you know any reason why you may not be united in marriage lawfully, and in accordance with God's Word, you do now confess it."

It was time for the moment of truth or ill:

"Royce, wilt thou have this woman to be thy wedded wife to live together after God's ordinance in the Holy Estate of matrimony? Wilt thou love her? Comfort her, honor and keep her, in sickness and in health, and forsaking all others keep thee only unto her as long as you both shall live?"

"I will."

The bishop repeated the questions to Tamra.

"I will, sweetie," she said, not a communicant of the Episcopal Church.

He smiled and then realized the service had just started. He attempted to squeeze her hand, but since she was holding onto his hands in a death grip, he could not get much traction. She only let go of his hands when they exchanged rings, and then she grasped them for the remainder of the ceremony.

The service proceeded at a pace slower than Royce remembered, having been to many Episcopal weddings: hymns; ministry of the Word; prayers ("Look mercifully upon this man and this woman…"); scripture readings; exchanging of vows; blessing and giving of rings; the pronouncement of marriage; the Lord's Prayer; another prayer so long Royce wondered if the bishop was being paid by the word, with one phrase that made Tamra wince ("may…forgiveness heal guilt…"), and the blessing of the marriage.

Royce whispered to Tamra to release his hands. She did not know they had come to the final moment. He fumbled lifting the veil over the back of the hat. He took her face in his hands and looked at her.

"I love you today and will love you always. You are in my heart," he said.

Tamra got tears in her eyes. "I love you, too, sweetie. We'll never be apart."

The congregation, believers and skeptics of the union, stood and applauded. Some whooped and cheered. She put her arm through his, and they walked up the aisle to the Wedding March from *A Midsummer Night's Dream*. They stopped under the trellis, and he grasped onto her waist with one hand and the back of her neck with the other. He planted one on her that was interrupted by Steven.

"People cannot get by you, old man."

Royce did not move. He continued to kiss her.

The reception was held in a covered tent on the tennis court. The floor of the court was covered in white carpet, and there were six long tables seating forty each covered in salmon-colored linens. Chandeliers hung down with golf ball-sized crystals. When the 30-piece orchestra played the opening of "When the Lights Are Low," Royce led Tamra onto the dance floor. Guests stopped in mid-slurp of their lobster bisque when Tony Bennett walked out from behind the orchestra and took his place on the stage. The applause almost drowned him out while he sang. They all put on quite a show, Tony Bennett and the happy couple, with the dance Tamra and Royce had practiced for two months, sometimes on Royce's patio while Sophie swam in the pool.

Best man Steven gave a toast. He had a Cuban cigar in one hand and a crystal champagne flute in the other. "I asked Royce if there was anything I couldn't say, and he said no. So Tamra, this is really his fault."

Sitting in the middle of one of the tables, Royce put his arm around Tamra's shoulder and gave it a proprietorial squeeze. She leaned into him.

"I'm glad Tamra came along into your life, Royce, because, otherwise, I was going to have the responsibility of putting you into assisted living." He took a long drag of his cigar.

Tamra gave Royce a besotted smile. Reginald put his elbow on the table and held his cigar like a Hollywood gangster. Evelyn had a smile that did not go away all night—except when she was crying.

"Tamra, since your new husband is ready to qualify for Medicare, you need to watch Royce's diet carefully," Steven said. "The junk we put into our stomachs is enough to have killed most of us sitting here years ago. Red meat is awful." This said to a roomful of people eating Kobe beef filet mignon with béarnaise sauce. "Soft drinks corrode your stomach lining. Chinese food is loaded with MSG. High fat diets can be disastrous. None of us realizes the long-term harm caused by germs in our drinking water. However, there is one thing that is the most dangerous of all, and we all have eaten or will eat it. There is one food that causes the most grief and suffering for years after eating it. Wedding cake." He waited a beat and raised his glass to the newlyweds. "Mazel tov."

The guests stood, raising their glasses. "Mazel tov."

Evening turned to night. Royce danced with Tamra's mother and then his mother, who was very happy indeed that her forty-one-year-old son finally got married, while Tamra danced with her father. She made her father-in-law happy, too. In front of his friends and clients she danced so nicely, almost primly, with him. And she had signed the prenup.

Royce and Tamra Kallas, a perfect confluence of naiveté and avarice.

PART TWO

Chapter Fourteen

Tamra moved into Royce's four bedroom and a den in Beverly Hills. She did not complain about the long hours he spent at the office. He was making money. What could be wrong about that? They still ran together, went to dinner and movies. They hosted dinners and small parties, Tamra employing a chef and servers. She needed help because all she could cook was Welsh rarebit and shepherd's pie.

She enjoyed time to herself and felt giddy living on the family dole. She filled her days mingling with millionaires' wives at the Riviera Country Club, yoga, acting class, and speech instruction. Tamra wanted to be a famous actress and socialite—without the bleeding-heart socializing. When they got engaged, she had terminated her employment as a, what, Royce had never been sure, and she didn't clarify for him.

"We have plenty of money, right?" she said, never having been told the extent of the Kallas fortune. "Why don't we do things with the money that are fun?"

"Sweetheart, having money is not fun or exciting. It is work to maintain and enhance the estate that is entrusted to me. It is my responsibility to mirror the accomplishments of my father, grandfather, and great-grandfather by being a good steward. I cannot be the Kallas who drops the ball. Actually, we did something fun with *the money*. You got the Ferrari you wanted."

She was startled by his dispassionate speech. He wasn't acting as though she had a right to know the extent of his assets. Although she acknowledged to herself that she probably wouldn't understand all his business dealings, she thought he should at least give her the bottom line. Exactly how much money did she have to spend?

Despite his lecture, Royce was generous with Tamra. She bought clothes that filled their closets: Chanel, Dior, Marchesa. He did not balk at the cost of the private acting lessons or the workshops that took Tamra to New York. Sophie was put in gymnastics and ballet, and, at her request, science camp. Tamra refurnished the house after she convinced Royce that the house was too masculine. Before the words "go ahead and get what you want" were out of his mouth, Tamra hired an interior decorator and a landscape architect—which pissed off Royce's gardener.

After the wedding, she asked him to buy another house.

"I thought you loved my house."

"Sweetie, I do. Your house is charming. I thought we would buy a bigger house now, for parties and a house that is ours, not just yours."

"Let us wait until we need to. When we have another child."

To that end Tamra did her level best to get pregnant, although she told Royce she would stay on the pill.

Chapter Fifteen

Ten months later in March 1996 Theodora was born. Tamra told Royce her birth control pills obviously were defective. Tamra had an uneventful pregnancy—except she was consistently irritated that her OB doctor weighed her during each visit. She wore designer maternity clothes and bought Burberry and Stella McCartney clothes for the baby.

Tamra chose the name Theodora because she thought it fit a rich girl, although she did not tell Royce that was the reason for her choice. Tamra also chose the baby's middle name, Evelyn, because she thought she would get a lot of mileage out of that choice, but she privately thought the name so beyond ancient and gross. "It's perfect," she said to Royce, who blushed, turning his golden-brown face crimson. He could only shake his head with pleasure.

Royce could not say the words to express his feelings about the baby because they were new to him. Sophie had come to him fully formed. Theodora was a brand new person. If pressed, he would have said he felt like a display of Hallmark greeting cards. The first time he held Theodora, still covered in blood and vernix, he had mixed sensations of ecstasy and revulsion. A nurse quickly and competently removed the offending goo, and he felt tightness in his breathing, a contraction to his heart, and punch in his stomach. He also felt a sob in his throat, but life's training did not allow it to escape.

He went to the hospital waiting room and brought both sets of parents and Sophie to see Theodora, but not before Tamra put on makeup, combed her hair, and threw a light pink lounging jacket over her shoulders. Tamra was in a VIP suite with soothing rust and muted turquoise wallpaper of cherubs and angels. The main room had recessed lighting, coffered ceiling, and a wet bar. Kenny G played on an unseen sound system. There was a bedroom off the main room for Royce to spend the night. Tamra covered her bed in a pale lavender satin bedspread.

Laramie cried quietly as he held the baby and rocked her oh so gently. "She reminds me of Sophie," he said.

Tamra told the four new grandparents the baby's name. "We're going to call her Teddy."

"Theodora's better," Belle said. "You call her Teddy, and it's going to sound like you've named her for a dead president. She seems like kind of a small baby."

"No, she's eight pounds twelve ounces, twenty-two inches long," said Royce, proud and cognizant of the criticism in Belle's voice. Tamra heard it, but maintained her *Mona Lisa* façade.

Reginald was pleased, of course, over the selection of the middle name, and he puffed up like the rooster in a chicken coop. Belle and Laramie left after an abbreviated visit, cut short by Belle who said they were having dinner with friends.

Evelyn cried and dribbled tears onto Teddy's face as she held the newborn. "My darling girl," she said, looking at Tamra, "you have created a beautiful daughter who, I bet, is going to look just like you."

It was hard to tell at that point whom Teddy would resemble because she had only a tuft of hair and pale eyes that might have been green.

Royce put Teddy into Reginald's shivering arms as he sat in one of the club chairs. The elder Kallas had not held a baby in forty-one years. He had not held Royce much, because he reasoned, he wasn't the nanny. "Are you having a good day?" Reginald asked Teddy. "She's a healthy charmer, she is," he said. Teddy for her part yawned and scrunched up her face.

As Reginald and Evelyn prepared to leave, Reginald took Tamra's hands in his, not having had physical contact with her since a dance at the wedding. "Thank you for the gift of this child." He took an envelope from his jacket pocket and, without fanfare, handed it to Tamra. He pecked her on the cheek, an act that Royce locked his eyes on.

After they left, Royce and Tamra looked at each other. She giggled.

"What did he give you?"

"Let's see. A check for a million dollars! It's in my name!" Tamra squeaked. She waved the check high in the air. She shrieked with such enthusiasm that Teddy, lying in her clear plastic bassinet, yelped. Tamra would get used to seeing million dollar checks, but that one was her first. "Do you think this means they aren't going to give us the carriage we asked for?"

Tamra hired a baby nurse, Portia, who worked twelve-hour days five days a week, and Emily who worked weekends. And Anne, a nanny for Sophie, worked during the week. Tamra slept most of the day. Something brewed under the surface of her skin. She had an uneasy feeling when she was alone with Teddy. During the nannies' time off, Tamra squeezed the wailing baby monitor willing Teddy to stop crying and go back to sleep.

When Teddy slept, she tiptoed into the nursery and stopped about a foot from the crib. With her hands behind her back as though she had been arrested for child abuse, she looked at the bundle asleep on her back, with a backdrop of copper and beige imported linen wallpaper. This was her baby daughter to nurture, unlike Sophie who had immediately been taken by Belle and Laramie while Tamra finished her school year in Arizona. Tamra had been away at school for the first three years of Sophie's life, only coming home on breaks. Teddy was a new living person. Tamra had never cared for any beings that drew breath, not human, dog, or parakeet. However, she had once grown bacteria in a biology class.

Royce was a super smart guy with education overload, and Tamra wanted Sophie to be smart, too. Sophie had moved in fulltime with Royce and Tamra at the end of her school year in June 1995. Not a great student herself except for acting, Tamra hired a tutor to help Sophie with her reading. Tamra sat at the dining room table and watched Sophie with the tutor until she got bored, and then she would polish her nails.

Tamra made sure that from Royce's perspective she appeared to enjoy being a wife and mother. She directed the chef on the menu and ensured the home was comfortable for Royce's return from the office, just as his mother did for his father. She walked Teddy in the carriage—that had its own generator that cooled and warmed the baby. Tamra sat in a rocking chair with Teddy, who made gurgling sounds in the key of C.

Six months after Teddy's birth, when the nurse's contract ended, Tamra told Royce she was going to hire an additional nanny for Teddy. "So I will have help and can have projects on my own where I will represent the Kallas name," she said.

"That is actually a good idea. Charities, yes," Royce said.

Tamra was not referring to charities. She had

involuntary muscle spasms when she thought of sitting through interminable charity lunches. She abhorred the videos of starving and sick children. They made her want to gag. No charity work. When she said she wanted to represent the family name, she referred to the name "Tamra Kallas" that would appear on a marquee, her name in ten-inch red plastic letters.

Tamra silently cursed her husband's industriousness when Evelyn called her and said that Royce had suggested that she extend an invitation to her charity luncheons and brunches. Evelyn was active in the Pacific Palisades Women's Club, Riviera Country Club, Episcopal Church Women, and the League of Women Voters, the latter of which did not show starving children; rather, the group discussed referendums, whatever they were. Tamra was then on the hook for several months, and, indeed, did see video presentations of starving children in India and in refugee camps in Kenya, children with AIDS (How did children get AIDS? Ew!), children with brain cancer, children with leukemia, children with cleft palates. After Tamra saw two video presentations from Doctors Without Borders in one week, she told Evelyn she was *frantically* busy with Sophie and Teddy and would have to—reluctantly—stop going to luncheons and meetings.

In a year and a half, Sophie learned that her sister was her mother, she was a flower girl in her sister/mother's wedding, she moved into her new mother and stepfather's house, she was adopted by her stepfather, and she became a sister to a new baby, all of which should have made her the poster child for mental health issues. She was five when she met Royce, and he was amazed that she seemed to handle whatever new challenges life hurled at her. She did not wet the bed, act out, or have problems at school. She was simply Sophie.

Although Tamra had been campaigning for twenty-five dollars, Royce gave Sophie an allowance of five dollars a week. He was firm about the amount. He said he wanted to teach her to value money, and Tamra said she could value money more if her allowance was higher. Royce began to teach Sophie about saving money and investing. He sat down with her at the kitchen island and opened the financial section of the *Wall Street Journal*. He asked her to give him the names of three toys she would like to own. Her first choice, no hesitation, was a Barbie doll. Royce said that a company named Mattel made Barbie dolls, and investors could own a piece of the company. That sounded good to her. He showed her the pages in the newspaper for the NASDAQ, found Mattel and taught her how to find the price per share: $29.75. She also picked Disney at $61.98.

"For my third pick, I want to give money to the Ronald McDonald House," Sophie said, looking at Royce's finger to see where it would point to her choice.

"That is not a stock. That's a charity. You give money to a charity, but you do not own a part of the company," he said and folded the newspaper.

"That's okay. Can I do that, too?" She put her elbows on the counter and rested her head in her hands.

"That is fine. Now we are going to check the prices of your stocks every day." Royce looked intently at her green eyes that spooked him as much as Tamra's had when he met her. "If the price goes up, your stock will be worth more, and if the price goes down—"

"I know, I know. I get it." Sophie was seriously squirming in her chair by that time.

"I will make the first buy for you. Let us begin with one hundred shares of each," Royce said. "You will have to make additional buys with your own money. Understand?"

She shook her head "yes" and rolled her eyes, as though she were listening to Sesame Street's Count von Count obsess over numbers.

"I want you to make some phone calls to find out how to make donations to Ronald McDonald House," he said.

"How is she supposed to do that?" Tamra asked, sounding more like a seven-year-old than her daughter, as she looked over Sophie's shoulder.

"She will figure that out, will you not, Sophie?"

"I can do it, mommy," Sophie said. "I can do all of this."

The mother of two children, Tamra returned to her acting classes, which Royce discouraged, because her absences did not belong in his tableau of a Kallas family. He had not minded the notion of the acting classes when they dated, but began to believe them to be unseemly for Kallases, who did not draw unnecessary attention to themselves. The prenup contained language that restricted Tamra's acting to taking acting classes only, no parts in productions, but she wasn't concerned by that prohibition, and he didn't make a fuss, so cool.

When fellow students asked why she had left acting classes, with mixed feelings she told them she had had a baby. The reactions of "Congratulations!" and requests to see photos of Teddy had an effect on Tamra. No one in the classes had an expectation how she should behave around the baby or how she should feel about Teddy. Just as actors adopt behaviors for their characters, Tamra assimilated other peoples' positive responses to her being a mother.

Teddy's grandparents provided additional strokes to Tamra. She gave her new nanny Julia half a day off when the grandparents visited. She was getting quite good at playing her role.

"Look how big you are," Reginald said to Teddy.

Tamra, assuming the observations were about her, opened her mouth to retort, when she looked over her shoulder and saw him lifting Teddy in the air.

"You're doing a beautiful job with her," Evelyn said.

Royce beamed. Tamra walked to where Reginald stood and put one hand lightly on his arm.

"You might not want to hold her like that. She has a tendency to—"

It was too late. The left lapel of Reginald's $2,800 suit looked like a pigeon crapped on it.

"Look how clever she is." Reginald laughed.

Royce, Evelyn, and Tamra looked at each other. Tamra sucked in her cheeks to keep from laughing. Evelyn charged in with a hanky for Reginald.

"Oh no, leave it, leave it," Reginald said. "I shouldn't have worn this suit to see this charming little princess." He handed off the new light of his life to Evelyn while he took his jacket off. "Now give her back." He nuzzled her cheek. Teddy drooled.

Tamra never thought of Reginald as a nuzzler. She did think he had lost more than a nice set of threads; with Teddy he lost his restraint in exhibiting emotions.

"Tamra, you are taking good care of my granddaughter," Reginald said.

There it is again, she thought. Like she was just the nanny for his angelic possession, but he did think she was doing well, so there was that.

When Sophie came home from school, Evelyn gushed over her, said how adorable she was. Reginald asked her if she was learning anything in school. When Sophie began to recite her part in a play, Royce groaned, "Not another actress." Tamra gave him a sharp look.

"I can count money," Poppa," Sophie said. "Give me the money in your wallet, and I'll count it for you." She put out her hand.

Royce and Reginald looked at each other. "Well, I do not know, Sophie—" Royce said.

"It's all right," Evelyn said and retrieved Reginald's wallet from his jacket's inside pocket. She handed the bills to Sophie, and sat down on the couch.

Sophie plunked herself down on the wide-plank hardwood floor, sat on her feet, and laid the money out in front of her. The bills were in order of denominations. Tamra was interested to see how much money Reginald carried around, and she walked from the kitchen to where Sophie was sitting.

"You have twelve one hundred-dollar bills," Sophie said. She furrowed her brow and said loudly, "I don't know how to do times yet."

"Add them, Sophie," Royce said, handing her a blank pad of paper. He kneeled down on the floor by her side.

Reginald, enamored with Teddy, walked up and down the great room, bouncing her in his arms.

Sophie dutifully wrote one hundred twelve times. "It's easy, because there are so many zeros. How do I say this number?" she said, pointing to the total.

Tamra was ready to answer that question. "It's twelve hundred. Or one thousand, two hundred," she said.

"How can it be two answers?" Sophie said.

"That is a good question," Royce said, looking at his father. "I guess it is like slang. Sometimes there are easier ways to say a number." He frowned.

Tamra thought he didn't look like he was satisfied with his answer.

"There are four fifties, and four fives." Sophie wrote out the problems. "Now what do I do?"

"The first thing you do is give Poppa his money, and, secondly, we will add these numbers together," Royce said.

"I don't get to keep Poppa's money?" She smiled at Royce and gave him a wink.

Desperate to love her new daughter just as she loved Sophie, Tamra found a head doctor in the yellow pages and begged for help. How to explain that she didn't want to be with Teddy? She didn't like the daily needs of the child—every day all the time.

"I really need for you to do something for me," Tamra said to the doctor. "I want to spend fun time with Teddy. I want my husband and his parents, his father really, to see that I'm a good mother, but I'm…I'm afraid of her."

Tamra sat on a rust-colored couch facing Dr. Nancy Herzfeld who sat in a tan straight-back chair. Tamra wore leggings and a tunic with sandals. She sat on her hands, which caused her diamond engagement ring to poke her thigh.

"Do you feel pressure from your husband or your father-in-law?" Dr. Herzfeld asked, taking notes.

"No, well, yes. It's not that they say, 'This is what you have to do.' Nothing like that. But they're kind of old fashioned, and they think…they hope I'll turn into a mother like my mother-in-law."

"What kind of mother is she?"

"Wow. I didn't think you'd be asking me so many questions. Can't I just have a prescription or something?" Tamra held up her hands in supplication.

"I need to get to know you first," the therapist said.

"Get to know me, huh?" Tamra snorted and shifted on the cushion, leaning back into the couch and fiddling with her diamond. "Everyone thinks I'm a rebel or kooky or something. But I'm not. I'm just me." She touched the zipper of her tunic.

"Tell me who you are."

"This is tough. I'm all in here," she gestured with her hands on her chest. She was getting frustrated with these questions, when she knew a pill would make everything better.

"Yes, it can be difficult to put your feelings into words."

Dr. Herzfeld looked like a nice person, dark brown hair, creamy light black skin. Tamra could fix her up, put a little volume into the hair, get her out of that no-shape suit. And the shoes. Blech!

The doctor asked Tamra questions about her childhood. Tamra told the doctor about being an only child, her confusion when she brought home report cards and her mother criticized her. Her dad not coming to her defense, even though she could see sadness in his eyes.

Feeling she was alone at home, her one salvation was her cousin Magda who was three years older than Tamra. When Magda got her driver's license, she took Tamra with her to various and sundry places: friends' parties, friends of friends' parties, completely unknown parties. Tamra was young, only thirteen when she began hanging out with Magda, but she learned how to dress (short) and to wear her hair (long and straight, sometimes crimped) and to handle guys (understand they were one pulsing hormone). At first, she was scared, but it came across that she was playing hard to get, which, of course, made the walking penises even more interested. Then two years later—bam!—Tamra was pregnant. Tamra began crying as she told her story. She put her hands in front of her face, which apparently gave her reassurance to continue talking. The doctor handed her a tissue, and Tamra blew her nose.

"You know what was really fucked?" She put a hand to her mouth. "Oh, I'm sorry."

"Go ahead. Tell the story in your own words." Dr. Herzfeld crossed her legs.

Tamra furrowed her brow. Whose words could they be but hers? "Okay, what was really fucked was my parents raising my first daughter Sophie." She emphasized her point by pointing her index finger at the doctor. "She was my baby, and my mother said I could only be her sister." New tears.

The doctor pressed on, mining Tamra's long-held hurts. Then the doctor said they would have to stop for the day. Dr. Herzfeld recommended more sessions. Tamra asked for prescriptions again, and the doctor gave them to her. Xanax and Elavil, with six refills. The last thing the doctor said to Tamra was, "good luck." Tamra smiled. She didn't intend to go back.

As Tamra left the doctor's office, she tried really, really hard to give herself a pep talk, because she not only wanted to love Teddy, but she also wanted to have another baby in a few years. She had five million reasons for wanting another baby, plus maybe another million dollar check from Reginald. Tamra took the medication, but didn't follow up on the sessions. The idea of telling a stranger all of her thoughts and feelings scared her a bit, but mostly grossed her out. She didn't tell Royce she had gone to a doctor. She hid her prescriptions in her makeup bag. Tamra didn't get instant relief from the meds. After a couple of weeks, she thought it had just been a waste of time.

A month after the doctor's visit, she wasn't as anxious as she had been and her fears of taking care of Teddy subsided. She spent more time with her. As she fed Teddy a bottle and cereal, she read from her class scripts. She became the characters and read all the parts. Or she made speeches like a politician at the Iowa caucus. Teddy looked at her mother with eyes that mirrored Tamra's: intense and green. As Tamra made strange vocalizations, Teddy laughed, pulling on her feet. Tamra curled her daughter's hair by winding strands the color of rice around her finger.

She dressed Teddy in tiny smocks and Sophie in cute dresses from Barneys and Juicy Couture so Royce would "ooh" and "ah" when he came home in the evenings or from business trips. But in her heart she didn't like sharing attention with her daughters. An acting chestnut: don't follow any animal act or children.

Chapter Sixteen

Laramie was collateral damage when Tamra decided to put in her claim as Sophie's mother. Belle let it be known she was upset that her role as mother had been usurped by her daughter, but no one considered Laramie's feelings. He had been named Sophie's father as part of the ruse after Sophie's birth. He was neither consulted about being Sophie's father nor about being replaced. He quietly accepted that Royce would be Sophie's father. Whatever anguish he felt, he never said it out loud.

And so in September 1996 Royce became Sophie's father. Royce's adoption of Sophie was final. An amended Certification of Birth was recorded. The transition for Sophie from Mr. Kallas, to Royce, to Dad had been an easy one. Sophie simply agreed to call people what they asked her to call them. In that way Tamra became Mommy, Mama became grandmamma, Daddy became grandpa, and Royce became Dad. Sophie was resilient, a quality she would call upon throughout her life.

To celebrate the adoption Royce and Tamra had a party, their first big party since Teddy was born. They invited both sets of grandparents, some of Royce's friends, and Tamra's new friends from the country club set. She did not invite any of her theatre friends. She didn't think Royce would understand them.

Royce was a puffed-up cock of the walk that night. Tamra wore an Alexander McQueen short black sequined dress, but not the "fuck me" heels, Royce was happy to see. He smiled at the thought that the cost of her dresses had increased exponentially since the night at Gramercy Welders

Society. Tamra had dressed both of her daughters in designer dresses because even babies could be fashionable. Sophie's dress was a Dolce and Gabbana apple green satin with a royal blue sash. Tamra brought a stylist in to do Sophie's hair, long and sleek, dark blonde, the color women would kill to have. Teddy wore a pale pink dress that covered her toes. Nevertheless, Tamra put her in white Mary Janes. For his part Royce wore a black Gucci shirt, black Dolce and Gabbana sports jacket, and black Montcler slacks. He apparently was going for the Darth Vader look.

Servers carried silver trays with marinated jumbo shrimp, crab cakes, lobster rolls, mini sandwiches with fillet mignon and imported cheeses, stuffed artichoke bottoms, sashimi, mini quiches, seared ahi tuna, crab-stuffed mushrooms, chocolate dipped strawberries, stuffed new potatoes with salmon mascarpone and caviar, gourmet brownies, and for the children—or not so children— macaroni and cheese cups, mini peanut butter and jelly sandwiches, and corndogs. As the evening lengthened, servers added snacks to their trays: Pringles, cracker jacks, M&Ms, Twix, and Chips Ahoy. For Reginald Mr. Goodbars. Royce saw Steven and Sophie doing a sword fight with two Red Vines. Wielding bottles of spirits, three bartenders made sure everyone was anesthetized. Teddy, too, had a bottle.

Valets ran long distances after parking cars several blocks away. Before the party, at Royce's request Tamra took gift baskets to all of the residents on the cul-de-sac to apologize for the vehicle jam-up he anticipated. Tamra had tall tables and stools installed around the pool. No one jumped in or was thrown into the water that night, although Steven came to the party in his fins and asked Royce if this was a swim party. Everyone stayed dry.

Royce watched as Reginald moved from group to

group showing off Teddy, lifting her dress a bit so whomever he had corralled appreciated the tiny shoes. And he said, proudly, that Teddy's dress was Dior. Although Belle had a full glass of wine whenever Royce saw her, she was not her animated and affectionate self. Laramie, as usual, followed along behind her, although he did entreat Reginald to give up the baby for a bit. Evelyn tried to keep Sophie close, but Sophie wanted to run around the house with her friends from school.

Royce heard Sophie tell Andie, a girl who lived in the cul-de-sac, "I have a new dad now."

"But you've always had this dad," Andie said, pointing to Royce. She had only known Sophie since she moved into the house after the wedding.

"But today he's special. We got to go to court and talk to a judge and everything. Everyone had to raise their right hands, but I raised my left by mistake, and I cried because I thought the judge would get mad at me."

An Episcopal bishop from St. Johns, the Most Rev. William J. Butler, gave a blessing to the family, Royce, Tamra, Sophie, and Teddy. Royce presented Sophie with a London Blue stone set into a platinum pendant on a slim platinum chain. It was made with Sophie in mind and matched the blue sash on her dress. Royce saw that Tamra had tears in her eyes as he put the necklace on Sophie.

Sophie ran off to her room and then ran back quickly. She handed Royce a handmade card on heavy lavender stock. She had used Magic Markers in blue, green, and red. On the cover, the card said, "MY DAD!!" Stars and hearts flew around the words. Royce opened the card, and inside Sophie had pasted pictures from magazines of a Maserati, a male model in a suit, a cruise ship, a house, and a dollar sign. He, too, had tears. The guests said, "Ah!"

———

121

Eating a corndog, Steven walked up to Royce who was watching his guests.

"You done good, my friend," Steven said.

Royce sighed, a happy, contented sigh. "Yes, is this not perfection?"

Tamra had been unable to convince Royce to buy a bigger house, even though he had told her he would when they had a second child. Tamra turned her skills into another perk: vacations. When Teddy was a year old, Tamra cajoled Royce to take a vacation in the way she knew best: sex. They had a lot of sex, which resulted in a number of vacations over the next three years. They vacationed during Sophie's breaks at the house in Rancho Mirage in the spring, and in the winter at the house in Telluride. In the summers they took trips in the yacht up to Alaska and down to Central America. They went through the Panama Canal and cruised the Caribbean. Tamra took her nanny Julia and new nanny Mary Ellen along so she could lie by the pool or on the deck or ski unhampered. Royce worked on the vacations when he wasn't skiing and snorkeling. In Royce's and Tamra's minds their world was perfect. Unfortunately, they didn't occupy the same world.

Evelyn, besotted with both Sophie and Teddy, invited Tamra to visit her during afternoons while the men of the family worked to preserve and grow money. She did not disfavor Sophie. She did not favor Teddy. In her mind they were the same: delectable.

Evelyn and Teddy sat on the floor of her great room in her 15,800 square foot house dressing Millennium Princess Barbie in a dark blue velvet gown with organza and shining lace. At the same time Sophie sat on the gold silk couch braiding Evelyn's white blonde hair.

"No, Nana, I do it," two-year-old Teddy said, although she had difficulty with the doll's thin arms.

"Tamra, you must be very busy with these two."

"Um hmm," Tamra said as she looked around the 1,000 square foot great room with covetousness in her heart. She mentally staged the room to her liking. She loved Evelyn and her taste in clothes, but this room did not look like Evelyn at all. Too masculine, dark colors, massive chairs. But she did like all the French doors going to the deck. "Is this house too big for you and Reginald?"

"Don't be silly, sweetheart. No house is too big. Ow, Sophie. What are you doing?" Evelyn said. She grabbed at her hair.

"Sorry, Nana. Your hair is really short."

Tamra wanted Evelyn to keep focus. "So, my house is too small?"

"Of course, I think your house is too small," Evelyn said, rubbing her head.

That was all Tamra needed to hear.

"Evie," Tamra said—Evelyn liked Tamra to call her Evie—"I like want to move, but I'm not sure he wants to."

"You've been married for four years. Haven't you learned by now that Royce wants to do whatever you tell him he wants to do?" Evelyn stopped putting the gown on Barbie and got a mini-Tamra stare from Teddy for her trouble. "Yes, Teddy. I've got her gown ready."

"Stop moving, Nana," Sophie said.

"Sophie," Tamra said, without much enthusiasm. She hummed tunelessly as she walked around the room, running her fingers on the backs of rust colored couches, built-in mahogany bookshelves, a casual table that sat fourteen, side tables with white marble tops, black leather bar stools. She picked up framed photographs and flipped through architectural books with pictures of magnificent homes. When she found a glossy spread of Julia Roberts' mansion, Tamra asked, "How large a home do you think I…I mean, *we* should get?"

"At least 10,000 square feet. You need bedrooms for the girls and then future children." Evelyn didn't notice that Tamra flinched at *future children*. "You need rooms for your staff, and you will need living spaces to entertain large groups."

Tamra joined Evelyn on the floor. "Will you help me convince Royce?"

"Of course I will."

"Evie," Tamra said dreamily, "how did you meet Reginald?"

"Well, my family is from New York City, and they all think I've gone down in class by marrying a working man," Evelyn said. "I told them, it's not as though he's working on a construction crew." Her mouth emitted a sound that was somewhere between a squeal and a laugh, with the result that dogs in Santa Barbara heard it.

"'Evie, you are scrumptious, and I want to eat you up,' Reginald said when we were together in the early years. He would nuzzle my neck and make me giggle. I am a good wife. I keep myself slim and wear only designer clothes. My hair and nails are always done. I keep lists of parties and who attends, and what I wore, and I give parties with a detailed eye. I travel wherever, whenever. While I defer to Reginald's judgment, his needs, and his beliefs, a large percentage of those beliefs were ideas I planted in his mind.

"He graduated from Rutgers with an engineering degree and from graduate school in international finance. I graduated from high school and worked at Bullocks. I got the job to irritate my father, who was inclined to dictate financial and life decisions to me. Reginald came into the store to find a necklace or something for his sister's birthday. 'How tall is she? What color is her hair?' I asked.' Uh, she is about your height, and her hair—he gestured with both hands around his head, looking like someone picking up a bowling ball—'is your color, I think.' What would you say her style is: maternal, professional woman?' 'Stop, stop. This experience was not supposed to be painful,' Reginald said. 'Who says?' I said and then put my manicured hand to my mouth. I believed I had gotten too familiar with a customer, which was forbidden by the management. 'I'm sorry. I shouldn't have said that.' Reginald let go with a belly laugh. 'Are you kidding me? It is so refreshing to hear someone give me back as good as I gave,' Reginald said in his stentorian voice, you know the voice I'm talking about."

Tamra nodded. Her daughters had wandered off to the kitchen in search of the cook's treats.

"'Thank you, sir. Let me see if I can ask you questions about your sister that won't tax you.'

'Okay, two things,' he said. 'One, find a necklace that costs at least $300 and two, give me your phone number, Evelyn Royce,' he said looking at my Bullocks nametag. I blushed. I bowed my head so that it wouldn't be so noticeable, but he saw it, anyway. I went to a lighted glass cabinet with jewelry. The cabinet was locked. It seemed to me that when I unlocked that cabinet, it gave me an air of wealth. You see, my parents carried their wealth on their backs, around their necks, and on the backs of all the people they employed, but I didn't feel particularly wealthy. That money was my parents', not mine. I selected three necklaces and matching earrings, both pierced and clip on, for Reginald.

"'I think your sister would like any of these, or all three.' 'What is this one?' Reginald asked, pointing to the red stones. 'Are those rubies?'

'Yes, indeed. This necklace is eight carats of rubies and three carats of diamonds. The metal is platinum.'

'Wrap it up, and what are those? I mean, I know they are earrings, but why did you bring them out?'

'Because they match the necklace. Each earring is two carats of rubies and one carat of diamonds.'

'All right, you have made yourself a sale. Now what about my second request?'

"I wrote my first name and number on an old receipt."

'And that boys and girls is how Evie and I met,' Reginald would say.

"He liked to tell that silly story because it showed he was in charge, he was thoughtful to his family, and he could have a good laugh. I like him to tell the story because it showed he cared about his sister, at least the value of accessories he purchased for her birthday."

"Evie, I believe that would be called a 'cute meet,'" Tamra said. "How did you get him to buy this house?"

"Oh, you know how to get Royce to buy you a house. I imagine you know just what to do."

Although Tamra made a concerted effort—that is to say fucked him frequently—to get Royce to buy a bigger house, he repeatedly said, "When we have another baby. We will be out of room then."

Tamra was torn between her acting career and her fermented desire to have a bigger house. Finally, in March 2000 the doctor confirmed that Tamra was pregnant. Royce relented and made plans to find *the* house.

"I do not want to buy a house, keep it for a few years, then buy a bigger one, keep it for a few years. I want a house now that will last us until they plant us in the ground," Royce said.

"That sounds fine," she said as she envisioned a 12,000 square foot house in Bel Air or a house on a cliff in Malibu with horse trails.

"I plan to buy land and build an estate where I do not have to put our grandchildren in debt," he said, imagining a 20,000 square foot mansion in Hidden Hills.

They blew their mutually exclusive bubbles as they sat together on the brick patio and watched Sophie swim and Teddy make bouquets with pink and white sweet peas.

"Where do you have in mind?" Tamra said, looking lazily at the backyard. She did like that house. But it was time to move on—and up.

"San Fernando Valley."

"Okay, sure," Tamra said, chuckling.

"I am serious. We can build a mansion that is as big as we want it to be. Even though I own and have lived in my house in Beverly Hills, I do not want to raise a family here. I do not want to overtly expose our children to the blatant materialism of this area."

Is he kidding? she wondered.

"San Fernando Valley isn't a good idea," she said. "San Fernando Valley is like Death Valley. People go in and never come out."

Royce disengaged Teddy from the vines. Tamra followed him. He gave Teddy a kiss on the top of her head. He threw an inflated ball to Sophie.

"I will hire an architect. You tell him everything you want in the house. Include a big garage for me," he said.

Even though she was nine inches shorter than he, she

could look in his eyes by gently putting her hand on his jaw and moving his head so he was looking down at her, a horse that learned to take the bit. "No, Royce. We have to talk about this. I'll find us something in Bel Air or Brentwood. You'd have at least a two-hour drive to your office if we lived in the valley." She crossed her arms, wondering what the trust fund was for if not for owning a mansion in the platinum triangle.

Royce kept his word and hired an architect, and he stayed firm in his decision to move—elsewhere. He bought ten acres of horse property in Calabasas at The Estates on Prado del Grandioso. Only four other developed properties within shouting distance. Three of the estates had horses on the properties, and Sophie was mightily interested.

In the following month, Royce and the architect worked on the plans. Tamra pouted. Royce imagined raising his family in the house, imagined every room, imagined Tamra and himself together for the rest of their lives, as his mother and father, who had been together for fifty-four years. His father knew how to sustain a family. Royce imagined he did, too.

The house was going to be over 30,000 square feet, three stories, with a pool, ten-car garage and tennis court. Teddy wanted a dollhouse built in her room, and Sophie wanted a game room. They wanted horses, two of them. Royce added a barn to accommodate six horses and paddock. Tamra's contribution to the house was a suite for herself. Not too close to the children's wing or the master bedroom. She added a sauna and spa next to the gym and a hair and make-up salon.

As construction on the main house began, Tamra wore a locket of desperation. She rationed sex with Royce.

They had enjoyed an active sex life, tempered only by the fact that two children and a nanny lived in the house. Tamra was nuts about sex, but she slowed it down so he would want her more. She often stayed up after Royce went to bed and she slept in Teddy's bedroom. She stopped running with him, too, using the growing baby as an excuse.

During the Mexican standoff, Tamra continued her acting classes. She got a small part in a regional production of *Les Miserables* as a pregnant French prostitute, where she sang "Lovely Ladies." She was not concerned that the prenup didn't allow for her to be in productions.

She came home from rehearsal one evening, and Royce was awake, watching a soccer match from Venezuela in the great room. He sat on the couch with a bowl of pretzels and a beer, wearing Bermuda shorts and a golf shirt. The girls were asleep.

"I do not understand why you want your own suite," he said as he turned the sound off on the game.

"The suite would be for me to use on nights when I come home late from a class or job. I don't want to disturb you." She waited a beat.

"You will not disturb me, and exactly how late do you plan on being? What is going on?"

"I'll tell you what's going on. *Calabasses* is what's going on," she said, deliberately screwing up the word. "If I have to live there, I will have my own suite," she said, hissing at him in a fake whisper. She didn't care if the girls heard her. She threw her large red shopper bag that she used to carry a pair of yoga pants, racing bra, makeup, and scripts onto the couch.

"It is called Calabasas," Royce said and sneaked a look at the television.

"I know what the fuck it is," she said, moving to stand in front of the television.

"What is with all this nastiness? What is wrong with Calabasas?" He tried to look around her to see the TV. "People just like us are buying land in San Fernando Valley. They have the financial ability to build an estate, and they do not want to pay premium dollars in Beverly Hills, Brentwood, Bel Air, and the rest of the Platinum Triangle. Are you this upset because we will not have a 90210 zip code?"

"You haven't begun to see how pissed I am," a portent of a blonde chimera. "And, FYI, there aren't Other People. Just. Like. Us." She backed up so that she was inches away from the television.

He gave up on the game and turned the television off. "Tamra, you need to work with the architect, so the house will have your imprint."

"I don't know what imprint means, but fuck that. You're moving out to Calabasses. You deal with the architect." She stood with her feet planted and her hands on her narrow hips.

As Royce slowly stood, she walked toward him, pulling her hoody over her head. She tossed it on the floor, then she took off her bra. He reached for her. She moved back a few inches while continuing to look at him, unbuttoned and unzipped her jeans and pushed them down to her feet and kicked them away. Her thong and sandals were next. Royce's eyes skittered around the room, probably worrying that one of the children or nanny would walk in on them. She walked up to him and stood with her breasts touching his chest. He attempted to put his arms around her.

"No touching of the merchandise, sir," she said, putting her finger up as warning. "Look only."

Royce grabbed yoga pants from the bag and wrapped them around her like a towel. He put her hand on it to hold it in place. "Come on," he said, picking up her discarded clothes.

He took her to bed. She crawled up onto the bed, looking like Griddlebone in a production of *Cats*. When she reached him, she lay on top of him and again told him he couldn't touch her. She fucked that poor man inside out. Any time he reached for her, she whispered in his ear, "No, no. You can only look." After she used him up, she stood up in bed straddling him.

"Wouldn't you miss this?"

He had a confused look about him. "Why would I miss you? Where would you be?"

"In 90210, sweetie."

"Oh, come on," he said. "Enough is enough."

Her voice turned icy. "I'll tell you when it's enough." She jumped off the bed, got a robe, left the bedroom and walked back into the great room. She flipped through the pages of a magazine, reading about celebrities' marriages and divorces and had an epiphany. She ran back into the bedroom and turned on the bedside lamp and shook Royce awake. He turned over onto his back.

"What is it?" He looked at the digital clock on his nightstand. Royce slept nude and Tamra, even in her pique admired the top half of his body, the lower half under a $2,000 sateen Frette sheet. He saw her looking at him and reflexively put his hands on the sheet in the general direction of his balls.

"I want to be myself, which is not going to happen while I am with you in a cow town." She looked out the French doors. She loved the tranquility of the moon reflected in the pool. Dome lights defined the patio and gave

131

amorphous texture to the landscaping. Small spotlights showed the height of the palm trees.

"You have never said that you cannot be yourself when you are with me," he said. He sat up and ran his hand through his hair that almost looked as good rumpled as it did during the day.

"Well, I can't. You want me to be something I'm not," she said.

"What do you think I am doing that makes you feel that way?"

"You want me to be your mother, be just like her." She flopped down on the bed.

"What is wrong with being like my mother?" He got out of bed and dressed in a pair of shorts. This conversation could not be carried out in the nude. He stood in front of her and reached for her shoulders. "And what does this have to do with moving to Calabasas?"

She shook her head and held out her arms to push him away from her. "Never mind about your mother. That's how you treat me, and I can't be myself, work on my craft."

He had a dazed look on his face. "If by your craft you are referring to acting, you have been taking acting classes." He sat down in a rocking chair.

"That's another thing. The way you talk. It gets on my nerves." She moved to a corner of the bed so that she sat opposite the rocking chair.

He held his hands out in front of him and motioned as in "okay." "Tamra, be quiet, please. You will wake the children. Is this diatribe…this *grievance* about Calabasas or a general complaint about your life and my role in it?"

"I need money to live. I need you to cover my expenses, my hair and stuff." She stood up and moved to a far wall so that she was in shadow.

"Turn that light on, please. I would like to be able to see you."

She didn't turn the light on.

"You are hopping from subject to subject, and I cannot keep up with you. Are you talking about a separation? My God, Tamra. And what are you talking about when you say you want me to cover your expenses? You pretty much spend as much money as you want to now."

They stayed frozen, like fish sticks. A minute passed. Then two.

"Okay, I will move to Calabasses."

She had decided she would torment him while she led her own life. She would have her own space in the huge house Royce planned, use his money, and then do whatever the hell she wanted to do, even if it meant distancing herself from his penis. She would ride out the marriage until it was time to divorce him. Tamra had enough integrity—or maybe it was simply too bothersome to do otherwise—not to fabricate reasons why. And as for waiting, she had reasons for waiting: for every year they were married she saw dollar signs with a prime number and lots of zeros. And she could get Reginald maybe to change his mind about the prenup.

She went back to Dr. Herzfeld for one session. She had decided she would tell the therapist flat out what she was thinking and planning. She liked the idea of saying the words out loud.

"What brings you back, Tamra?"

"My husband is building a huge house, which sounds nice, except he's going to put it in Calabasas. Damn. It's like a mediocre reflection of reality." She had learned that quote in one of her acting classes.

"What's wrong with Calabasas?" Dr. Herzfeld

asked.

Tamra thought she might have made a mistake going back to the doctor. What good was her advice if she didn't know that the entire San Fernando Valley should be blown up like a foreign country the U.S. didn't like? "I live in Beverly Hills and plan to stay there." She sat back against the rust-colored couch. The doctor sat in an oversized leather chair. The office was nice. Wall of windows, glass conference table, aquarium in a built-in bookshelf. Of course, Tamra thought, she charged ridiculous rates to pay for the upkeep.

"Are you planning to leave your husband?"

Fair question.

"No, I was just expressing myself," Tamra said, laying her hand over her heart. "I'll move. But I'm staying in my acting classes. I'll get a driver to take me back and forth. See, I have to find myself again. My husband has used duress to hold me against my will." She adjusted a thigh-length tunic and then crossed her legs, the leather of her knee-high boots squeaking.

"Your husband abuses you? You didn't tell me that last time." Dr. Herzfeld quickly perused her notes.

"Yes, well, no, not *that* kind of abuse. He doesn't touch me or anything like that. Huh, that's one of our problems. He doesn't touch me..." Her voice faltered for effect. "He's a really good father. Much better than I am a mother. He adopted my Sophie, and you can't tell the difference how he loves both girls. And that's the thing, you know. I think I should leave and have the girls stay with him. Royce would always have nurses, nannies, and private schools, you know." Tamra waited for Dr. Herzfeld to tell her what to do.

"How are your daughters? How do you think they

would handle a separation?"

She wanted to talk about her problems, not about her daughters.

"Do you think you might lack maternal sensibilities?"

When Tamra got a puzzled look on her face, the doctor defined sensibility.

"Yeah, maybe. It kind of sounds like me." It felt good to say whatever the fuck she wanted. "I like the *idea* of children, but the actual beings I gave birth to, I'm like not sure, you know. Do you think I'm a monster?"

"You aren't a monster. I've seen monster mothers, and you don't qualify, but you need help so that you don't become one. If you leave your children, they will be affected, the degree depending on the arrangements that are made for visitation. You can help them by including them in therapy…"

Tamra tuned out the rest of Dr. Herzfeld's comments. She was thinking about the fun of looking for her own house. She could spend as much money as she wanted. She was young, too young to die in the valley with two breathing samples of herself. And another one growing inside her. Holy crap!

Construction went on for seven months. It easily could have been a two-year project, but Royce paid the architect and contractor shamefully well. He wanted to move in before the baby was born. Lights flooded every dusty inch of the site every night, which gave the other residents the sense that the rapture was coming.

Tamra refused to hire an interior decorator or to otherwise purchase furniture. She would not do anything about paint, wallpaper, tile, marble, wood, doors, windows, chandeliers, any of it.

"We have hired an interior decorator, Philip Comcast," Royce said one evening after he got home from the office. "Please work with him."

She followed him into their bedroom after he checked in with the girls.

"Who's we?" she asked.

"Steven recommended him."

"So Steven's been told what a total bitch I am, I suppose."

Sophie and Teddy lumbered into the room.

"What is the matter?" Royce asked them.

They looked concerned about something. Tamra assumed the children heard them argue. Hell, that's all Tamra heard growing up, Belle beating on Laramie's head about something.

"Nothing," Sophie said.

"Nothing," Teddy mimicked.

"Steven has seen the house, he knows you are pregnant and that it is difficult for you to be on your feet," Royce said, pulling the girls to him.

She sighed. Royce was quick to defend himself. Tamra liked that power she held over him. "Do what you want," she said.

"Come on, girls. Back to bed," Royce said as he steered them out of the room.

When the move was imminent, Tamra was too fatigued to do any of the packing. Of course Royce hired a moving company to pack dishware, clothes, linens, CDs, books, Royce's entire study, and toys before the move date.

Royce walked into Teddy's room five days before the move was scheduled.

"How was your day?" he asked her.

"Fine," she said, stringing the word out, sounding melancholy. It seemed she had already learned the "fine" and "nothing" responses to most questions her parents asked her. She sat on her knees on her floor with several outfits for her American Girl doll Julie in front of her.

"Just 'fine'?" Royce knew he wasn't going to hear an answer to his question of more than one syllable. He picked up a doll's dress, only to have Teddy frown at him and take the dress back. "Ask me how my day was," he said.

"Daddy, that's silly," Teddy said, combing her doll's blonde braids with a tiny white comb.

"I think you will want to hear what I did today."

"Okay, tell me." It was clear she was more interested in dressing her doll than listening to him talk.

He stood up and walked aimlessly around the room. "You might want to ask me."

"Come on, Daddy. Just tell me." She had reached the stage in their communication where she got impatient.

"I bought the horses today." Actually, his assistant Lew had purchased them, but that was a technicality.

Teddy shrieked. Tears began falling down her face. Sophie heard Teddy yell, and she ran into the room, and they hugged each other and then him.

"Where's your mom?" he asked them.

"She's gone," said Teddy. She was still hanging onto him.

"Gone where?" Royce asked, separating from them.

"Mom went to a spa," Sophie said, as she picked up a dress for Teddy's doll.

"She left today for a spa?" Royce knew he was sounding like an uninformed idiot, but he seemed incapable of changing course. He crouched down and idly looked through a box of Teddy's toys. "Which spa?" he asked.

"I dunno," Sophie said. "It's in Palm Springs, close to the Rancho Mirage house. I wrote down the name on a piece of paper. I put it on your desk. I don't think she wanted to tell me, but I practically begged her 'cause I was afraid she would go somewhere else to have the baby."

Would she do that? "Did she say how long she is going to be gone?"

"Five days. She said she's too pregnant to help with the move," Sophie said.

He kissed the top of her head. Then Teddy's.

Chapter Seventeen

During the Christmas season in 2000, a phalanx of movers carried all of the furniture out to the truck. Teddy was so excited her tummy hurt because she was getting horses, and she was so upset she cried because she didn't know what it meant to leave her house and move into another one.

"Who will live in my bedroom? Will someone else sleep in my bed?" she asked. As she watched the movers pack her toys, she cried, "I don't want someone else to be in my bedroom."

"You are going to have a new bedroom that is bigger, has a built-in doll house for all your dolls, and has shelves for your books and toys. You will not have to put them under your bed any longer," Royce said.

"But my bed is on a truck," Teddy said, lower lip fully inflated like an inner tube.

"When we go to the new house today, all the furniture will be in it. How is that?"

"Daddy. What's wrong with Clabalasas?"

What indeed.

That night the girls raced through the new house looking in every room, turning on every light, hiding from each other, running up and down the stairs, stomping their feet and shouting so they could hear echoes. They had been to the house during construction, but had not seen it completed. Royce wanted their first official visit to be a surprise. Sophie and Teddy sat inside Teddy's 100 square foot dollhouse and opened and closed the windows and door. They lay on Sophie's custom-made bunk beds with queen-sized mattresses, opened drawers in her walk-in closet.

"Sophie, can I sleep with you?" Teddy bounced on Sophie's lower bed.

Sophie put her books in her built-in white bookcase that covered one wall.

"The new household staff will put your toys and books away," Royce said, standing in the doorway.

"No, I have to do it, Dad. I want to get them right." She put up three Harry Potter books and *Charlotte's Web* and *Where the Wild Things Are*. Royce watched her handle each book with care. He walked to the windows that looked out on the patio, with its ground lighting that created pockets of light.

"Your bedroom is going to look just like you," he said, turning toward Sophie.

Teddy laughed. "You're going to look like a bedroom." She found that statement funny and bounced harder.

"Why do you want to sleep in Sophie's room?" Royce said.

"Quit bouncing on my bed. You're messing up my bedspread," Sophie said to Teddy.

"My room is so big, Daddy. I will be in there all by myself," Teddy said and plopped down on the bed and straightened the bedspread. But since she was still on the bed on her knees, her effort wasn't effective. As she scooted on her knees toward one corner, the diagonal corner came undone.

"Please stop! You're making a mess. You can stay in here, but only tonight," Sophie said, taking movie videos and her CDs out of boxes. Her room was wired for sound—and had been soundproofed. "Is that okay, Dad?"

"Sure, but then Teddy you need to sleep in your room. It will be a nice room."

Royce wondered if someone was going to be sleeping in his room.

Two days after the move, Tamra emerged in Calabasas, with a slight tan. She listed to port side and walked as though she were trying out her legs for the first time, like a baby elephant. She was nine months pregnant.

"Nice of you to drop in," Royce said that night in his study. He was putting books on the mahogany bookshelves that, like Sophie's, covered one wall. He, also, like Sophie, wanted them "just right." Then he looked at his wife pregnant with the third heir to his trust. "Please walk through the rooms with me to talk about buying furniture to fill this house. It is huge. I have only furnished a few rooms. Most of the furniture came from the Beverly Hills house."

He motioned for her to walk out of the room, and he followed her into the two-story living room, separated into two spaces by a large arched doorway with mahogany pocket doors.

Tamra gazed around the room and dropped her red overnight bag. "I'm going to replace all of this furniture. You should have taken this stuff to Goodwill."

"You could not live without this furniture before we bought it." He sat down in a pale grayish green Tuscan high back chair.

"I'm over that now. I want a different look in these rooms." She walked through the room assessing the couches, chairs, tables, lamps and rugs as though she were in a furniture showroom.

"Tamra, talk to me. Please tell me what is going on with you." He followed her as she perused the room.

"How many times in how many ways can I tell you?" She ran her fingers over the keys on the highly polished custom white baby grand. "I don't know anyone here, and my friends and my acting—"

"You are going to keep going to acting class? What about the girls and the new baby?" Their none too quiet voices struck the walls and floors and echoed through the rooms. Royce stood and followed her. He stood by the piano as she played a nonsensical tune.

"I'll have a new baby nurse and new nanny to take care of the kids." She stopped playing. "Where's my suite? Are my clothes in it? Do we have a map to this fucking mausoleum?"

A week after the move, Royce invited his parents to look at the estate. As with the children, they had seen it during phases of construction, but not the finished product. Royce folded and unfolded his arms and then settled for putting his hands in his pockets. He stood back waiting for his father's assessment. He was not familiar with praise from his father, but at forty-seven, he still sought it.

They began in the front yard with plants and thirty-foot tall palm trees that bordered the house: barrel cactus, yucca, prickly pear, saguaro, and wild grasses. Bougainvillea lined the outer eight-foot tall walls to the property and would one day define the perimeter of the estate. The buildings had red clay tile roofs. The exterior stucco walls of the main house were the color of Caribbean sand. Royce and his parents walked by a fountain with hand-painted tiles in pink, turquoise, yellow, and light green that sat under a portico, the size of which rivaled a boutique hotel. They walked through two fifteen-foot curved oak front doors with pewter handles. The house, that appeared to be two-story from the exterior, ran parallel to the street to the west and east of the portico. On the first floor, sets of double floor-to-ceiling curved windows were evenly spaced along the walls on the street side. On the second floor balconies large enough to fit Reginald's ego.

"This house is so big, Royce," Evelyn said. "Who is going to live here?"

Both Reginald and Royce looked at her with concern, but neither of them acknowledged the question. They were beginning to worry about her "forgetfulness" that occurred more and more frequently.

If one rode in a helicopter over the property, one would see three sides of a square that formed the main house (and eighty-five-year-old Mrs. Jenner down the road sunbathing in the buff by her pool, with a tattoo of a lion on her left butt cheek that was hot when she was twenty years old, but now because of her wrinkly ass looked like a map of the London Underground).

"Your family will grow with this house," Reginald said. Royce could not read him.

The elder Kallases took a little stroll with Royce. Twelve-foot high curved French doors opened onto a red brick-colored Mexican paver patio with round and rectangular glass-top tables and cushioned chairs and umbrellas in cobalt. Beyond the patio a hole had been excavated for the pool. On the right side of the hole a pool house was framed, behind which would be the tennis court. A ten-car garage was connected to a corner of the main house. The cars had not yet been brought to the house from the storage facility, so the garage could have been rented out as a blimp hangar. Two horses took up residence in a paddock and barn behind the garage. A putting green was also going to be on the backside of the property. Royce had moved in before the back of the property was completed so they did not have to move with a new baby.

"Who's going to take care of the horses?" Evelyn asked, as she patted the mane of the black one. "Have the girls named them?"

Royce looked surprised. He had not asked the girls what they were going to name their horses. He tentatively also patted the black one. Horses had never been his thing, neither riding nor betting on them. "I do not know, Mother."

"Is the baby going to ride?" Evelyn asked.

"That's a silly question, dear," Reginald said. He looked at Royce, apparently worried.

Reginald, Evelyn, and Royce walked back into the house through the foyer, large enough for soccer games that extended to the front doors. It had a twenty-foot ceiling. Twin staircases stood to the left and right of the foyer. As Royce and his parents walked on the wood floor—made from eucalyptus trees with a light blue-green tint over brown—their footsteps echoed. The smells of paint fumes, leather, alder, eucalyptus and grout competed in their noses.

His parents toured Royce's study, library, two kitchens, eleven bedrooms *en suite*, six additional bathrooms, breakfast room, nursery with bedroom for the baby nurse, dining room, playroom, and den. Sophie's room was a sophisticated cream suite, while Teddy claimed the pink bedroom. When they walked by Tamra's suite, in which Tamra had secreted herself for the duration, Royce made no comment.

"Where is Tamra today, dear?" Evelyn asked, apparently reading his mind.

"I am sorry she is not available to visit with you today. She is completely exhausted."

"Of course she's exhausted," Reginald, who had been uncharacteristically quiet during the tour, said. He gave what Royce interpreted as a disapproving look. "Tell her we miss seeing her and that we understand why she needs to rest. This was a big move. Probably more than she could handle."

His parents were sympathetic toward Tamra, not just because she was nine months pregnant, but because Evelyn enjoyed Tamra's company beginning with their meeting and the Champagne-logged ride in the limousine. Reginald was smitten when she popped a baby out of her. If Royce's parents were in her favor, was he wrong to have built the house out here? Should he have bought land in the Platinum Triangle so that Tamra would be happy? Certainly he had the wherewithal to buy land and build a house anywhere in the world, but he hoped his parents would see that he was being conservative in his spending—at least by *his* family's standards.

They took the elevator to the basement that was still under construction and was going to be a play center. It was divided into the gym, spa, sauna; theatre; game room with pool and foosball tables and arcade games; laser dance floor with a soda fountain, counter, stools and red vinyl booths; a bar with tan leather club and lounge chairs (and a locked cabinet); wine cellar with dining room (also locked); a poker room. An HO gauge model railroad had its own room set up with a small town.

"Do you need all this?" Reginald asked.

Again, what sounded like disapproval from his father. "We do not need any of it," Royce said, defensively. "This floor is for fun. The children will love it." Royce felt his pulse in his neck.

Reginald sniffed, and Royce had the familiar feeling of inadequacy. He said nothing else about the basement. As they went back to the elevator, Royce walked with his hands behind his back like a criminal.

"How many square feet do you have here?" Reginald said.

"Thirty-one thousand five hundred, including the pool house."

"What are you doing out there?" Reginald asked. "The pool house?"

"A living slash entertainment room for parties, kitchen and two bedrooms and baths."

"This is a fine property, son," Reginald said, folding his arms and taking a wide military stance.

"Do you really like it, Father?" Royce's heartbeat began to decrease to a normal number. He rubbed his hands on his upper arms and walked into the elevator behind his parents.

"I think you made a wise choice building here."

"Thank you, sir." Royce extended his hand and Reginald shook it.

"Your family will be happy here," Reginald said. It sounded like a directive rather than a forecast.

"It is beautiful inside and out," Evelyn said. "You must be very proud. You have a new home, and you are about to have a new baby." She stood on her tiptoes, kissing Royce's cheek.

Royce was embarrassed—happily so, until he thought of his wife installed in her private square feet. His father had said he had made a good purchase in Calabasas and directed his family to be happy there. Royce would ensure that that happened. He would do everything, everything within his ability and his extended resources to make that happen. Even Tamra. He would make her happy, too. He did not know how at that moment, but he would carefully analyze her issues and come to a resolution.

Chapter Eighteen

Before the move, Royce's assistant, Lew, made arrangements for an agency to send several candidates for Royce to interview nannies and baby nurses.

Royce interviewed three candidates for nanny and chose one. He interviewed five applicants for the baby nurse position, including Nichol Laurent. They met in his office. Tamra had taken care of the arrangements when Teddy was born, and he had no real experience in asking the right questions, but he had interviewed people around the world, so this should not be that difficult.

Nichol Laurent was a regal woman about six feet tall, slim, dark skin. She sat in one of his visitor's chairs with her ankles crossed and her hands relaxed in her lap. She did not seem nervous at all, which surprised him, because the size of his office and the views outside his windows generally intimidated people. When she came in the office, she had shaken his hand, firm, warm.

"You have a French accent, Ms. Laurent. Where are you from?" Royce leaned back in his chair.

"I was born in Port-au-Prince, Haiti." She wore a flowered dress and flats. The dress looked like one his mother would wear going to church on Easter. He liked that, to the extent it registered with him.

"How long have you lived in the United States?"

She furrowed her brow, and he realized he sounded like an immigration investigator.

"My family moved to the United States when I was a teenager, but my parents also had responsibilities at a hospital in Port-au-Prince, so I stayed with my aunt and uncle in Florida. To answer a question you cannot legally ask me, I am thirty-five years old."

———

Royce smiled. "Where did you receive your training?" He folded his arms over his chest and wished he could pace, not tuned into the fact that he could do exactly that. He owned the place, after all. Why was he thinking like that?

"I have a B.S. in nursing from the University of California, Irvine. I have an M.S. in Child and Family Development from Cal State San Diego. That degree emphasizes child mental health. I also have a certificate in CPR. I am a registered nurse. I attached my licensing information to my resume." She hadn't moved since the interview began, her only reaction appearing on her forehead, which still looked a little—what—puzzled?

"Have you always been a baby nurse? How long have you been working as a baby nurse?"

"To answer your first question, yes. To the second one, eleven years." She sat still like a statue, but somehow also managed to look relaxed.

"Tell me about the families you've worked for." The more relaxed she looked, more tense Royce got. He wanted to rub his temples.

"I have worked for eight families—some for multiple assignments—since graduating. I have stayed for three months with five families and two times for more than two years because the couple had second babies. I worked for one family three times." She had blue eyes and hair closely cropped to her head, showing the fine structure of her skull.

"Why did you leave their homes?" he said.

"I left as the parents no longer needed me. Most parents use my services as auxiliary to their own childcare."

"My assistant, the one you met, Lew, has called your references." He held up a piece of paper with Lew's notes. "They were all complimentary about your work ethic."

She sat silent for a moment watching him. Then she leaned forward slightly. "Yes."

In that single word Nichol conveyed confidence. She reminded him of Mary Poppins in that way. Except Mary Poppins could fly, and he hoped Nichol could not. "Tell me your philosophy of raising children," he said. He did decide to stand up and walk behind his desk, hugging his arms. He walked from side to side, and he could see her eyes following him. But she otherwise did not move.

"I believe children need to be loved. That's the most important ingredient in raising a child. Secondly, children need structure. A newborn is wrapped tightly in a blanket because that makes him or her feel safe. As a child grows, the same premise holds. Schedules work well as long as they are not dogmatic." She finally moved. She wrapped her arms at her chest. Mimicking him? "What is *your* philosophy of raising children?" she asked.

Royce was gob smacked for two reasons: he had not thought she would ask a question of that nature and he had no idea what his child-rearing philosophy was.

"I was raised by a strict father and a loving mother," he said. "Sounds like a combination of your points." But his childhood had not been just love and structure. His father had been the dominant parent, and he had instilled his beliefs at an early age: loyalty, fealty, responsibility, value of education and personal relationships. Why was he answering her question with personal information of his childhood? He picked up Lew's notes. "Your references also said you have a genuine interest in their babies."

"I love babies. I love children in general."

He knew he could not ask her if she was married or had children, but he wondered.

"I do not have children. I have never married."

Whoa! Spooky. "I have had many children, but I have given them back to their parents." She pressed her hands together in front of her.

He nodded. "What is your philosophy of life? Where do you fit in the world?" he said, not sure why he was asking such a strange question.

"Existential questions. Hmmm. I believe in being fair, hardworking, and loving and expecting the same qualities in other people. I fit in the world as someone who can take care of people who can't take care of themselves. I don't just mean babies. Anyone who cannot speak up for themselves. I believe our world consists of 'haves' and 'have nots.' I believe 'haves' have the responsibility to take care of the 'have nots' and speak for them." She stopped, but Royce could tell she had much more to say.

"Have you worked for any families that were…well to do?" He held onto the back of his chair.

She appeared to be concentrating. "I don't think I know what you're asking me."

"If you work for my family, you will be exposed to evidence of, for lack of a better word, affluence. I cannot have someone working for me who is overwhelmed or smitten, if you will, by opportunities that will be available."

"Some of the families I've worked for have provided me very comfortable surroundings."

She fascinated him. She wasn't shy about letting him know her opinions. "Those are the only questions I have." Royce stood behind his chair. "Do you have questions?"

For the next hour Nichol pummeled Royce. "How will the new baby fit within the family, that is will the baby be the center of everyone's universe or will it simply be the third child?"

He had no idea, but did he favor Teddy over Sophie?

He didn't think so. He sat down at that question and thought for a moment before answering her. "The new baby will be both," he ultimately told her.

She seemed to like that answer because she smiled. Those blue eyes held the light from the windows. She recited a list of her duties generally. "Will there be additional duties you wanted me to assume?"

"Tamra will tell you," he said, although he was not certain of that at all.

"Give me an idea of the personalities of your daughters."

Such difficult questions. He had not thought about their personalities. He had simply provided for them. "Sophie wants to please everyone. She's studious and responsible, even looks out for Teddy." He thought about telling Nichol Sophie's background, but decided that was information that might be appropriate only if he decided to hire her. "Teddy is inquisitive, constantly in motion. She expects more from the world than Sophie does." After he gave her that answer, he knew that was true, and he silently applauded himself for knowing that about his daughters. He wondered about Teddy's assumption that the entire world was available to her, as opposed to Sophie who worked hard to get rewards. Was that a function of Sophie being raised for the first six years of her life by Belle and Laramie, rather than by Tamra and him?

"What role do you play in your family?" she said.

"That is an easy question for me to answer. I am the protector of the family." Then he thought that sounded dumb, like he was a caveman or something. "Tamra manages our home and has primary responsibility for our children."

A normal answer for a father, he thought. He

squirmed in his chair a bit as though he had an itch that needed scratching. Nichol looked at him as though she were evaluating the merit of his answer.

"If I am hired and live in your home, I will be available for twelve hours a day, which can be broken up through a twenty-four-hour period, with two days off a week. I generally stay three to six months, depending on the needs of Mrs. Kallas and the baby."

Royce knew he would hire her. Nichol was smart, calm, and a bit provocative, the last a characteristic he appreciated in an employee, since so many of them treated him as though he were in a different class than them and agreed with everything he said. Nichol's manner was refreshing.

Christmas Eve baby girl Truesdale was born. Tamra insisted on the name, and since they argued with no resolution about the house, Royce did not balk.

"Where did you come up with Truesdale?" he asked at the hospital, sitting in a chair next to Tamra's bed. They were in a VIP suite at Cedars-Sinai with all the fixings: pale blue walls, except one wall was wallpapered in tan and blue leaves, bar, microwave, hardwood floor in a dark oak, French doors looking onto a lanai, flat screen television and separate room where Royce slept. The last item a portent of what was to come.

"Trousdale Estates, part of Beverly Hills," she said. "I think Bob Hope lived there."

"Why are we spelling it T-R-U-E-S, instead of T-R-O-U-S?"

Tamra looked at Royce's face as though she were reading tea leaves in the bottom of a cup. "What do you mean?"

"You are spelling it differently." Royce thought of each word before he said it. They had been having a nice moment from the deliciousness of having given birth to a healthy baby girl. Tamra was not on his case. Royce could see the sweet Tamra he had met so many years before. He selectively forgot she had been a handful from the beginning.

"Trousdale Estates isn't spelled the way it says on her birth certificate?" Tamra asked, seemingly too tired to ratchet up an argument. She was simply asking him a question.

"No, it is not."

"Hmm. No big deal."

Two days later in the morning Tamra and T-R-U-E-S-D-A-L-E came home from the hospital. Royce went into the nursery with the sleeping baby in his arms, while Tamra headed for her suite.

Nichol had told Lew she generally moved in before the baby was born, so that she could set up the nursery. Lew told her that would not be necessary, one of the few mistakes he made while working for Royce.

Royce found Nichol going through cupboards in the nursery. She did not look happy as she opened empty drawers. No wipes, baby oil, lotions, Q-tips. Not even diapers. But Truesdale would sleep in a stunning custom crib with a canopy that, mercifully with all its gilt surfaces, had proper baby bumpers.

"Is Tamra breastfeeding?"

"No, no, she will not be."

Royce and Tamra had had no conversation about breastfeeding, but he remembered her argument for not breastfeeding Teddy: "It will make my boobs stretch and sag."

———

153

"I found only a couple blankets and one set of sheets. No onesies and no pajamas, although I did find six storage boxes marked 'Teddy' with Armani dresses and Ralph Lauren sweaters and tops for a three-year-old. Is this little baby going to have five hundred-dollar dresses, but no diapers?" She turned from the counter and looked in his eyes for the answer.

Royce opened his mouth to apologize, but for what? Having an irresponsible wife and being neglectful himself? For overspending on Teddy? "Make me a list of everything you need and tell me the stores to go to. You will have everything you need immediately."

"Do you have the pediatrician's instructions for formula? Did anyone understand a baby was coming home?" She was being pretty bossy for someone wearing a tunic with winged pink hippopotami and blue elephants.

Royce felt appropriately chagrinned. He looked down at the floor, very un-Royce-like. "We have been busy moving. Mrs. Kallas has been exhausted by this pregnancy." He gave her a page of instructions that he had in his wallet for the formula.

"I do not know my way around here," Nichol said. "Is there a Babies R Us or Baby Toytown? Or a Walmart? Walmart would be good."

"We have an account at Bergdorf?" He said it as a question. "I do not know if we want our children, even the baby, dressed in clothes from Walmart."

Nichol pulled her lips into her mouth to keep from speaking. She shook her head "no." She swore in a language Royce did not understand.

"I am sorry. I do not speak French," he said. He pressed on. "We will have to ask Lindy about stores. She is our new house manager. We just moved here." As though he would know the names of local stores at any time.

Angel, a new housekeeper, was given the list and dispatched in a black Cadillac Escalade to bring back exactly what Nichol asked for. From Walmart.

While they waited for Angel to return, Nichol looked through the bag the hospital had provided for the baby: two newborn diapers and a bottle of formula. She thought about this family she was, apparently, going to be a part of. No one had thought to buy the necessities for the baby. How could that be?

Royce decided to take the time to tell her his schedule.

"I begin my days early. I run."

"I am a runner, too," she said, leaning against a counter.

"Tamra is, too. At least she was before she got too big with the baby."

"May I run with you?" Nichol asked. "When the baby is with Tamra, of course."

"Of course. Yes, of course, I would enjoy the company when Tamra can't join me." It surprised him that he made that statement, because it wasn't true. He didn't think through how running together was open to misinterpretation by his staff. "I have to warn you, though, of two things. I run early in the morning. I start at 5:30, and, secondly, I finish up the run with the weight circuit." Maybe that would scare her off.

"I will see you in the morning if the baby is sleeping. Do you think that Mrs. Kallas can come down here now so we can discuss my duties?"

"Tamra went to lie down when we got home. I don't think the house's phone system is working yet. I'll be right back."

Royce had to make the awkward trek to Tamra's suite. The blackout drapes were closed. The room was dark. It was ten o'clock in the morning. She had come home from the hospital and immediately gone to sleep.

"Tamra? Tamra, stay awake for a minute."

She lay under a winter white duvet and wore a white eye mask. "I'm so tired. What is it?" She was lying on her side away from him and did not move. She smelled of strawberry oil, her usual fragrance.

"I know you are tired. We need to speak to Nichol about her responsibilities, about the schedule to bring the baby to you."

"I just want to sleep. Have the nurse person take care of the baby."

"You do not want to meet Nichol before she begins caring for Truesdale? You do not want the baby with you?"

"I need some sleep, okay."

Royce went back to the nursery, briskly told Nichol Tamra was resting, and said he needed to go to work.

When the baby supplies were delivered to Nichol, she began to organize the nursery. Later as she nestled the baby with a brown fluff of hair, golden skin, and blue eyes in her arms, Nichol heard a door bang and a feminine squeal. Teddy was home from school. She clomped on each stair, skipped down the hallways, ran into the nursery, and then put on the brakes.

"Oooh, hello, I am Theodora. I am called Teddy."

Teddy with long straight dark blonde hair put out her right hand toward Nichol. She wore pink tights under a short white dress with thin pink stripes and pink tennies. Propping Truesdale against her chest with her left arm, Nichol shook Teddy's hand.

"Hello, Teddy. I am Nichol." Nichol watched her wrap her arms around her shoulders and, from under her eyelashes, look at the person who held her new sister. The child, just over three feet tall, swayed from side to side.

"Can I touch your hair?" Teddy said.

"Of course." Nichol knelt down. "Why do you want to feel my hair?"

"Because." She patted the top of Nichol's head with one hand and the top of her own head with the other. "My hair is soft, and yours isn't."

"That's right. My hair is different from yours. Don't you have friends at school with hair like this?"

"You talk funny." Teddy apparently was finished with the topic of hair.

"Do I? Je suis très heureux de vous rencontrer. Vous êtes une belle jeune fille."

Teddy laughed, a sparkling, mountain-stream laugh. "I don't understand what you're saying. Is it a secret language?"

Nichol swallowed the chuckle in her throat. "No, it is French."

"Oooh. I get it. I know Spanish. !Hola. Mi nombre es Teddy. ¿Cómo lo haces?"

"Muy bien, gracias. Good girl. Tell me about school."

"Well," she said, stretching out the word, sounding as though she had been doing manual labor, "I used to go to Montessori. It sounds like dinosaury." She giggled and twirled around twice. "Dine-o-sorry."

Nichol stood rocking Truesdale, who slept through Teddy's performance, and watched Teddy pirouette.

"Now I go...to..." She stopped to take a breath. "...to Carden, um, I don't know how to say the next word."

"Conejo. Your daddy told me your school is Carden Conejo. Co-nay-ho."

"Co-nay-ho," Teddy mimicked Nichol, including the accent.

"What grade are you in?" Royce had told her, but she wanted to listen to Teddy talk.

"I'm not in kindergarten yet. Next year I'll be in kindergarten. Now I'm in before kindergarten. Have you heard of that? You're tall. My Daddy's tall. May I hold the baby?"

"Use the soap in this dispenser," Nichol said, pointing with her head, "so you have clean hands when you hold your sister."

"I know where the sink is. We moved here—we used to live in Beverly Hills—I went through all the rooms. Every. One. I know where everything is." She started to wiggle and hum as she dried her hands on a white towel with pink roses. "You want to know where a room is, ask me." She pointed her thumb to her chest.

"Thank you. I'm not going to be able to find the rooms by myself. Now, you can sit here, and I will put the baby in your arms."

Teddy sat down on a white lacquered chaise lounge and patted down her dress, her legs straight out in front of her. Teddy's tennies thumped on a white cushion. Nichol held onto Truesdale with one arm, cradled her head. With the other hand, she put a blanket on Teddy's lap and a pink towel with a "T" under Teddy's shoes.

"That's my towel!" Teddy said, the volume turned way up.

The baby yelped and shuddered against Nichol.

"My girl. You will need to speak softly...like this...until your sister is a little bigger."

Teddy put a cupped hand on either side of her mouth like parentheses. "Okay," she said, whispering.

Nichol put Truesdale's head in the crook of Teddy's little arm and wrapped Teddy's other arm around the baby's torso. Nichol opened the baby's blanket, exposing Truesdale's arms and bunched up legs.

"What's that?" Teddy asked with a high squeal, pointing at Truesdale's umbilical cord stump.

"That is what's left of the umbilical cord." Nichol kneeled so that her face was level with Teddy's and waited for the next question.

"Okay, I guess."

Teddy stuck her tongue between her teeth and touched her finger to her sister's face. She traced her eyebrows and touched her closed eyes and her nose and ears and mouth. Truesdale stirred in reaction to Teddy's movements and bleated. Teddy squinted at Nichol, a worried look from her green eyes, green like green eggs and ham.

"I didn't yell. I didn't say anything," Teddy whispered.

"She is fine. What are you going to call this tiny baby?" Nichol asked.

"Her name is Truzzzz-dale. It sounds kinda long. How about Truey, or, I know, Tru."

Tru swung her arms in wide arcs and bunched her miniature hands together into fists, her first effort at self-preservation. She let out a tremulous cry and pouted. As Tru opened her mouth, Teddy peered in at the soft pink gums and the quavering tongue. Tru let a cry rip.

"I don't want to hold the baby any more, thank you," Teddy said, shaking her head.

Nichol picked Tru up from Teddy, who jumped up from the chaise lounge and opened drawers and looked at the new treasures they held. Nichol walked to the changing table and asked Teddy if she wanted to change the baby. Teddy squinched up her nose.

"No, thank you. Perhaps another time."

"Perhaps," mirrored Nichol.

"How come you have a blouse with elephants? My mama doesn't wear blouses like that. My mama wears pretty dresses and I dress pretty, also. My sister Sophie wears a uniform for school. Do you have any pretty clothes?"

"This is my nurse uniform. I also have tunics with babies and frogs. Yes, I have pretty clothes, but I don't wear them when I am working. I am sure your mama has *lots* of nice clothes."

"What color are you? Julia, she was my nanny until we moved, she was kinda brown, and she had different eyes from me. I'm pink, and I have green eyes."

"Yes, you certainly are pink. What color do you think I am?"

"You're like chocolate. A chocolate brownie. Yum, yum. Do you taste like chocolate?" Teddy put her hand over her mouth and laughed into it, sending a muffled giggle into the room. "You're very, very pretty," she said and paused as though she were trying to solve a difficult riddle. "I'm going to go see my mama."

"I think she is sleeping, sweetheart. She needs some rest so she can manage you three." She put Tru in her majestic crib.

"My mama will let me come in." She sauntered from the room, looking, Nichol thought, secure in her beliefs.

Teddy returned ten minutes later with two bananas. "My mama wants to sleep," she said.

Nichol watched her negotiate trust. Could she trust Nichol? She stuck out her hand to give a banana to Nichol.

"Where's my nanny?"

"You have a new nanny, and she was hurt in a car accident. She is not able to come for a few days."

Teddy withheld the previously proffered banana. "I'm gonna take care of myself?" she asked.

"No. A temporary nanny will be here tomorrow. In the meantime, Lindy and I have the privilege of taking care of you." She began reading through the instruction manual for the carriage.

Teddy gave back the banana. "Humph. This is our new house. Nobody lived here before us. My bedroom is pink. Wanna see it?"

Nichol grabbed one of the new baby monitors and followed Teddy, who pinged off the wide hallway walls and walked into the middle of her room and held her arms out like a ringmaster. She opened drawers and her closet, a walk-in, of course. She pointed out her favorite shoes and told Nichol the brand names. Next was the dollhouse that was actually a separate room with a connecting door four feet high and large windows to the outside.

"Most girls do not have all these clothes and toys." Nichol lowered herself to the floor to look at the titles of Teddy's books.

"They don't? How come?"

"Because their mamas and daddies don't have enough money to buy them this much."

"My daddy has this much money." She stretched out her arms and stood on her tippy toes.

"Do you thank your daddy and mama for your nice things?" Nichol was walking to the middle of a not quite frozen lake. She had been on the job for about three hours and already acted on the compulsion to teach the child to respect her material possessions and her parents for providing them. Perhaps Teddy's parents did not share Nicole's worldview.

"I don't know. Maybe." Teddy went inside her dollhouse and closed the door.

A few minutes later back in the nursery Teddy took instructions from Nichol and helped her put some of the supplies in their new places. Nichol had blankets, lotion, wipes, pink and yellow onesies, pajamas with feet, t-shirts, pants, shirts, sweaters, two dresses for presentation to grandparents, boxes of diapers, formula, bottles, plastic bath tub with recliner insert, towels, Q-tips, socks, cushions for the rocking chair, detergent for the washer that, along with a dryer, resided in a closet in the nursery. An eight-pound baby and a ton of shit, although Nichol would never say "shit."

At three o'clock Sophie arrived home from school. She wore a uniform of navy sweater, white wide-collared blouse, navy and green plaid skirt, knee-high socks and Nikes. While not as giggly as Teddy, Sophie was also excited to see Tru.

"I saw a new baby before, when Teddy was born."

Nichol repeated the process about holding the baby. Teddy announced the baby's new nickname.

"Tru. That's cool," Sophie said.

"Tell me about your new school," Nichol said. She lay Tru in Sophie's arms.

"Everyone has to wear this uniform," Sophie said, touching her collar. "That's kind of groddy, but the school, that's cool." She gently touched the top of Tru's head, and then kissed it. "She smells good. It's weird, isn't it, that babies have a smell all their own. It's like a car. Everyone wants the new car smell." She thought for a moment as she hugged her new sister. "Where is my new nanny? I'm old enough to take care of myself, but my mom and dad said I have to have one.”

Teddy repeated the story.

“So, I can like do whatever I want?”

“No, Lindy will supervise you, but you sound like a young woman who can make good decisions.”

It was the “young woman” that did it. Nichol could tell it made an impact.

“Okay, first I’ll change my clothes so I don’t get my uniform dirty,” Sophie said. “Then I’ll get a snack. I’ll get Teddy one, too. *Then*”—she dragged out the word as though it were a heavy burden—“I’ll do my homework.” She began to walk out of the room and then turned. “Would you like a snack?”

“Yes, I would like a snack. Surprise me.”

The next morning after only about three hours sleep, Nichol met Royce in the foyer at 5:25, wearing a t-shirt under a hoodie, tights, shorts, gloves, and Adidas. Mornings were chilly. Nichol told Royce that all three girls were asleep and that she had given the baby monitor to Angela. If Angela heard the baby stirring, she would call Nichol’s cell phone.

“All right, let us see what you are made of,” Royce said. He looked at her legs, the only part of her that was exposed. Through the tights he could see they were muscular.

They ran onto the horse trails. She kept pace with him, and her long legs—those legs again—were as long as his. After running three miles, they reversed course, which meant they had to run up a hill. Royce’s legs were giving out on him because he had been tense the entire time they ran, worried she would not be able to keep up with him, worried she would. He ran as though he were pulling a Ford F-150, while Nichol handled the hill without effort. This was a new experience for him. She gave him a run for his money. No, that was his wife.

When they returned to the house, he handed her a bottle of water and opened one for himself. "You are not a bad runner, but I went kind of easy on you," Royce said and then cringed. Was he being a typical misogynist pig?

She checked on the baby, who was sleeping. She recovered the monitor from Angela and went to the basement where the gym was located. She left the baby monitor on a shelf.

Royce went down to the gym and put on a CD of fifties music. She turned the music off.

"You do not like doo-wop?" he asked.

"I cannot hear the monitor."

People, most particularly employees, generally asked Royce's permission instead of usurping his authority. He stared at one of the speakers for a moment and decided against saying anything. He taught her the circuit, although, if he was honest with himself, he would admit she knew her way around the equipment. As they went from machine to machine, he would set the weight for her and begin to explain the moves or posture, and Nichol would set a higher weight.

Tamra walked in, and Royce and Nichol stopped moving. "The baby is crying," she said in a tone that could have frozen Lake Tahoe. She wore shorts and t-shirt, and she had bed hair. She did not make eye contact with Nichol. She turned around and walked out.

Nichol checked the baby monitor. "It's functioning properly. No sound came from the nursery."

"Uh, Mrs. Kallas is just going through—"

"I understand," she said, as she held up a hand to stop

him from explaining.

"You can assume that for the most part Mrs. Kallas will not be up at 5:30. As for running with me, I think it is a good idea for you to run with me. You will make me work harder than I do alone, and we can use that opportunity for you to keep me up-to-date on the baby."

Nichol nodded and left the gym.

Breakfast was served in an alcove that looked onto the patio and got the morning sun. Nichol, Sophie, and Teddy sat on forest green wrought iron chairs at a glass table. Neither Royce nor Tamra joined them. Sophie told Nichol that her mom did not get up early, and her dad had already left for the office. As she gave Tru a warmed bottle, Nichol looked at Sophie who was eating her breakfast and Teddy who was not. Teddy did not want the oatmeal the new two-star Michelin chef Noel put before her.

"Eat the oatmeal, please." Nichol said to Teddy.

"She won't eat it," Sophie said.

Teddy sat up straight and looked in Nichol's eyes. "Are you going to tell me, Nichol, are you going to say, huh, if I eat it, I will save a *starving kid*?"

Sophie held a spoon to her mouth and looked at Nichol.

Nichol almost, not quite, asked Teddy if she had ever seen a starving child. "It won't save a starving child, Teddy, but perhaps it will make you grateful—to have the oatmeal."

"But maybe I want something else," Teddy said, and she stood up as if to leave.

"Teddy likes pancakes," Sophie said. "She always gets them if she asks for them." She drank her orange juice, and Nichol saw that her glass was shaking a bit.

Nichol put Tru on her shoulder to burp her.

———

165

"Teddy, please sit down. It is time for breakfast. Today we have oatmeal."

Teddy looked stunned. Without saying a word, she sat down and put milk on the oatmeal and ate all of it.

Nichol winked at Sophie.

Although the temporary nanny was at the house, after school Sophie and Teddy gravitated toward Nichol, because she was in close proximity to the baby and because they liked being around her. In the following days the nanny dressed the girls, they had breakfast with Nichol, and when they came home from school, they tagged along with her and Tru.

As they ran on the fifth day of her job, Nichol gave Royce abbreviated reports on the girls. For the most part they ran without talking. Nichol asked Royce about Tamra. "Mrs. Kallas has only come in to see the baby a few times. Is she ill?" Nichol kept her eyes on the trail, a path strewn with ragweed, sagebrush, and saltbush.

"I do not believe so. The end of this pregnancy wore her out. I think she is taking advantage of your being here. I do not think I characterized her lack of contact with the children very well." He stopped running and put his hands on his thighs and looked down at the trail, trampled by horses' hooves. "She is appreciative of your being here, and I have given her glowing reports." He had not talked to Tamra about Nichol at all, because all Tamra said was, "I'm tired." Five days in, he fabricated Tamra's state of mind. *Why is Tamra acting this way?*

Nichol invited Teddy to go on walks with the baby and asked her how her day at school had gone. Along with the nanny, Nichol watched at the paddock while Teddy and Sophie took riding lessons. The permanent nanny was still recovering from the accident, and a series of temporary nannies came through the Kallas home.

After school Teddy was deposited by a school bus on her doorstep like clean laundry. She ran through the house calling "Nic-a-Nic-a-Nic!" and an echo rattled through the large unfurnished rooms. She would find Nichol in the living room or the kitchen or the nursery or on the patio. Teddy plopped herself down on the nearest chair or couch. She bounced up again and asked, "May I have a hug now?" and held her arms up. Nichol hugged her, once for herself and once for Tamra.

"May I hold the baby, please?" she asked. "I washed my hands. Ta da!" She held them up for inspection.

Nichol took a packet from the bag that accompanied Tru. "Here, these are special towels."

Teddy looked at Nichol. The sun punctuated her green eyes, left no doubt what was on her mind: wonder and, alas, suspicion. Teddy wiped her hands on the towel. "Ta da now, okay?"

Nichol placed the squirmy body onto Teddy's lap and reminded her how to properly hold Tru's head. Teddy made silly noises to the baby.

Every day Nichol, Teddy, and baby Tru, in her $3,850 custom carriage, walked down Grandioso until it turned onto Parkway Calabasas. Nichol was embarrassed to push the carriage. It was outrageously, egregiously too too much. The cost of the carriage would pay for thirty children to go to school for a year in Haiti or would pay for vaccinations for over 3,000 people. Since her parents were doctors, Nichol had enjoyed a middle-class life growing up, but still she was barraged daily with the pervasive poverty that affected all classes in Haiti.

She was conflicted, her duty to the girls who were raised, in her view, in a materialistic environment versus her love of her poor country. She had not experienced those feelings in her previous positions, because, although the parents appeared to have money, they were not wealthy like the Kallases were wealthy. They did not live in 30,000 square foot mansions. She continued the walk and with each step moved further and further away from her heritage. She no longer complained about the carriage.

Sophie seemed to have adjusted well to the move and change of school. One day after school, Nichol found her in the kitchen. Sophie sat on the white marble counter eating an apple. She was still wearing her school uniform, except that she had loosened her tie, taken her shirt out from the waist of her skirt, and rolled her socks down to her ankles.

"When your mother had Teddy, was she sick afterwards?" Nichol said.

"My mom's sick? I just thought she didn't like us anymore. She didn't like me when I was born." Sophie was expressionless as she chewed. She banged her feet against a custom Italian-made cupboard.

Nichol wasn't expecting that response. "Why do you think your mother didn't like you when you were born?" She put her hands on Sophie's shoulders.

"Please don't tell my mother and dad I'm telling you this," Sophie said, whispering. She jumped down to the floor and took Nichol's hand. She walked Nichol into the walk-in pantry and closed the door.

"I know now that Tamra is like really my mother. No one will tell me why she pretended to be my sister. All I know is what my moth…I mean grandmother has told me, that like Tamra didn't want me, but I don't know why."

Royce had told Nichol some of the history related to Sophie being raised by Belle and Laramie for the first six years of her life. Nichol accepted that Tamra and Royce had the prerogative of telling Sophie many or few details of those six years.

Sophie ran her fingers over a large package of Rwanda Blue Bourbon white bean coffee. Nichol saw that she was trying not to cry.

"I'm sure your mother loves you. Sometimes new mothers get afraid of taking care of babies. That's what I meant by sick."

"I dunno. I better do my homework," Sophie said and left the pantry.

Nichol didn't know if Tamra was suffering from postpartum depression, but something was going on that wasn't healthy for any of them.

One day Teddy ran into the house and called for Nichol. Tamra stood on the landing.

"I am trying to rest." Tamra said. "Why are you always so noisy?"

Teddy raised her eyes to the landing and wrapped her arms tightly around herself. Tears ran down her cheeks. She tossed her head to shake them off her face and smiled, a tight smile quickly gone. "I'm sorry, mama," she said in a small voice. She looked down at her shoes and then up at the landing. Tamra was gone. Teddy walked through the house head down, arms at her sides, feet slow, until she found Nichol, Stella the temporary nanny, and Tru on the patio.

Teddy politely said "hello" to Stella, who told her she would help her change her clothes. Teddy gave a vague nod of her head and then turned toward Nichol.

———

"Hello, my girl," Nichol said. Tru was asleep in her carriage. Nichol opened her arms, and Teddy walked into the hug.

"Nic?" Her voice was muffled because she was talking into Nichol's abdomen.

"Yes, my girl."

"May I love you?" Teddy whispered.

Tamra continued to walk around the periphery of motherhood.

Royce and Nichol ran in the mornings. One morning as they stood in the gym, she took the hoodie off while they did the circuit, and Royce gasped. But only in his head. She wore a tank top and jogging shorts, exposing her abdomen and shoulders. Nichol's body was athletic, great shape, like a statue. Tamra's body was also athletic, but smaller, at least with his tremulous recollection of that body.

"The permanent nanny we hired is not going to be able to begin work," Royce said. "Her injuries were too extensive. I hate this parade of temporary nannies going through here." He did pull downs, but had lost count.

"I can ask a couple of the people I went to nursing school with," Nichol said. Nichol set weights for the shoulder press.

"I know you are helping the nannies, and my daughters like you very much. I am going to double your salary until we hire a permanent nanny," Royce said, moving to the curl bench.

"Mr. Kallas, that is not necessary."

"Yes, it is, and we will have no further conversation about it." He was attempting to sound jolly, but feared he sounded like an asshole.

That day Tru tested her lung capacity. Nichol rocked her and walked through the halls with her. Tamra opened her door with the ferocity of a daytime drama leading actress.

"Why is she crying so hard?" Tamra said, looking as imperious as she could, considering she was eight inches shorter than Nichol.

Nichol paid attention to how Tamra looked: light makeup, blonde hair pulled back in a neat ponytail. She wore a RENT t-shirt over shiny black leggings. In contrast, Nichol wore a light blue uniform with babies and angels.

"Just establishing world dominance," Nichol said.

"I asked you why she is crying like that. I don't expect a sarcastic answer." The height difference was clearly not an issue for Tamra.

"I don't know, Mrs. Kallas, so I am just going through my bag of tricks."

"Well, if you are such a hotshot nanny—"

"I'm not a nanny. I'm a baby nurse." She walked up and down the hallway next to Tamra's suite. "It's okay, Tru. It's okay, sweetheart."

Tamra leaned one arm on the doorframe. "I would like to give her a bottle now."

"I've already tried that, Mrs. Kallas," Nichol said and turned to walk back toward the nursery.

Tamra followed along behind. Tru's cries had wound down to a whimper. Nichol began to put her in her crib.

"I said I'm going to feed her." Tamra sat down in the rocker. She stared straight ahead instead of looking at Nichol, cleared her throat, held her arm in front of her and wiggled her fingers.

Nichol sighed, handed Tru to Tamra and prepared a bottle. Tru began to suck with vigor.

"There, you see, she wanted her mother," Tamra said, a self-satisfied look on her face.

Nichol turned to walk out of the room.

"Stay in here," Tamra said, loud and venomous.

Tamra would never admit to Nichol that she wanted her to stay in the room because she was afraid to be alone with Tru. What had probably been postpartum depression turned into chronic low-grade terror at being a mother. Added to that element was Tamra's mother. Tamra was both angered by Belle's emotional abandonment of her as a child and repelled by her own abandonment of her daughters. Whenever she thought she could regain relationships with Sophie and Teddy, she was either shot down by the girls or she panicked.

One day Tamra was sitting by the pool and heard Sophie tell Teddy to hurry up or they would be late for their lesson. Tamra walked out to the stable behind them. Sophie turned around when she heard Tamra's sandals "whap-whap" on the deck as they slapped against the heels of her feet. Teddy turned around to see what Sophie was looking at.

"What are you doing?" Teddy said. She stopped walking. "The pool's that way," her little girl voice strong and dismissive.

"I thought I would ride with you today," Tamra said, continuing to walk toward them.

The girls turned back and began walking again toward the stable.

Over her shoulder Sophie said, "Please don't come out to the stable dressed like that."

Tamra reflexively hugged herself, attempting to hide

her abdomen. She was wearing a bikini under a sheer floor-length caftan, emphasis on sheer. "I want to watch," she said. "Or maybe I can get changed and ride with you."

The three of them reached the paddock.

"We only have two horses," Teddy said, climbing over the fence, not looking at her mother.

"I've ridden with Sophie before. Remember Soph, we went to Griffith Park?"

"I was younger then, smaller." Sophie stood by Tamra, giving her an apologetic look.

"We'll fit. I'll be right back. Don't leave without me." Tamra ran to the house and into her suite. Her heart was beating fast as she pulled on a pair of jeans and t-shirt over her bikini. Would they wait for her? Such an impulsive act, possibly self-destructive. She put on a pair of boots and ran back to the stable before she could think too much.

They had waited for her. It was time to put up or shut up. Tamra asked the trainer if she could ride behind Teddy and let her daughter control the reins. Teddy shot the trainer a look that Tamra couldn't exactly decipher, but didn't look friendly. The trainer said it was fine with him as long as Teddy followed his directions.

Teddy clicked her tongue and scuffed her boot in the dirt. "This isn't going to work," she said.

Tamra climbed onto golden brown Shampoo behind Teddy, and Sophie rode Velvet, black and sleek. They set off on the trail.

"How often are you riding, Teddy?" Tamra asked, leaning her chin into Teddy's shoulder.

"Shush! I have to concentrate," Teddy said, trying to shake Tamra off her.

Tamra felt the familiar dread come up through her torso into her head. She felt like she was going to cry. She couldn't breathe, couldn't take oxygen into her lungs. She tightened her grip on Teddy, who swung her upper body around as though engaged in Olympic hip hop dressage.

"You're holding onto me too tight," Teddy said.

"I, I just remembered something, something back at the house. I need to leave," Tamra said.

Teddy obliged her mother by walking Shampoo close to a slatted fence. Tamra inelegantly swung her leg over and climbed onto the fence. Her vision was impaired by tears.

"Have a good ride," she said, head down, talking to the dirt.

Chapter Nineteen

Four months after Tru entered the world, Tamra stayed out overnight. She had been leaving the house on whims, auditioning for commercials, plays, and musicals and, of course, taking acting classes.

One of the auditions panned out, and she got the part of Berta the servant in a local production of *Hedda Gabler*. Rehearsals lasted six weeks. Her loose-fitting housedress of a costume hid her post-Tru tummy. After the first night's performance, some of the crew and actors went clubbing, and Tamra went along, happy to hang with people her age again. Rather than go home at four o'clock in the morning, she stayed with the makeup person Marissa. Later that day when she awoke, she felt free and unencumbered.

Royce knew she left the house, but did not know she stayed out that night. Tamra's suite, by her express direction, was located in a part of the house a time zone away from the master suite.

One day he called her at home from his office.

"Teddy has been telling me you are not home very much or you are sleeping when she gets home from school. What are you doing?"

"My acting classes."

"You have a new baby. You need to be home for the baby, in addition to the other girls."

"Tru has a nurse. She's in good hands. And there are nannies. Look, I gotta go."

"We need to talk about this. We need to reach a resolution."

"It is resolved. I'm going to take my classes. Nichol takes care of the girls."

She hung up.

She had a vague sensation that she was incapable of taking care of a baby and raising children, but reliance on her staff assuaged her guilt. Fear tickled at the edges of her heart. She had no clear reason for not telling Royce about the play. While she assumed he would not approve, she no longer cared about his opinions regarding her life. But while she found it fun to be elusive, she felt some guilt about not being home with her daughters. Her initial fear of taking care of newborn Tru settled into a generalized squeamishness about being with all her children, three children by the age of twenty-seven.

Tamra generally acknowledged Teddy by kissing her on top of her head and Sophie with a brisk hug. On occasion Tamra sat and listened while Teddy played a piece on the piano. She looked like she was in a doctor's office waiting room expecting bad news. Teddy stretched her little fingers as wide as she could onto the smooth, slick keys, a smile on her face and flush on her cheeks because her mama was watching her. This Tamra knew. This was not the Teddy who brushed her off horseback riding. This was the little girl she loved. From a distance.

Royce managed billions of dollars and hundreds of employees, but could not manage one wife. Of course, his anguish was caused in part by his thinking he *could* manage Tamra and *should* manage her as though she were a mutual fund.

He worried about Sophie and Teddy. Occasions when Tamra deigned to spend time with them meant the world to Teddy—unless she felt like being a brat. Sophie seemed self-sufficient. When asked, Sophie said she missed her mother, but then shrugged her shoulders as in, "What are you going to do?" Royce wondered if Sophie still considered Belle her mother. He was afraid to ask her. He thought about Teddy who described in minute-by-minute detail how Tamra listened to her sing a school song.

He decided to talk about the Tamra situation with Belle and Laramie. He invited them to dinner at Delphine's on Hollywood Boulevard. The Woodens visited and infrequently took the two older girls for a sleepover. They neither offered sage advice nor complained to Royce.

Sitting in a gray leather-backed banquette, they made small talk through the ahi tuna poke and crispy calamari appetizers. When the entrees arrived—scallops, salmon, and jumbo wild Pacific prawns—Royce dove into the middle of his distress.

"I need your help with Tamra. She is out there somewhere." He pointed vaguely toward the street. "She is not—"

"I know, Royce. I know exactly what she's not doing," Belle said, dropping her fork onto her plate, with more intensity than the restaurant setting allowed. "I am so angry at her. She wanted to be a mother. Or so she says."

"Of course she wants to be a mother," Laramie said. "Maybe she's feeling overwhelmed now that she is responsible for raising three children." He attempted to navigate the prawns.

"But that is the point," Royce said. "She has *not* taken responsibility for our girls. And we have Nichol, a live in nanny or nurse, or whatever her title should be, and a temporary nanny to take care of them."

"She's a good person, Nichol is," Belle said, with a mouthful of scallops. Looking over her shoulder, she saw herself in the large oval mirror on the gold wall behind the banquette. She wiped her mouth on a white linen napkin. "I call her at least once a week to get a rundown on how the kids are doing. *Without* their mother."

Laramie kept his head down, concentrating on the prawns, as though fascinated by their texture.

Even though Royce had his opinions about Tamra's behavior, he flinched when he heard the venom in Belle's voice. "I am glad you are staying in touch with Nichol. You know you are always welcome—"

"Thanks, but it doesn't feel right," Belle interrupted again. "Tamra's not there when we come over. It's embarrassing, really."

Royce felt the conversation was being directed by Belle, that she was using it as a forum for her laundry list of complaints against Tamra. He looked sadly at his plateful of salmon. He did not feel that he could swallow, thinking of the ever-reaching repercussions of Tamra's actions, thinking of all the people affected by her dogged determination to be…to be Tamra. Oh, he loved that woman, still under the illusion of a white picket fence marriage—although in his case, it would be eight-foot tall electrified walls. Tamra was the one chink in his otherwise impressive armor. She had him by his Achilles penis.

Royce was reluctant to ask his parents for advice because he did not want to admit he might have made a mistake marrying Tamra. Perhaps Reginald was correct and Royce had been wrong; perhaps he should have investigated Tamra's background; perhaps he would have found something that told him she was a manipulative gold digger. Wouldn't his father berate him for confessing that he should not have married Tamra? Also, his mother and father were, since Teddy's birth, members in good standing of the Tamra

Fan Club, and he did not want to change their opinions of her. He wanted them to think that the mother of their grandchildren was doing her job, pulling her weight, and other clichés. All very confusing for him.

He asked his friend Steven for suggestions to help his daughters. Steven, never married and childless, but an uncle to his sisters' children, recommended Royce talk to their pediatrician. Royce was apprehensive to make the call because he had never gone to Teddy's or Sophie's doctor's appointments and had not met Dr. Jacob Elderson. He expected a lecture from the doctor, but, instead, got objective, yet sympathetic advice: spend as much time with Sophie and Teddy as he was able to, substitute a caring mother figure for Tamra, and get counseling.

After he watched Nichol with the girls for several months, he knew she was not a substitute for Tamra, but was, rather, a mother in her own right. His observation did not connect with him on an emotional level, but, rather, on a practical level: he needed a mother to care for his children, and Nichol filled that role.

He then spoke to Sophie's principal who said Sophie was a conscientious student and was not acting out at school, except what was expected because of her age. "Raging hormones" was the way the principal described seventh graders. Before that moment, he had not thought about Sophie's changing mind, changing body. She was a child. A child needed to be provided for. But he remembered his early teen years. Sophie needed expertise he did not have. Nichol would probably know what to do. Thank God for Nichol.

———

He arranged his schedule to work from home one afternoon during the week and on Sundays, and he attempted to come home before the girls went to bed. When Royce returned home in the evenings, if Sophie and Teddy had made themselves stay awake, they told him about their day. He listened, as he would to one of his analysts give him a report.

One day after a week's trip to factories in the Dominican Republic, Royce came home to his family. He was told by Angela that Tamra had gone out for the evening. Royce went into Teddy's room, which was empty. He tiptoed into the nursery. Tru was sleeping, twitching and softly snoring, and Royce assumed Nichol was sleeping in the adjoining bedroom. He walked into Sophie's bedroom. She was lying in the top bunk on her belly with an open schoolbook. She high-fived Royce.

Teddy was laying on the bottom bunk. Her green eyes sparked when she saw him, and she jumped up and hopped from foot to foot. She had a tight smile, looked all around the room and wiggled, a human Slinky. Royce, unable to converse well with a five-year-old, loved Teddy in his self-described feeble way. He looked for signs that she was holding in feelings and questions about Tamra, as advised by Dr. Elderson, the pediatrician, and Dr. Redland, the psychologist, both of whom he had on speed dial, but considering he had no relationship to his own feelings, he didn't know the signs to look for.

Sophie was cool, almost bored talking to Royce about a science project that she was submitting to a district-wide contest. Royce still marveled at the size of her bunk bed. Two queen-sized mattresses, enough to hold a sleepover group of four. She had chosen Ralph Lauren bedspreads, one in cream and the second one in pale gray. Sophie had proudly shown the bedspreads to him when she chose them from a catalog. Sophie must have had thirty to forty stuffed bears of various sizes and colors. They occupied space all around her.

Sophie told Royce about the English literature anthology she was reading. She looped some of her hair around her right hand, sat up as though her name had just been called to win the Oscar for best actress. "Mr. Hepperson, his name is Matt, he's my drama teacher. He tells us we can call him Matt. He is so cool. We do improv, and I made people cry."

He saw how animated she became. "Well, that does not sound good, making people cry."

"No, Dad, you don't get it. We do made-up stuff, like having a conversation or something. Sometimes it is funny, and sometimes it's sad. If we do our job right, the audience will laugh or cry."

Since he seemed to have her attention, he decided to try another topic. Steven coached him on rock bands that were popular. "I understand there is a band from Agoura Hills. Have you heard of them?"

Sophie tried to look nonchalant, uninterested even. "Dad, *everyone* knows about Linkin Park. I couldn't believe it when they said the band started like close to Calabasas. I want to meet Chester Bennington. His voice is like so radical." By that time, Sophie was sitting cross-legged and squeezing one of her stuffed bears.

Royce reached up and kissed her on her cheek. "Radical, huh? Well, how about these?" he asked, as he took four concert tickets out of his pocket and showed them to her.

She read the words on the tickets, but it seemed she didn't recognize the significance of them.

"Do you not like them?" He thought about the effort his assistant Tiffany had made to find a concert appropriate for a young teenager and then to score sold-out tickets. Royce knew the producer that financed the concert.

She held his hand that had the tickets, looked at them a second time, and then looked at his face. He could see the light go on. She jumped up and almost hit her head on the ceiling. She shrieked. "Are these real? You're not kidding, Dad? These are real tickets to No Doubt? In Washington, D.C.? Seriously?"

He nodded his head and sighed, a deep, satisfied sigh.

By that time she had taken the tickets from him, and she clutched them to her chest. "Dad, these are the best. Just the best. I love you, Dad."

"I love you, honey. Now, one of those tickets will be for a chaperone. And no one is coming back with a tattoo or piercing."

"I don't need a babysitter," she said, with the beginning of a pout, and then thought better of it. "Oh, I'm just so excited!" She jumped down to the floor and wrapped her arms around his waist and laid her head on his chest. "No Doubt! And we get to go to Washington, D.C. Oh, I want to go to the Smithsonian."

At that second, Teddy figured out that she wasn't included in the upcoming trip. "Daddy, you got Sophie tickets to No Doubt? I want to go."

Royce had no idea how Teddy would know about No Doubt. There was so much he did not know. "These are for Sophie, Teddy. You get other treats."

Sophie put one hand on Royce's back and the other hand on Teddy's to push them out of the room. "Go! You have to go. I have to call my friends. Right now!"

Teddy shrugged. It appeared she was trying to figure

out if there was something for her in that deal.

As he walked from the room, Royce turned. "Sophie, how did you make the audience cry during your improv?"

"That was easy," she said, pointing to her sister. "I pretended I was Teddy after Tru was born and mom turned all weird."

Chapter Twenty

The psychologist suggested Royce and Tamra participate in couples' therapy. Dr. Redland also said that, based on Royce's cataloging of Tamra's behavior, Tamra might suffer from postpartum depression and should see a therapist on her own. There were medications that were effective in minimizing the symptoms.

Since he had minimal success in phone calls with Tamra, he had to get her while she was sleeping. He thought she would be vulnerable if half-awake, which would give him an opportunity to control a conversation with her.

One morning he tried her door. It was not locked. He walked in and opened the blackout drapes. He sat on the edge of her bed with his back to her. She lay on her side on lilac and white cotton sateen sheets.

"We need to talk about what is going on with you," he said.

Her hair lay in clumps, unlike her usual sleek look. "What does it look like? I'm sleeping. Leave me alone." She turned over onto her stomach, turned her head away from Royce and pulled the white duvet tightly around her. She looked like a white chocolate tootsie roll.

"No, I want an explanation for your absences from home and your abandonment of your children." He turned toward her and put his hand on her soft tan shoulder.

She rolled onto her back and pushed two pillows behind her head. She let the duvet fall off her chest. "Bullshit. You want to know why I'm not in your bed. You're not here for the girls most of the time. What's the difference? Why is it okay for you to be away, but not for me?" So much for her vulnerability.

He willed himself to not get a hard-on, but was not

successful. Even though he wanted to ring her beautiful neck, he was aroused. He felt he had the sword of Damocles an inch above his penis. He turned in such a way that she couldn't see his crotch. He did not answer her question. "I am working, providing for this family. My responsibilities require my time. Why are you not spending time with your daughters?" He clasped his hands together, hung his head, and looked at the floor, to keep himself from becoming enraged. Or aroused. Upset was about all he would allow himself.

She pushed the duvet off the rest of her body. "I do spend time with them. I didn't know I had to punch a time clock every time I'm with them. Besides, we have a nurse and nanny or whatever they are to take care of them. By the way, why is Nichol running with you? I thought that was going to be a once or twice kind of thing. She's supposed to be with them. Is *she* one of your responsibilities?"

Royce was silenced for a few minutes. He had not worn a bulletproof vest to protect his heart and other vital organs. He looked back at her. His voice was soft and suffused with concern. "Tamra, do not attempt to make an innocent activity vulgar and do not transfer your anger toward me onto our daughters. Do you not feel badly that someone else is essentially raising them?"

"I want to go back to sleep," she said, rolling back onto her side.

"Tamra, Tamra. Look at me."

She turned her head away from him.

"Good Christ, what is the matter with you? Are you ill? I think you should see a doctor. I went to see that psychologist who counseled me before I adopted Sophie. She has been very helpful in teaching me about taking care of the children. I told her about your symptoms, and she thinks you are suffering from postpartum depression. It is really important for you to see a therapist. I am so worried about you."

"Oh, stop." She pounded her fists into the bedclothes, again and again. "Get. Out. Of. Here."

"You need help, Tamra."

He looked down at her. He walked to the window and looked out onto the pool and patio. He waited until his erection was gone. He did not want his children or staff to see him like that. Royce closed the blackout curtains and left the room. She had tossed his balls into the trash like yesterday's French fries. He never thought about counseling with Tamra again.

After he left the room, she got up and walked into her bathroom to look at herself in the framed mirror. Tamra couldn't explain herself to herself, much less to Royce. Being angry toward him gave her a buffer against exposure of her fears. Hatred camouflaged self-loathing for her apparent inability to be a mother. When Sophie was born, Tamra had no opportunity to be a mother. When Teddy was born, she was caught up in the attention she received as a new mother. But a feeling had prevented her from fully connecting with her babies. She wondered if she should go back to the shrink to get more anti-depressants. She hadn't taken any since Teddy was a toddler. She'd think about it.

Royce went back to his bedroom, stood looking at nothing and then noticed their wedding album in a built-in bookcase. He sat on the bed and thumbed through the photos, a gorgeous, sexy Tamra, looking like an angel in her ball gown. Sweet Sophie, six years old, years away from acting in a scene that reflected his family's malignancy. He felt he was in an aphasic fog.

Chapter Twenty-One

In June 2001 one morning as they stretched in the foyer before their morning run, Nichol said, "I have been here six months. How long do you want me to stay?"

Royce was startled by the question. "I assume you are a permanent member of the staff," he said, holding one knee loose and one leg straight angled in front of him to stretch his hamstrings."

"I hope I have been taking care of your daughters in a way for their best development," Nichol said. With her right hand she held onto her right foot and lifted it to her buttocks. She stood on her left leg and held onto a foyer wall for balance. She talked to the wall. "I am managing well, with Sophie in school all day and Teddy part time. I have plenty of time for Tru. I have become quite attached to your girls, more so, if I may speak frankly, than other children I have had in my charge. I am enjoying taking care of Sophie and Teddy. It is a new experience for me."

"I have feared Sophie and Teddy would act out since their mother suddenly aban…stopped spending time with them. They have not, and I give you all the credit and my gratitude." He did not add that he would have come unglued like a Tijuana wallet if she left. He had come to enjoy their runs together, much to his surprise, and she brought much-needed normality to his life. "I hope you will stay indefinitely. Would you agree to be responsible for all three girls on a permanent basis? With nanny and other staff support, of course, for managing the girls. This is a good time to raise your salary."

"The increased salary you have been already paying me is quite enough for me to save and to send money for my parents' projects in Haiti." She began to twist from side to side. "Perhaps, in lieu of increased salary, you would make donations to a particular project I support."

"Your parents are not in Miami?" He did not remember Nichol's job interview.

"No, they have always had a home base in Haiti. They are doctors at a hospital in the capital for people who cannot afford to pay for medical care, which is actually almost everyone in the country."

"It is settled then. I am giving you a raise. I am doubling your salary. No, no argument. You did not sign on to take care of a thirteen-year-old and a five-year-old."

"I enjoy watching over them. I am not trained as a nanny, but I think mothering is instinctive. How do you envision my responsibilities indefinitely?"

"I think pretty much what you have been doing. Tru will continue to need close supervision, and Sophie and Teddy seem to be thriving on the attention you pay to them. I am, of course, away from home for long periods because of my heavy work responsibilities, and Mrs. Kallas, well, Mrs. Kallas has her activities that take her time."

"I believe children need structure and consistency to feel secure. I would, of course, defer to Mrs. Kallas, if she expressed an interest—" Nichol said, stalling out.

"Mrs. Kallas suffers right now from the baby blues," he said. Curious he should tell her his opinion, which was based on his naked need to have a tolerable explanation for Tamra's behavior, seasoned with input from the psychotherapist. Royce was embarrassed by his wife's behavior and his apparent inability to correct the situation. However, he was afraid of the volatile repercussions of addressing the issue again with her.

"I can remain here to take care of the girls. I will need you to hire a permanent nanny to relieve me in the evenings and nights and my days off. I would ask that you give me two months' notice when you want to terminate my services. That way, I can line up another position."

"I am not going to want you to leave anytime in the foreseeable future, not until Tru is in high school," Royce said.

"Oh, my!" Nichol said, putting her hand to her heart. "If I may, Mr. Kallas, let me draw up a list of my duties as I see them within the structure of this family on a permanent basis. And I will need an annual vacation to visit my parents and the rest of the family in Miami. And one weekday and one weekend day off. I will work from seven o'clock in the morning until seven o'clock at night. I have Tru on a schedule, and I will be able to take nap breaks throughout the day before the older girls get home."

"I understood you to say your parents live in Haiti."

"Yes, they do, and my family gets together once a year in Miami."

"That sounds just the ticket," he said. "Of course, you will take vacations. We will work out the logistics of your days off. I think we should talk about getting you a proper bedroom. I don't want you to have to sleep permanently next to the nursery in that small bedroom. We have several suites available." He sounded like a front desk representative from the Beverly Wilshire.

They walked down a hallway, and then Royce stopped in front of a door. "This suite includes a living room." He opened the door and walked in.

Nichol stayed in the doorframe. "This is too much, Mr. Kallas. My room is fine."

"It would make me happy to do this for you, so you know this is your home, not a way station to another baby nurse position."

———

191

After that conversation Nichol examined her feelings about the girls, about her job. In her prior assignments, she had loved the children, but was able to leave them without looking back. She had worked hard to obtain her degrees, had enjoyed her time as baby nurse, yet one rather simple thing was the deciding factor in accepting Royce's offer to be his children's primary caregiver. She had become a part of the family. And, if she was honest, she was influenced by the grandness of the estate.

Throughout her career, she had given no thought to having children of her own. She had never had a long-term relationship, preferring to casually date, since she moved from location to location. In the time she had been at the Kallas home, she acknowledged to herself that she coveted that family. She loved those girls. She asked herself how she could manage a marriage with children of her own, while continuing to work as a freelance baby nurse. The answer came back: she couldn't. Not the hours she worked. So she would embrace a surrogate family and continue with the Kallases "indefinitely." It would be nice not having to get acquainted with new families every few months.

Nichol protested when Lindy gave her bedding choices. "I can't have sheets that are this expensive. I do not need designer sheets."

"The rooms must be furnished to meet Mr. Kallas's standards for the family."

"But no one's going to *see* my sheets."

"Ralph Lauren or Frette."

Nichol got a whiff of jealousy from Lindy, who, although she had Ralph Lauren on her bed, had a suite in the staff wing. *They think I'm getting special treatment,* Nichol thought. And she was. Nichol sensed that Lindy reinforced the deepening divide that existed between her and the other staff. Nichol ran with Mr. Kallas, she worked out with him, she spoke to Mr. Kallas as though they were equals. She was not concerned about their opinions.

Royce directed Lindy to hire a painter to decorate Nichol's rooms. And so painted in soft yellow, pink, and lavender, melted ice cream colors, Nichol's new rooms reminded her of the vibrant colors of Haiti and her townhouse in Pasadena. She was going to have to think about selling the townhouse and buying something closer to Calabasas. A Frette mauve satin comforter and baby blue sheets lay on a custom Italian mahogany four-poster. The custom nightstands, dresser and armoire complemented the bed. A two-sided fireplace sat in the middle of one wall. The entrance to the suite was through the living room. A door connected the living room and bedroom. She had a walk-in closet, at which she laughed because she did not have enough clothes to fill it. Tunics with angels and frogs did not take up much space. In the lavender bathroom an oversized bathtub sat next to a large window that viewed the tops of palm trees. *Goodness, is this my life now?*

It was her life, and she imagined her parents at the hospital with skeleton-like children who roamed the grounds. Children who wore shorts and t-shirts and no shoes. How could she reconcile that she slept on expensive sheets, while her parents slept on a bed with a thin mattress, a rusted frame, and sheets that had been washed to such an extent the color had faded to gray?

Nichol had worked for families in Eagle Rock, Marina Del Rey, Beverly Hills, and Century City. Every home had a bedroom for her, every house was large, and it appeared that her employers were living comfortably. But not on this scale. Not like this. Not with an oversized tub that overlooked palm trees.

How could she reconcile that she shared a life with Tamra?

While Tamra's primary motivation in cozying up to the elder Kallases was to have Reginald and Evelyn in her camp in the event it all went south before her planned D-day, she also liked them. She enjoyed the time she spent with them, unlike her visits to her parents, where she was berated constantly by her mother. She called Evelyn at least once a week and occasionally drove to Pacific Palisades to take her out to lunch and a movie. The elder Mrs. Kallas still believed that Tamra had to drop out of charity events because of her schedule with the children.

Royce suspected Tamra stayed away all night more and more regularly and was confronted with the evidence, an empty bed. He knocked on Tamra's door at 7:00 one morning. She did not answer. He knocked again and called her name. No response. He opened the door. The blackout drapes were closed, the suite was dark. He felt for a light switch, and the lamps gave the sandy-colored walls warmth not otherwise found in the room. Tamra was not in the suite. Her bed was made, as it was every day by a housekeeper when she decided to get up.

He left the suite and walked down the long hallway and stairs into the east hall. He checked the girls' rooms on the possibility Tamra slept with one of her daughters, and he imagined opening Teddy's door and finding Tamra lying in Teddy's big girl bed, nestling her in her arms. He did not find her.

After going to his office he called home about 10:00 that morning. He had already called her cell several times, and the calls went to voice mail. Lindy said Mrs. Kallas was not home, and, no, she had not seen her all morning. Royce knew better than to ask Lindy to give Tamra a message to call him back. He tried again at 1:30. She was not at home. At 4:00, Lindy reported that Mrs. Kallas's Jaguar sat in the driveway, but she had not seen her.

"Look in her suite, the gym, sauna, theatre, pool. I will wait."

As Lindy checked each of the rooms, she came back on the phone. "No, Mr. Kallas, not here."

Then Royce heard Lindy's part of a conversation: "Mr. Kallas expects to speak with you. Yes, I understand, ma'am, but Mr. Kallas has called three times today, and it must be important. No, I am not going to tell him that. Mr. Kallas, Mrs. Kallas is in the sauna and in quite a mood."

"Tell her to stay in the house. I am on my way home."

When he got home, Royce saw her car in the driveway. He walked in, looked in the usual places for her, and asked Lindy where she was.

"She left with a small bag after you called. A taxi picked her up."

"What did Mrs. Kallas say to you when she was in the sauna?"

"I will not repeat what she said. She cursed me."

That night and for the next four nights, Royce waited for Tamra in a barrel chair in her bedroom, sitting in the near dark. On the fifth night he heard a car. Cold air followed Tamra as she walked in.

"Where have you been for five days?" He didn't move.

"Jesus Christ!" She searched the dark room for the body that accompanied the voice. She found his silhouette.

"You jump me in the middle of the night to ask me where I've been? You haven't cared where I've been for the past year." She smelled of cigarettes and beer, but the predominant smell was strawberries. Tamra still wore the strawberry body oil. After all those years.

"You have made it clear you are a free spirit, able to come and go as you wish, but you are the mother of three young girls and married. Again, where have you been?"

"Well, Mr. Curiosity-Killed-the-Cat, I've been in New York auditioning for an off Broadway play. I got called back and got a part."

"How in the hell are you going to perform in New York? This is something the two of us should have discussed."

Tamra turned on a light and began taking items out of her carry-on bag. Royce stood up.

"*We* haven't had a discussion since you moved us out here, and—" she said.

"Stop it! Do not re-hash an old, tiresome complaint. We live here." He punctuated his words by pointing his index finger toward the floor.

"Look, as much fun as this is, I'm going to bed," she said.

"No, you are not." His voice got louder, like the sound of a fire engine as it gets closer and closer to an accident. He took hold of her shoulders. He could have lifted her off the ground and carried her fireman style. He guessed the appropriate name would be firefighter.

She stood toe to toe with him, but did not attempt to free herself from his hold on her. "Do you believe that if you order me around and bully me that I will fall into your arms and become your mother, the devoted wife?"

The last collapsed in on Royce, and he made an effort to take in air. He let go of her shoulders and moved closer toward her as in a hug, in an effort to find a place on his body that could touch hers. Tamra stood with her arms crossed and her feet planted.

"Tamra, I have loved you since the day I met you." He did not whisper. He was beyond masking, beyond caring about their privacy. "We were happy for five years, were we not? How did you change so much? The children, you never see the children. If you are experiencing postpartum—"

"I'm not *experiencing* anything, so shut up about that. I didn't change two years ago. I changed six years ago and became the house *frau*. *You* made the decision, the inter-lateral, unit-lateral, whatever it's called, and *you* made the decision to move us here, even though y*ou* knew I hated it. So I like decided I could make that kind of decision myself. I gave you your three children, and now I do what I want to do, you know."

"But you wanted children, too. I adopted Sophie." His confusion stemmed tears that threatened to fall. He blinked again and again.

"And you don't think I'm a good actress? You gave me five million dollars for each of those girls."

Royce moved away from her and leaned against a wall. "What are you saying? You have three beautiful, intelligent, curious daughters. Sophie has lost two mothers. I am thankful she is resilient. Teddy. She does not know what she did to make you so angry with her. At first she blamed Tru, because you changed drastically when she was born. Tru does not know her mother at all. Why are you being cruel?"

"I don't know, man. I just don't know." Tamra

walked by Royce, who reached a hand out to her, but did not attempt to stop her.

He left her room and slogged through the house and walked up each stair, feeling the heaviness in his back and legs as though he were pulling weights up the steps. Teddy sat on the landing, a blanket pressed to her mouth. He picked her up and felt her wet face. He carried her to her room and laid her in her bed. He knelt by the side of the bed and tucked her in, the universal salve to comfort children.

"Daddy, why doesn't Mommy love me anymore?"

"My sweetheart," he said, "some things I do not understand about the world. Your mother loves you—" His voice trailed off. "I know I love you and Tru and Sophie and will never leave you." He waited. "Do you believe me?"

"Uh huh," she said as she turned toward him and touched his tie.

"I want to protect you all the time, but some things in life I cannot protect you from. I will always be with you and your sisters, sometimes only in my heart when I am at work." He folded and unfolded the pink blanket that lay at Teddy's feet.

"And Nichol?"

"Nichol what?" he asked.

Teddy sat up on her knees and put her arms around his neck. "Nichol, too, Daddy. Protect her, too. Please."

Royce kissed her on the forehead and left the room. Protect Nichol? Did Teddy think that he should love Nichol, too? Was that what Teddy was saying? He supposed he did love her, the person who cherished his children, but the emotion stopped there. Ah, he thought he had registered a feeling. Dr. Redland would be proud of him.

Although Royce went to dinner, plays, and Lakers

games with friends, he was ashamed of his non-marriage and turned down invitations for events that required a partner. He reduced his philanthropic work because he did not want to explain Tamra's absence from fundraisers. His threadbare excuse that she had just had a baby only worked for so long. He had envisioned inviting friends and groups to the mansion for casual evenings or full-on tuxedo-required dinners, but he did not want to host them without his wife. Since moving to Calabasas, the mansion only hosted family parties, friends' gatherings, corporate events that did not require Tamra's presence, tennis—with Steven, Royce's cousin Larry, and friend Bianca—and some of his college friends for pool. When the prenup was drawn up, it contained language requiring Tamra to act as hostess, with the penalty for non-participation a reduction in the annual "stipend." Royce had not dinged her yet, despite his attorney's insistence that Royce use the prenup for its intended purpose: protect Royce's assets and his station in life.

He only spoke about the "Tamra issue," as he referred to it, with Steven. Steven's only, and not unreasonable, conclusion: divorce her.

"Man, she's using you like a hotel. She has a place to sleep and a closet for her five hundred pairs of shoes."

They were sitting in the theatre at Royce's home watching a Sunday baseball game with Steven's favorite team, the Boston Red Sox.

"I have done some research on postpartum depression, including a consultation with the psychotherapist," Royce said. "She did not think depression would have lasted this long, but, on the other hand, she said since Tamra is not being treated, the depression could have become chronic."

"Do you think Tamra would go to a shrink?" Steven reclined his chair and ate a handful of popcorn.

"That is never going to happen." Royce took a sip of his beer.

Steven suddenly shot up out of his seat, causing Royce to spill his beer. "Did you see Varitek nail that fucker. Right over the Green Monster." He sat down. "Sorry." He handed Royce some napkins. "Does she have any contact with the kids?"

Royce mopped up his arm. "Minimally. She talks to them at dinner when she deigns to spend time with them. Tamra is out of touch with the girls' lives." He placed his glass in the beverage holder and leaned forward in his chair. "I dread dinner when she's there. Sometimes I stay in the office even when I don't have to so I can miss dinner the nights I know she is going to be there. God, it is so fucked! I want Tamra to act like my wife. I am uncomfortable being around her because she is so withdrawn. It is as though she were a distant relative visiting who doesn't speak much English."

Steven took a good-sized gulp of beer. "So basically it's you and Nichol raising your daughters. Still behaving yourself in that arena?"

At that remark Royce wished he had never introduced Nichol to Steven. One day the fourth for tennis had bailed, and Royce had suggested Nichol play. Sophie was in school. Nichol took the baby monitor with her, although the part-time nanny Carmen was in the house. Royce thought Nichol played very well and used her height to her advantage. During the fourth game in the third set, Tru began chirping, and Nichol said she should stop, a shame because she and Steven were leading.

"You know, my friend," Steven said. "If Nichol

weren't your nanny, you two would make a good couple."

"You are bordering on being out of line, my friend. Also, I think you're getting off the topic, which was Tamra."

"Oh, shit, Kallas. Dump her, the sooner the better. You're making a martyr of yourself."

He had to think about that one for a while.

"Tamra comes to visit us," Reginald said over the phone one day while he and Royce were at the end of an analyst's report on computer parts assembly factories in Peru. Perhaps he intended to irk Royce or, more probably, to embarrass him. "The three of us go to dinner. Don't you know where your wife is?" Reginald sounded disapproving. But of whom? Royce could hear his father chewing on something. Probably his chocolate candies.

"She did not tell me," Royce said, as much response as he was able to give. "Neither did you." He stood up to pace, but decided, instead, to cull old pens from his Harvard coffee cup.

"You're not managing your family, son."

Here we go, Royce thought. He sighed. "Tamra has not been, she is not...I think she is ill. I think she has postpartum depression, and it seems she is afraid to be around the girls. The result is she alienates herself from the family." He dumped some pens that made a dull thump in the wastepaper basket.

"That's nonsense. She talks about the girls when we're together. Shows us pictures. It's your responsibility to take charge. I know how to run a family, and you should go by my example."

"Humph," Royce said. He thought about the early days dating Tamra. He thought she looked like his mother, and there was a big age difference between his mother and

father like him and Tamra. He based his belief that Tamra
would be an exemplary wife and mother like his mother on
those similarities. How wrong he had been. How wrong.

Chapter Twenty-Two

After the play closed in New York, Tamra had returned to Calabasas, but she left again without announcing her departure. The household learned she was gone simply by her absences from the house. She returned about the time the girls' school break began in the summer.

One day Tamra sat on the deck by the pool on a yoga mat. She did the child's and extended puppy poses. A Zen Lizzie Borden. Nichol brought the younger girls out to play in the water. Both girls had taken swimming lessons so they were water safe. Teddy dove into the deep end, while Tru played in the shallow end with Nichol. Royce had designed the pool so that the shallow end was like a beach.

Tamra finished the intense extended side pose. "Hello, my babies. Come here and give me a kiss." She held out her arms.

"I don't want to kiss you," Teddy directed to Tamra and emphasized her point by slapping the water.

"Teddy, can't you come say hello to your mama?" Tamra asked.

"Goodbye, Mama," Teddy said and dove to the bottom of the eight feet.

While she watched Tru patting the water, Nichol walked to the edge of the pool. "Mrs. Kallas, Teddy is very hurt that you don't spend time with her. The way she's talking today is because she's angry," Nichol said, her back to Tamra. Nichol knew she was taking an enormous risk, the risk that Royce would think she was being insubordinate. But at that point she didn't care. She hoped she could either embarrass Tamra sufficiently that she would start participating in her children's lives or simply irritate her.

"Do not speak to me that way. I am your employer. This little show of Teddy's is because of you."

Nichol was close enough for Tamra to knock her in the pool. Nichol knew exactly where she stood, figuratively and literally. "I am responsible for the welfare of these girls, especially when you are not here."

"Me and *my* husband are professionals who are very busy. You, uh, serve at our pleasure." She confused herself with the president.

Tru sat in the water. Nichol sat down beside her. Tru looked at Nichol, held out her arms and said, "here," Nichol's cue to give her a hug. Nichol reached over, and Tru threw her small wet arms around her neck.

Tamra sighed loud enough to be heard in the back row of a theatre. She stood up, threw her shoulders back, tossed her hair, and began to walk away. She turned her head back. "Remember what I said and don't mistake your role here." She did not wait for a response.

Nichol thought Tamra must be auditioning for a role in a soap opera. Tamra did not say goodbye to her daughters.

Nichol stood and held Tru, who drenched her. Teddy had been treading water during her mother's performance. She looked at Nichol with concern on her face. Nichol blew her a kiss. Teddy blew one back and dove deep.

Chapter Twenty-Three

Nichol had not taken much time off since she began working for the Kallases because Tamra's long absences were jarring enough for the girls. As they completed a run, Nichol asked Royce if she could speak to him about her vacation. "My parents have started a new program of training nurse's helpers, and I would like to see it."

"So you are off to Florida," Royce said as he began circuit training.

"I will stay in Miami for two days visiting my aunt and uncle. Then I fly out of Miami to Port-au-Prince."

"Your parents work in Port-au-Prince?"

"Yes, Port-au-Prince, Haiti."

"Extraordinary," he said, as he stood near the pull-down machine. He gave Nichol his full attention.

"They work at Grace Children's Hospital," she said and hoped her exasperation was not obvious to Royce for not remembering she had already told him about her parents' work. "I am going to revive my nursing skills for a short period of time taking care of orphaned children."

"Is it safe for you to go to Haiti?" Royce had never been to Haiti, but he had spent time in the Dominican Republic, a country that shared the island of Hispaniola with Haiti and he knew about the country's political instability.

"Of course. It's not Calabasas, but I'll be fine."

Royce's posture changed from workout buddy to employer. "When would you like to leave?" his voice authoritarian and his manner unengaged.

"Are you upset with me for telling you my plans?"

"No, of course not," he said.

The next morning Nichol and Royce warmed up before their run.

———

"I have made my plans. I will be gone for twelve days, beginning August thirty-first. I am interviewing temps today. Do you want to make the selection, or shall I?"

"You make it," he said, sounding like his father. All right. Now, let us run." Royce did not change his demeanor for the rest of the week.

Nichol felt the sting of his new attitude toward her, but she thought she should keep her feelings to herself. She wondered if Royce was irritated with her because she was leaving.

Teddy, without knocking first, although Nichol had schooled her in respecting people's privacy, walked into Nichol's living room. Then she saw a suitcase on the bed. "Are you sure you want to go away?" Teddy asked.

"I do not want to leave you, but I have not seen my mama and papa for two years," Nichol said as she looked through her closet for warm weather clothing. She walked from closet to suitcase and back again.

"I have not seen my mama in a long time, either," Teddy said, as she fingered the buttons on a blouse Nichol had just put in the suitcase, commiserating in her own five-year-old way.

While attempting to temper Teddy's distress, Nichol found Sophie to be inconsolable. She was convinced Nichol would not return.

"You're going to be just like my mama," Sophie cried. "You aren't going to come home."

Nichol promised she would be back in less than two weeks.

"Who's going to take me to school?"

Nichol almost canceled her vacation. She did not know how to respond to Sophie. She wanted Sophie to feel she had someone to rely on.

"We have your uniforms ready, and Carmen will take you to the store to get school supplies and she'll take you to school. I'll be home on the second day of school."

"Why do I have to go to *Walmart* for my school stuff?"

"Where would you like to go, Barneys?" Nichol said, hoping she sounded friendly and fun. She couldn't think about Sophie's feeling of loss. She couldn't. She had to see her parents.

On the day Nichol left, Royce offered a driver to take her to the airport. "Have a good visit with your family. We will see you in two weeks."

"Twelve days."

"Yes, that is fine."

Two hours before Nichol's flight, Royce's driver carried her suitcase to the car. While Sophie was in school, Teddy and Carmen, who carried Tru, walked to the driveway. Nichol had given Carmen detailed written and oral instructions about taking care of the girls on her own. United States' invasions of Haiti had not been planned as well.

"Please come back home. You live here, not with your mama and papa, you know," Teddy said, with her thumbs in the back pockets of her jeans.

"Dear one, of course I will come home. In twelve days. Hold out your hands."

Teddy obeyed.

"Twelve days. All of your fingers and your big toes. Every morning is one less." She bent one of Teddy's small fingers down onto her palm. "After today it will be only eleven days." Nichol squatted so she was face-to-face with Teddy. "I love you."

———

207

Teddy wavered, but put her arms around Nichol's neck. "I love you, Nic-a-Nic-a." Her bottom lip quivered.

Tru blew kisses and then held her arms out for Nichol to take her from Carmen's arms. "Here," Tru said.

Nichol saw Tamra standing at her bedroom window, watching the leave-taking, her hands balled into fists.

Tamra channel surfed through her daughters' lives while Nichol was gone. She decided to stay home, although she didn't know how long a vacation Nichol planned to take. She would have to ask the nanny, although she really didn't want to have to talk to her. Maybe she could ask Sophie or Teddy.

Later that day Teddy practiced the piano while Tru sat on the bench with her and swung her chubby legs back and forth. The nanny watched them.

Tamra walked into the room and stood next to the piano and pretended she was reading Teddy's music. She laid one hand on Teddy's shoulder and sang the lyrics, "Rock-a-bye Baby." Teddy flinched and moved her shoulder to extricate herself from her mother's touch. Tamra turned back to the nanny, asked her question, received an answer, and left the room.

Sophie continued to find refuge in her bedroom on the phone with her friends. Tamra went to her room, but Sophie said she wanted to be alone.

"I haven't been home for…a while, and I'd like to catch up," Tamra said.

"That's not my fault," Sophie said.

Tamra cleared her throat. She sat down gingerly on Sophie's beanbag. Its cream-colored leather squished as she tried to find a comfortable spot. Sophie looked at her with what Tamra could only call as derision, another word she had added to her vocabulary from acting class, where her coach commented on one of Tamra's scenes: "You are supposed to be wanting this man who doesn't want you, as he looks at you with derision. Work past the wall he has thrown up." If Tamra worked that scene again, she would know exactly how to play it.

"I know, I think I know what you're feeling," Tamra said. "It's my…fault for not being here. I'm sorry, Soph, but my acting career is so important to me. I don't mean to leave you here, but I can't take you with me. My mother, your grandma, left me, kind of."

Tamra squirmed in the beanbag and finally gave up and stood. She walked to Sophie's bed and sat down on Sophie's bottom bunk. She talked to the upper bunk where Sophie sat polishing her toenails with OPI Bikini Envy, a light celery green color that shimmered as she wiggled her feet. "Grandma left me in a different way. She sent me away to boarding school."

Sophie sighed. "So why don't you stay home?" Her voice cracked.

Tamra stood up and put her hands on the mattress Sophie lay on. She waited a few beats. She had learned the art of timing. "You were my first love, Soph." Her hands inched toward Sophie's leg. "You will always be my first…and best…love. I have to, I just have to act, and I have to go where there are opportunities." Tamra began crying, which surprised her as much as it surprised Sophie.

Sophie looked down at her. She had a look on her face flavored with sadness, and Tamra thought she got it, that she understood. Tamra would work harder at being a mother, especially to Sophie, her baby. She cried harder as she watched Sophie's face crumble. She grabbed for Sophie's hands and succeeded in making Sophie spill the polish on her shorts.

"Look what you've done. Jeez!" Sophie climbed down from the bunk and ran into her bathroom, coming out with nail polish remover.

"Here, let me do that for you," Tamra said, taking the bottle away from Sophie. "I'm so sorry. I'll buy you a new pair of shorts. You…you can come with me. We'll go shopping together. It will be fun."

She kneeled in front of Sophie and scrubbed on the cotton material as Sophie stood impatiently before her. Tamra knew the polish would never come out. She knew her scrubbing was futile.

Royce may have fooled Nichol that he was uninterested in her vacation plans. He definitely fooled himself until the first morning he ran without her. He felt a pain in his chest unrelated to physical exertion or warning of an imminent heart attack. The pain expressed his feeling of loss. He stopped, leaned over, put one hand on a thigh and his other hand balled up to knead his chest. He breathed in and out through his mouth. Royce turned around to go back home, not completing his usual mileage for the first time since a heavy rainstorm forced him to curtail his run.

That night he ate dinner with the girls. Carmen sat with the girls to help Tru eat. Tamra joined the diners. That meal was awkward times a zillion. Royce made small talk with Carmen, Tamra corrected Sophie's slouching posture, Sophie told Teddy how to use a fork, Teddy stuck out her tongue at Sophie, ignored Tamra and talked only to her daddy, and Tru attempted to clutch a cherry tomato. Tamra, defeated for one evening, sat down to dinner two additional nights without success. Thereafter, she ate dinner only in her

suite. Something dangerous affected and infected her family
that worried even her. She thought about asking Royce to
take her out, but decided she would rather stay home and
watch "Popular" on TV.

Chapter Twenty-Four

Tamra escaped the exhausting antagonism of the house, playing the role of the wounded bird. She met up with her "fuck buddy" Morgan Breedlove at the Beverly Wilshire Hotel, where she and Morgan got some endorphins bubbling while screwing each other's funny bones.

They laid waste to the mini bar, every Barbie-sized bottle of beer, wine, vodka and whiskey sucked out of the miniaturized refrigerator. She had a chocolate attack, while Morgan ate the nuts. Then they turned their attention to room service, requesting, no demanding, magnums of Champagne, cheesecake with strawberry sauce and killer chocolate cake. They weren't rock stars, but they were acting like it. Those two liked spending someone else's money. Morgan thought he was spending hers, and she knew she was spending her husband's.

One of them fell asleep staring at the television in the living room, and one of them passed out in the bed. Or maybe it was the other way around. She woke up to candy wrappers all over the bed, with some stuck to her nakedness. She needed water desperately; that is, until she raised her head off the pillow. "Help! Help me! Please!" she cried.

Morgan's cheek stuck to the fabric of the sofa. He was lying on his stomach. "Wha...what you are?" He couldn't bother putting together words that required cognitive function. He slid off the sofa onto the floor and the soft carpet, where he was unconscious again faster than one can say "Seconal."

Tamra stopped screaming. She stared at the ceiling with her mouth open. She began a low moan of "aaaah, aaaah," a mantra for the tone deaf. "Water, I want water. Waaa-terrrr." She raised her head with the same result as the first time. She decided to sneak up on it. Keeping her head on the pillow, she scooted to the edge of the bed. She felt with one foot and hand as she lowered herself to the floor, bringing the pillow with her, dropping a few candy wrappers as she went. Lying on the floor on her back, she did a variation on a crab walk, scooching first with her feet and then with her butt, and finally with her arms, feet, butt, arms, until she reached the counter with the bucket of ice. The counter was too high for her to reach up and get the bucket. She was going to have to do the next part quickly. She was going to have to get on her knees and grab the damn thing. Quick was going to be better than slow. Lying on the floor on her back, holding the pillow against her head with one hand, she got on her knees, grabbed the bucket, which hit the pillow and upended, spilling cold, cold water from the melted ice on her neck, her breasts, her stomach, her crotch, loosening a few more candy wrappers. She fell to the floor and rolled up like a sow bug, wailing into her pillow, "Whaaa, whaa," until she was hoarse.

After they both regained consciousness, they went to Mastro's Steakhouse in Beverly Hills, where they were able to get in at 10:30 because Tamra threw her name about. They wanted raging, bloody steaks and Alaskan King Crab Black Truffle Gnocchi and colossal onion rings to replenish their muscles, tissues and sinew depleted by rampant fucking. They ordered Cabernet Sauvignon that came from Stags' Leap Winery in Napa, California. As he gave the waitperson the order, Morgan said, "It's always good to support local businesses."

Tamra asked him, "What are you talking about?"

"Instead of buying French wine," he said.

"Since when did you pay for dinner, and since when

are you interested in supporting local businesses?"

"I care about things, whatever, beside myself. Speaking of caring about yourself, in all the times we've talked, you've never told me about you when you were growing up. The only thing I know about your personal life is you don't like your mother."

Tamra dropped an unopened oyster onto her plate of crushed ice. "What the fuck? What are you doing? You working for the FBI?"

"No, I'm just a guy who'd like to know a little bit about a girl I'm fucking." He put so much energy into the statement that the couple at the next table looked over, then looked at each other and laughed out loud.

"Jeez. My life as a kid isn't very interesting. I lived with my parents, went to school, hung out with my friends. Pretty normal."

"You are so lying to me," he said.

Morgan put his head down with his jaw on his chest, looking at the plate of oysters protected by their shells until someone came along with an oyster knife. He pushed the plate away.

"What the fuck, huh?" she said. "Why are you all up in my business? I thought we were going to come here for a nice dinner. Chill, you know?" She knew she sounded like a rapper Goddess.

The waitperson brought their entrees, the steaks sizzling with butter dripping down the sides.

Morgan and Tamra were quiet, taking the first bite of their meat, an orgasmic experience. It was so good that Tamra enjoyed it even though she was usually so careful about what she ate. They stabbed at the gnocchi and onion rings and opened a second bottle of wine.

"Do you think we can handle this much alcohol

considering last night?" Morgan asked.

"Of course we can. We're professionals," Tamra said. She paused with her knife and fork poised over the steak. "You know, I don't...I don't like to talk about my childhood. There are only six people who know about it, and two of them are dead. I, um, I was raised by my grandparents until I was six."

Tamra continued eating, alternating looking at him and at her food. She ate an onion ring, the crunchy coating jiving around on her tongue, her teeth biting down on the soft, slick center.

"My grandparents were killed in an accident," she said. "My parents couldn't, they uh, didn't know what to do with me. They were better at taking care of other children than me, you know."

"What do you mean?"

"Although she's a complete ditz, my mother is an orthodontist and my father's a pediatrician."

Morgan looked at the red meat of his steak. He pushed the tongs of his fork down on the top of the steak and watched blood run in rivulets on his plate.

"After my grandparents died, my parents warehoused me in programs before and after school. On weekends either I was free to hang with my friends, or do stuff with my dad."

"I'm sorry," Morgan said. "That must have been a life-changing blow when your grandparents died." He reached his hand out to touch Tamra's arm. He was still watching the blood pool. "How did they die?"

Tamra had a piece of steak in her mouth. She kept chewing and shook her head from side to side. "No, don't think so," she said. "I'm not going down memory lane about my grandparents. I'd wind up as a fucking puddle on the floor." She pointed to the floor with her fork. "Nope. Not looking for a cathartic experience."

"That's exactly why you should tell me, so you'll be a better actor, so you can mine the feelings."

Tamra looked at him for a moment while she decided what she would tell him. "They were taking a train up to Santa Barbara, and the train jumped the tracks. Sixteen people were killed, forty-five injured. I still remember the numbers." She stopped and took a gulp of wine. "That morning me and my dad took my grandparents to Union Station. Nonny bought me an engine, the Pacific Surfliner. That was the name of the train they took from Los Angeles. That evening I found out when I was watching cartoons, and the program was interrupted by news. You know, like breaking story."

Morgan nodded and chewed.

"So I'm sitting on the floor playing with my new engine, and I hear the news report. I was the one to tell my parents." Tamra took a piece of onion ring with her fork and created a pattern in the steak juice. "My mother went into the bedroom. She wouldn't come out, and she wouldn't let me in. My dad was consoling her or something. I was crying because I didn't understand why the train broke and why my grandparents weren't coming home. After a while, I went out to the garage and got a hammer. I started smashing the engine. My dad heard me and came out there. He asked me what I was doing, and I told him, 'Getting poppy and nonny out of the train.'" She took a deep breath and blew air out through her mouth.

They had ordered dessert that would be prepared while they were eating their entrees: chocolate sin cake for her and Johnnie Walker Flight Tray with Mastro's warm butter cake for him. She ordered ice wine. When the desserts arrived, she was staring at the pattern in the carpet. They were both quiet while eating their sweets.

Tamra sucked on her fork, having polished off the cake. "Teach me," she said. "Teach me how to be a better actor, so I can make a living at it," a curious request considering she was set for life financially.

"Are you shitting me?" Morgan said. "You've got a major league scam going on right now. Getting a man who's got serious coin, telling the man you love him and want to have babies with him. And then you go off and do your own shit. That tops anything I've done and must require a fair amount of acting."

What Morgan said made her angry. She wasn't the one who changed the game plan after she'd been married for five years. She had thought Royce wanted to make her happy, and he knew that building a house in Calabasas would not make her happy. So, it wasn't her fault that he lied to her. He didn't really want to take care of her. Like her parents, making her go to boarding school when she didn't want to go.

Tamra thought about her grandparents and the train accident. *Nice touch with the train engine*, she thought.

Chapter Twenty-Five

Away from the Tamra drama, Nichol spent the time with her parents in Port-au-Prince at Grace Children's Hospital, treating children with tuberculosis. The hospital was housed in the former residence of Spain's ambassador to Haiti. The ward was on the second floor. Iron beds filled the room, with thin mattresses and one blanket on each bed. They were brightly colored and had appliques or were quilted. Nichol guessed they had been made by women from a U.S. church group. Since tuberculosis bred in closed spaces, the windows were always open. Sweat was dried by Caribbean breezes.

Nichol and her parents cared for children with tuberculosis whose parents were dead, had abandoned the children because they could not afford to care for them, or had left their children in the care of the hospital until the TB was under control. She saw malnourished children with extended bellies and orange hair. Dehydrated children walked about the ward connected to IV poles. Nichol brought a Polaroid camera with her and took photos of the children, who posed by jutting out a hip, putting their hands on their hips, or sticking their tongues out. Why in the world was that particular pose universal? When she left the floor that day, every child had a photo on the flimsy tables by their beds.

Nichol's back dripped with sweat. She had not been exposed to that level of heat since the last time she had been in the country. She held children on her lap, who wore simple cotton gowns to their knees and who were barefoot. Her skin stuck to theirs. She sang songs to them in Creole and assisted her parents as they made rounds.

———

She was able to keep it together until she got to a section of the ward set off by itself: the AIDS children. One baby, about six months old—or older but stunted by the disease—stared at her from her crib. The baby lay on her back with an IV running into her tiny hand. Nichol picked up the baby, who weighed only about ten pounds. Nichol held the little girl with one arm while she pulled the IV pole along with the other. She found a rocking chair and sat with the precious child in her arms. The girl wore only a diaper, but didn't need other clothes because of the extreme heat. The baby grabbed at her finger, held on, and put it into her mouth to suck on. Nichol wore no protective clothing or gloves, but had no fear of being infected, even though her training taught her otherwise.

After holding the baby for a while, she noticed a woman watching her. She wasn't dressed like a nurse. She wore a dress whose floral pattern was faded, had a satchel over her shoulder, and wore flip flops on feet that had walked many miles. The woman approached Nichol.

"Ti bebe," she said.

"Eskise m'. Tibebe w la se bèl," Nichol said in Creole as she stood, handed the woman her child and gestured toward the rocking chair.

The woman smiled with the pride of a parent who has been told her baby is beautiful. She sat down gingerly in the chair as though she wasn't allowed on the furniture.

At that moment, Nichol was overtaken by the tears she had successfully kept at bay. She thanked the woman for letting her hold her baby and left the ward. She stood in the stairwell painted a faded yellow, holding onto a wrought iron windowsill and cried. She cried for the baby girl, for every child in the hospital and every sick child in the country.

Late at night when she lay on a cot at the Coconut Villa, a motel close to the hospital, Nichol could hear other guests speaking English, French or German as they walked the outside corridors. They were government contractors and entrepreneurs who ran private companies in the country. They were church groups from Indiana and Michigan touring charities. They were U.N. military. Nichol heard the noise of the generators that came on periodically through the night because the city's electricity was sporadic. There were periods of blackouts every night. The air conditioning units were loud and ninety-five percent worse than worthless because they spewed hot air.

For the first few days Nichol felt displaced. She had become acculturated to her life in wealthy surroundings. She felt she was home in Haiti, yet how to reconcile her love of this country with her life in California. She let herself cry again. She cried for her confusion and for the children of both the hospital and Calabasas. While the Kallas girls had material comforts very few people enjoyed, they lived with the madness that was their mother. They would probably never experience sickness exacerbated by poverty, but they suffered their own version of poverty. Of course the children in the hospital would choose to live like the Kallases, that is if they had any knowledge of such wealth, which, of course, they didn't. The Haitian children's point of reference was villas behind tall walls in the hills above Port-au-Prince, guarded by men with guns. She understood her sadness for the patients in the hospital and clinics, but the Kallas girls? To cry for them?

Nichol returned from Port-au-Prince to Miami at the end of her vacation and spent the night with her Tio

Maxamel and Tia Allegra. She called the house to talk to Teddy, but instead Lindy transferred the call to Royce.

"Nichol, we have missed you."

"Oh, Royce. I expected a little girl's voice. How is everything at home? How are the girls?"

"The house is upside down without you."

"The nanny. Isn't Carmen doing her job?"

"She is doing exactly what you told her to do, except she probably still has not completed that extremely long list of instructions. And Tamra has not left the house."

Nichol did not react to that news, because she thought Tamra would leave again when she got home.

Nichol had a nine a.m. flight to LAX. She boarded at 8:30 and read a book for fifteen minutes while the plane loaded.

As some passengers stood in the aisles and stowed their carry-ons, one of the passengers screamed, which led to general murmurings from the other passengers and, a flight attendant moved toward the sound. Nichol looked up. Her first reaction was to provide aid to whoever was injured. From the back of the plane a passenger bellowed, "Oh my God." A few passengers bolted out of their seats apparently to get off the plane and pushed past those in the aisles. Flight attendants told them to return to their seats. Nichol stood up to help people who were screaming, but no one in the aisles was moving. She pushed the flight attendant button.

A voice spoke over the intercom, and people yelled, "Shut up," "Shut the fuck up." Finally, the shrieks and general disturbance curbed sufficiently so the voice could be heard.

"From the flight deck, this is Captain Jack Williamson. We are going to be held at the gate here for a few, so just sit tight, and we'll let you know when we can push off."

"What the fuck is he talking about, push off? The whole world is blowing up, and he thinks we're going to get in the air?" a passenger asked.

"What is it? What's happening?" a woman cried.

"The World Trade Center…a plane flew into it," another passenger said, holding his cell phone above his head. "My wife just called me. It's on CNN."

The passengers exhibited fear, rage, disbelief, and denial. Arguments broke out about the veracity of the reports, whether it was a twin engine or turbo, private or commercial, or a bomb.

Nichol's heart rate accelerated, while her demeanor was calm. She continued to wonder if there were people on the plane who needed medical help. Although she had pushed the flight attendant button to tell a flight attendant she was a nurse, none responded. She watched a man fumble with his cell phone and a woman cried with her hands over her face. Perhaps Nichol could soothe that woman's dread.

She called Royce. It was five thirty a.m. in Calabasas. He would be on his run, but he carried his cell phone in the event of an emergency with the girls. "Please pick up," she prayed into the phone.

"Hello?" his concerned voice said. He was breathing hard.

"Royce, please listen. There's been a bomb or an explosion. I don't know. CNN is reporting a plane crashed into one of the World Trade Center towers."

"My God. Where are you? Are you all right?"

"I'm fine, I'm in Miami. My plane is still at the gate. They aren't letting us off the plane, and we aren't taking off yet."

223

More shrieks, more screams, more "Are you bullshitting me?"

"P-people around me are saying there has been another plane. I will call you later."

"Come home. I will send my plane."

"We'll talk later."

Nichol sat with the phone in her lap. She talked to no one but listened. She began to believe CNN's reports, and the hand that held the phone shook, which caused her to hold it with both hands. She looked around her. Her seatmate cried into his phone. The woman across the aisle clutched a rosary. She heard people praying. That seemed like a reasonable and necessary activity, but she refrained. Her skepticism as to the power of deities prevented her from asking for strength or absolution. She asked herself the questions others would ask without answer in the following days: how could God let those hijackings and crashes happen? If half, if only a quarter of what she heard on CNN was true, a sinister, evil element had been unleashed on the United States.

Another plane: the Pentagon. Another plane: a field in Pennsylvania. What was the destination of that plane? Where was God when those planes were hijacked?

On the other side of the impassable chasm Royce flipped channels between network and cable and read reports as they were generated on Google. He learned the New York Stock Exchange had ceased trading. He told Carmen to keep Sophie and Teddy home from school. He called senior vice presidents and directed them to contact the personnel departments to inform employees to stay home. They argued about whether it should be a paid day, and Royce said he would cover the expenses if necessary—which translated into make it unnecessary—and to contact the travel departments to obtain current locations of all traveling employees and to make arrangements for their return home based on current FAA information. He called his assistants and asked whether they had family traveling. He stayed at home, not knowing if the earth still spun about its axis. He learned throughout the morning that Cantor Fitzgerald, the leading bond trader with whom he did business, was decimated.

He heard his children giggle and knock on his study door, and he remembered Nichol had not called. He tried her cell number several times, but only got a recording saying the circuits were busy.

She called in the afternoon. "I am back at my tio and tia's," she said, whispering. "I do not want Tia Allegra to hear me. She would get very angry if she knew what happened at the airport. We were kept on the plane for three-and-a-half hours. Then we were herded—that's the only word to describe it—into a small room, and one by one we went to a counter and were interviewed, more like interrogated, about our travel plans," Nichol said, out of breath. "They asked when we made our travel plans, online or through a travel agency. We had to tell in detail what we had done when we reached our original destination, whom we had been with, what we did in Miami. They went on and on about our time in Miami." Nichol experienced fear that day, real bone crushing fear, an emotion with which she was not familiar. Fear transitioned into anger as she talked. "We learned three of the planes involved were destined for Los Angeles. They wanted evidence of addresses or other legitimate connections to Los Angeles. After they—"

"Wait, wait. Who is 'they'?"

"Airport security, FBI, and I don't know who else. Oh, yes, Customs. We are in the United States flying to another city in the United States, and Customs got involved, because of the high number of Haitian and Dominican passengers."

"You sound so, I do not know, angry, I guess."

"Yes, I am angry." It was difficult to whisper as her wrath increased, and she wound up hissing. "Anyone flying with a foreign passport was kept back as other passengers were released. It was not just me who was mad."

Are you saying you were kept back?"

"Yes, that's what I'm telling you. Because I have a Haitian passport—"

"You do?"

"Do you want me to tell you what happened?" Nichol asked. "I am sure this has been an extremely sad and stressful day for you, too. I have not talked about the way I was treated today to anyone. If I have crossed a line, I apologize. I thought I could tell you." She thought she could tell him that the FBI agent grilled her about her employment in Los Angeles, about the family she cared for.

"Of course you can tell me. This has been an incredible day of surprises, none of them good."

"Is my being Haitian a problem? You know I'm Haitian." She was itching for a fight, and Royce was the nearest target. On the flip side, she craved a strong presence to protect her.

"I made an assumption, and I should not have done so," Royce said. "Please tell me what happened next." Royce put the call on speaker so he could rub his temples and pace. The day was not over, not by a long shot. He still had to re-check Latin American markets and the Tokyo Stock Exchange. He had friends at Cantor Fitzgerald and had not been able to talk to anyone in New York because calls were not going through due to—as the recorded voices reminded him again and again—high call volume.

"I was kept back because the hijackers went to a flying school in Miami, three of the hijacked planes were headed for Los Angeles, I have a foreign passport, and I'm of color. Evidently the hijackers were dark skinned."

"Nichol, you do not think you were detained because you are black, do you?"

"This is obviously too much for you to hear. I will stop now. Do you want to tell me what is happening with your company?" Her tone was sharp.

"You have heard that the New York Stock Exchange shut down. The NASDAQ canceled trading, the London Stock Exchange closed in fear that whatever malevolence had struck would travel across the Atlantic. I should spend some time with Sophie, Teddy and Tru. Please call me tomorrow with news about when you can fly."

When Nichol hung up, she was angrier than she was when she called. Nichol was a black woman in a white man's world, and Royce was part of that world. It would be a week before she remembered that he had offered to send his plane.

The next two days were filled with chaos and nascent recognition of the enormity of the loss of life and property. The FAA continued its prohibition against civilian planes flying. The NYSE remained closed.

Four days later, Nichol got a flight to LAX. Royce dispatched Colwin to pick her up. After she claimed her baggage that had been raked through three separate times, she saw Colwin waiting in a line of people who held up signs. He simply stood with his hands behind his back and

———

227

waited for her to find him.

"Welcome home, Nichol," she muttered to herself.

As she settled into the town car, Nichol asked Colwin if there were any messages from Mr. Kallas.

"No, ma'am. Just told to pick you up and deliver you to Calabasas."

She called Royce's cell, and Tiffany answered. "No, Mr. Kallas is not available. Can I take a message?" Nichol disbelieved it.

"Yes, tell Mr. Kallas I am home."

"I'm so glad you made it back in one piece," Tiffany said. "The children will be happy to see you."

The children. That was her job after all, wasn't it?

When she walked into the house, she felt she needed to go through a decompression chamber to re-enter her Calabasas reality. She walked past her suite and into Teddy's room. She tried to reconcile Teddy, the immaculate child with the dark blonde hair with the dark brown children with orange hair that she had held for ten days. Teddy sat on the floor with a board game intended for at least two people.

"May I play with you?" Nichol said, getting on her knees.

Teddy looked up at her. She did not appear to be surprised Nichol was home. "No, thank you."

Nichol didn't know what to say, but she wanted to say something, something that sounded like "I love you." She rested a hand on Teddy's footboard. Her hand shook slightly. She wanted to hug that child and kiss her. When she had thought about being home with the girls during the days she waited to fly to Los Angeles, she imagined them laughing, squealing, wrapping their arms around her neck when she came home. She had never imagined they would not be happy to see her.

"What's wrong, Teddy?"

"Nothing's wrong." Teddy scattered the pieces of the game and moved as if to stand up, and Nichol held onto one of her arms.

"Don't," Teddy said, although she didn't attempt to pull her arm free.

"Please, tell me. I will listen."

"You haven't been here for sixteen whole days. You said twelve. You promised only twelve, all my fingers and two toes." With that she removed Nichol's hand from her arm.

Nichol allowed herself to cry while she held children with distended bellies, babies with AIDS, children missing limbs and blind. She had whispered to the children "Tanpri, padonnen nu," "Please forgive us." And on that day in Calabasas, tears filled her eyes and her voice was high and begged for forgiveness. "Oh, sweetheart, please. I am so sorry. Let me tell you what happened. Planes were not allowed to fly for four days. I couldn't get home. I came home on the first plane I could get."

Teddy walked to the doorframe of her room. "I don't believe you. Planes fly *all* the time." With that, she flounced down the hallway, as only an entitled five-year old can.

Nichol blinked away her tears and guilt and went into Sophie's room, but it was empty. She relieved Carmen. When Tru woke from a nap, she was happy to see Nichol.

"Here," Tru said.

"Yes, my sweetheart, here."

When Sophie came home after spending the day at the mall with her buddies, she shrieked and ran to Nichol. They hugged each other hard. Nichol kissed the top of Sophie's head.

"You came home."

Sophie talked nonstop until the exhaustion of the past days released, and Nichol got tears in her eyes.

"I'm sorry, Nic, what did I say to make you sad?"

"No, sweetheart, not you. It has been, uh, stressful, huh, yes." Nichol shook her head.

For two days Teddy rebuffed all of Nichol's efforts to mollify her. She let Nichol help her dress, but didn't talk to her. She pursed her lips and avoided eye contact. Royce hadn't known Nichol had told Teddy she would be gone no more than twelve days. When Royce confirmed to Teddy that the planes had not been allowed to fly, she forgave Nichol, but initially only gave her a one-arm hug and let Nichol kiss her on the cheek.

Royce's reaction to seeing Nichol ran somewhere between the girls' reception. Nichol didn't see him the first night. He did call to tell her he would be home late because as the financial world took steps to right itself, he had to keep up on the markets. "Glad to have you home," he said with effort, approximating friendship.

"It's so nice to be home." She swallowed hard on that sentence. Was it nice? Was it home?

Tamra lurked in the background. She saw Teddy ignore Nichol, but she wasn't prepared to take on a maternal role herself. She flinched when she heard Sophie greet Nichol. Tamra didn't receive that kind of reception when she came home. Tamra deflected motherhood essentially in the same way her own mother had. Tamra would not have responded well to the comparison, because she believed her mother simply didn't like her, while Tamra suffered from postpartum depression and couldn't help herself. Right? And she wouldn't get applause for being a mother, so let Nichol do the boring stuff.

On her first morning home, at precisely five thirty, Nichol joined Royce by the front door. She wore her running clothes.

"I haven't been able to run for over two weeks," she said.

"Oh, you startled me. Are you going to run again?"

"Yes, of course. Why would I stop?"

"I just thought—"

"Thought I wouldn't want to run with you because I am an angry black woman?" She regretted her tone, but not the words. The genie was not going back in that bottle.

"Nichol, please." He turned his hands palm up and held them chest high. He sounded as though he was asking for world peace.

"I'm sorry," she said. "I've had a rough few days." She touched his bicep and then took her hand away as though she had gotten a shock. "I know you have, too. I would enjoy running with you if it's okay with you."

Royce touched his arm where her hand had been.

They had breached each other's facades. After a few days, they settled into a combination comfortable-cautious relationship. They did not discuss international treatment of third world countries, the politics of world hunger, or the reaction of stock markets to 9/11. They discussed more difficult subjects: themselves. Because of Nichol's experience in Miami, they related to each other as individuals, not employer-employee, as people who had the shared experience of loving three fragile, yet resilient children, of deflecting anticipated barrages from Tamra. Nichol had to do a lot of thinking to figure out if her role had changed minutely or profoundly because of the trip.

Chapter Twenty-Six

Evelyn said she would love the opportunity to talk to Nichol, but at Thanksgiving dinner? When Royce told his parents he was hosting Thanksgiving 2001, they asked why Tamra wasn't going to join them, but Nichol would. He and the girls insisted Nichol join them. Noel would cook dinner with the help of two temporary cooks, and he and the housekeepers who worked Thanksgiving would eat dinner in the staff kitchen while the family and Nichol ate in the formal dining room. When Reginald and Evelyn were told that Tamra would not be joining them because she was in New York, Reginald, ever the Tamra fan, said she was an enterprising girl. When they were told Nichol would be at dinner, they refused to understand why an employee should be included at the Kallas dinner table. Royce talked to his father on the day before Thanksgiving, and Reginald said it would be "highly inappropriate" for Nichol to join them. Royce told his father he and the girls wanted her to share a meal with "the most important mother figure in the girls' lives."

Nichol learned of the disagreements among not only the Kallases, but also the staff. Even though they knew she ate dinner with Royce and the children generally, the staff chaffed at the idea of her being included for the holiday meal. The *only* people in the house who understood why Nichol would eat with the family were Royce and the girls. Nichol told him she should eat in the kitchen.

"The only time you eat in the kitchen is for late-night ice cream raids," Royce said, as though that solved anything.

The family was served a turkey roughly the size of a 1995 Ford Thunderbird. The elder Kallases were polite to Nichol, although Reginald did not make eye contact with her. Evelyn called Nichol "Tamra" twice. The girls thought Evelyn was teasing. Reginald gave Royce a concerned look, but they did not talk about her errors.

In 2002, perhaps as a New Year's resolution, Tamra turned to her "fuck buddy" Morgan Breedlove. In acting class Morgan was laid back, yet could bring passion and pathos to his scenes. And to sex. She did not see him with any regularity; she enjoyed the randomness of their couplings.

He told her about a troupe that was forming in the spring to do Shakespeare outdoor theatre, traveling from San Diego to San Francisco in the summer. If accepted into the troupe, she would practice five days a week for three months and then travel up the Pacific Coast, like the circus, for four months.

She had never been in a full-on Shakespeare play, only scenes, so she hired an acting coach who specialized in transforming the Bard's work to the stage. She met him every evening for a month, during which time they had a scorched earth affair – in addition to her trysts with Morgan that were like a pick-up game of basketball. Tamra coached the coach in his bed, on the floor of the theatre, in her Jag, and in his hot tub. When the Shakespeare coaching ended, so did the sex. She moved on. The coach did not.

She did not return he coach's phone calls, so he called Royce at the office.

"I have a personal matter to discuss with Royce Kallas."

"What is the nature of the matter?" Haley asked him, signaling to Royce's personal assistant Tiffany to pick up.

"The *nature of the matter* is that I am banging his

wife, and I wonder if he would prefer to keep it quiet."

Tiffany took over the call, and with exaggerated politeness asked him to hold. She buzzed Royce.

"A man who says his name is Puck is on the phone. He wants to speak to you about a very personal matter."

"This is Royce Kallas."

"For purposes of this conversation my name is Puck."

"And?"

"Do you know it's possible to have sex in the front seat of your Jaguar?"

"Why are you calling me?"

"I am an acting coach hired to prepare Tamra for her excursion with Shakespeare. Your wife has quite a range."

"I am not interested in discussing her acting ability. You have fifteen seconds to tell me why you are calling."

"You probably don't want me to go to the *Star* or *In Touch* and sell my story."

"Listen, punk…"

"No, my name is Puck."

"…sell the story to whomever you wish. Understand?" Royce hung up. He was embarrassed, humiliated, and sick at the vision of Tamra, the Tamra he knew eight plus years before, and another man in her car, of all places.

He called his assistant, Lew. "Sell the Jaguar immediately."

"It's not even a year old. You're going to take a bath selling it. Jags keep their value, but not the first year."

"Sell the damn car."

No one bothered to tell Tamra why it was sold, but she was not concerned. A silver Maserati was in the driveway a day later.

———

Puck or punk evidently did not contact anyone, because Royce asked Lew to have the company's media monitoring service specifically check for mention of Tamra and affairs. He hated, hated having people aware of his faithless marriage.

Because of his daughters, because of his father, because of his inability to cut his losses, Royce did not throw Tamra out on her skinny butt. A part of him, a part where memories of the happy years together dwelled, believed he could get Tamra back.

Tamra tried out for and was added to the Shakespeare troupe. In March 2002 she began rehearsing five plays that would rotate: *Midsummer Night's Dream, All's Well That Ends Well, Measure for Measure, Taming of the Shrew,* and *Twelfth Night,* comedies for a fun summer.

One spring day Tamra met Royce getting ready for his run. Nichol approached, and Tamra waved her over with a limp uninterested hand. "I'm leaving tonight for three months of rehearsal and then four months of travel putting on Shakespeare." She raised her chin.

"You are going to be gone seven months?" Royce asked as he hid his distress behind a stretching exercise, twisting his torso from side to side with his hands on his hips.

His movements forced Tamra to move her head from side to side to maintain eye contact with him. Nichol stood to the side and let the gyrations go on without her participation.

"During rehearsals I'll be home in the evenings and on weekends. I'll have the helicopter take me. The rehearsals are going to be in San Diego. I don't know why you didn't have a helipad put in here."

Royce let that go. "Seven months and then?" He stopped moving and put a hand on his chest and touched the cuirass he wore in his encounters with Tamra.

"Whatever happens."

Tamra moved closer to Royce. While she was bored with his interrogation, she was also sexually excited and one leg brushed his leg like a whisper. Royce took a step back, but his face blossomed pink like a cluster of sweet peas. Let Nichol bear witness to Tamra's ability to control her husband.

"Are you concerned at all—? Never mind," he said. His naked vulnerability in full view, he walked out the front door.

The two women considered each other.

"Mrs. Kallas, your daughters love you and miss you," Nichol said.

Tamra frowned, but quick witted she responded, "Fuck you."

After Tamra packed two large suitcases and an overnight bag to hurry out of her family's lives, she went into Sophie's room. Sophie lay on the top bunk talking on the phone. Teddy sat on the floor doing her homework. Tru lay on the bottom bunk and played with Sophie's scrunchies. She wrapped them over her thin arm.

"You're all here. Good. Don't you look cute together." She stood just inside the door. Teddy looked up with a trained expression of boredom; Tru imitated Teddy. Sophie did not look over at Tamra.

"I will be gone. For a while. A little while."

Sophie continued her call and spoke louder, saying, "There's some noise in my room."

———

"Okay," Teddy said and went back to her homework.

"Don't you want to know? I'm an actress. I'm very good. Maybe you'd like to come watch me on the stage. We're doing Shakespeare. You will learn about him in…someday."

"What a shake spear?" Teddy asked and jumped up. "Shake a spear?" Teddy demonstrated with one of Sophie's hangers.

"It's a man, Teddy," Tamra said.

"Shake a spear at a man?" Teddy asked, lunging toward Tamra.

"All right. I'll see you later." Tamra reached out to corral Tru, but the baby danced around the room behind Teddy.

"Knock it off, spaz," Sophie said.

Teddy sat back down on the floor and watched as Tamra walked out the door.

"Go away," Teddy said, as tears made blobs of her mathematics homework.

"Go 'way," Tru said.

Tamra sent the girls postcards that sounded as though she were a cousin off on an extended coastal train trip following surfers. "This is the Globe at Balboa Park in San Diego where we perform. Having fun." "I'm in Santa Barbara. Lovely beaches. We are at the Casa de la Guerra." She and the troupe followed the routes of the Franciscan monks that settled California: San Diego, La Jolla, Laguna Beach, Oxnard, Santa Maria, San Luis Obispo, Santa Cruz, San Jose, Fremont, San Francisco. The postcards tracked her like a GPS. Nichol told Royce when the first postcard arrived. He went into Sophie's room. She said Teddy had it.

"Teddy, you got a postcard from your mother?"

Teddy, lying on her bed, staring at a poster of Pete Wentz on her ceiling, pointed to her waste basket.

Chapter Twenty-Seven

Tamra did not discuss her acting with Royce except to defend her belief that she was entitled to her gypsy existence within their marriage. Beyond telling him early in their relationship that acting was "righteous," he did not know that her work was praised by her fellow actors and she had developed a fan following. She received mail, one-third of which complimented her work, one third was of the "I want to fuck you" variety, and one-third told her to go to beauty school or take up another hobby.

The troupe performed *Taming of the Shrew*, in which Tamra played Bianca. She had tried out for Katherine, but the producers thought she didn't have the disposition to be over-the-top angry. One night after a performance when they were in Laguna Beach, she was told some fans wanted to say "hello" to her. She left on her stage makeup and waited in the crowded dressing room where the other actors high fived each other, sat quietly as they took off makeup, or kibitzed about what worked and didn't work that day.

Tamra was signing some of her headshots to give to the fans.

"Tamra, you have guests," the actor who played Lucentio said.

Tamra stood up and turned toward the curtain that served as a door.

"Hello," Royce said, holding a playbill.

Tamra stared at her husband, Sophie, and Teddy. She didn't move toward them, so Royce walked through the group of actors, and her daughters followed. Royce leaned in to kiss her, and, looking around the room, Tamra quickly gave him her cheek.

"Why are you here?" Tamra asked him, with equal parts venom and curiosity.

But then Sophie held out her arms, and Tamra, looking surprised, embraced her.

"You were really good," Sophie said.

"You liked it? You really think I was good?" Tamra said, holding Sophie's hands.

"Yeah. We studied Shakespeare in my English class this year. I don't know the play you did, though. You made an awesome Bianca," Sophie said. She looked around the room at all the actors, some still wearing their makeup and costumes, with other costumes hanging on racks. A lengthy table with brushes, wigs and tubes and bottles of makeup sat below a wall of mirrors and lights divided into individual spaces for the actors.

"Thank you. That means a lot to me," Tamra said, smiling for the first time since she created a separate life for herself.

Tamra turned toward Teddy who stood with her arms folded over her chest and looked everywhere in the room except at Tamra.

"Did you like it, Teddy?" Tamra said.

Teddy didn't answer her. The child's mouth was an angry sneer, and her eyes were squinted in a personification of hatred. Sophie poked her with her elbow.

"Teddy, why not tell your mother what you thought of the play?" Royce said.

Teddy looked at Royce without relaxing her face and body. "I didn't understand what anyone was saying. It was like they were talking in the foreign language. You..." she said looking at Tamra for the first time, "were just peachy. I think you should keep acting..."

"Oh, thank you, Teddy. That means..."

"…and not come home ever again."

Royce put his hand on Teddy's shoulder and tried to pull her toward him, but she shrugged him off her and stomped out of the room.

"So, is this your family?" Tamra's "fuck buddy" Morgan asked as he walked up to the majorly awkward little group.

Tamra took in a breath and imperceptibly shook her head "no."

Morgan got a shit-eating grin on his face and extended his hand to Royce. Tamra made no effort to introduce them to each other.

"They are just leaving. We can run lines together in a while," Tamra said, grasping Morgan's shoulder and turning him away from her husband and daughter.

"Oh," Morgan said, maybe the light bulb going off in his head. "Well, nice to meet you," he said to Royce.

"Who is that?" Royce asked, in a minimally interested voice.

"No one. He's just a guy in the company," Tamra said.

"Well, I guess we should leave, Soph," Royce said.

"Yeah, okay," Sophie said, her eyes following Morgan. "Goodbye, Tamra, uh, Mama." She held her arms out, but then changed her mind, turned away and walked out.

"Goodbye. You were great," Royce said. "Well…" Although Tamra wasn't giving him attitude, he didn't reach out to hug or kiss her. He walked out.

Tamra watched his retreating back. She stood looking around the room, as though she were waiting for stage direction. She realized she had not asked about Tru.

———

Chapter Twenty-Eight

When Tru was old enough to sit at dinner without decorating the floor with her unwanted food, Nichol began a new tradition. She gave the girls a treat at the end of the school week: she decided that every Friday evening she would take the girls out to dinner. The girls got to choose the restaurant. Sophie and Teddy usually got their pick because three-year-old Tru didn't know the names of many restaurants, except Chuck E. Cheese. Fifteen-year-old Sophie was generally more interested in high school football or basketball games than dinner with her family. She brought friends, when she could be enticed to come. Seven-year-old Teddy was at an age where she thought going out to dinner was pretty cool. Nichol asked her to select the restaurant one night.

"Not Chinese, glak. The food's squirmy," Tru said. "They make worms," and then she cackled. Cloud Nine was scratched from the possibilities.

That Friday night the four ladies and friends returned from dinner, drunk on hot fudge sundaes, giggling and pretty silly in general. Royce was home.

"May I join you next Friday?" he asked.

"Oh, Daddy. Oh, yes, please, please come," Teddy said.

"But not Chinese, Daddy," Tru said.

Even though Sophie was beyond bored with the idea of family dinner, she wanted part in any activity that let her spend time with her dad and Nic. Teddy did not really believe he would join them, but he came home on Friday ready to take them out. Royce had Tiffany put "dinner with the girls" on his office calendar and accompanied them each week he was not out of town. He felt the odd man out sometimes, because he did not get the jokes that the others thought were so funny. The females clutched their chests and high fived with great frequency.

With a few weeks of Friday night dinners under his belt, he felt comfortable enough to join in.

"Knock knock," he said.

"Who's there?" Teddy played the straight man.

"Doris."

"Doris, who?" Sophie joined in out of curiosity of her dad telling a joke. She had brought Kaylie as her guest.

"Doris locked. That's why I am knocking."

General groans from Nichol and Teddy.

"Good one, Daddy," Tru said, not understanding much except for "knock, knock."

Embarrassed, Sophie went back to being bored and talking to Kaylie.

Royce chose at least two star restaurants, which meant the girls wore dressy clothes and only engaged in their versions of French. The first time they went to a classic French restaurant, Tru was worried when the waiter set plates covered in cloches in front of her and the others. She did not take her eyes off the dome. She watched the waiters remove all of them at the same time and expected butterflies to fly out. She was disappointed it was just food.

On the odd chance Tamra might be home, Royce debated asking her to join them for dinner, but, frankly, he was tired of being shot down by her truculent words and gratuitous swearing. And he enjoyed the dinners as they were. He watched how the girls interacted with Nichol. All the girls vied for her attention, even the girls' friends, but there was no jealousy among them. As he looked at them, he imagined that his intact family sat at that table, and he got a sensation he identified as pride and another sensation he would have to deliberate about for a few years before he could articulate it.

When he found an opening to talk, he asked Nichol about her social life. "What have you been doing for fun recently?" he asked.

Her eyebrows scrunched "Social life?" she asked, stretching her arms out to indicate the girls and the restaurant.

"Sure, of course. But what about adult fun?" More than three years in and Royce was just at that moment asking Nichol about her personal life.

"I am happy, very happy here," she said and squeezed the girls' shoulders. "This is my fun now."

"You do not want to do something besides taking care of these three miscreants?" he asked.

Teddy turned her head and looked for a miscreant, whatever that was.

"Never mind, Ted," Sophie said. She furrowed her brow. She knew what miscreant meant. Her dad always sounded like a dictionary.

"Are you trying to get me fixed up with someone?" Nichol asked.

"Uh, no, of course not." He had never thought about Nichol dating. He could not see her with another man. *Another* man?

"When I went to university, I took my lessons very seriously. Great competition existed for nursing school slots. And then I followed that with my master's program, which was intense. I did not have much time to socialize. Now I go to concerts, plays, dinner with friends. I have run since high school, and I like to find new tracks, hills, or paths to run on.

Since I bought a townhouse in Hidden Hills, I have found trails at Ahmanson Ranch—”

“You run at Ahmanson Ranch?” he asked and interrupted her.

“Yes, sometimes when the girls are in school and on my days off.”

“Well, I will be darned.”

“Why, Daddy? Why are you darned?” Teddy said.

“It is an expression, Teddy. I was surprised that—” He could not finish the sentence without getting himself knotted up in something he could not at that time untangle.

“In high school I was on a girls' basketball team and in college I was on a co-ed team.” She paused. “I love to go to the movies. Right now everything I see with the girls is G or PG. I like most everything except for movies with lots of car crashes, high body count, and no plot. I leave those for my guy friends.”

“Maybe we could go to the movies. I am an Alfred Hitchcock fan.” He realized what he had said. Sophie and Teddy did, too. “With the girls, of course,” he said, too late. “Or you can check out, maybe through a Y, to find a basketball team. I was guard on my high school team. I stopped playing when I became too short to play with the big guys.”

“Okay, if you will play, too, I will find a basketball team for us,” she said, as a joke. She knew he wouldn’t do it.

Nichol did find a co-ed team through Pierce College. She met Royce for their run one morning. “First we have to try out,” Nichol said. “Games are on Saturdays.”

“Hmmm. I do not know if I can do it,” Royce said.

"I understand." She was not surprised and was ready to drop the idea.

The next morning they met at the front door for their run.

"I have thought about it. I would like to play basketball."

And so it began.

On the ride home after tryouts—they both made the team—Royce said, "I have a favor to ask you."

"Of course," Nichol said. "What do you need?"

"Would you, please, not call me Mr. Kallas when we play basketball. It was embarrassing to hear you saying 'Mr. Kallas, step it up. Move your ass, Mr. Kallas.'" He raised his voice to a falsetto.

Nichol laughed. "I'm sorry. Do you want me to call you by your first name or some embarrassing nickname from childhood?"

"For your ears only. I do not know if Tamra even knows this. In boarding school my nickname was Phallus. Guys tried to find something that sounded close to Kallas, and there it was, the very object foremost in boys' minds. So, thanks for the opportunity to go down memory lane, but no nicknames. Royce will do just fine. Call me Royce at home, too. I am not going to have dinner with you gaggle of women and, while you are all singing some—in my humble opinion—inane song, you say, 'Join in, Mr. Kallas.'"

"That will take some getting used to, but I agree it is awkward calling you 'Mister' in front of the rest of the team." In fact she had stopped calling him Mr. Kallas unless it was necessary since she returned from the 2001 trip. Most of the time she didn't address him by name.

The girls got wind that their daddy and Nic joined a basketball team. Teddy said she wanted to watch them play, followed by Tru who just wanted to go wherever everyone else was going. The girls soon argued with referees' calls and yelled to the other team, "Baby, baby, baby." Even three-year-old Tru understood the basics. "Daddy throws to Nic. She makes the basket. Team wins."

Chapter Twenty-Nine

In 2004, Tamra continued to go home in between engagements and assignations, and Royce led a double life. In one, he was married to an unfaithful peripatetic vagabond and could not divorce her, lest he lose his father's love and respect. And money, although Royce was conflicted as to the significance his parents' trust played as he continued to be the cuckold.

In his shadow life, he invested himself in his daughters and—although he would still deny it—Nichol. As he became more a part of his daughters' lives, he recognized, after such a long time, they did not need him just to provide a golden roof over their heads and designer clothes on their backs. He had always followed his father's model: work hard, accumulate wealth, and let his wife raise the children. He felt heavy guilt because he had not spent more time with Teddy when she was a toddler. He learned how to be a father from Nichol. Whereas up to eight years before, he had concentrated on amassing his personal fortune, he became, under Nichol's tutelage, a nurturer and safety net.

By the spring of 2004, Royce had become a person with whom he was only marginally familiar. He broke a firm resolution of the Kallas men: he talked to his father about his cumbrous marriage. He found Reginald at home in his study.

"Father, I look at you and Mother, and I want the same marriage." Royce sat down in a guest chair.

"Each marriage is different, the people are different," Reginald said, leaning back in his black leather chair, identical to his office chair and identical to the conference room chair. His body language said he was uncomfortable discussing something personal.

"Yes, I understand that," Royce said as he dragged his ponderous heart, "but you and Mother have a relationship based on trust. Right?" He slapped his hands on his thighs.

"Yes, that is true. Your mother is an exemplary woman." Reginald leaned forward and put his elbows on the desk.

"Mine is not. Tamra has a rapacious appetite to lie." He crossed his right leg over his left and prepared for a razor-sharp rejoinder.

"Do not be crass. She is a delightful girl." Reginald slapped his hands together.

"When did you become her champion?" Royce leaned back in the chair, thereby making himself completely uncomfortable. He straightened his spine.

"Do not be disrespectful. She has given you two outstanding children."

Royce stood up and looked down on his father. "Three, Father, three children. What can I say so you will understand the severity of my situation? I cannot take more of this."

"Royce, such a flagrant and unnecessarily dramatic representation." Reginald reached into a desk drawer and pulled out a crystal bowl holding an assortment of Hershey's miniature candy bars. He rooted around in the bowl for his favorite, Mr. Goodbar. "Son, it is your responsibility as the man to keep your house in order." Reginald's punctilious righteousness offended Royce.

"What if I have to divorce her to have order?" Royce knew he wasn't presenting his arguments well. He was on the defensive with his father and thought of ways to take control.

"Absolutely not. I know that today people divorce for no reason. You made a vow to be married until death do you part. You remember that? You cannot leave your family."

"I would not leave. Tamra would. She is already gone more than she is at home. She does not enjoy spending time with the girls. I would keep them with me, with Nichol as nanny."

"You are not…with…?" Reginald sighed and looked out his study window.

"Of course not. Absolutely not. I am telling you, it is Tamra."

"Kallases do not divorce, son," Reginald's orotund response. "Four, five generations, with no divorces. That is your heritage and will be your legacy."

The next day, Royce chose a moment to call Tamra. She was in rehearsals for the Shakespeare tour. He felt something needed to be resolved, something, or he would go mad. Since he would adhere to his father's edict not to divorce, he decided to go one hundred eighty degrees out. He asked her, pleaded with her to come home. He realized he wasn't sure he wanted her home.

After thought and reflection, she articulated her feelings about his request: "Fuck you and the horse you rode in on," Tamra never to be confused with an intellectual leviathan.

The silent war continued. When Tamra was home, she moved through the house like a stealth specter. Sophie and Teddy expressed an absence of interest in her, while Tru saw her like a toy she lost, forgot about, and later found. With Nichol's efforts, Royce kept the bubble in the level centered. He sometimes found himself dissembling when

Tamra left and then returned. His entire body suffered a repetitive stress injury.

Chapter Thirty

In July 2004 on a Saturday night, Sophie had a sweet sixteen party in the pool, pool house and tennis court, complete with lifeguards and a DJ. All of her friends from school came, some just to check out the estate, some to compare properties because theirs were probably larger. Royce stood with Nichol and the parents of Sophie's friend Kaylie, talking about children growing up. He thought about Sophie at six, a green-eyed giggling blonde. Both sets of grandparents came to the party.

Reginald appropriated Tru for the evening. She was easier to talk to than a tennis court full of teenagers.

Evelyn talked to Laramie and Belle about the grandchildren and watched Reginald talking to Tru. "Isn't it lovely a big wedding like this." Tamra's parents gave each other quizzical looks. They had no idea what she was talking about.

At that moment Tamra made an appearance. She introduced herself to Kaylie's parents, who, until that moment, thought Nichol was Sophie's mother. Tamra put her arm through Royce's and waxed poetic about Sophie turning sixteen. Sophie was too busy with her friends to notice Tamra until Noel rolled a cake onto the tennis court. Tamra took the mic from the DJ and insinuated herself next to the cake.

"Quiet, everyone. Please, quiet." She was playing to the crowd.

Sophie looked for Royce, and when she saw him, shot him a worried look. He took charge. He simply was taller than Tamra. He took the mic away from her.

"Thank you for coming tonight to celebrate Sophie's sixteenth birthday with her family," Royce said. He managed

---

to position Nichol, who was holding Teddy's hand, next to him.

Tamra seemed lost at that point. She looked dejected. After a moment of standing very still and listening to the toasts, she regained her Tamraness and plowed into the crowd, introducing herself to Sophie's friends. She went into the pool house and changed into a bikini and then settled herself on the pool deck, dangling her feet into the warm water. Belle put enough real estate between herself and Tamra to keep the proceedings civil.

Everyone sang "Happy Birthday," and Tamra disappeared.

Royce then said to the partygoers, "Sophie, can you come over here, sweetheart? I have a small present to give you."

Everyone started clapping and chanting: "Sophie, Sophie."

As she walked over to Royce, he held out a small ring box. She kissed him on the cheek and tore the wrapping off the box. When she opened the box, she screamed.

"Oh my God, oh my God. Where is it, Dad?"

She held a key over her head and began working her way through her friends to get to the garage.

"No, Soph. Look out on the street," Royce said over the mic.

Sophie screamed again, and a group of her friends ran with her. The mob reached the street where a silver Mercedes Cabriolet convertible sat waiting for her. The remainder of the night Sophie gave her friends rides up and down Grandioso and made big plans with her buddies to go to the mall, to the beach, to pick up her friends for school. Unfortunately for Sophie's plans, Royce had plans, too. The car and the perks it allowed were not going to interfere with

Sophie's grades.

Chapter Thirty-One

In the fall of 2004 Teddy, the week before the new school year started, lay on her bed and stared at a poster of Linkin Park that had replaced Pete Wentz on the ceiling.

One day Nichol knocked on her open door and walked in. "Get up. We're going riding."

"I don't want to go riding." Teddy was lying on her queen-size bed that replaced her little girl bed, but she still loved pink.

"Up. Not a request."

"No. Leave me alone."

Nichol sat on the edge of Teddy's bed. "I am not going to leave you alone," she said. She opened her arms. "Come here. Please."

"No. Stop."

Nichol stood up. "Fifteen minutes at the stable. I am tacking up two horses, and I can't ride both of them."

Nichol went to the paddock and talked to Velvet as she brushed her mane. "Help me with this girl."

"I want to ride Velvet. You ride Shampoo," Teddy said, as she walked up behind her.

Nichol smiled at the horse and turned around. "Okay, and you get to tack her up."

"There are child labor laws, you know."

"Did you learn that in school?"

"Of course."

They led the horses out of the gate. Teddy used a log stump to help her mount Velvet. She went ahead of Nichol. They rode out onto the trail and let the horses choose a walk. Nichol pulled Shampoo even with Velvet. She smelled the sagebrush and horse remains.

"Are you angry with your mother?" Nichol asked.

"I'm not mad at you." Teddy patted Velvet's mane.

"Your father loves you, you know."

Shampoo kicked up some pollen-filled dust.

"I know. And you love me, and the world's wonderful." Teddy sounded as though she had saddle sores on her heart.

"This is not bad, my dear one. You are growing up. You are beautiful. You get excellent grades. You are healthy."

"Please stop. I'll go back."

"No. Talk to me."

"Why? I say something, and you tell me how great my life is."

"Do you know how far away my mother lives?"

"You're a grownup."

"I came to the United States when I was a girl. I missed my mother. When I was at home in Haiti, my mother was gone working in clinics."

"Your mother is a doctor, saving lives. My mother is in a minstrel show." She started to cry. She drew back on the reins and stopped Velvet. "Do you know at school everyone thinks you're my mother? Since we don't look alike, they ask me if *I'm* adopted. I tell them you are. There are lots of nannies that come to pick up kids, but I guess you don't seem like a nanny."

Nichol reached over to Teddy and gave her a light punch on the arm. "I will be your adopted mother." She paused. "You know, all girls have issues with their mothers. It's required."

"You're doing it again. Can't I say something and you don't act all la-de-da?"

Nichol turned Shampoo to face Velvet. The horses nuzzled each other. She waited.

"I hate her!" Teddy said. Velvet, spooked, stepped back. "I hate her, and I wish she'd never come back."

Too angry to edit herself, Nichol said, "You and your sisters, such loving, exceptional girls. And your father—" She slammed on the verbal brakes. "He is a nice person and takes good care of you. Even if you are spoiled. A little bit."

"Do you like my father?"

"Yes, I said—"

"Do you like him?"

"I-I – "

"Uh huh. I thought so. And what do you mean, I'm spoiled? You live here, too."

"I certainly do, my love. I guess I am spoiled, too."

They continued to ride down the trail, Teddy in front of Nichol, the latter of whom wondered if she was going to fall off an emotional cliff.

In September 2004 wearing a ruffled pink and white skirt with a pink t-shirt and pink tennies—modeling herself on Teddy's attire—that Nichol helped her dye to get the color just right, Tru walked up the stairs to the door of her three mornings a week preschool, wearing her long brown hair in two braids. She carried a Dora the Explorer backpack. Royce and Nichol watched from the sidewalk, and they sniffled, cleared their throats, and smiled, wan heart-breaking smiles.

They had already taken Teddy, who looked smart in her new uniform, to her third-grade building, after she unsuccessfully argued with Royce that she wanted to walk to class alone so she would not be embarrassed. Sophie had driven herself to school, lord help us. After they dropped the girls off, Royce went on to his office, and Nichol went back home.

She was surprised to find Tamra not only at home from the tour, but also in *her* bedroom. Tamra sat on Nichol's mauve satin comforter. Nichol never sat on the comforter herself because she wanted to maintain its pristine appearance. Thus, she was both irritated with Tamra and curious as to why she was in her room.

Tamra's eyebrows were professionally groomed, and they arched with acidic cynicism. Her toenails were professionally pedicured, polished in a French style with white tips. Her feet dangled off the edge of the bed. Dressed in simple but expensive black yoga pants, white oxford shirt open over a silver t-shirt, and flip flops, Tamra leaned back on her elbows. Nichol, dressed in jeans, a pullover blue shirt and moccasins, felt mannish and enormous by comparison. Nichol paced the floor next to the bed, not sure if she should be deferential, consider Tamra her equal, or something else entirely. Tamra had her ass on Nichol's comforter, after all.

"I haven't been in these rooms since Royce moved you in. Very nice, very cozy. Fireplace. Interesting colors. Does this feel like your home?" Tamra asked, aloof and enigmatic. She could have been interviewing Nichol.

"I am very comfortable here. Thank you for asking. May I ask you, please, Mrs. Kallas, to not sit on my bed, on the comforter?"

"Right at home, eh?"

"Yes, it feels as though it is home."

"And the rest of the house, too, is available to you. Correct? My husband using his good manners would have told you to consider the rest of the house part of your home."

"Yes, Mr. Kallas told me to make myself at home. Three *years* ago. I asked you not to sit on the comforter."

Silence.

"And my children, too. You consider them to be your daughters."

"I have been with them almost every day for three years. I love your daughters." Nichol gave as good as she got, without the sarcasm.

"Like they are your own. Right?"

"I am very close to them." She paced, like a prisoner in a six by four cell.

"The last piece of this house that you consider yours is my husband. You consider him yours, too. Yes?" Tamra said.

"I do not know what you mean." But she thought she did know.

"You've got a close relationship with my husband. I've seen the two of you together. You run with him in the morning and eat dinner together at the dining table I picked out." She ticked the offenses off on the fingers of her left hand, the hand with a monster diamond. Her hands were professionally manicured, too.

Nichol waited.

"I wonder what you talk about while you're running, while you're eating. I think you discuss how you can keep me in the dark when I'm gone for a few months so you can fuck each other," she said, her pernicious meanness delivered to Nichol prepaid.

"Your husband and I…your children always come first. What you are suggesting is vile and immoral. I will not say more. Please leave my room."

Tamra bolted off the bed and impeded Nichol's path. "This is my house, these are my rooms, and my furniture— although these pieces are falling down ugly. I'm the one telling you to leave." Tamra's veins showed in her forehead and neck, like sluggish tributaries to the Mississippi.

———

263

"I will wait for Mr. Kallas to come home."

"No, I don't think you will. I think you will get all your shit together and leave this house now."

"I have to pick up the girls from school."

"I'll pick them up. What school is Tru going to?"

"And you think I have cast an evil spell over the girls so they think I am their mother, but you cannot be bothered to take Tru to her first day of preschool or Teddy to third grade and you do not know their school schedules and, unbelievably, you do not know what school they go to. If I sit here and do nothing, you are going to get phone calls from school. The girls will be embarrassed. So, if you don't mind—" She attempted to get by Tamra without knocking her down. Nichol had height over Tamra, but Tamra had nastiness in spades.

Tamra grabbed her arm. "I do mind. I mind very much. You are my employee and as such you should speak to me with deference," a line out of one of Tamra's plays. "I'm going with you to get them."

"You are not coming with me. The girls will pick up on your energy."

"Don't give me that airy fairy shit. And do you think you can talk to me this way?"

"I will get the girls, and then Mr. Kallas can give his opinion." Plus, and Tamra probably did not know this, there was a clause in Nichol's employment contract that provided she would be given no less than sixty days' notice of termination, except for cause, which was defined in detail as inappropriate behavior while in the Kallases' employ. Nichol felt she was on firm ground since the only thing she had said was for Tamra to get off her comforter.

Tamra grabbed at the comforter and scratched it with her lacquered nails, threw it on the floor, and kicked it against a wall. She walked out of Nichol's suite.

Nichol shook. She closed and locked her door and hugged herself to put warmth back in her body. She stood in the doorway between the living room and bedroom and rocked from side to side. Do I have to leave my girls? What have I done wrong? Will Royce take Tamra's side? How can I live without my girls? Without Royce? The last question came to her unbidden. She understood it was not an appropriate question. He was married. Why would he be interested in her? She implored herself to stop that kind of thinking. Absurd thoughts, romantic nihilism.

She cried. For a moment she focused on her comforter. Long scratches cut into the precious threads, and she ran her fingers over them. As she put the comforter on the bed with intentional tenderness, her tears bruised the satin.

Before she picked up Tru, Nichol called Royce. "I am sorry I am disturbing you at work. Can you please come home early today?"

"What is going on? What is the matter?" Royce said.

"Tamra fired me."

"Where are you now?"

"I am leaving to pick up Tru. I thought I would take her to lunch. Then I pick up Teddy at 2:00. Sophie comes home by herself after 3:00." Nichol did not trust that she would not start crying. She needed reassurance from Royce.

"Get the children. I will be at home at 2:00," a noncommittal response.

Nichol picked up Tru at noon and told her they would not eat at home for lunch; instead, they would go out for lunch, a grownup lunch to celebrate her first day at preschool. Tru squeaked and clapped her hands together. She got Nichol all to herself. Tru talked in a sing song voice about preschool without stopping for punctuation: "I have to raise my hand to talk like this I have to raise it if I need to go to the bathroom my teacher is Ms. Cambria isn't that pretty Ms. Cambria my new best friend is Kaia."

They went to Ruby's. Tru was excited she was allowed to have her own chocolate shake. She sat on her knees instead of sitting in the baby booster seat. Tru showed Nichol how to turn her napkin into a tent. Tru wanted a cheeseburger, and Nichol said they would share. Tru pouted, but was happy again when her shake arrived with a cherry on top of whipped cream. Throughout the meal Nichol's thoughts flashed by like a strobe light as she paid attention to what Tru said and simultaneously thought about the showdown with Tamra. She felt she was walking from a normal mirror to a funhouse mirror, normal house, funhouse, normal, freak.

They picked up Teddy. "My teacher is nice—"

"What's her name?" Tru asked.

"There are two new boys in my class, and my friends got all freaky over them—"

"Did you get freaky?" Nichol asked.

"*I* ignored them."

At about 2:15, Nichol walked in the kitchen door with the girls. Tru still talked like rapid gunfire, to stop only to catch her breath in a dramatic way with her hand on her chest. "Whew!"

"Well, there are my girls," said Tamra, as she walked in the kitchen in gold kitten heels that clicked and whapped as she walked. "Where's Sophie?"

"Nic took me to lunch," Tru said as happy as a brand-new preschooler could be.

"Why is Tru calling you 'Nic'?" Tamra asked, turning her head toward Nichol, but not looking at her.

Tru looked at Teddy to see if she had done something wrong.

"That's what we call Nichol because she's our friend. We love her," Teddy said.

They all stopped in the living room, as if it had been pre-arranged. Nichol sat down in a Tuscan high back chair, and Tru plopped herself in her lap. Tamra, who sat in a matching chair, held her arms out for Tru and made a clucking noise in her throat.

"You're a chicken," Tru said, guileless.

"Good one," Teddy said and snickered. She jumped up on a couch.

Nichol bit the inside of her cheek. She waited a moment. "Teddy, no jumping on the furniture."

Teddy sat down, dramatically putting her hands in her lap. "Nichol's with us every day, all the time." Teddy fought back tears. She wanted to sound like an adult. She was saved by the sound of the front door opening.

All four of them looked toward the front door as Royce walked in.

"Daddy, oh, Daddy's here," Teddy said as she ran to him and wrapped her arms around his waist.

Tru pushed herself off Nichol and ran to him.

"I am sorry I am late. Girls, I need you to go into Teddy's bedroom for a little while."

They started to object, but they met three angry faces, and so they left.

"There you go. Thank you," Royce said.

Teddy led them upstairs where they lay on the floor of the landing, out of sight of the adults below.

"Why did you call Mr. Kallas? He's a busy man and doesn't need to be disturbed by a minor matter that I have taken care of." Tamra stood by her chair.

Royce looked at Tamra. "Nichol told me you fired her. Number one, what prompted you to do that and number two, you do not have the authority or ability to fire anyone."

"I fired her because stuff she does is just not right. Why can't I fire an employee?"

"You abrogated your position as mother to the girls and manager of the house the day we moved here and hired Nichol as the baby nurse. You have been a ghost in this house for almost four years, materializing and disappearing as you see fit. I have tried and tried to get through to you, asking if you are ill, asking why you gave the responsibility and joy of raising our daughters to Nichol." A paroxysm of anger fueled him.

"I think you have been under this one's spell since the day we hired her," Tamra said as she walked around to the back of Nichol's chair. She patted the top of the chair, cognizant that scenes required movement to compliment the dialogue. Then she arched her back, which resulted in pushing her chest out, right in Royce's flight path. "She's charmed the pants right off you."

"What are you saying? Are you telling me you think Nichol and I have made love?" Royce's voice got higher and louder as he talked. He moved further into the living room.

Nichol had not told him that Tamra accused her of having sex with him.

"Answer me. Is that what are you saying?" he said.

Tamra hesitated. "No fault of yours, Nichol has done some kind of voodoo on you."

"Are you making this up because I'm Haitian?" Nichol did not turn her head to look at Tamra and made no pretense of being subservient to her. "Do you think I put a special potion into Royce's coffee and then wave a dead chicken over my head?"

Any chance of Nichol backtracking to employee status evaporated that moment. She was aware that she had referred to Mr. Kallas as Royce.

"She's saying that she knows about spells," Tamra said and looked at Royce. "Please do this for me, for our girls. Please fire Nichol so we can re-claim our relationship."

"No, Tamra. What is best for *our* girls is the consistency that Nichol provides. Sophie is lost to you. Teddy does not understand why you stopped being a mother to her as soon as Tru was born. I am beyond caring why you quit being a wife and mother. We are managing very nicely."

"You sound as though you are—" Tamra said.

"Do not interrupt me." He wanted to give her an opportunity to actually listen to his words. Royce believed everything he said, and he also visualized all the lawsuits Nichol could bring.

The muscles in Tamra's face stopped flexing.

"You have to know you sound *nuts* talking about spells and, vulgar when you talk about a sexual relationship between Nichol and me. You are confrontational and delusional. At the very least, you owe Nichol an apology and you owe the girls an apology. And if you do talk to them, do not disparage Nichol." He walked to the chair in which Nichol sat.

Tamra stood behind that chair. He put a hand on each wooden arm and leaned over. His face was even with Nichol's, but he was looking up at Tamra. Nichol's head sailed somewhere near nirvana.

"My girls need a mother in their lives, and Nichol provides that role," he said. He enunciated each syllable. "Tamra, do you have any other hallucinatory paranoia to share? Any other allegations? Any other flat out lies?" Royce stood up and took in oxygen.

Nichol was also able to breathe. She had almost been in Royce's arms. She got a sensation she could not define.

He walked back into the middle of the room, looked around, then back at Tamra, who had not moved. "I have been trying to figure out why you decided today to attack Nichol and wanted a best mother award," he said. "You have been having an affair, and it ended on the tour. No, stop shaking your head 'no.' That is the answer. Do not try to get back in our girls' lives now and then leave as soon as another affair begins."

"N-no. I want to be a good mother. I—"

"Have enough integrity to recognize your limits and enough compassion for the girls to care about the impact your absences have on them." He spoke in a whisper—with attitude.

Tamra walked around Nichol's chair, with soft, quiet movements as though she were moving in slow motion, picked up her handbag, which was conveniently in the living room as though she had placed a prop and planned a quick exit in advance, and walked toward the kitchen. Royce followed her. Nichol heard him tell her that all he had ever wanted was to be a husband and father. Tamra said something Nichol couldn't hear, but the tone of her voice was not pleasant. Tamra bolted back into the living room, stood about ten feet from Nichol, pointed her finger toward her and said, "Don't get too comfortable, *Nic*, because you will be out the door soon."

Royce charged back into the room. "I swear to God, Tamra, if you do not—" He looked at Nichol and stopped himself.

Tamra first looked angry, then terrified, then superior, as though she didn't know which emotion to feel. She froze with an expression of resignation on her face. She looked like a Madame Tussaud wax figure of herself.

Neither Tru nor Teddy understood what had happened, but they did recognize at some primal level a sea change happened that day. Teddy attempted to fill Sophie in on what had happened, but she didn't have the right vocabulary. Nichol was subdued and cautious with her demonstrations of love, and their daddy was sad. For about a month Tamra stayed home. She seemed lost, dropped from the sky into that house with that family, and she didn't know what role she played. She didn't fit in with the girls' routines. Tru in her joyous pink heart did not remotely feel Tamra was her mother, Teddy felt too much that she was, and Sophie did not know who her mother was.

Chapter Thirty-Two

On Halloween 2004, Tamra walked in the front door of the mansion dressed as Titania, queen of the fairies, and showed she had learned to vocalize. She boomed into the foyer as though she stood before an SRO crowd. "Trick-or-treat!" Her voice echoed throughout the first floor. Lindy, Angel, and Noel came on a run from the dining room where they had a game of Texas hold 'em going. They thought someone had broken into the house. When they saw who it was, a process that took a couple beats, they mumbled "hello" and returned to the dining room. They were neither disrespectful nor churlish, but had individually and collectively had as much of Tamra as they needed. They felt the impact of Tamra's conduct on the family about whom they cared.

Nichol, Sophie, Teddy, and Tru were out. Sophie and her friends were trick-or-treating in Hollywood with Kaylie's twenty-two-year-old sister as chaperone. Sophie was dressed as a zombie, thanks to Nichol's efforts.

"Tell them you are a Haitian zombie. That's special."

Nichol accompanied Teddy and three of her friends, plus Tru, dressed as five of the seven dwarfs, to other mansions in The Estates. Nichol had an ulterior motive for taking the girls. She wanted to see inside some of the other glamorous homes. Royce was in the theatre watching "North by Northwest" and "Rebecca" to put him in a Halloween frame of mind.

"Boo!"

"Good Christ, Tamara. You scared me to death. What are you doing here?"

"I live here. Remember?"

"I am not the one with memory problems."

"You've got an answer for everything I say, don't you? Where is everyone?"

Royce did not react or respond.

"Sophie, Teddy and Tru, I was talking about them, of course."

"Of course."

Cary Grant ran to get out of the path of an airplane. Royce turned up the sound.

"Why aren't you out trick-or-treating?" she asked, talking loudly to be heard over the noise of the plane. She touched his shoulder.

"I am not much for wearing costumes." He didn't move her hand.

"That's right. You were the kid who dressed in a suit on Halloween. Okay, I'm going to bed."

"With whom?"

"Wow! Welcome home, Tamra."

Again, no reaction or response.

"We missed you," she said in a low singsong voice. "We're glad you're home." She left Royce in the theatre and went to her suite. Her bed was covered in confetti. She smiled. *They wanted to surprise me.* She picked up a handful of the small pieces of paper. They were bright colors, and Tamra began to feel sunny inside. She held some in her hand. It took her a moment to figure it out: they were the postcards she had sent the girls while she was on a Shakespeare tour cut into half-inch squares.

By the end of 2004 Royce was a pro at working anywhere under any conditions. He was plugged into his laptop and phone. He traveled for business frequently, but was able to reduce the number of trips by using Skype and GoToMeeting. In his view, technology made him work more efficiently. Royce was fifty-one years old, had three children from three-and-a-half to sixteen. He was fit, still running every day, but got tired, where earlier in his professional life he had been energized.

Royce and Nichol spent the second half of 2005 visiting universities with Sophie. Royce commented to Nichol that he had no idea how much time was needed to properly raise children. They went to Stanford, Harvard, University of Chicago—Royce's request—and the University of California at San Diego, which was Sophie's first choice.

"Sophie wants to be a doctor," Royce told Steven.

"That's good. Tell her to choose geriatrics so she can take care of us. By the time she becomes a resident, we should be ready to retire."

"You will have to move to Haiti because she plans to practice in third world countries."

"Nichol has had a good influence on her," Steven said. "How does it feel, dad?"

"My friend, I spent the first forty years of my life learning not to have feelings—not to put too fine a point on it—to strap on a set of stainless steel balls. I've spent the next ten learning to grow a heart. When Sophie graduates in June I will be a sobbing mess."

In June 2006 Sophie did indeed graduate from high school, and Royce did indeed tear up as he applauded in the audience next to Nichol, who also cried. Teddy didn't cry. She was jealous she wasn't graduating. Tru didn't understand all the emotion being displayed. Tamra made an appearance as the proud mother, sitting with Reginald and

Evelyn. Laramie and Belle sat with Royce and the girls, and Royce detected a cross between pride and jealousy from Belle.

For Sophie's graduation party, Royce booked Magic Mountain amusement park during its closed hours, from 11:00 p.m. to 5:00 a.m., for her entire senior class. Sophie was a very popular girl at the party, and, Royce thought, she deserved to be. Nichol, Teddy, and Tru joined Royce. The grandparents bowed out of the party. The kids rode on Apocalypse and Colossus, the iconic rollercoaster, danced to the Velocity band with special effects lighting, and met Looney Tunes characters.

Sophie was accepted to her first choice, University of California, San Diego, where she was going to double major in Biochemistry/Cell Biology and Public Health. Unlike some of her friends who got boob jobs for graduation, Sophie got a trip for two to the continent—the continent!— of her choice. She chose Africa because Nichol had sparked her interest in third-world countries and being of service to people in need. She did some research and found projects she could work on in Kenya, Nigeria and Sudan. Also, she and her pal Mariana had scoped out primo beaches, but they didn't say that to their parents. Mariana was a world traveler thanks to her parents who owned a boutique travel agency that catered to wealthy clients. The graduates left the week after graduation.

One day in the summer of 2006, Royce felt the weight of his Sisyphean labor; it weighed down his shoulders, his arms, his head, his wooden legs in his encapsulated doom. He called Tamra's cell from his office.

She answered her phone, and Royce was surprised and curious to hear her live voice.

"You are there."

"Yes, I am. I want you to stop calling me. We have nothing to talk about."

"We do, Tamra. You have built a cushy life for yourself, taken me for granted, abused your daughters—"

Her voice jumped like a fighting gamecock. "Abused them? How in the hell am I doing that? I'm not even there. You're out of your mind."

"By abandoning them, by treating them as though they are someone else's children—"

"Tell me right now why you're calling or I'll hang up."

Royce heard the virulent yet gleeful voice with which she hated him and had fun doing so. He stood up from his desk and paced the room.

"I will pay you for twenty years of marriage, which is another $9,000,000 and give you the Beverly Hills home, which is worth four point two million. You can have two of the cars. I will consider giving you more money if you agree now," his voice louder than appropriate for his office, which was not soundproofed.

Tamra had been quiet while Royce spoke, uncharacteristic for her. "Give me $50,000,000, and I'll be gone." She erroneously thought that giving her $50,000,000 would wipe him out. That was her goal. She wanted to leave him with nothing as he had left a hole in her life when they moved from Beverly Hills. "It is only fair," she said.

"You know I cannot give you that amount of money," his voice a plea.

"On the contrary." Tamra had played a character that used that phrase and added it to her repertoire. That phone call was an opportunity to show Royce she had learned to speak like he did. "I know you *can* give me that amount."

"The major part of the family's money is in trusts. An additional nine million, and you give up your rights to the girls."

"You're going to have to give me $50,000,000," she said, a growl like the old hag with a poisoned apple.

"I can give you a different house in the Platinum Triangle, in addition to the money." He made the point with his hands, freed by Bluetooth. "Why are you demanding such a large settlement? You could not spend that much money in your lifetime."

"A house in the Platinum Triangle? Please just give me what I want," her voice tender and playful. "And it doesn't matter what I plan to do with the money. You have an obscene amount of money, and you do what you want to with it. I've been married to you for eleven years, and you don't want to give me any of your money. So you aren't even close, sweetie."

He remembered another lifetime when she called him sweetie.

"What you want is impossible. I do not have the ability to appropriate funds from the trusts." He had $50,000,000 and more available to absolve himself of that disease, but his negotiating genes wouldn't let him pay her that amount. Another consideration: he did not want her to know exactly how much money he had in his personal largesse. He paused and stopped pacing. "Tamra, did you ever love me?" An entreaty in the form of a question that was always on his mind when he thought of her. He heard her breathing and background noise of people talking and laughing.

"Yes, I did. You like treated me like a queen for four

years, let me be myself, adopted Sophie, and traveled with me. I liked being your wife." She paused. "Then you broke my heart. You made a huge decision without me. I will *never* forgive you." The sentiment was true—although the dialogue and delivery came from her auditions for soap operas. She had become a victim of the louche world of the theatre. She had turned his moving to Calabasas as her ballad of sorrow.

He felt as though he were in a traffic jam. "And Teddy and Tru?" He sat down and put his hands on his chest as though he had to confirm he indeed had a heart, like the Tin Man.

That question was trickier for her to answer. She did not want to expose her conflicted feelings. "This conversation is over."

Chapter Thirty-Three

After the activities surrounding Sophie's graduation, the house settled in to enjoy summer vacation. One July day Teddy, Tru, Carmen and Nichol sat on the floor in Teddy's bedroom playing Clue. They were about to find out if Col. Mustard committed murder in the Library with the Rope when Royce walked in.

"We have stuff to talk about," he said.

"Stuff?" Nichol and Teddy said simultaneously. He said "stuff"?

He rubbed his hands together, as though a magician in a county fair carny show. He looked like a Champagne bottle under pressure.

"Mesdames, how would you like to cruise the Mediterranean?"

Tru, for starters, didn't know what Mesdames and Mediterranean were. Teddy looked skeptical. She hadn't been on the yacht since moving to Calabasas, barely remembered it. Nichol waited.

"I moved the yacht to France. I thought, if you would like to, we will take a cruise." He didn't tell them that when he moved the yacht, part of him hoped Tamra would sail with him, and he admitted to himself to being the poster child for insanity.

Teddy hugged Tru. They looked like orphaned monkeys. Next they jumped up to hug Royce. "France, Paree," Teddy said over and over. Tru repeated what she heard Teddy say.

Picking up the scattered game pieces Nichol rattled off a few sentences in French, to which Teddy, correctly, responded.

"Speak English," Tru said, copping an attitude. "I

don't know French that fast."

"I emailed Sophie, but she is quite content in Morocco at the moment," Royce said. "I will have to work while we are sailing, but I thought, I do not know, a couple of weeks. Three weeks. And you, too, Carmen, if you can be away from your family that long."

More shrieking.

"Can we bring some friends, Daddy? One friend a piece. Please," Teddy said.

"Yes, you may. That is an excellent idea. I will have to talk to their parents, of course."

"Can Nichol bring a friend, Daddy?" Tru asked.

Nichol and Royce gave each other side glances. Teddy poked Tru with her elbow.

"Ow!" Tru said.

"If she would like to," Royce said.

Nichol shook her head and chewed on her upper lip.

"You do not want to go?" he asked.

"Oh, yes, of course I want to go. Fly in a private jet to a yacht and cruise the Mediterranean."

And so an adventure began. It required them to shop, of course. Royce told Nichol to buy a cruise wardrobe for herself and the girls. She did not know what a cruise wardrobe consisted of, but she wanted to be part of the entire experience with the girls and knew, since he had made the offer, he expected her to dress like a Kallas. So they were off to the Bs: Bergdorf, Barneys, and Burberry.

Teddy invited Xandy and Tru, Kaia. Royce invited their parents to the house to explain the yacht's accommodations, safety precautions, including elite nannies (similar to German Shepherds trained for combat) for each of the girls and security personnel. He provided international powers of attorney to be signed and notarized by the parents to give Royce authority to act in their stead in the event of an emergency.

The day arrived. They flew out of Burbank in Royce's 737 for the trip across the Atlantic. Teddy and Tru showed off the plane's features to their friends, who were duly impressed, as was Nichol, who had only been in his G4. The nannies, including Carmen, retained for the trip hung back from their young charges until the girls included them in their general squealing and yelping. Nichol would not be the nanny on the trip. She didn't know who she was on that plane. She wasn't Royce's wife. She wasn't a family friend.

Royce and Nichol faced each other in recliners. Teddy and Tru were too busy being flight attendants to notice them. They sipped wine and noshed on sashimi and California rolls.

Without preamble Royce began his lament. "I feel like such a failure. My father has a solid marriage. I am stuck in limbo because my father is against divorce. Even at my age I cannot defy my father because it is not just his edict, it is generations of Kallases. No divorces. With Tamra what did I do wrong? Did Tamra go wild as a result of feeling abandoned herself as a child? Is she still blaming me for moving out here?"

Nichol responded with a small voice. Royce had to move his head closer to hear above the cabin noise. "I think the move scared her. She had grown into a self-perceived notion of privilege, and you upset the status cart." Nichol continued to take risks. Would there come a time when she went too far, said too much?

"Why should she still be mad six years later?" he said.

———

An un-Nichol façade dropped into place like a faceplate on medieval armor. "I don't think she is still mad. I think she uses your moving to Calabasas as an excuse, but she is actually quite happy with the arrangement. She leaves as she pleases for her acting jobs, she has no responsibilities here – she has convinced herself of that – and she has money and a soft landing spot between jobs."

"You left off her other hobby—men. Six years of waiting, waiting for her to come back to me, waiting for her to divorce me, waiting for I do not know what."

"Maybe you're not waiting for anything else. Maybe you already have it, but you don't realize it." Nichol's voice faded, and she looked out the window. "Do you mind if we choose another topic?"

Royce looked at her, puzzled. Nichol's straightforward look-you-in-the-eye-with-strong-voice did not correspond with the reticent person sitting before him.

"Did you go on vacations as a child?" he asked.

She looked back from the window. Distracted, but not by what was outside at 35,000 feet.

"Hmm?" Vacations?" She blew out dread and jealousy through her mouth. "My parents worked all the time, so the only vacations we had were to Miami. My tio and tia took my cousins and me to Disney World. Afterward, all I wanted to do was to go back there again and again."

Royce, no longer sure why he had asked the question, thought Disney World was a fine vacation spot, but to become fixated on it?

The group flew into Nice Cote d'Azur Airport and took a limousine to the harbor of Port Vauban, Antibes. Royce introduced Nichol to his yacht. He told Nichol to pick out the yacht she thought belonged to him. The girls followed along behind, giggling and strutting like their versions of super models. Nichol stopped in front of a white yacht with cobalt blue trim. Ten crewmembers in blue golf shirts and white Bermuda shorts stood ready to receive their guests.

"It's this one. *Greek Seas*," she said and pointed. "This is outstanding." She had to lean her head back to take in the height of the yacht's decks.

He led the group down the gangway.

They boarded, and a crewmember showed the girls and nannies to their cabins. Each girl shared her cabin with a nanny to ensure no one dove off the bow in the middle of the night. Nichol stared at every bit of the forward and main salons. She tried out the tan couches and ran her hand over the teak walls and mother-of-pearl dining room table. She peeked into the main galley.

"There are three chefs in there," she said to Royce.

"Yes, there are. I have chosen a suite for you." He gave her the owner's cabin. "This is your head and private shower." That was the long and short of it for that trip, they were not going to share a cabin.

"I feel like I did on our first trip to Disney World. I want to look at everything and don't want to miss anything."

"You will have three weeks to explore my little tug."

They settled in the forward salon. The girls could be heard laughing while they rode the elevator from deck to deck.

"What prompted you to get a yacht?"

"I had worked hard in college, law school, graduate school, and wanted to reward myself."

"Yes, but the difference between you and most of the rest of the world is when we want to reward ourselves, we buy a watch or a pair of shoes." She looked out at the other boats.

Royce decided to ignore what could be a contentious issue. He showed her the rest of the yacht.

For three blissful weeks they cruised from port to port. They stopped at Monte Carlo to say they had been there. Genoa, Elba, Naples, Civitavecchia for three days in Rome, Athens, Rhodes, Mykonos, Samos.

The trip, at first exciting, settled into peaceful surrender for all of them. The ship's polished teak and metals mirrored shinier versions of themselves. Royce and Nichol played Trivial Pursuit and Clue with the girls and nannies. They had kayak races, snorkeled, slept, and ate their way from one end of the ship to the other. Royce and Nichol raced each other around the ship on jet skis, the circle tighter and tighter with each revolution. While he worked in his office, the girls, their nannies and Nichol dove again and again off a ramp lowered off the bow and jumped on the inflatable trampoline. Royce joined them for sightseeing in each port where they also ate. They bought gifts for Lindy, Noel, Angel, Francisco, and the other staff. Only Tru suggested they buy a gift for Tamra. She had a generous heart and her dad's wallet. For three weeks they were a family with a patina of saltiness and sunshine.

Nichol wore clothes she had purchased on instruction from Royce: cotton and linen for day, silk for evenings. The bathing suits she wore were her own, not bikinis, not even two-piece. She was a respectable member of the Kallas family, if even for only three weeks.

The cruise ended back in Antibes, where they took the train to Paris. They stayed at the George V, and Nichol was charmed by the opulence, the plush, and the rarified air of the wealthy. She was both appalled by her weakness to be seduced and challenged to retain her beliefs about the duty of the haves to provide for the have nots. That said, Royce indulged her desire to have afternoon tea at the hotel, where guests spoke using their indoor voices and moved slowly as though they were underwater. Nichol's stomach churned with conflict. After they were seated, Tru expressed suspicion about a cucumber sandwich. Nichol thought about Haiti, how it was not even in the same solar system as the parts of Paris she was seeing.

"Where were you just now?" Royce asked, as he nursed a glass of pinot noir.

"Haiti. The Bel Air slum in Port-au-Prince. Such a strange name for a slum."

"Why that particular place?"

Tru and her friend Kaia smelled their sandwiches.

"It is one of the worst slums in Haiti. Oil, excrement, and garbage pollute the ditches that are supposedly providing clean water. Babies walk around wearing only t-shirts. No diapers, no shoes. There are no toys. The only thing in abundance is dirt."

"Nice talk while we're eating," Teddy said. She and Xandy drank their tea with their baby fingers extended as though they were waiting for battery-operated parakeets to alight.

"Do you think all this," he looked around the room, "is decadent, immoral?"

"I'm not judging the value of the chandelier above our heads versus the value of a child if that's what you mean."

"Do you think that I, and people like me, should sell our possessions, the planes, yachts, cars, houses, stocks, businesses, and donate the proceeds to Haiti? Here is nine hundred million dollars. Spend it any way you want to, but, please, at least buy diapers for the babies." His tone was sharper than she had experienced the previous few weeks.

"Dad," Teddy interrupted, "you said we should never talk about money."

"You are absolutely correct, but this conversation is—is about poverty. Nichol, go ahead."

"No, you shouldn't give away all your money, *and* I think we have a moral responsibility to care for those people who cannot care for themselves. However, that said, if you sold everything you own today and gave it to Haiti, that gesture probably would not raise the country's standard of living. People have thrown money at Haiti for years, and there is no appreciable difference."

"So what should rich bastards like me do with ourselves?"

"Daddy, bad word," Tru said.

Nichol heard familiar tension in his voice. She wondered if he was mad at her. It was clear his mood had changed.

"Educate yourself and your friends about life-threatening situations in the world. Involve yourself in politics to affect change in U.S. policies," she said.

"Are you not aware of my philanthropy... and...never mind, never mind." He seemed to catch himself. He looked upset.

She knew she had said too much. She sensed he resented her bringing up such a hot topic while they were supposed to be enjoying themselves.

They retreated into their teacups.

They walked through Paris with the four girls, their nannies and security staff and practiced their French on shop owners. At Hermes in Paris' 8th Arrondissment, Nichol, Teddy, and Xandy looked at $10,000 handbags that were kept behind glass. Royce told Nichol he would buy her one. She didn't know if he was teasing her, but she was glad he was happier. She didn't buy a handbag. She just wanted to pretend she was a lady who bought $10,000 handbags and belonged in Royce's class. The sensation was familiar to her, one she had not been able to shake, like a cold that lingers: she was black and was from a poverty-stricken country no one wanted to know about. Other people would think she wasn't entitled to possess such excess, but why did she want it?

That evening the entire menagerie were the guests of President Chirac at the Élysée Palace. The girls were delighted to speak French with the president and a group of French school children Chirac had brought in just to meet the American girls. Royce did not appear to be delighted. His French was barely understandable and, besides, his mood was gloomy.

The plane waited for them on the tarmac at Orly for the flight home. Nichol thought Royce's demeanor could only be categorized as stiff. He told her to pick a movie, and he took some papers out of his briefcase to review.

When they got home, the staff greeted them, and the four girls talked at once while they presented the gifts. Nichol's eyes were on Royce. He smiled briefly at the girls and then his mask fell back in place.

The next morning, while their out-of-shape bodies were on Paris time, Nichol and Royce met to run.

"I have a gift for you." She handed him a small box wrapped in cobalt and maroon shiny paper and a lavender envelope.

"Read the note later, but I want you to open the gift."

He handed the envelope back to her while he unwrapped the package. It was a snow globe of the Parthenon. He gave it the obligatory shake. "Thank you." He kissed her on the cheek. "I am curious about the contents of the note," he said.

She smiled and they slogged through a run, not talking.

He put the note in his jacket pocket to read at the office. As he stopped at lights, he argued with himself about when he should look at the damn thing that was bugging the hell out of him. He exercised self-control and drove down Wilshire with the note still in his pocket.

Everyone at the office welcomed him back, some of whom had worked with Royce on matters during the three weeks he was out of the office. He closed his office door and hung up his jacket. He looked at his desk top, swollen with paperwork. Royce flipped absentmindedly through the top layer of files on his desk and then remembered the note. From the envelope he took a sheet of lavender paper with NL imprinted on the top of the page.

"Dear Royce:

My thank you will be inadequate, but I do sincerely thank you for including me on your family's vacation. You are very generous to give me three weeks with your beautiful daughters and magnificent floating home. I fear that my superlatives are not enough to express my gratitude for the once-in-a-lifetime gift."

Royce stopped reading. Why did Nichol say "once"? Why did she not know he would always include her? He continued.

He was stunned. Stunned as if struck with a Taser. Stunned, both by the content and the implication. He had two women in his life, and he was not going to have peace with either of them. Nichol apparently thought she was an indentured servant to whom he randomly threw crumbs, while she also felt she had a higher sensibility and purer moral code than he. Tamra thought he owed her the moon and transportation to get there. He was not a stupid man, and he realized that when he exposed Nichol to the yacht and his version of vacationing, it could either give her a sense of entitlement or a blunt reminder she was not one of them.

He quarreled with himself about what end result Nichol expected, for it was his experience that women desired a specific resolution to a request or demand. She might just be suggesting—if the last sentence of the note was a suggestion—that he stop talking about divorcing Tamra and take action. He wanted Nichol in his life—the trip cemented his feelings about her—but he had to work through how a different relationship with her played out.

Then he chastised himself for letting personal (and personnel) matters distract him from work. He put the note in his pants pocket and opened a file. He looked for problems

———

291

he could solve.

Chapter Thirty-Four

Nichol was not a teenager in the throes of unrequited love, yet she was not too old or jaundiced to believe in happy endings. Exactly how delusional was she? And why was she thinking of Royce in romantic terms?

Royce read the note several times, trying to figure out what Nichol wanted him to do. But he did not want to think more or overanalyze. He wanted to fix something, wanted to act. He would take Nichol on a date. That, he reasoned, was what she was after. And so, on a Thursday evening when he returned home from work two weeks after his receipt of the note, he went to her suite and knocked on her door. She invited him into her living room. She had framed photos on a credenza of her parents, her at graduation, her aunt and uncle with her cousins, and her with what looked like a group of friends skiing.

"Are you a good skier?" he said.

"I can usually get from the top to the bottom of a run without falling down or plowing into other skiers. Before I took this position, I had three weeks' vacation a year, so I spent two weeks with my family and then in the winter I went skiing with friends. From college."

"We will have to look into the possibility of your taking an extra week," Royce said. "And staying at our house in Telluride."

The built-in bookcase housed not only her books, but also hand carved wooden figures: a woman with a basket on her head, a man walking a donkey. An oil painting of a man in a white robe with angel wings. She said the painting was Jean-Bertrand Aristide, a former controversial president of Haiti.

"But I guess they all are," she said.

They made small talk, a curiosity of western culture they both despised, but on that occasion it gave them a buffer. His nerves betrayed him, and he hid his shaking hands in his pants pockets, a posture he employed frequently when Nichol was near.

"I would like to invite you to dinner on Saturday evening," he said.

She faced him, almost as tall as he, dark brown skin to his golden brown. "That will be nice for us. Dinner twice in one week."

He wondered if she thought he was throwing her another crumb. "I mean just for the two of us. I thought we might try Chez Jay. Are you familiar with it?"

"No, I—"

"It is in Santa Monica. It is a cool place. Tourists, locals, celebrities all like it." He wondered if he had just said "cool"? "You can drive the Maserati."

Nichol nodded as though her tongue were heavy with anesthesia.

A wagon wheel rested against Chez Jay's exterior wall, and ivy climbed the wall. Another wagon wheel sat near the bar that was covered in a red and white striped awning and Christmas lights. The restaurant was crowded, the bar full of laughing patrons.

During their runs and on their drives to and from basketball, Nichol and Royce had become comfortable with each other. However, that night they acted like a typical couple on a typical first date, and they used the menu for conversation. They ordered filet mignon béarnaise for Nichol and swordfish for Royce.

They stayed on their own sides of the table, acting

the role of mature adults. They shared chocolate cheesecake as they talked about this and that, mainly anecdotes from the cruise: Tru wondering why the pizza in Florence only had cheese and no pepperoni, Teddy and Xandy discovering that a pair of sunglasses at Dior in Paris cost 34,500 euros or $25,000 US. Nichol kept the conversation poverty free, and Royce silently breathed in.

At the end of the evening, with the Maserati safely tucked away from the vicinity of Nichol's lead foot, they walked into the house through the kitchen, walked up the stairs and parted company at the landing. Royce walked in one direction to his suite and Nichol walked in another direction to her suite.

They felt their way through the alien relationship they had invented, a hybrid neither could define. They were deluded into thinking that if their burgeoning relationship did not work out—whatever that meant—they still had the running trails and basketball court. Their runs and basketball games did not become more intimate, but, rather, continued as before the vacation, as though those activities were in a different universe from their dates. But would they stay casual if it all went south?

On occasional weekends that his daughters went to his parents' home, Royce took Nichol to the beach, hiking, even bowling. He cleared his calendar on those days and worked longer hours during the week. They did not hold hands, whisper sweet nothings, or giggle together at home or, for that matter, when they were alone together.

Nichol gave Royce an opportunity to be happy, to be calm, to love his daughters without feeling he had to continually apologize to them for being an inadequate father. Royce's feelings for Nichol developed from curiosity to admiration to love for her maternal instincts. He remembered the sensations of adult love with Tamra. If he had mined his feelings and had been honest, he would have said he had been infatuated with Tamra because she was a free spirit, even though that was a cliché. Then Tamra eviscerated his ego and left thick scars that influenced his reaction and response to Nichol.

On a Thursday before a grandparents' weekend, Royce approached Nichol with caution. He put his hands in his pockets, a clear sign that he was not in his element.

"I would like to ask you if you will join me for a weekend in Santa Barbara. Steven has a house in Montecito. He and his wife Lysie invited us." He stopped and then looked at her as she checked Teddy's uniform skirts to make sure Teddy hadn't shortened the hems. "He surprised all his friends by getting married last year. I did not think the guy would ever settle down."

"Us? There's an 'us?' Steven knows about us? Did you remember the girls will be at your parents' house?" Her voice reflected her bewilderment.

"Yes, the two of us." Royce's scalp burned. "That is why I am asking you." She hung up the skirts and closed Teddy's closet door.

She nodded her head, unable to speak.

Steven greeted them both with hugs, which pinched Royce's heart with happiness. It appeared Steven approved of Nichol as a friend of Royce's, not as the nanny. Lysie, too, had big smiles for them. The house was Spanish, like Royce's, but on a much smaller scale. Dark oak beams cut across the white ceiling. Curved French doors led to a pool and patio. The furniture was dark, heavy and ornate, with scrollwork on the dining chairs and sideboards. White couches lightened the rooms. Overall the look was masculine, except for arrangements of flowers and accent pillows. Lysie had not made her mark yet.

When Nichol and Royce arrived in Montecito, the sleeping arrangements became an issue in everyone's mind except Nichol's. Royce had bedded his share of women, but didn't want to broach the subject with Nichol. He didn't want to presume and didn't want to insult her. He believed he must handle her differently from other women. The reality was—no matter how many dinners they shared—she was his children's nanny. There were legal issues to this assignation. But he forged ahead.

After the tour of the house, Lysie walked with Nichol and Royce down a hallway toward the bedrooms.

"This is your room, Royce," Lysie said.

Nichol continued to surprise him, shock him. She followed him into the room, dropped her overnight bag on a chair and left with an enigmatic smile. A mute Royce followed her back to the living room. He decided he would not say anything to Nichol about her unilateral arrangement. He continued to believe that on some occasions he was in better shape if he said nothing. How curious that his confrontational skills abandoned him in Tamra and Nichol environments.

After a dinner on the patio of grilled shrimp, steak kebabs and wine, the foursome sat in tan and red lounge chairs near a fountain that had a sound of dwarfed waves. They ate chocolate mousse out of cups. Their spoons clinked as though they had been tuned by a tone-deaf piano tuner. Conversation dwindled out into the air that still smelled of grilled meats.

"What time is it, Lysie?" Steven asked.

———

"Time to go to bed," Lysie said. "We're getting to be old people."

Yes, we are," Steven said, feigning a yawn. He took Lysie's hand and they both stood up.

"I am, too," Nichol said and stood up.

"Nic, could you wait for a moment?" Royce asked and reached for her hand.

"Okay, sure," she said and sat on Royce's chaise.

Steven gave Royce a clownish grimace. He and Lysie left them on the patio. Nichol looked at Royce with one eyebrow raised as in "What's up?"

He held her hand in his. He noted that hers was smooth and dry, while he was sure his hand was sweaty. She was polite enough not to say anything. "I prepared bullet points for this conversation, but I cannot remember any of them," he said and stalled out for a moment. "I love you, Nic."

The only sound came from water slipping over the lip of the shelf in the fountain.

She cleared her throat. "I have not let myself have feelings for you, because you are married to someone else." She had an opportunity to mock him because she had heard for the last five years that he wanted a divorce, yet had done nothing to make it happen. She didn't take it. "I work for you." Nichol cried, quietly at first and then sobbed. Her shoulders shook.

Royce hadn't expected that reaction. He sat by her, waited, watched her, and then it occurred to him he could console her. He put an arm around her shoulders. She wore a red silk blouse, and it slipped on one side, revealing her cocoa-colored shoulder. She leaned into him, and so he put the other arm around her and sucked in a breath as though he had been punched in the gut with a bowling ball. Nichol got his shirt wet with her tears. She talked through her hands. He couldn't understand her, and he took them away from her face.

"I said, yes, I could love you. Royce, I want to jump into your arms."

"That is good. I hoped that is where this conversation would end," he said and surprised himself for saying his thoughts out loud.

"I told myself I would wait until the divorce is final to make love with you. I have very strict parents," Nichol said.

"You are a grown woman." He regretted saying that. His mouth tightened, and he clenched his jaw, which felt as though he had chewed a big juicy wad of bubble gum. He said things he didn't want to say and did not say what he wanted to tell her. Was he going to have to have one of his daughters translate for him? And shouldn't he be applying the same statement to himself? He was a grown man.

"My age doesn't matter. I have never been married. To please both my parents and myself, I thought I would not be your lover," Nichol said. "And Tamra. Until—"

"I know, I know. Until I am divorced."

"Worse. Until we are married."

They looked at each other. They wanted something different from their exchange, but didn't know how to accomplish it. Did they read each other's minds, communicate on some astral plane? They moved apart from each other.

"Why did you put your bag in my room?" A legitimate question.

"Because I want to show my feelings for you without saying them."

"But you just said…about your parents—," he said.

———

She shook her head as though he, a male, would never understand. Royce wanted to change the direction of their deteriorating conversation. Holding hands, they walked into the house and into the bedroom.

"You must think I am easy if I sleep with you," he said, hoping he sounded playful. "You just said you were going to wait, but here you are."

"Yes, here I am."

"What changed?"

"I have to take my own advice," Nichol said and pantomimed reeling in a fish with a fishing pole.

There was no fumbling with clothes, no grasping of body parts, no breathy expressions of love and lust. Nichol simply stood in front of Royce and took her clothes off, not too fast, not too slow. She didn't gyrate, didn't have a diamond in her belly button. She hung up her clothes as though that was just an ordinary day, an ordinary experience.

He did not attempt to touch her. He was respectful of the sleek lambent creature with supple grace that stood before him. Royce watched her and waited for an invitation. He received his enticement when she got into bed. Royce stared at her, laughed, and shook his head.

"You are an original," he said. Who was this woman whom he thought he knew?

"Yes, I am, as you will find out if—"

He cut off her talk with his mouth. And so the night began. The night was an absence of manipulation, lies, rancor, comparisons, neediness, desperation, hearts, flowers, professions of undying love. The night was a presence of acceptance. However that is expressed.

No morning-after regret. No clumsiness. They each felt a rightness about their time together, but neither articulated their feelings because at that point they thought it was too corny. Or too risky, for both had their lives in the game. In the morning—actually about one o'clock in the afternoon—they appeared in Steven and Lysie's living room, where their hosts watched a game between the Angels and Red Sox. Boston led.

"Look, Lys, they have risen from the grave."

Royce blushed, Nichol did not. She looked like it was commonplace for her to sleep with her married employer in another couple's home. She exacted no proprietary holds on him.

"What would you like to do today, kids?" Steven asked. Royce wondered why he had been apprehensive about Steven liking Nichol in her new role.

"I would like to have a short conversation with Royce. And then go to the beach," Nichol said.

Royce snorted into his coffee cup. Another conversation?

"We'll load up the car with beach stuff. Come outside when you're ready," Steven said.

Nichol patted a spot next to her on the couch. Royce abrogated his controlling interest in his wellbeing and handed it to Nichol. He sat on the couch next to her as instructed and attempted to hold her hand, but she demurred.

"I need to have a clear head when I say this," she said, her voice soft yet also commanding.

"You are going to tell me that…what happened last night and today will never happen again."

"Stop talking. You are not in charge of this conversation."

Royce had trouble keeping up with Nichol, like a Chihuahua chasing after a Great Dane.

"I need you to do something so I can tell you I love

you," she said.

"Of course, I want to hear you say you love me." He had not heard those words from an adult female in the twenty-first century—except for his mother. He reached for her hand again, and again she held it in her lap. "What do you want me to do?" he said.

In that instant he knew he had made a mistake. She was on to him: she knew he would *never* be able to get a divorce. With sweetness and finesse she would make her demand. He compared her to Tamra, who used sex and threats to have him fulfill her every desire.

"No surprise. I want you to take action now to terminate your marriage. Whether Tamra files, you file, I leave that to you. But I need it done for me to fully invest myself in you." She had made finances part of the equation in exchange for her love, but she probably did not know that.

He agreed it was no surprise. Royce felt heaviness in his head and a sparking sensation in the region of his heart like a busted carburetor on a 1995 Dodge Neon. "Yes, you are entitled to and deserve that resolution. I think we both are—"

"Good, let's get changed for the beach."

"But, is that it?"

"That's it."

Nichol drove the Maserati on the trip back to Calabasas. Royce kept an eye out for the California Highway Patrol, because Nichol drove eighty-five and could not be persuaded to lighten up on the gas. What was it with females and sports cars?

"Steven and Lysie like you," he said.

"That's nice to hear," she said. "I like them, too."

"He thinks you are good for me. Steven has

encouraged me to file for divorce. I want to ask you. Did you see this weekend as a one-time liaison or us spending more time together?" He thought about how they could rewind the tape if neither wanted to go forward. He waited for Nichol's response before he decided what his would be. Nichol held the power.

Nichol looked surprised. "Of course."

The look on his face was blown by the wind shear on that low-flying missile. "Of course, which one?"

"We won't do this at home."

"I agree," he said and realized he had been concerned she might insist on their taking on the roles of a married couple.

"I won't sleep with you at the house until you are divorced and take the next step," the scope of which she did not share with him.

He pretty much knew what she meant. He looked straight ahead—much like a dog sitting in the front passenger seat—hoping that would dissuade her from taking her eyes off the road to look at him.

"Could you slow it back down?"

She shook her head "no."

"The girls know something is up," he said. "I think we should let our relationship grow organically for them." When did he start using a word like "organically?" He knew they needed to figure out the parameters of the relationship. If there was to be a new status. He needed to think about her status as an employee; she could file a sexual abuse case if things between them did not work out. But Nichol would not do that. Would she?

"Lindy, Noel and rest of the staff," she said, "that's a different story. They will resent me. I've already gotten a few comments since we have dinner and play basketball together."

"What are they saying? Who is speaking inappropriately? Do you see yourself as just a member of the staff?"

"Of course, I do. Because I am. It's fine. I can handle remarks as long as it doesn't affect my caring for the girls. At least I've been able to up to this point. So we will not hold hands and skip down the hallway or take stolen kisses," she said. "And I will not tell you I love you."

Their subterfuge didn't impress one person. Tamra returned to Calabasas after her tour and smelled something different about the house. She honed in on Royce who did not seem angry with her or petulant. He was indifferent. Not a good sign. Better when he begged her. She watched Nichol, who, Tamra was bitter to observe, had become her own designer children's mother.

Tamra followed Nichol into her suite one night.

"You are not welcome in here and do not even think about pulling a stunt like you did before," Nichol said.

Tamra was impressed with the bite in Nichol's voice and body language. She had grown a set of balls. "I just want to ask you a question. Have you become my husband's mistress?"

Nichol put one hand on Tamra's back and walked her to the door, like shooing a dog outside who messed in the living room. She exercised her territorial prerogative and closed the door. Tamra let Nichol kick her out of a room in her own—ostensibly—house. Being escorted out of the room so boldly by the hired help told Tamra what she wanted to know: Royce and Nichol were on. Whether Royce fucked Nichol or didn't, Tamra knew she would get what she wanted. And she knew, if he was fucking Nichol, he would want to marry her, and, therefore, get Tamra out of their lives. She wondered if Nichol knew she was helping her walk away with a multi-million-dollar deal. At that moment Tamra was rooting for Nichol to keep Royce occupied.

Chapter Thirty-Five

In the fall of 2006, Sophie was a college freshman; Teddy entered fifth grade and Tru, kindergarten. Ten-year-old Teddy went through the pre-teen awkward, self-conscious stage, while five-year-old Tru was a confident, charming adolescent, to the extent adolescents are charming. Nichol grew with them, adjusting to each stage. Teddy was accepted into the musical theatre ensemble, which made Royce nervous. Also, Teddy was a pitcher on the school's softball team, which made him excited. Tru played soccer.

Royce took no action to file for divorce himself, but on three occasions during the year told Tamra to file. Demanded. Begged. If Tamra filed, the wrath of his father would be manageable; he could blame her, he thought, probably irrationally. Each time she told him she would only go away when he gave her $50,000,000, plus $9,000,000 for nine more years of marriage, and the house of her choice. He told her to retain an attorney who could advise her. She didn't respond. He carried an almost unbearable heaviness because he did not accomplish the task Nichol had given him.

Neither he nor Nichol addressed the topic, and she didn't tell him she loved him. They continued to go out with Tru and Teddy and continued to go on their dates. They were both disciplined enough not to cross the line between what they deemed to be appropriate and inappropriate behavior in front of the girls and staff. Teddy hoped they had lots of sex together. She had paid attention in health class.

When Teddy and Tru visited their grandparents,

<hr>

Royce and Nichol took off for weekends in La Jolla, San Francisco, and Nichol's favorite, the house in Rancho Mirage. They didn't stop during the weekdays for a quickie because Nichol had two girls to raise and Royce had businesses to run.

One weekend they helicoptered with the girls to San Simeon and had a private tour of Hearst Castle. A gift to the Hearst Foundations was helpful, but not necessary.

One Sunday evening when the girls returned home from visiting Reginald and Evelyn, Reginald found Royce in his study, sitting at his desk.

"Son. We need to have a serious conversation."

"You have my attention," Royce said. He stood and shook his father's hand. Reginald stood on the opposite side of the desk.

"Teddy let it slip that Nichol is now, I cannot believe I am saying these words, your *girlfriend*. She said you are being nice to Nichol and going on dates. Dates, Royce! And Tamra told Evelyn that she thought something unseemly was going on between Nichol and you. Explain yourself." Reginald held his right elbow while he rested his right hand on his cheek. He looked like Jack Benny.

"Nichol and I have gone out to dinner and the movies. Yes. And I will continue to do so as long as she wants to accompany me." Royce fiddled with paperwork on his desk, looking for the right words to say to his father.

"Have you lost your darn mind? What has come over you?" Reginald asked.

"Tamra has come over me. She treats me and this house as though this is a hotel and I am an ATM."

Reginald walked around the desk and stood over Royce. "You are her husband. What possesses you to cheat on your wife? I didn't raise you that way."

Royce looked up to the person of his father who controlled his life in significant ways. "No, Father. You raised me to believe that Kallases do not divorce. What you failed to teach me was what to do when I have an unfaithful, conniving—"

"Do not talk about Tamra that way. She is your wife. Never speak about your wife using such terms. You wanted to marry her over my objection. You wanted not to have a prenup. If Tamra is a…a gold digger, you could have known that before you married her. You have made your bed—"

"Fine. Fine. I will not say anything more about Tamra," Royce said and stood up, going toe to toe with Reginald. "I will, however, conduct my life as I see fit. Nichol is good for the girls. And for me. She has filled the holes left by Tamra. Do you understand that Tru does not consider Tamra as her mother except in name? And Teddy feels betrayed by Tamra."

Reginald turned and left the study.

Royce heard the front door close. He sat down heavily in his custom-made executive chair.

With each hookup between Nichol and Royce, she was no longer in the working class. She shared Royce's wealthy status. She was seduced by the opportunities provided to her. While Royce didn't flaunt his money and didn't lavish her with absurd luxury gifts—because he learned she flat out did not want them, except for a fast car, which she got, a red Maserati GranSport Coupe—his way of looking at the world influenced choices she made. And the reverse was also true. She gave him information about various charities in Haiti to which he could contribute, and he did. He resumed fundraising events at the house—without a hostess—including one for International Child Care, the organization Nichol's parents worked for.

The temptations outweighed her moral code and professionalism. She willingly was a participant in an affair, albeit one in which she had levied the ultimatum. Years before Royce had given her a credit card to use for the children's needs. He now told her to buy clothes for herself for every day, not just cruise clothes. She believed he wanted her to dress to Kallas standards, that is to say, expensive. She stopped wearing tunics with frogs and, instead, wore Michael Kors tops and pants and Missoni dresses where the hangers cost more than the frog tunics.

One day Nichol stopped in the middle of the weight circuit, while Royce changed the weight on the bench press bar. He lay down on his back and raised the bar. He pressed 220 pounds.

"It's been over a year," she said.

He anticipated that moment, practiced for many, many months his contribution to the foreseen conversation. Every day that she did not bring up his divorce was a reprieve. He wanted to be with her, wanted to marry her. He looked at her, with his brain devoid of a snappy comeback.

"Should I assume that your inaction is the answer to the question I haven't asked you?" she asked.

Royce looked at her. She stood tall. She was muscle and tenderness. He loved her body. He sat up on the bench and took a hundred-pound weight off the bar. "I know I have failed you. I should probably be in therapy to figure out why I have such a strong, impossible to get beyond, reverence for my father." He chuckled, the sound grating and false, as though the laugh flew out of his mouth backwards.

"I respect my parents, too. I told you their stand on

pre-marital sex," she said, her voice neither bullying nor apologetic, "and I decided you and the girls are more important to me than my parents' edicts."

"Tell me how I can do this, how I can go against my father's *decree*."

"We make choices. You've made yours."

"No, Nichol, please—"

"Don't do this to yourself. I accept your decision," she said.

"I will—"

"Stop. You're making me a hard woman, and I don't want to feel the way I do." A paroxysm of anger. "I wonder if I am a fool, if I made a fool of myself in Montecito and every day since then. Maybe earlier I shouldn't have accepted your first invitation for a date and shouldn't have given you the note. God, I *am* a fool, an idiot."

She had up a good head of steam. He had come to believe she wanted that family any way she could get it. He believed she would not walk away from the part she played in that family. The two of them, unindicted co-conspirators.

Nichol walked out of the gym, and Royce dropped the hundred-pound weight on the floor where it landed with a heavy thud and clang as it hit the leg of the bench. Her needs collided with his pathological veneration of his father.

Chapter Thirty-Six

By 2007 Royce and Nichol had known each other for seven years. She stayed with the family and continued to fulfill her role with the children, but not the role Royce had apparently carved out for her. The five of them were a fully dysfunctional family, dysfunctional because by that year reality television proved that every family was dysfunctional. Nichol was their glue, their grout, their mortar, and Royce was grateful for her and loved her. She refused to tell him she loved him. He acknowledged to himself that if God, a Christmas elf, or a coal-based energy source asked him what he wanted that he did not have and could not buy, he would have answered "Nichol as my wife." He grumbled and pouted that he had to get Tamra out of his life and was faced with the prospect he would have to spend some serious coin to get Nichol. Fifty million of them. Yes, he said he wanted Nichol as his wife—his father's stand on divorce notwithstanding—yet would not meet Tamra's demand.

Another financial reality impacted Royce. Nichol somewhat understood his business dealings. She knew he was a heavy hitter: he bought businesses, especially technology based, invested in emerging markets. He had investigative teams that traveled the world to find new investments. She didn't know the value of his assets, other than the conversation they had in Paris. She had not asked him if he had given her a hypothetical amount or if he really was worth $900,000,000. Nichol worried about him, how he was handling the serious financial crisis that affected global economies.

While they waited for their starters one evening at Mastro's, she flat out asked him.

"I do not mind your asking me," he said. "First, there are industries that actually thrive during rotten economic times or survive unscathed, most of which are related to catering to the super wealthy, such as art and expensive real estate. I will give you an example: Bottega Veneta is an Italian purveyor of high-end shoes, handbags, and clothing. Right now the company sells a $1,350 wedge heel sandal and $18,400 leather tote bag, and women buy them with no regard for the status of the world's economy. I have investments in the leather manufacturers that supply to Bottega Veneta."

"Okay, I understand what you're saying. But I have another question. Why do you know the prices of shoes and handbags?"

"My policy is to look for long-term growth potential—" Royce missed the humor of her question, and he was off to the races. He talked about his investments for the next hour, through their entrees and into the after-dinner wine.

Nichol accepted his work ethic and commitment to the firm. She just wished he was quicker on the uptake when she thought she was being funny.

In the summer of 2007, the little family that could, along with the usual suspects, including Sophie and her boyfriend Raphael, sailed to the Society Islands of French Polynesia: Papeeta, Tahiti, to Moorea, to Raiatea and Bora Bora, then onto Samoa, Fiji and Tonga. Tru and Teddy brought friends. Royce thought himself a very modern father when he accepted Sophie's announcement that Raphael would be sleeping in her cabin.

Close to midnight near Bora Bora with the engines stopped, Nichol and Royce laid on matching blue chaise lounges outside in the sultry darkness. White wicker tables sat on the sides of the chaises. A sliver of a moon provided enough light to see black silhouettes. Nichol and Royce heard low voices, the crew that spoke to each other just above a whisper.

"I have a gift for you," Royce said. "It is not a big deal. It is an incentive gift." He reached into the pocket of his shorts. "I will be right back." He put his wine glass on a table. He returned with a flashlight.

She gasped when she saw a small blue Tiffany box. "Incentive to do what?" she asked as she stared at the box.

"It is an incentive for you to stay with me."

She responded to his non-proposal. "Have I taught you nothing these past years? Do not buy jewelry retail."

He was encouraged that Nichol was in a playful mood. "But the box is pretty," he said.

"We'll have a conversation after I open this box." She took it out of his hand and shook it lightly.

"Yes, you can open it now."

She undid the white satin ribbon and opened the box. Inside was a ring with a dark stone. He shined the light on it. The ring was a blue diamond solitaire. The color reminded her of the Pacific Ocean that lapped against the hull. "Oh no."

"That comment frightens me." He had planned what to say, but it appeared that plan had gone all to hell, leaving him with shambolic badinage, of which he was not fond.

"It's beautiful. I have never seen a color like this."

"Will you wear it now? Oh, wait. I forgot something. Will you marry me?"

Nichol hesitated long enough to stop Royce's heart.

———

315

"What precipitated this?" she said with enough velocity to crack the diamond. She held the box in front of her. "Why are you asking me now?" Her voice was frosty and sucked up the froth of the tropical air. "How can you ask me now? Ask me when you have a divorce. When you can marry, ask me to marry you. It's been over a year since you professed you loved me and would get a divorce. You have done nothing about the divorce. Am I supposed to be seduced by this expensive ring?"

She would have been seduced by the ring to the point of catatonia if she had known the price: the six-carat natural blue diamond cost $7.8 million. However, the ring did not appear to seduce her out of her anger. Her heart was too big for the yacht, too big for the Pacific Ocean to contain her.

He was so outside his element, he had no rejoinder. A furious father he understood. A furious mean woman he understood, but for a furious justified woman he had no compass. His misplaced munificence led to a five-heart pile-up. Royce and Nichol were yoked together by the love of three girls and separated by the breadth of his fealty for his father and rapaciousness of his wife.

She tossed the box in the air with one hand and caught it with the other. Back and forth the box went. Back and forth. "Do you know what I want to do with this ring? Do you know? I want to throw it into the ocean. In fact, that's what I am going to do."

The advantage and problem for Royce was that because of the dark he could not see her tears, did not see her face, but he felt the heat. He watched as Nichol's shadow walked to the rope at the bow. He saw her extend an arm over the hull. Slowly, as though trying to stop someone suicidal from jumping off a four-story building, he walked toward her.

He hoped his voice was calm. "Do not throw that ring overboard. That ring is the most expensive gift I have ever given anyone, and it means a lot to me because I love you. Please." He extended his hand.

"How much? How much did it cost? Over a million, I bet. I am so angry I want to throw it overboard and you right after it." She walked toward him, her body taut.

As she reached him, she hit his chest with the box. Not expecting her to give it to him, he dropped it.

When the vacationers returned home, Nichol stopped running with Royce, was cordial at the Friday night dinners, and cut off the dates. They stayed on the basketball team, ostensibly as support for the team. The drives to and from the games were quiet and fragrant with tension. She continued to focus her attention on the girls.

One evening a week after they came home from the cruise, Teddy confronted Royce in his study. He sat behind his desk looking back and forth at three monitors that sat on the desk extension to his left. He was still wearing his suit from that day at work.

"Daddy, why are you and Nic acting just like you and Tamra? You aren't talking to each other. How come?" She plopped down in a chair in front of his desk.

He did not want to say the answer out loud. "I hurt Nichol's feelings."

"What did you do? Did you tell her you are sorry?"

"I have apologized to her at least a hundred times."

"Then you must have done something awfully bad if she's still mad at you."

"I think you are right. I did not mean to hurt her feelings. I thought I was doing something nice, but I know

now it was not."

"Tell me what you did. Go ahead, you can tell me."

He took in a breath as though instructed to do so by his doctor while having a rectal exam. "I proposed to Nichol. I asked her to marry me."

She laid her hands on his desk and leaned over so her face was level with his. "But you're still married to Tamra. Right? You can't marry Nichol. You can't have two wives, can you?"

"You are one hundred percent correct. I cannot have two wives."

"So, why haven't you divorced Tamra?"

He died a little because he had exposed Teddy to fractured lives for so long.

"I am going to take care of it," he said, with all the conviction of a bank offering a thirty-year mortgage to a man on death row.

He consulted John Phelan in January 2008. He had paid Tamra $12,000,000 for 12 years of marriage and $15,000,000 for the births (and adoption) of their children. Royce decided he would give her an additional $50,000,000, the amount she demanded. As a parting gift. He was finally going to divorce her.

"Considering what she has done to you and the children over the years, I want you to fight based on her abandonment of your marriage and evidence of extra-marital affairs," Phelan said.

"No, I am not going to do that for three reasons: first, she will oppose me and drag this out longer than I can endure. Secondly, I have had an affair, albeit a short one, with Nichol. You know, you've met her, my…the children's nanny. Thirdly, I do not want the children to hear about abandonment from their friends whose parents read gossip magazines."

Royce's admission didn't seem to faze Phelan. "Does Tamra know about the affair?"

Royce was surprised by the question. He had never considered the possibility that Tamra knew. Or cared. "I do not think so."

"Didn't you have a problem already with the bastards that tried to blackmail you? Crap was published then about you."

"Those exposés were a damnation of Tamra, but not of her treatment of her daughters. That is what I want to avoid."

They could not pinpoint the day of separation. While Royce argued that the separation began in 2002 when Tamra went on tour, she could argue she simply had employment contracts that required her to be away from home. The attorney said he would put "To Be Determined" on the Petition for Dissolution. Royce decided he was not going to tell Nichol he was divorcing Tamra until she was served with the dissolution petition. He rationalized he didn't want to be stringing her along worse than he had been to that point.

In March 2008, the family gathered at Go's Mart sushi restaurant—in a crappy strip mall between a dance studio and massage parlor—to celebrate Teddy's twelfth birthday: Royce, Reginald, Evelyn, Laramie, Belle, Sophie, her boyfriend Raphael, Teddy, Xandy, and Tru. Nichol didn't participate. She said she wasn't feeling well, and she told the truth. She was broken inside, confused and pitiful, feelings she had avoided through her life while she concentrated on her education, her profession. She missed the intimacy with Royce.

The family returned home to eat cake and open presents. The song "Footloose" was playing. Royce did not remember leaving music playing when they left for the restaurant. He and Reginald found Tamra in the theatre with the sound turned up to atmospheric and selected to play in surround sound throughout the entire mansion. The final scene of the movie by the same name played.

Tamra did not look surprised to see the men. She had been crying. Her face was wet and her eyes were red. She held a bag of popcorn in one hand and had a box of tissues in her lap.

"Hello, gentlemen. I guess I missed dinner. Was it nice?"

"Are you upset about something, dear? Why didn't you come to dinner with us?" Reginald asked as he patted her on the shoulder. The bag of popcorn shook.

"I'm not upset. It's the movie. Sweet," she said, her voice low and modest.

"Why are you here?" Royce asked, standing in front of her.

"Son, be kind to your wife."

For her part, Tamra dabbed at her eyes and blew her nose. She looked up at Royce and Reginald like a little girl asking for a puppy at a designer doggie store.

As they left the theatre, Royce put a hand on his father's arm. "Please do not treat her as though she functions in this family."

"Of course, she does," Reginald said. "The girl's got spirit. She likes boysenberry pie." He paused in his assessment of her. "She looks like your mother. And look at the beautiful granddaughters she made."

Even though he had taken the enormous step of telling Phelan to file for dissolution, Royce continued to drag his feet. While Royce was committed to getting the divorce and spending time with his children, a day distracted him and a good portion of the rest of the United States. On September 29, 2008 the stock market lost $1.2 trillion. Royce's investments in transportation stocks fell 12.8 percent in one day. Even though he was saved by his investments in China, India, and Latin America, he told Phelan he was changing his mind about the amount he would pay Tamra. He reduced it from $50,000,000 to $25,000,000.

That November Royce did not let the economic downturn distract him from his daughters. He took Teddy and Tru to the father-daughter dance that was held at the Sherwood Country Club. They made a production of the girls walking down the staircases, Teddy on one side, Tru on the other. Nichol, Lindy, Noel, two housekeepers and Royce watched them descend. They clapped and Lindy hooted. Royce had hired a photographer and videographer. Light from the chandeliers was reflected in Teddy's short black sequined dress. She was allowed to wear short heels. Teddy's enigmatic smile signaled her growing confidence and poise. Tru had a big Tru smile and a knee-length pink—it had to be pink—satin dress. She had begged to wear heels because Teddy got to, but Royce—who consulted with Nichol—didn't give in to her. Royce wore a Hugo Boss suit. He hoped the girls were proud to be his daughters.

The Sherwood clubhouse was ringed with covered porches accented with white columns, beyond which were ancient oaks on green rolling hills. The clubhouse had been transformed into a nightclub—rated PG nightclub. White translucent drapes covered the walls. White tufted velvet settees sat at one end of the room with a piano, and white lacquered chairs encircled tables for eight. Recessed lighting changed the colors of the room from pale pink to yellow, then blue.

Tru bounced on her feet when she saw the room. "Wow! Daddy, look."

"Don't talk so loud," Teddy said. "Be cool." She wanted people to look at her, but not because her dopey sister was being a child.

Chapter Thirty-Seven

Reginald and Evelyn stayed for a few nights to be together for Thanksgiving 2008, along with Steven and Lysie. Even when his boysenberry loving partner in crime was not at home, Reginald enjoyed visiting his granddaughters and playing pool with Royce and Steven. While Evelyn and Lysie made blondies with the girls, the men played a drama-free game of Go Shit, Royce's game from college modified to Go Shoot in the presence of Reginald. Always to ensure that Royce was embarrassed, Reginald asked what Royce was doing to convince Tamra to come home.

"Why aren't you able to manage her, son?"

Royce stared at his father, his cue stick pushing into the tile, his jaw setting.

"Oh, I'm just joshing you, Royce. Don't mean anything by it."

That was the closest thing Reginald said to Royce that resembled an apology.

"I think she's in New York, Father," he said, when in fact he had no idea where she was.

Nichol had begged off. She told Royce Reginald had never warmed up to her, and she was embarrassed at being Royce's Haitian mistress. He bristled at the description.

On Thanksgiving night, taking a break from the football games, Royce, Reginald, Steven, Raphael, and Laramie, who had come for the day, joined Sophie, Teddy, Tru, Evelyn, Lysie and Belle. Reginald begrudgingly put out his cigar when he placed himself at the head of the table.

Royce was surprised to see Nichol join the group. He looked at her with a question in his eyes. She walked up to him as everyone else was settling into their chairs.

"Your mother came to my room. She brought Sophie as a reinforcement. She invited me, said I belong here. I told her I wasn't feeling well, and she said I could feel unwell after dinner. How was I going to turn down your mother?"

Royce pulled a chair out for Nichol and then walked up to his mother and bent down to hug her as she sat at the foot of the table. "Thank you, Mother," he said.

That night Royce dreamed he was making love to Nichol. No, it was Tamra. In a hypnopompic state, he felt her body on his. But whose was it? He awoke with Tamra, naked, stretched out on top of him. She rubbed her breasts against his chest while she fondled him.

"What the hell are you doing here? Are you mad?" He pushed her away, covered his erection and exposed his mortification. He vacillated between screaming as loud as he was able to and whispering so he did not wake anyone and become an unwilling participant in a farce.

Tamra lay on her side. She reached her arm across the divide and headed toward his penis, but Royce grabbed her arm none too politely.

"Get out of here now, or I will have you removed from the house in perpetuity," he said sibilantly.

The woman with all the tricks stood up in the bed straddling Royce. She gyrated her hips and fondled her breasts. "Come on, sweetie. I know you want me."

Royce fought between bliss and loathing. One of them won.

After that night, Royce could wait no longer. Every day of inaction was disrespectful to Nichol—and himself. He dreaded the thought of giving Tamra what he considered to be an obscene amount of money. Royce knew he would have to speak to his father. He waited a month. Phelan called him twice to find out if he was ready to proceed.

He went into his father's office—without an appointment. The office had the best views of Wilshire, and Los Angeles spread out to the horizon. His father was on the phone shooting the shit with a client.

Royce walked about the office with his arms crossed. On the walls hung awards from the Red Cross and American Business Men's Association, city council proclamations from Pasadena and La Canada-Flintridge, photographs of Reginald and men wearing hard hats standing at construction sites with one foot on shovels; another photo of a group of men wearing golf shirts and holding drivers in front of a lake on a golf course; a third, the girls at his parents' house at Christmas the year before; and then one of Royce and Tamra at their wedding. Royce took that one off the wall. His father scowled at him while he listened to his caller.

Royce sat down in one of the chairs in front of Reginald's desk. His father had two photographs on his desk: one of his and Evelyn's wedding day and a second of Evelyn taken the previous year.

Reginald ended his call. "Well, son?" He thumped his hands on his desk. "You called this goat roping."

Royce had been staring at his parents' wedding picture and was startled when his father addressed him. "I need to speak to you about something important."

"Oh, son, what now?" He wiggled the fingers of one hand, indicating he wanted Royce to give him the photograph Royce had taken off the wall.

"No, this photograph is not going back up on the wall. I have contacted John Phelan to divorce Tamra."

"Royce, that is impossible."

"Why should I stay in a marriage when Tamra is gone more than she is home? I have not told you this, but…" He put his hands on his father's desk.

Reginald put his hands on the arms of his custom-made chair—to accommodate his girth—and leaned back as though he was repelled by Royce being close to him. "Maybe you should not tell me. Maybe it is between you and Tamra. In fact, I am sure it is. But having said that, I have something to tell you about Tamra. She came to see me two weeks ago."

"She what? When? You did not tell me." Royce stood up and splayed his fingers out on his father's desk.

Reginald leaned back further. "The girl needs security. She does not feel secure with you. She said you do not want to have another child."

"You are talking to my wife about personal matters, but you will not let me tell you something about her that you need to know."

"What is the matter with you?"

"With me? Why do you think something is wrong with me?" He walked back to the far wall, turned around, and crossed his arms.

"Why don't you want the baby?" Reginald's voice boomed through the room.

"Who? What baby? Wait, what are you saying?"

"Your baby."

Royce shook his head and walked toward the wall of windows. He put his hands high on the glass as though he was obeying an order from the police. He stared out the window. "Does Tamra say she is pregnant?"

"She showed me the x-ray or whatever it is called. It was the size of a raisin."

"It probably was a raisin."

"Do not be insolent. You wanted to talk about something important, and here it is."

"Were you planning to tell me this?" Royce continued to talk to the window.

Reginald stood up, but stayed behind his desk, holding onto the back of his chair. "Tamra knew you were up to something. She said you would probably see an attorney when she told you about the baby." He talked louder, as though he could command Royce to turn toward him merely by raising the volume.

"There is no baby," Royce said.

"Why would a woman lie about having a baby? She is already married, so she cannot hang that over your head."

"No, she has got something better."

"Would you move away from that window? It looks—inappropriate."

He walked back to Reginald's desk. "Tell me, *Father*. How shall I stand or sit *appropriately* while I listen to this shit?" He stood by the front of the desk with his arms spread out like Christ, ignominy overriding servility.

"I will not tolerate this." Reginald walked in front of his chair and hit one of his knuckles hard on the desk. "I do not care how old you are. You will not speak to me disrespectfully."

"Respectfully, sir, do you have *any* idea the degree of Tamra's perfidiousness?"

"And I ask you, what is her motivation? She knows my stand on divorce. She does not need to make up a baby."

"Let us *pretend* for a moment she is not pregnant."

Reginald shook his head "no."

"Now hear me out, Father. No baby. No conversation with Tamra. I come to you and tell you I am filing for divorce because I have valid reasons to file, reasons addressed in the prenup. *Valid reasons*. The prenup that you forced me to have Tamra sign," Royce said enunciating each syllable. He raised one finger by his face and shook it in tempo with his speech. Yes, the prenup protected most of his assets, he thought. Thank God.

"Even assuming no baby and valid reasons, you will not divorce."

Royce wondered if his father filtered out some of Tamra's behavior because he did not want to appear wrong about having championed her after Teddy was born. His father was intractable. Royce walked out of the office. He carried the photograph he had taken off the wall.

He thought Tamra was in rehearsals for a play. She did not return his phone calls. He had to think, he wanted to speak to Nichol, and he needed to talk to Tamra. He would have his office find out where Tamra was.

Then a thought hit him like a nine iron to the head: *Thanksgiving.*

He walked down the hall to his office. He passed Tiffany's desk. "Call Nichol. Please."

A moment passed. A moment of staring out the window.

"Hello, Royce."

"I talked to my father today. Tamra went to see him. He is sympathetic to her."

Nichol sighed. "He believes his Greek dynasty will be sullied. You will not convince him to change his mind."

"Wait, I have more. Tamra told him she is pregnant…"

"Oh, Royce."

"…and that it is my baby. Which, of course, is impossible," he added quickly.

"Is it?" She immediately hated that she said that even

though she thought it was a valid question. Nichol understood that Royce had a gravitational pull toward Tamra. Even now. "What does she want?"

Royce did not answer the first question. "What she has been after for years. A lot of my money."

"What are you going to do?"

"Help me here," he said.

"What can I do for you?"

"If I divorce her, I will incur my father's wrath for the rest of my unnatural life. If I stay married to her, I will go crazy or kill her."

"I will stay as long as you need me for the girls. And I can care for another baby, too."

"Why are you talking to me as though you are only my nanny? And why do you think we would be taking care of someone else's baby?"

"Because that is what I do. I take care of someone else's babies now." Nichol knew when Tamra had been at home. Thanksgiving. She could do the math.

Royce stayed up that night to catch Tamra. She came home at 2:30 in the morning. Royce stood in the kitchen with his hands in the pockets of his gray bathrobe. Tamra walked into the house and jumped when she saw him walk out of the darkness.

"Checking up on me, Royce? That isn't your style." Her hair looked as though it had not been brushed in days. She wore no makeup. She was wearing a pale green long-sleeved shirt and jeans and brought the smell of coffee and beer into the kitchen.

"No, I am not checking up on you. I am filing for dissolution of marriage. My accountant and attorneys will work with your attorney on dividing assets. Do not forget the prenup. Do you have any questions?"

"Why the fuck now?"

"I should have filed years ago, but I kept waiting, waiting and waiting for you to acknowledge your life here with the girls and me. But you never have. It is past time. You are gone with great regularity so I am assuming there is a place for you to stay temporarily."

"What's the hurry? Oh, oh, I get it. You are expecting Mrs. Kallas wannabe to take my role. She's waiting in the wings. You want me out of here so you can marry her and make an honest woman of her. Well, I will not be rushed. I'll move out when I'm ready to," Tamra said.

"I anticipated that attitude," Royce said. "I will be filing an *ex parte* petition to remove you from the residence because your strange comings and goings are stressful for the girls. They do not know if you will be home by midnight or in three months. That conduct creates great confusion for them."

"Bullshit. Absolute bullshit. The girls aren't close with me because you and your new missus turned them against me."

"I am not going to engage you in a conversation that is based on falsehoods. Tell me if your attorney can accept the dissolution petition. Then, rather than having a process server sit out at our curb until three in the morning, the papers can go directly to him or her."

"Fine. I'll get you the information." She did not tell Royce she already had retained an attorney, Laura Wasser, divorce lawyer to the stars, with whom she was going to attempt to void the prenup and walk away with half his assets not in the trust. Without breaking a sweat.

Tamra had already invested the annual and baby monies she received from Royce with his guidance, although he didn't know it. She had paid attention when he talked—back in the day—and he mentioned particular stocks. She believed that because he was wealthy, then he could make her wealthy, too. She used another investment firm, probably one of Royce's competitors, but she didn't know—or care. Royce had never asked her what she did with her money, which she found peculiar.

With the under-counter lights creating pockets of light in the kitchen, she walked up to Royce, and he, surprised by her sudden movements, did not step back. She reached her hand inside his robe. "Waiting for me, I see. That's my sweetie."

Chapter Thirty-Eight

One morning in February 2009 as he drove to the office, Reginald felt strange sensations in his left arm, heaviness, burning, shooting up into his jaw. He thought he might need the assistance of a doctor. While the sensation spread to his chest, he drove his Jag to Good Samaritan Hospital. Although he passed other hospitals and urgent care facilities, he would only go to Good Samaritan where he was on the board of directors and the hospital specialized in cardiac care. He drove the speed limit.

When he arrived at the hospital, he told the clerk he was having a bit of chest and left arm pain. He demonstrated with his right hand. He was immediately taken into an examining room by wheelchair, where he was outfitted with a blood pressure cuff, EKG leads and pads, oxygen, and an IV that initially dripped saline solution. His initial blood tests and EKG were inconclusive, but the ER doc Samuel Reynolds told Reginald he wanted to order more tests. Dr. Reynolds thought "something is going on." It was interesting to Reginald to have the perspective of a patient.

A nurse asked him if he wanted to call anyone. It had not occurred to him to contact anyone. He asked her to call his son. Even in this situation he wanted someone else to do his bidding.

"Hello, Father."

"I'm having some unpleasant symptoms, so I have come to Good Samaritan."

"Good heavens. What is it? What is the matter?"

"Something with my heart, I gather."

"Father, I am coming to the hospital now. Are you in the emergency room?"

"Yes, I am, although now I am going somewhere else

---

for more testing."

"Testing? I am on my way. Call my cell if you need me."

Reginald underwent a stress test where, with electrodes connected to his chest, he walked on a treadmill at a speed that made him gulp for air. Then he underwent an echocardiogram, where a technician smooshed his chest with an instrument that looked like a stainless steel pear. Orderlies wheeled Reginald back to his examination room, where Royce paced.

"Oh, Father. I do not know how you managed to get here with chest symptoms. Why did you not call an ambulance? Why did you come here instead of a hospital closer to you?"

"I didn't call nine-one-one because it's too much bother. Sirens and all that. I came here because I'm on the board. Not right to give another hospital my business. Royce, it is absolutely fascinating all these tests they run. Fascinating."

Dr. Reynolds introduced Dr. Adam Maltefusco, a cardiologist. The results of the two tests: reversible heart condition.

"I think we need to do an angiogram and angioplasty," Dr. Maltefusco said.

"And what will those tests tell us?" Royce asked.

"The angiogram uses X-ray imaging so I can see your father's heart's blood vessels. We will catheterize your father. A dye is injected into the blood vessels of the heart, and a series of images gives us a detailed look. Then I'll do an angioplasty if appropriate for treatment," said Dr. Maltefusco.

Reginald was wheeled into the Cardiac Catheter Lab. He was positioned on his back on an examining table with monitors placed at eye level where the doctor could see the images. A nurse sat by Reginald's head and talked to him during the procedure. Reginald was given Versed, a medication to relax him and provide pain relief from the catheterization. He remained awake, but, due to the medication, would not have cared if the doctor removed his heart and had a pickup basketball game with it. He felt giddy and flirted outrageously with the nurse. He had not flirted in over fifty years.

The doctor talked to the technicians who assisted him. At one point the three of them reviewed the images with such intensity they could have been judges who determined the winner in a photo finish at Churchill Downs.

Dr. Maltefusco left the lab and found Royce in the Cardiac Care waiting room. He told Royce his findings: "Your father has several arteries that are between eighty to ninety percent blocked. I cannot continue with the angioplasty. It could kill him. We need to operate immediately." Dr. Lue joined the men. Dr. Maltefusco introduced him as the surgeon.

"What will you be doing? Specifically."

"We will graft new arteries in place of the blocked arteries. Your father is not in a condition to make decisions for himself, because he has been given medication. Do you have a power of attorney?"

"Yes, I am his agent under his power of attorney for health care. And you have my permission on his behalf." He asked Dr. Lue for his qualifications. The doctor said he had gone to the David Geffen Medical School at UCLA, Stanford for his residency, and fellowship at Loma Linda University. Royce didn't ask the doctor his kill rate.

The doctor left Royce alone in the waiting room. Royce stood, saw the magazines he had been ignoring for the past hour and a half and a television mounted on a wall. Since no one else was in the room, he changed the channel to CNBC and listened to people discuss trends in the current market downturn.

The doctors, nurses, and techs moved around the operating room in a well-choreographed dance. Reginald was anesthetized, cut open, and a rib spreader gave the doctors access to the heart.

Royce waited until his father went into surgery, and then he walked outside to call his mother. He did not want to minimize his father's physical condition, but also did not want her to be alarmed. That was his job, to take the heavy blows. Royce's voice was calm and well-modulated. His mother was not a hysterical person, but she had seemed to be frequently confused in the past year. As he talked to her, she told Royce several times that his father did not have a board meeting at the hospital that day. Royce made arrangements for a car service to pick her up and bring her to the hospital.

An hour-and-a-half later, Royce was still waiting for his mother. He was watching CNBC when Doctors Maltefusco and Lue came into the waiting room and talked to him. Dr. Lue used the same calm voice Royce had used with his mother over the phone. Dr. Maltefusco put his hand on Royce's shoulder. Royce felt the weight of the hand and wondered if he would float away if the doctor had not kept him anchored in place.

His father was dead. As Royce had listened to a report on CNBC on how global warming affected rice production, his father was dead. Royce later thought that if he hadn't gone outside, his father would still be alive. If he had not let his mind wander and focus on CNBC instead of the surgery, his father would still be alive.

Royce walked outside to wait for his mother's car, although he did not remember walking, did not know how he got from one point to the other. He did not remember what he told his mother or what people said when he told them of his father's death. When he got home, the staff greeted him with expressions of sympathy. Nichol did not let recollections of Reginald's reserved demeanor toward her affect her words to Royce.

"Your father lived for the Kallas family. He left the legacy to you."

Royce would later add guilt to his grief. He thought of the last difficult conversation they had. He wondered if that argument led to his father's death. Doctor Maltefusco, in response to Royce's question, said that the way his father lived caused his death. Royce did not know what the doctor meant, because during his life Royce filtered out anything that could be perceived as negative about his father. Reginald had influenced every day of Royce's life.

Tamra went to the funeral. She walked into St. John on the arm of an usher. She wore a short veil on a black hat and dressed in a loose black calf length dress that was big on her small frame. She leaned over and kissed Evelyn on the cheek and sat on Royce's other side. Sophie, Raphael, Teddy and Tru had to move further down the pew. Tamra turned her head to look at the pews on the left side of the church, interested to see who had seen her walk in. Tamra peered over her shoulder at the mourners on the right side. She looked like Linda Blair moving her head around. She saw that Nichol sat in the second row.

After the funeral, graveside service, reception, and family gathering at Evelyn and Reginald's house, Royce took Teddy, Tru, Sophie, and Nichol home. His mother stayed in Pacific Palisades with two of her sisters. Tamra, who excused herself from the family group due to fatigue, was already in the house. She wore a loose blouse with flared sleeves and pants.

"Royce, you have my condol—"

He grabbed her arm with a noticeable effort to move her in the direction of his study. Everyone else dispersed upstairs.

Royce slammed the door behind her, and she winced.

"What's so important you have to talk to me now? You must be beside yourself," she said, standing in the middle of the room, looking around her as Royce paced. The force of his gait made Tamra shiver, he was happy to observe.

He walked over to her and yanked up her blouse to reveal well-defined abs, a flat belly with a diamond in her belly button, and sensuality to burn.

"I won't be showing for a while. It's early," she said, pulling her blouse back in order.

"No, much too late."

"I want this baby. I want to show you I can be a good mother."

"I want a DNA test, because the baby is not mine."

"You'll have to wait until the baby's born."

"I will write you a check tonight. Pack your bags and leave."

"Things have changed."

"Nothing has changed. You are still lying. Either you are not pregnant or, if you are, it is not mine. Not considering your extra-curricular activities."

"The law in California says that a child born during a marriage is presumed to be the child of the marriage."

"Fuck the law and fuck you."

"Well, sweetie, you've added some new words to your pompous speeches."

"Do you remember your acting coach? Do you remember a director in one of your plays? They thought they were real shakedown artists. Except I will not be blackmailed. I will, however, present their letters to a judge."

"I think you should let this go for a few days and concentrate on your father. You've experienced a big loss."

"Would you please stop talking?" He opened the door. "Out," he pointed to the hall.

"As usual, you're bluffing," she said. "You haven't had me kicked out of the house yet. And you have threatened like forever." She giggled a self-satisfied giggle, shrugged her shoulders and walked toward the kitchen.

Royce sprinted up the stairs, looking for his children and Nichol. They sat on the floor in Teddy's room looking at photos of Papa.

Tamra was correct. Although he had filed the petition for dissolution, he told John Phelan to hold off on the exclusion order. He rationalized twenty different ways, all of them creating paroxysms of anguish. He did not think he could toss her from the house on her pregnant ass. However, he called Phelan and asked him when a paternity test could be done, because certainly he did not believe Tamra.

"As early as the tenth week. Do you want me to petition for one or will Tamra willingly have the test?"

"She is not going to agree, so do what you have to do to get it accomplished."

"I want you to anticipate Tamra's response. She will say that the testing is not safe for her or the baby."

"Is that true? Is the testing dangerous?"

———

339

"It has been established that there is only a small risk of miscarriage."

Royce hated himself for thinking that a miscarriage would be a solution.

A month after the funeral, Royce, as beneficiary of the Kallas Family Trust, met with the two institutional trustees—presidents of banks—and his mother, who was primary beneficiary of his father's portion of the trust. As he anticipated, one half of his father's assets rolled into Evelyn's portion of the trust. The second half was left to Royce and Tamra's children held in trust until a child reached the age of thirty, at which time he or she would receive ten percent; at the age of forty, thirty percent; at the age of fifty, sixty percent. All children born of the marriage and adopted would share equally.

A provision was retained for Royce's benefit. Except that it was not. For his benefit. The trust stated Royce was to receive $500,000,000 and interest accrued when he reached the age of sixty unless he divorced his lawful wife Tamra Belle Kallas before his sixtieth birthday. In that instance the money bypassed Royce and inured to the benefit of the children.

Royce closed his eyes for a moment. He felt light-headed. His father took his disapprobation to the grave. If Royce divorced Tamra sometime in the next four years, he would not receive any money. And he wondered what he would do about Nichol. He did not want to lose her. He was determined not to let his father have the last word, the word that ensured Reginald's ability to dictate the rest of Royce's life.

Royce noted that the Kallas Family Trust had been amended one week after Tamra told Reginald she was pregnant.

Royce walked into the foyer late one night. Teddy ran up to him. "You have to come with me," she whispered.

"You scared me. Why are you whispering and skulking around?"

"Please, shush! Come into your study." She grabbed his arm and pulled him down the hall. She closed the door as if a thief. "Talk softly, Dad. Okay?"

"What is it, sweetheart?"

"Do you want to know what Tamra's been doing?"

"Do I want to know?" He groaned and started to pace, but Teddy grabbed onto his arm again.

"Stand here and listen to me. Please."

He crossed his arms and nodded.

"Tamra is snooping around, trying to find out something about Papa's will."

"His trust. All right, you have my attention." He rubbed his hands up and down his arms, a coldness penetrating his bones.

"She's been looking in here, but you don't have anything out on your desk, do you?"

Royce grinned for the first time that night. He shook his head "no."

"She called Nana today."

"She told you this?" Royce said.

"No, I found out. I went with her to Nana's house. Dad, something is wrong with Nana. She kept confusing me with Tru and called Sophie Sasha."

Royce sat down. "Will this never end?"

Teddy felt disappointed. "Don't you want to know this."

"I did not mean you, honey. Go on."

"Nana asked Tamra how *she* was feeling. I didn't understand, 'cause Nana is the saddest. Just the saddest. Nana sat next to Tamra on the couch and patted her stomach!" She paused for effect. "Do you know what that means? It means she's pregnant! She's going to have a baby."

"She went to see Papa a few weeks before he died," Royce said. "She told him the same thing."

Teddy was *super* disappointed. She thought she had exciting news for him.

"What else?" Royce stood up and paced. Teddy did not stop him. She sat down in his chair and swiveled.

"Nana told her, 'you will be taken care of. I am so sorry Royce doesn't want this baby.'"

The presumptive mother-to-be stopped going to Shakespeare rehearsals. She stayed in the house, watched movies in the theatre—she chose "Dumb and Dumber" and "Friday the 13th"—worked out in the gym, and lounged by the pool on warm days. She had marathon phone calls with friends. She approached Teddy and Tru and asked them if they wanted to go shopping. Normally salivating at the mention of shopping, they shut her down with a curt, yet polite, "No, thank you." Everyone waited for Royce to file a petition to have Tamra excluded from the house. And yet Royce waited.

A family law judge ordered a paternity test, in spite of Tamra's attorney's arguments that the testing was not safe. John Phelan produced two obstetric expert witnesses who testified that, as long as an SNP microarray procedure was undertaken in an accredited facility, there was little risk to the mother or baby. Tamra was ordered to appear at DNA

Testing of America at 9:00 a.m. in one week's time.

A couple of weeks later Royce passed her where she sat in the dining room, tears dripping down her face. He walked back and stood on the opposite side of the table. "Practicing your new part?"

She put her head down on her arms that were folded on the table and cried harder. Her shoulders shook. Tears smeared the glass.

"You got the paternity test results, did you not? I did. Since you are here, I want to speak to you." He crossed his arms and looked at the glass and steel table Tamra had picked out that he disliked. So cold.

Tamra stopped sniffling, but did not otherwise acknowledge him.

"I want to know whose baby this is, and I want to know if he knows."

She raised her head, straightened her back, but kept her arms folded. "Why do you care?"

"Do not misunderstand me. I do not care. I want to know if he is accepting responsibility."

"I don't know."

"You do not know who the father is?" He stood still and faced her, the coldness of the table separating them.

"I haven't told him, so I don't know what he's accepting." She sniffled loudly and wiped her nose with her hand.

"Should you be leaving for your California tour soon?"

"I'm not going."

"Why? You do not want to play Beatrice pregnant?"

"The baby's father is with the company." She looked at him, searching for answers. "I didn't think you would do it.”

“What? Call you on your lies? If you will not leave voluntarily, I will have you removed. I am willing to put you back in the Beverly Hills house. And do not ask my mother for money.”

She sighed. “I want another chance. I know I messed up.”

“Yes, I would say you have. Unwanted pregnancy.”

“You kept telling me to spend time with the girls. And you.”

“Too late.” He pulled a chair out to sit down but changed his mind.

“It was hard. I don’t know why, but I couldn’t be around them when they were babies. I don’t know what’s wrong with me.” At that, she cried harder and kicked her flip-flops off under the table. “Don’t you think I can get the girls to love me again?” She looked up at him.

“Are you daring me?” He pounded on the back of a chair.

“Asking.”

“I am not going to entertain that question.” He turned to walk away.

“This can be our baby. I can be a good mother.” Her body language, straight back, hands in her lap, beseeched him to accept her illusion.

“You have got an opportunity to find out.”

“Oh, thank you. I’ll be the best.” She smiled. Her red-rimmed eyes reflected the crystals in the chandelier. She stood up. “Look,” she said. She turned to her side and lifted the material of her shirt. She put her hands around a small but definite protrusion that stretched the waist of her yoga pants.

Royce chuckled, a dry chuckle as though a

windstorm blew through the dining room. "I certainly did not mean an opportunity with me."

He left her standing alone in the dining room, her outcrop exposed. Her heart flopped like a Broadway musical.

"I am going to do it." Royce and Nichol made popcorn from the machine in the theatre. The smell of salt and oil and popping corn filled the room. "I am going to tell my attorney to file the exclusion petition."

She looked back toward the closed door, turned toward Royce, and touched his arm.

"But I have to admit. I'm wondering. The money—" he said.

"Don't be childish. You are not going to have to live on the street. You own this house. You own the Rancho Mirage and Telluride properties and the New York apartment. So you can become a ski bum."

"I will need a ski bunny." He sounded—and knew he sounded—like a romantic male star in a circa 1960 *Gidget* movie. They sat down in the soft leather recliners in the first row.

"I am sure there will be plenty to choose from," she said.

"Nichol. You know what I am saying."

"Tell me about this movie, but do not tell me the ending."

And so his cerebral Ping-Pong ended—without a score.

Chapter Thirty-Nine

Royce felt he lost both of his parents when his father died, because of his mother's all-consuming grief and her advancing forgetfulness and confusion. After the funeral service, she dropped her façade of being a hostess. She got worse, not better. Sixty-five years together. She stopped calling to see how her granddaughters were doing, and she did not invite the girls for sleepovers. Evelyn, who was living alone in her estate in Pacific Palisades, isolated herself from the rest of her world. Then her disintegrating brain further isolated her, her mind filleted like a catfish.

Royce got calls from Evelyn's neighbors and housekeeper Florrie saying Evelyn ordered her to move out. The neighbors knocked on her door and she did not answer for three days in a row.

He went to her home and let himself in with his key after no one answered the door. The house was cold. He called out to his mother, but got no answer. He smelled something burning that was coming from the kitchen. He found a coffeemaker that had dripped coffee directly onto the hot pad, because there was no coffeepot in place. Clean, stacked Christmas dishes filled the center island.

Royce went upstairs and continued to call out to his mother. He found her in bed. She lay on top of her bedspread and wore a bathrobe and orange cowboy boots.

"Mother. Mother, are you all right?" He shook her shoulder as though he was afraid she was dead. Royce put on his father's face so that he would not cry. He knew it was time to move his mother into his house.

She opened her eyes. "What do you want, dear?"

"Mother, you have to get up. Where is your staff?"

———

"What?"

"The people who work for you. Magdalena, Florrie, Baron. Does any of this sound familiar?"

"Where did Magdalena and Florrie go? I had to dress myself."

"What are you wearing?"

"You can see. I have this on," sweeping the general area with her arms.

"I am going to take you to my house."

"That's nice, dear boy. When did you get to be such a big boy? Now you go outside and play for a bit."

After a protracted effort to convince Evelyn that he was an adult with his own home, Royce packed a Louis Vuitton suitcase with pants, sweaters, shoes, and underwear. He helped her get dressed. Her skin hung loosely off her arms, and her legs had lost tone. She refused to take off the cowboy boots. He took her home. On the way, she commented that he had a nice car, a 1954 coral red with white top Pontiac Starchief. She said it reminded her of a car his father bought when Royce was born.

Royce choked up. "Mother, this *is* Father's car." He coughed. "Remember you gave it to me after he died."

"Of course, I remember."

When they got to Royce's estate, Evelyn said, "Oh my. When did you buy this house? You should have told Daddy first."

Teddy and Tru ganged up on her the minute she walked in the front door. "Oh, Nana's here."

"Hi, Nana, come to my room first."

"Awesome boots."

Royce took that opportunity to look for Tamra. She was in her suite and sat on a celery-colored settee. She was barefoot and wore a colorful shift. She was reading a *Vogue* magazine. *When did Tamra become a cliché?* he wondered.

They looked at each other out of the corners of their eyes as if they were two strangers on an airplane sharing an armrest.

Royce stood in the doorframe. "I have got a bit of a crisis. My mother cannot live alone any longer," he said.

"So get her a live-in companion," Tamra said. She flipped pages in the magazine. She tunelessly whistled and tore out pages from time to time, running her hands down the smooth, silky color pages.

Royce raised his voice. "No, I have heard horror stories about caregivers in that situation. She needs to be supervised, and her *caregiver* needs to be supervised."

"Los Angeles has lovely facilities," Tamra said.

"I am bringing my mother to live here." Royce was running downhill.

"What? Oh, jeez, why do you have to do that? I love her, but I don't want to have to take care of her."

"I am not telling you this to initiate a discussion. I am telling you because I am giving her this suite," he said looking down at her. *Hang on, I am almost finished*, he thought. Portraying the bad guy constantly with Tamra was tiring.

"Yeah, fat chance of that happening." Tamra threw the magazine down on her settee and stood up.

"You will be leaving soon."

"No, Royce. No."

"She is here now. I signed the petition, and my attorney is going to serve you with that document and a temporary restraining order excluding you from the house. Call a moving company."

She whimpered. "Can't you give her Nichol's suite?"

"I am going to use this suite because it is separated

from the noise of the children's wing. You know something about that, separating yourself from the girls." Royce stood before her, arms crossed over his chest.

She looked at him, a rarer and rarer occurrence in the Kallas married limbo. Royce was fifty-six years old. His brown hair—he still had most of it, knock wood—was turning gray. They had been married for fourteen years.

"I will not move," she stood as tall as her five foot three allowed against his six feet, "until I'm ready."

"Get ready."

Royce walked from the room, and she followed. "It's a boy."

He walked, did not look back, did not miss a step; his heart had been stomped on by those "fuck me" heels.

Two days later while Tamra worked out, a moving company drove up to the estate. Royce's assistant Lew drove in right behind the truck. He instructed the movers to pack up Tamra's clothes, other personal items, and furniture. By the time she had finished with her workout, half of her furniture had been taken out to the truck.

"What are you doing?" she said when she got back to her suite. She stood close to Lew. Her abdomen almost touched him. She yelled into his face, spitting venom. "This is my house, and these are my things."

"Tamra, you were served with the petition and temporary restraining order," Lew said.

Her hands shook.

"Here is your key to the Beverly Hills house," he said.

"The house will be mine?"

"He'll discuss it with you. The movers will take your things to the house. Since you have the key, you will need to go with them. Arrangements have been made for you to meet with an interior designer.”

She called Royce’s office, but he would not take her call.

For five hours the movers emptied drawers, hung clothes on prepared racks, wrapped jewelry with tissue paper. Then they moved the rest of the furniture onto the truck, followed by the boxes. Lew checked on the progress from time to time. When the movers took the settee, she sat on the floor, legs stretched out. The movers finished.

“It’s time,” Lew said, the warden leading her to the electric chair.

He walked closely behind her down the stairs.

“What?” She stopped on the stairs. “Are you afraid I’m going to steal the silver? Which should be mine, by the way.”

“You and your attorney will need to address items in the house with Mr. Kallas’s attorney.”

“You sure know a lot about my life.”

“Occupational hazard.”

Tamra walked to the driveway where her black Maserati Spyder was parked. She turned back toward Lew. “Do you think I can take one of the Escalades, too? I will need a back seat soon.” She touched her abdomen.

“You and your attorney—”

“Yeah, yeah. Me and my attorney.” She waved her hand in the air and walked to her car. She peeled out of the driveway and down the street.

The house quiet, Nichol came out of her suite. She walked down the long halls to Tamra’s suite. Everything was gone. Her body was quaking.

After she officially became a part of the Kallas

———

household, Evelyn walked around the mansion, attempting to remember the location of Teddy's and Tru's bedrooms. On her third day in residence, she walked outside to the front lawns. She did not understand why desert weeds were planted everywhere. *You would think Royce could have pulled these out of here by now and planted some flowers.* She found some gloves in the pantry and went back to the front lawn. She yanked the plants out and laid them on the lawn. Any plants with needles, she expertly pulled up by the spindly roots. She pulled up the wild grasses and succulents. She deracinated one entire section of carefully chosen plantings. Laid them all on the lawn.

The gardener Francisco walked down the driveway and saw that Evelyn had pulled out all of his plants on the left front of the house. He jumped up and down and screamed "¿Qué estás haciendo a mis plantas?" He ran toward the back of the property and ran back to where Evelyn stood, picked up a succulent that had been ripped from the earth, and rang the front doorbell. Lindy answered the door.

Francisco yelled *"la señora loca tira mis plantas,"* and waved his arms like a seagull ready for takeoff.

Lindy went out the front door and looked at the result of Evelyn's efforts. Evelyn continued to pull up plants while the gardener talked to Lindy.

Lindy said *"Tendré cuidado de ella. Calmar,"* which, roughly translated was "The lady of the house thinks she is helping, so relax" and went out to fetch Evelyn into the house.

"*Señora*, Ma'am, Mrs. Kallas, ah, hmm, you must not dig those up from the ground," Lindy said. "Senor Francisco is very, very mad." Lindy had difficulty not laughing, both at Francisco as he jumped about and at

Evelyn with her whacked out determination.

"Those ugly things need to be pulled," Evelyn said. "You wait. Royce will be glad they are out of the ground. Some of these things look like artichokes." She continued to yank succulents out by pillowy petals.

"Ma'am. You please wait to talk to Mr. Kallas. Don't do anymore digging, okay. Hmmm?" Lindy said.

Evelyn sat in the grass to get better leverage on the plants, *not much more than weeds.*

"Fine. I'll wait until Royce comes home. I wanted to finish the job, because there are more weeds over there. I will get back to it tomorrow."

Lindy helped Evelyn to her feet and pivoted her around so that she was facing the front doors.

They walked under the portico, with Lindy's arm around Evelyn, who wiped her hands together to get the dirt and sand off her gloves. "Who are you?"

"I am Lindy, ma'am."

"I would like a nap now, please. All the fun has gone out of the day," said Evelyn, a deflated balloon.

After Royce was told about the exhumation of the plants, he made sure Evelyn and his landscaping were safe. He hired three full-time caregivers, each working an eight-hour shift. They alternated days off. Maricio was the midnight to 8:00 a.m., Jason was 8:00 a.m. to 4:00 p.m., and Pete was 4:00 p.m. to midnight.

Royce hired a contractor to remodel Tamra's former suite for his mother. It consisted of a small living room, fireplace, bedroom, and bathroom. Elgin's men painted the walls lemon yellow. Elgin laid skid-proof tile in the bathroom. From Evelyn's home Royce brought a lady's desk, two plum-colored tufted velvet wingback chairs with matching tea table in cherrywood. The chairs and a cream tufted velvet loveseat were placed in front of the fireplace. Evelyn seemed satisfied with the suite out of which Tamra had been unceremoniously dumped.

The tumult in the house was temporarily eclipsed by summer in the valley. The sun finally arrived in July 2009, after flirting with the fog for a month. It warmed every tree, plant, blade of grass, and horse's tail in its path. Teddy and two of her friends lay by the pool, damaging their skin, for which they would pay in later years. Royce looked out at the girls from the library. *Teddy is doing much better with Tamra gone*, he thought. Tamra called from time to time, asking for something: money, another car—he gave her an Escalade—and a larger house, because she was going to hire a live-in baby nurse. One time she suggested that Nichol work for her since the girls didn't really need a nanny anymore.

After filing the petition for dissolution, Royce and Tamra had a court date, where a judge made temporary orders. Based on the declarations in Royce's petition, Tamra's response, and their testimony, the judge ordered custody of Teddy and Tru to Royce and reasonable visitation to Tamra (Although she told Royce she probably would not ask to see the girls for a while), temporary spousal support to Tamra of $100,000 a month, and the Beverly Hills house.

Chapter Forty

Morgan Wooden Kallas was born on August 25, 2009. Tru was excited about the baby. She asked to go to Tamra's house to see him. Tamra suggested she bring the baby to Calabasas, but Royce nixed that idea. When she returned from Tamra's, Tru was wound up. She told everyone in the house she held the baby, and he was "so cute." After she listed his vital statistics, brown hair and blue eyes, she turned to Nichol.

"Was I a cute baby? Was I that little?"

"Yes you were, sweetheart. You were almost a naked baby after you were first born, but you were definitely cute."

"Groddy. That's like so embarrassing. Why was I naked?"

"We didn't have the supplies we needed for you. Lindy and Angel made an emergency trip to Walmart, and the day was saved."

"I didn't have *any* clothes?"

"You had a diaper and were covered in a warm blanket."

"How totally sad. And I wore stuff from *Walmart*?"

"Oh, sweetheart. You were never deprived. And your fashionista standing is safe."

Royce went home one evening and found Teddy, Tru, and Nichol in the theatre, where they watched *Cloudy with a Chance of Meatballs*. Tru held one of her dolls. Royce had not seen her play with a doll for at least a year.

"Hello, my beauties," he said.

"Hi, Dad."

"Hi, Daddy. Aren't you going to say hello to Nichol, too?" Tru asked.

Teddy gave her an elbow to the ribs.

"Owww! Look, Daddy. This is Morgan. Say hello to Morgan, too." Tru moved a piece of the blanket, and the doll bleated.

"Yes, I see," he said. "Why is he here?" he asked, looking at Nichol.

"Tamra called. She sounded so un-Tamra like," Nichol said. "One minute she complimented me on the way I have raised the girls, the next minute she cried. She said she felt sick, flu-like, and she did not want to make Morgan sick. Her parents cannot take care of him because her mother had back surgery and is in the hospital. When Tamra came to the house, she was quiet. Like I said, so un-Tamra."

"Daddy, he's an awesome baby," Tru said. "I'm helping Nichol. See?"

Royce walked in front of Tru's recliner. "Tru, he is not our baby. He will not stay long."

"He is no bother," Nichol said. "He actually has a sweet disposition. I do not mind taking care of him at all. I would have liked advance notice, though. The nursery has not been used for a long time." She re-positioned the baby so that his head rested on Tru's slender shoulder.

"Why is her baby nurse not taking care of him?" Royce said, turning to look at Nichol.

Nichol stood and faced Royce. "Tamra said she was so sick she did not want him in the house with her."

"Nic, Tamra may be taking advantage of you. Her mother probably is not even in the hospital," Royce said.

Nichol leaned against the wall. "We will be fine taking care of him. He is just a small baby who needs to be fed and held. I can understand Tamra's concern."

"Ladies, all three of you, would anyone like snacks?"

"Awesome, Dad. Carrot sticks, celery, and peanut

butter." Teddy took the baby from Tru and clucked to him.

"I don't want vegetables. Can I have a PB and J?" Tru said.

"I think we can manage that. Nichol, will you help me?"

They walked into the kitchen.

Nichol looked at him hard.

"I agree to this arrangement for a few days. I do not want Tamra to think we run a babysitting service," he said.

They stood next to the island in the main kitchen that was roughly the size of Maui.

"I would ask you to separate your feelings about Tamra from Morgan," Nichol said. "He has not hurt anyone in this family. His sisters want to get to know him. The difference between you and me is that she does not push my buttons any longer."

"Why, oh why, does everything related to Tamra have to be so complicated? It feels so much…lighter in this house since the judge had her removed," Royce said. "I knew we would all feel better when Tamra left, but I did not anticipate feeling this good. But now with the baby here…a boy she said was mine." He sighed.

Nichol put her hands around his neck. "I like taking care of a baby. I didn't realize how much I missed it until she brought him here today. Please, do this for me." She had not been affectionate with him since the Bora Bora debacle. He touched his forehead to hers, and then, throwing Kallas veneer of control to the winds like a spring kite, he kissed her. Wrapped his arms around her waist, pulled her to him and kissed her. They seemed to realize what they were doing at the same instant, as though hit with a rated PG Taser, and separated.

Royce looked for the fixings for the PB and J and the

vegetables. It was apparent that he was not well acquainted with his kitchen, and he opened and closed cabinet doors, looking for bread. "Can you help me here?" he asked.

Nichol pointed toward the pantry and the refrigerator, rather than speak, perhaps afraid her voice would give her away.

He juggled the peanut butter, jelly and celery. "It has been four months since she left. If the girls miss her, they are masking it very well," he said.

"Your divorce will be final in a few months. Let go of her."

Actually, Nichol did not know about the negotiations going back and forth that held up the final order. Although Royce probably could have successfully fought Tamra on the provisions of the prenup, she was arguing that Royce also spent large chunks of time away from home. Tamra's lawyer had threatened Royce's lawyer that she would depose Royce's appointments assistant and recite every date he had been away on business. She promised a full-color chart. She would depose Nichol and ask her any number of embarrassing questions about dates and locations where she and Royce had "hooked up." The fact that Royce knew the expression made him feel ill.

They added an iced tea for Teddy and a glass of milk for Tru. Nichol fetched the missing butter for Tru's sandwich. Tru could not abide a PB and J without butter.

"Tell me, how about you? How do you feel now that she is gone?" Royce asked.

"The girls are content now. They think they know how everyone in the house fits."

"How do you fit, Nic?"

"Why ask me how I fit? I am simply a member of the staff." A bolt of anger sliced through her and struck Royce.

He had mistakenly thought she was warming up to him again. He almost dropped the chunky peanut butter jar, but he caught it in time to keep it from crashing and littering the floor with tiny peanut pieces. "What is that about? Do you feel that we do not show you every day how important you are? I was waiting to divorce Tamra before—"

"Before what?" The words came out strong, yet ponderous, as though they had come from a long distance.

Royce had seen her anger after 9/11, the day years ago when Tamra accused him and Nichol of having an affair, and the night on the yacht in Bora Bora. Otherwise, she was so even tempered, a description a woman probably would not want to hear because it sounded like a family's faithful Labrador retriever.

"I did not think it proper to talk to you again…about…us…until I am divorced, which at least in theory should happen in a couple months. We are bifurcating the dissolution. The finances will be handled separately and, if Tamra has her way, can take years to resolve."

Nichol spread peanut butter into the celery pieces as though laying fresh concrete. "After I take these plates in to the girls, I am going to take Morgan upstairs," she said.

"No, wait, please. I have apparently—obviously— said or done something that upset you. It was not my intention to be cavalier about this. I seem to step in it every time we start to have a conversation."

He held out his arms as though an evangelist at the pulpit and then touched his heart. He took the plates she held, put them on the island, and took her hands in his. He looked at the floor. He cleared his throat—not a habit of his—raised his eyes, and whispered, "Please be patient just a little while longer. I, I love you, Nichol. No, do not say anything. After Bora Bora I thought I was being respectful by not pursuing you until Tamra left the house, and I was divorced from her. I am afraid that what I have done, instead, is give you the impression I do not think we are important. I want you to be happy and have the same feelings I have. I did listen to what you said in Bora Bora."

"Can we talk about this another day? I really need to tend to the baby."

She picked up the dishes, and he, rendered mute, followed behind her with the girls' drinks. He pondered what her demeanor meant. And how did Tamra get between them, yet again?

Three days passed, and Tamra did not call to check in, did not answer her phone. Nichol stayed busy with Morgan. A temporary baby nurse gave her time to sleep. After all the years she had been a baby nurse, she still had the ability to function on little sleep. One of the stable of nannies who worked for the Kallases filled in for Nichol.

On the fourth day of Morgan's visit, Royce called Tamra's parents' home.

"Laramie, how are you and Belle doing? Excited about your new grandson?"

"It's nice to hear from you, Royce. I'm sorry about the way things turned out. You're a good man. The baby is beautiful, but such sad circumstances."

"I agree. Not ideal."

"It's a damn shame the two of you couldn't work it out for the baby's sake. And the girls, too, of course. A child needs both parents," Laramie said.

"I agree," Royce said. Laramie had evidently been fed the same line as Reginald that the baby was Royce's. He did not correct him.

"Belle is in the hospital having back surgery,"

Laramie said.

So it was the truth. Amazing.

"Do you know when Tamra is coming to see her mother?" Laramie said.

Or not.

"I do not have any idea where she is. Do you know where she might be?" Royce said. "She left her baby with Nichol to take care of."

"No, not a clue. Sorry I can't help either of us. I've got to concentrate on Belle. Speaking of her, I need to get to the hospital."

Royce called Nichol and told her Tamra had left for parts unknown.

On that same day Tamra came to the house. She let herself in and arrived at the house while the girls were in school and Royce was at work. Nichol heard footsteps in the hall and was startled when it was Tamra who walked into the nursery. She was rocking Morgan who was asleep.

"Say hello to mama, little man," Nichol said. She stood and gave the baby to Tamra before Tamra could come up with a reason why she couldn't hold him.

Tamra looked at Morgan as though he were a fish slapping for his life in the bottom of a boat. "Can I sit with him here for a while?" she asked.

"Of course. I will leave the two of you alone. I will be—"

"No, don't leave. Please." She never took her eyes off her son and held onto him as though he were wriggling out of her arms, instead of sleeping.

Nichol motioned for Tamra to sit on the chaise lounge, while she folded clothes from the dryer.

"Are you feeling better?" Nichol said, with her back

to Tamra.

"I thought I was."

Nichol turned to face Tamra, holding a onesie.

"I'm afraid to hold him, touch him," Tamra said. "Before he was born, I was terrified thinking about raising him on my own but excited to have a son I could be a real mother to, not like with the girls. When he was born, it was like a wave hit me. I was afraid I would hurt him." She opened his blanket to let his little legs stretch out.

"I think most new mothers have the feeling of being overwhelmed, even mothers who have already had children. That feeling goes away with time and practice."

"No, Nichol. Not that kind of overwhelmed. It was so strong, it was like I didn't want him. Like what I felt with Tru, but worse. Or maybe it wasn't worse, because you took care of her, and so I didn't have to think about it. But I do love Morgan." She looked down at her not quite one-month old son, watched him stuff a fist into his mouth in his sleep.

Nichol got a bottle from the small refrigerator and heated it in the microwave. She tested the temperature against the inside of her wrist and then handed the bottle to Tamra. "He will probably drink the entire bottle."

"But he's asleep," Tamra said, looking up at Nichol. She did look terrified.

With his eyes squeezed shut and his arms pumping, Morgan yelped, then yelped again, sonar on a submarine, releasing pulses of sound, listening for echoes.

Tamra fed Morgan. She watched him suck on the nipple, and looked up at Nichol as though waiting for a critique from her. When the bottle was empty, she gave the baby to Nichol.

"I'm going to get a soda from the kitchen. Will you burp him?" Tamra said.

As soon as Nichol scooped him up, Tamra almost sprinted from the room. After fifteen minutes passed, Tamra had not returned to the nursery. Nichol went into the kitchen. Tamra had left. Nichol was sad, but not surprised.

Nichol called Royce at the office. "Tamra was here. Are you far away from anything breakable?"

"Why? What?" He stood and actually looked around his office to see if he had anything he could damage or destroy.

"Tamra is still sick. She has been at home, but not answering the phone. And her parents cannot take the baby because—"

"—Belle is in the hospital," Royce interrupted.

"It looks like we have a boarder."

"No! I am not going to let Tamra pull one of her tricks so that she can irresponsibly jet around. We will take him back to Beverly Hills."

"You don't know she is jetting around. She may really be sick, depression sick, postpartum sick. For a moment, please, let's do what we can to make the little guy feel safe. Tamra was adamant that he could not stay at home with her," Nichol said.

"But Tamra—" he said.

"Please hear me. I don't ask you to do anything *for* Tamra. I ask you to let Morgan stay where he has family."

"He is not family, Nic. And you already have two girls, not counting Sophie, to care for. Why would you want to take him on? A new baby. And Tamra's baby to boot."

"He is your daughters' family. We have a temporary baby nurse for nights and my days off and a nanny for the girls."

That night Nichol and Royce had basketball practice.

They drove to the college in his black Maserati.

"Please trust me with this situation for a little while longer," Nichol said.

"How little?"

"I don't know. I think it is important that Morgan stay here; it's probably safer here, based on what Tamra told me. Let me take care of him and you take care of your Tamra fatigue."

"I will trust you. Now can we talk about something more important?"

"Oh, Royce, not now. I am not sure I can handle any more right now." She sat with her hands in her lap and stared straight ahead.

Royce looked at her, her face lit by cars driving in the opposite direction. He was affected by her features, so dear to him, a face he had known for ten years. Her face showed her intelligence and her heart. He realized he was sounding moony and stopped.

"I do not want you to handle anything. I want to continue our conversation of a week ago. Will you talk to me?" he said.

Nichol looked over at him, turning her head to a slow beat.

"Do not do it if it is such an effort," he said, an Arctic wind.

They drove for a few minutes in silence, each moment a year, a past year.

"We went places together for years," she said. "Like a couple. We held hands, we hugged, we told each other stories about our lives and about nonsense, and we made love. We discussed politics. But Tamra is always right here. Right here." She gestured as though Tamra were an apparition sitting on the dashboard.

"Wait," he said.

"No, I told you I want to say this."

"You will. Let me pull off the road. We are foregoing practice tonight." He turned onto a side street and found a place to park. He leaned his back against the driver's side door. "Now."

"Sometimes when we go to dinner with the girls and you are talking to them, I look at the four of you and say, 'Please give me this family,'" she said. "Then I felt guilty, because I ask to tear your family apart. Now, even with Tamra gone, she is still with us."

"We will send Morgan back immediately," Royce said.

She held up her hand to stop him. "No, the baby needs love, and Tamra may not be equipped to give it to him right now."

"But if she—"

"Shush, please."

"Do not shush me," he said. "I thought you said Tamra does not push your buttons, as you called it. If the baby, understandably, gives you thoughts of Tamra, let us end this."

"It is not the baby." She poked his chest none too softly with her fingers. Nichol turned her head toward her window and gulped hard to keep herself from crying.

"Dammit, why does our first real argument since Bora Bora have to be about that woman?" He hit the steering wheel with the heels of his hands and then grasped onto her shoulders. "I cannot believe we are talking about her, instead of us. I know I have dragged this out. I am sorry I have put you through this. Please, let me hold you. You have no idea how sorry I am."

Nichol turned as though she were trying out her

———

365

upper body for the first time. Arms reached out to effect purchase onto Royce. Their shoulders and arms touched. The black Italian leather console restricted the embrace. Nichol released her tears. He patted her back as though comforting a child with a nightmare.

"I know, I know. I am sorry, so sorry," he said. "Yes, after October. Then we will sit down with Sophie, Teddy and Tru and tell them, although I think they will probably say, 'It is about time.' We will have a meeting with the staff, where I will make it clear to them that you are the lady of the house and must be treated with respect. Friends will be easy. You have met some of them already."

"Not too long to wait," she lied.

A week later, Laramie called Royce at the office.

"How is Belle doing?" Royce said. He turned the snow globe Nichol had given him upside down and shook it.

"She's fine, fine. She'll be laid up for several months. We have a hospital bed, and she can either lie down or walk." He paused. "No sitting. Uh, Royce. I'm calling about Tamra. She's in the hospital." Laramie cleared his throat.

"I'm sorry to hear that," Royce said. *What kind of scam is this?* he wondered.

"She's being treated for postpartum."

Royce was surprised. He did not know a woman would be hospitalized for having strange thoughts about one's baby. "When Tamra had what I assume was postpartum depression after Tru was born, I had research done to acquaint myself with the condition. I thought it could be treated with medication and therapy. Why was she hospitalized?" He sucked in a breath. Royce could hear Laramie's voice catch.

"It's not just depression. It's psychosis. Oh, God,

Royce, she's being treated for postpartum psychosis! She will be an inpatient for at least ninety days. I don't even know what psychosis means, but it must be serious because they're talking about something called electroconvulsive therapy. I'm going onto the Internet to learn about it."

"I'm sorry. What can I do to help?"

"Well, here's the thing," Laramie said. "It turns out that Tamra has a power of attorney. Evidently, she had one done at the same time she prepared her will. Right after Morgan was born. The power of attorney names you as guardian of the baby in the event she is incapacitated. I don't know why she did that since you're the boy's father." There was an edge to Laramie's voice now. "Do—"

"Laramie, I am *not* Morgan's father." Royce stood up and walked to the corner windows. He looked down twenty-five floors to the ant people scurrying about. He gently knocked on the glass. "I'm sorry that Tamra led you to believe otherwise," he said. "I have the results from a paternity test. Now the baby is at my house, has been there almost from the day he was born. Tamra told Nichol she was afraid to be with the baby, and so kind-hearted Nichol said she would take care of him." Royce felt a pinch of regret that he was trying to make Laramie feel bad.

"Oh, Tamra. My God. I don't know what to think about her sometimes. She's so sick. If you could keep the baby, that would be a tremendous help. I just can't manage now with Belle and all."

Royce could see Tamra in the hospital bed the night he beaned her in the summer of 1993, her face bruised, an ice bag on her head and eyes. He resisted the urge to ask where Tamra was hospitalized.

367

PART THREE

Chapter Forty-One

On January 12, 2010 a friend of Nichol's called and said something had happened in Haiti. Nichol turned on the television and listened to a CNN reporter say, "A 7.0 earthquake has decimated the poorest country in the Western Hemisphere. Port-au-Prince, the country's capital, has been reduced to rubble. It is believed that over 250,000 people have been left homeless. Casualty numbers are expected to be in the thousands."

Royce called her a half-hour later from his office, telling her the same thing.

"Where are your parents?" he asked.

"They are both practicing at a hospital in Port-au-Prince. I called their cell numbers. Nothing. I tried the hospital. Communication with the country is nonexistent. I called the Red Cross, but did not get any information. I'm going to call my Tio Maxamel to see what he knows."

"Call me here when you learn something," he said.

Nichol called Tio Maxamel and Tia Allegra in Miami.

"We are afraid, not only for your manman and papa, but also for Pierre, Alfonz, and Max," Maxamel said. Maxamel's and Allegra's children, Nichol's cousins, had returned to Haiti after completing their university educations in the United States.

Nichol stayed close to televisions for the next two days. Sophie and Nichol spoke on the phone and by text. Sophie wanted to go to Haiti, but she had just started a new quarter, and Nichol did not want her to miss school.

"But this is why I'm in school, to be involved in third-world countries."

Nichol convinced her to wait until spring break. "The

need for volunteers will be ongoing with a catastrophe like this one."

Teddy, age thirteen, unlike her usual protocol, did not slouch into the house after school with a bored look on her face, her skirt rolled up six inches shorter than it was supposed to be, and hole up in her room. Instead she sat with Nichol and Tru, age nine, as the drama played out, and the news gave only a few positive reports of people dug out of the rubble alive. Most of the reports told of bloated bodies filling the streets, bodies that were not identified or claimed. Who could pay for a Haitian funeral with a band, coffin, mausoleum, and cross at the gravesite? The smell of decay filled the city.

Maxamel called on the third day after the earthquake. "I have made contact with a man named Charles Erwin, who has his own plane. He is taking medical supplies into the country and has seats for three people. You can come with us, Nichol, but he is leaving in two days."

"Thank you, Tio. You have no idea how grateful I am."

Nichol called Royce and told him what she had learned. He told her *he* would fly her to Port-au-Prince. She told him only humanitarian planes were allowed into the airport, already crowded with media planes. He asked her to at least let him fly her to Miami to meet Erwin's plane.

Teddy and Tru sat with Nichol as she watched television news and talked to relatives in the United States. They knew this was not a week's vacation. Nichol had not scheduled a return flight.

"When are you coming back?" Tru asked.

Nichol took Tru's and Teddy's hands. She seemed dazed. "I don't know. First I have to find my parents."

She called an agency that specialized in providing nannies and tutors. She told them she did not know how long she would be gone. She set up appointments with possible replacements for the next day. She also made arrangements with the baby nurse to stay indefinitely and hired a second one, assuming Tamra would remain hospitalized.

Royce seemed to not know how to react, how to move, what to do, except to tell her he was paying all her expenses to Haiti, including paying for all the gas for Erwin's plane.

"I would be honored to help you and your country in this way." He did not know what he felt, except that it was painful.

Nichol had two suitcases open on the bed—after taking off the comforter, of course—and chose and folded clothes.

"Can I talk to you for a minute?" Royce said. He closed the door and sat down on her bed between the two suitcases.

"Of course. By the way, I have six appointments set up for tomorrow for my replacements."

Replacements? Plural?"

"We need a part-time baby nurse on Kristina's days off and a nanny."

"Oh, that baby. I have to do something about him." Who's Kristina? When was she hired?"

"Remember, we talked about getting a temporary nurse. I found one. Lew handled all the paperwork. Any supplies Kristina needs will be handled by Lindy. You don't need to do anything about Morgan." She continued to move back and forth from the closet to the bed. She looked up from the cotton blouses she held in her hand. "I am sorry I have to upend your family."

"I understand why you are going. You have got to find your parents."

"There is more. I have to go back to my broken country to see if there is anything I can do to help mend it. Medical people are needed. Haiti is a wealth of injured, broken, and homeless people, which has been exacerbated by the earthquake. Medical people are always needed."

"I had almost forgotten you are a nurse. You have been so much more to my family," Royce said. "Please stop folding clothes." He put his hand over hers. "You know I love you and I know you love me. I cannot believe I am talking this way." He cleared his throat. "I could give you a list of reasons why I love you, but we do not have the luxury of time. You fly out of our lives in two days."

"I have been here nine years, Tru's entire life. I stopped being concerned about not having a job as a baby nurse by the time Tru was six months old. I'm now a nanny-tutor-companion-comfort station, and I have accepted that. Your daughters are so precious to me. When we had the episode with Tamra all those years ago, I told her I love your daughters like they are my own. My feelings have not changed. If anything, they have gotten stronger."

Royce spoke. "I want to marry you. You know that. I never had the intention of having an affair, but you said—"

She nodded.

How will I talk to you?" Royce said.

"I will call you as soon as cell service is restored or I find a landline I can use. It may be a week or so, but don't worry. My reasons for not getting in touch with you will have nothing to do with how I feel about you," Nichol said.

"The girls asked me if we could take you to dinner tomorrow night. Do you think you are up for it?" he said.

"Yes, that would be very nice. I have to get packed tonight because I'll be interviewing most of tomorrow."

He attempted to put all his feelings, known and unknown to him, into a kiss without slobbering on her. Then he left her room.

The next day Nichol juggled chauffeuring and interviewing. She let Tru and Teddy sit in on the afternoon interviews for nannies. The three of them decided they would rank each person on a scale of 0-10. They agreed on categories they would vote on: experience, age, flexibility, sense of humor, opinions of teenagers, but there would be no swimsuit or talent competitions. After the interviews finished, Nichol discussed the morning appointments with the girls. They agreed on the two finalists.

When Royce came home, the three of them summarized each interviewee and told him why they had picked the two applicants for him to consider. Royce weighed in and told Nichol to make the final decision. The "winner" was Emaline Trouffert, who got points simply for having a name that looked like Scrabble words. She was forty-five years old. She had been an English Literature professor at Cal State Dominguez Hills, where she taught for almost twenty years. She had retired early because her husband had been quite ill. He subsequently died, and she didn't want to sit at home staring at the walls. She had two grown daughters. She agreed to coordinate her schedule with Morgan's baby nurse.

For Tru, Emaline's attribute was that she had been a swimmer in high school and college. She had been in the swim club and did synchronized swimming. Tru had begun showing an interest in synchronized swimming and was in the pool or at practice almost every day.

Teddy was not as enthusiastic, not because she did not like Emaline, but because she was almost fourteen. In her mind, she did not need a nanny. She just needed a chauffeur.

Emaline was available for temporary and permanent positions. She lived alone and could live in with the Kallases. Nichol called the agency and left a message that they had chosen Emaline and wanted her to start the next day.

Business concluded, they went to dinner at Wolf Creek Restaurant. They sat at a pine plank booth with gold cushions. Sophie was helicoptered in from San Diego. The girls held court all evening, talking over the din of the other patrons, taking turns for their daddy's and Nichol's attention. They talked about cheerleading squad (Teddy), cookie sales (Tru), surfing (Sophie), synchronized swimming (Tru), microbiology (Sophie), and *West Side Story* tryouts (Teddy). Everyone was electrified, speaking quickly, talking, talking. All of them afraid to stop talking. At some point in the evening, they got quiet when they thought about why they were at dinner together at a restaurant on a school night.

Tru speared pieces of pasta in her Ale Mac N' Cheese. She whimpered. She reached over and put her thin arms around Nichol's neck.

That gesture got Nichol started. She laid her fork on her plate of The Big Easy, a shrimp dish.

Teddy put her head down toward her chest and sniffled. She took Nichol's hand and held it between hers.

Sophie, chowing down on jambalaya, didn't cry. Not yet. "I want to go with you, Nic. I need to be down there with you."

Nichol looked across the table at Sophie. "You can't go down there now. You have to stay in school."

Sophie began to protest.

"Based on the news reports about the number of wounded people and the degree of devastation, there will be plenty of time for you to come down," Nichol said. "Besides, there isn't a seat for you on the plane I will be on. Soph, I love you for wanting to help. Just wait a while."

The four of them looked at Royce. "Girls, you don't have to go to school tomorrow. We will all take Nichol to the airport," Royce said.

"Emaline is coming in the morning," Nichol said. She leaned into Tru who was hanging onto her as though she were a baby koala.

As they drove home, there were noticeable snifflings. The darkness was punctuated with streamers of white light from streetlights.

"Nic, can I tell you something and you won't get mad?" Teddy said from the backseat.

"Oh, boy, Teddy. Don't put me in a bad spot or anything."

Teddy talked to the back of Nichol's head. "Okay, I'll tell you, anyway. I wanted to be so mad at you because you are leaving. I wanted to not talk to you so you'd know I was really mad. But I couldn't do it. I couldn't be mad at you, because then I wouldn't be able to say good bye."

"I'm sorry this is making you angry. I think I understand why it is. Please believe me that I'm not leaving you. I will be back." Nichol was barely holding it together.

That night Teddy and Tru asked Nichol if they could sleep with her. The three of them decided to have a sleepover in Sophie's room. They each gave her a present and asked her to wait until she got to Haiti before opening them. She read a story to Tru and discussed a love triangle with Teddy, who claimed not to be a part of the drama, just an interested bystander. Sophie talked about Raphael, some things Royce probably shouldn't know. Nichol put the three presents in her suitcase.

Nichol and Royce had not been running together for over a year. Yet, without prior arrangement, they both appeared at the foyer at 5:25 the morning she was going to fly out. Nichol felt that she had to brief Royce on every minute detail of the girls' lives, because he was going to be directly responsible for their sanity and well-being for an undetermined amount of time.

"Do you have a plan for how long you will stay?"

"No, I don't. First, I have to find my parents. I may have to find temporary housing for them, although what I'm hearing is that there are more displaced people than shelters. Secondly, I want to see what the need is. I am sorry I can't be more definite."

They were silent for a moment, each adjusting gloves that did not need to be adjusted and tying shoes that did not need to be tied.

"So I am going to have a nanny for Teddy and Tru because you are leaving me. On top of that, I am going to have a baby nurse for a child my ex-wife has left here like a pair of shoes she no longer likes," he said.

"Why such anger?"

"I am not angry. I am frustrated. Tamra leaves her baby here and takes off to wherever she goes, without a care. Four motherless children."

"She's in the hospital," Nichol said.

"I know, I know."

They ran for an hour. When they returned to the house, Royce went to the gym, while Nichol checked on Morgan. He was asleep. She took the baby monitor out of Sophie's room and walked into the gym. As she placed it on the counter where she always stowed it, she saw a box from Tiffany. She turned and looked at him. Noncommittal.

He took a ring out of the box and held Nichol's right hand and put the ring on her finger.

"I am going to keep doing this until I get it right," he said. "When this goddamned divorce is final, we will put this ring on your left hand."

"You are such a smooth talker." She looked at the ring. It was the one he had given her in Bora Bora. She did not take the ring off and did not look for a large body of water in which to throw it.

"I am going to miss you more than I can describe," he said, "Probably more than I even understand. I have been watching CNN, too, and there is desolation and more desolation. Please be careful." He held both of her hands, and she let him.

"Yes, I will consider that warning. Don't forget. I was born there."

"And do not forget, you have been living in Calabasas, California for nine years where very few people carry machetes, and before living here you were in the wilds of suburban Irvine and San Diego. Do you see a trend here?"

"I get your point. I will accept this gift as a, let's see, a dinner ring only. If you propose when I get back——"

"You want another ring? You are killing me here."

Morgan's squeal came over the baby monitor.

"Please keep this in the safe until I return from Haiti. I can't take it with me. I would be murdered in broad daylight wearing that ring."

That morning Nichol, Emaline and the temporary baby nurse Kristina, went through the schedules.

Royce, Teddy, Sophie, and Tru, a send-off

———

contingent that was in the throes of loss, accompanied Nichol to Burbank Airport. None of them knew if they would see her in two weeks or a month. The girls were true to their emotions. They did not attempt to disguise how they felt. The more they cried, the more the adults presented stoic faces. Teddy's reaction was unexpected. She considered herself cool and tough beyond her years. As she stood on the tarmac next to the Kallas plane, she was either unconcerned to let strangers see her cry or was so fully engulfed in loss she had no control over her eyes or her mouth that bled tears and sobs. Sophie was not able to console her sisters, because she was frightened for Nichol. She had learned enough about Haiti to know danger lay in wait behind poverty. She held Nichol and whispered to her, "Please, please be careful."

Standing behind Nichol, Tru wrapped her arms around her waist and looked as though she were using Nichol as a flotation device. She cried into Nichol's back, "Nic, Nic, please don't go. Please don't leave me." Nichol felt that leaving the girls was the cruelest thing she had ever done. If only she knew how long she was going to be gone, they could mark the days off in a calendar. She laid her arms over Tru's.

The adults portrayed people who would miss each other, but did not—they thought—reveal the hole they already recognized as absence of a cherished love, although Royce would not have known to use those words.

They boarded the jet with Nichol. It was time. It did not matter how much they cried or how much they postured. It was time. Nichol wrapped the girls in her arms one more time.

"Be good to each other while I'm gone," she bawled. "Teddy, Tru, don't give Emaline too much grief. Sophie, go back to school. Pay attention to your studies. I'll talk to you as soon as there is phone service. I love you."

For public consumption Nichol and Royce gave each other polite hugs, which gave them away more than if they had gone into a clutch. But they also whispered into each other's ears "I love you," "I love you best." That was the first time Nichol said "I love you" to him.

Moments later she was gone.

Every day Royce, Tru, and Teddy asked each other, "Did you hear from Nichol?" For two weeks, the answer was the same: no. They limped through their days.

Chapter Forty-Two

In addition to missing Nichol, being responsible for his daughters, and attempting to run a multi-billion-dollar company, Royce was responsible for his mother. He let his assistant Lew supervise her caregivers.

The daytime caregiver Jason had tea with Evelyn every day. They sat in the chairs by the fireplace with the tea on the table between them. The teapot, cups, sugar, and light cream, and a three-tiered dish with scones, clotted cream and raspberry jam, and cucumber sandwiches sat on a silver tray.

Jason was not above manipulating Evelyn for his gain. Inasmuch as all of Evelyn's expenditures were checked closely by an accountant, Jason's largesse was limited to her buying him clothing while she was also buying something for herself or her granddaughters.

Two weeks before they had gone to Saks Fifth Avenue where Evelyn had two personal shoppers who were available with only a phone call. Evelyn was looking for clothes for the girls. She was aware she wasn't knowledgeable about adolescent and teenage girls' likes, wants, needs, and acts of desperation. Personal shopper twenty-two-year-old Dennie knew Teddy's and Tru's sizes and kept lists of the clothes, handbags, shoes, and jewelry the girls wanted. It was a game that Sophie didn't play. Teddy and Tru would go into the store and walk around with Dennie, showing her their latest "got to have" and "I will die if I don't have this." Then Evelyn went into the store, and Dennie said, "I have a few things the girls might like."

Jason followed along, saturnine and listless, sometimes commenting on an item. "Mrs. K, do you think nine-year-old Tru needs an $850 Gucci handbag?"

At that point Evelyn noticed Jason for the first time since they arrived at the store. "Oh my, you dear boy. I think you have worked hard and deserve something, too. Dennie, what do you have for my boy Royce here?"

Jason didn't correct her. Menswear was in a separate Saks, but Dennie found some unisex sweaters and such. A $499 Michael Kors cream-colored sweater and Armani $395 hooded jacket later, the "boy's" mood improved, and he made no further comments about Evelyn's purchases. They totaled $4,380 and would make Teddy and Tru giddy for a good twenty minutes, squealing "Nana, what did you get me," "I love it, Nana. You got exactly what I wanted," "Nana, you are so clever. I love the purple." Jason returned the jacket for cash.

That day having tea, Jason complained about the other two caregivers, Maricio and Pete, saying they were lazy and left the lion share of the work for him.

"Who has a lion?" she asked.

"I just told you, Pete and Maricio. There is no lion."

Evelyn's erratic brain function drove Jason nuts.

"I can't imagine such a thing." She reached for another scone, even though she had told Jason she was only going to eat one. "What do they do?"

How was Jason going to describe tasks that she would understand?

Evelyn put jam and clotted cream on top of the scone and licked her fingers, something she could only do in her home with Jason present. She trusted Jason.

She attempted to talk, but she had too much food in her mouth to be understood. Jason waited with what he believed was a thoughtful look on his face, waited for her to swallow all that brain-clogging mush.

The next morning at 6:45 a.m., pumped full of information Jason had repeatedly drilled into her about the other caregivers, Evelyn was wearing black linen pants, a pullover top, and black and gold sandals. Each day one of the caregivers laid out her clothes because Evelyn, who her entire life had been a clotheshorse, had lost the ability to dress herself in the clothes she loved. Left to her own devices, she would wear her bra on the outside of her sweaters, would put on several layers of clothes in the middle of August.

She stood in the foyer so she wouldn't miss Royce before he left for the office. She stopped him as he was ready to walk out the door, coffee thermos and *Wall Street Journal* in hand.

"Royce, I demand you fire the caregivers, except for Jason." Her demand sounded like a brood of baby chicks.

Royce, in his charcoal Giorgio Armani suit, Hugo Boss white sea island cotton shirt, Boss black and red raw silk tie, and Prada black loafers, believed he could allot five minutes to comprehend, analyze, and act upon his mother's complaint. "Why should I fire Maricio and Pete and keep Jason?"

"Because —" Evelyn was prepared. She understood the dynamics of her son's budgeting of time in one-minute increments and need to question any request, suggestion, and directive placed before him, but she couldn't remember where he was going. "—I have learned Maricio and Pete are stealing from me. Jason is completely trustworthy."

She got Royce's attention with her allegation of theft.

"What have they stolen?" he asked.

"What?"

"You said they've stolen from you. What have they taken?"

"Hmmm, I wonder—" Evelyn said.

"Mother, focus," Royce said.

She thought he sounded so much like his father. She remembered Jason saying to her, "I think sometimes your son forgets about you. If it weren't for me, no one would take care of you." Evelyn thought of Royce now: in command, authoritative, like her husband had been. But Royce not wanting to be with her? She thought of Royce as a young boy when he raced in the house after school, shouting "Mater, where are you, Mater?" Some of the boys at Royce's private day school thought it was stylish—and hilarious—to refer to their mothers as "Mater." Royce told her about his day while eating the peanut butter cookies she made for him every day, banging his black with white flares Adidas Superstars against the chair leg, the banging louder as he ate a cookie, his dark green knee socks somewhere around his ankles. *Why did his school insist on knee socks with sneakers?* Evelyn wondered.

"Royce, please do as I ask. Jason said he knows two trustworthy caregivers to take Maricio's and Pete's place. In fact, Jason can train them."

"All right, Mother. I will have my assistant Lew look into it." Royce was making no effort to hide his looking at his Movado black-faced watch with diamonds at the twelve, three, six and nine positions. He picked up his Hermes briefcase, kissed his mother on the forehead, walked out the door, and left Evelyn standing in the foyer wondering why she was there.

Royce's assistant Lew fired Pete and Maricio, not because he found any evidence of malfeasance, but because he did not want to continue to have conversations with Evelyn on the subject. Lew interviewed Jason's friends at the house, which just frosted Evelyn because she believed she should conduct the interviews. She picked off an offending piece of lint from her baby blue St. John sweater and pants in Santana wool, as she hung around in the foyer. She waited for each of the interviews to be concluded in the living room. As each candidate came out of the meeting, Evelyn moved with a quickness she had not thought possible because of arthritis in her left hip. She introduced herself and gave each of the applicants a wink while shaking his or her hand. She was happy to see one of the caregivers was a woman, because, although she enjoyed her talks with Jason, she missed having a hen party. Evelyn and Alma talked for a few minutes, standing in the foyer.

"Where are your people from, Alma dear?"

"Wisconsin. I broke ranks and moved to California after I graduated from college. Year after year I watched the Rose Parade on TV. It was January, and the sun was shining on the floats. People in the stands wore light jackets or short sleeves. I decided I would come out here and find out for myself if it was as wonderful as it looked on TV. You know, the American Dream California-style."

Evelyn scrutinized Alma, who was brunette with blonde woven through. Her hair was braided. She had brown eyes and soft brown skin like toast. Her best feature was her smile that had the added benefit of making her eyes look happy.

"I would like you to work for me, dear," Evelyn said.

"Ma'am, I would take good care of you."

Chapter Forty-Three

After Nichol had been gone fourteen days, Royce opened his email, and there among 129 other emails were two from Pierre Frere. Royce was ready to delete them when he stopped. The name looked French and was not from any of his French contacts. He opened the first email:

Royce: I have the luxury of sending you two emails, so one will be for you to read to my girls, and this one is for you. I sweet talked my way into using Pierre's email. That and $50.00. You see, you are very precious for me to spend $50 for two emails. I miss you.

It is heartbreaking here. People dig through the broken pieces of concrete that used to be houses or businesses, looking for someone alive. I think 'I will tell Royce about this,' but you aren't here. Phone service is sporadic. Telecommunication companies are focusing their capabilities on NGOs (non-governmental groups, such as International Child Care) so that medical operations can communicate with out-of-country doctors, pharmaceutical companies, hospitals, in-country clinics. The need is so great for everything.

There are also companies that have brought in satellite equipment and set up sites where people can make a free three-minute call anywhere in the world. But you should see the lines of people who wait to make calls. Some people pay for someone to stand in their place in line. Other people in line get mad Haitian style. Everywhere people think that someone else gets something they do not get—a tent, a bottle of water, a phone call—and the already tense days escalate into fights and killings. This amid generosity I have not seen before. If someone has two small bottles of water, that person will share with a stranger.

I found my parents. At the time of the earthquake, they were at International Child Care's Grace Children's Hospital in Port-au-Prince. The same hospital I went to back in 2001. During the quake nurses led the children out of the buildings into an open lot. No one could communicate with the hospital for three days. Whoever was at the hospital during the quake stayed. They used the generators sparingly, because they didn't know how long they would have to get by with the amount of fuel they had. As soon as people came back to work, they relieved the nurses who did not know the status of their own homes.

My parents went into the hills to bring out injured people or to treat them in their villages. Staff at Grace had an idea where they were going, but not exactly. They simply rode off on a Yamaha they borrowed from the hospital with a full tank of gas. I went into the hills with a nurse who travels to the remote clinics International Child Care set up pre-quake. He wanted to see the amount of damage done to the clinics. We found my parents, and I was so relieved. I didn't know the extent of my worry until I found them. They had slept only a few hours since they went in-country. I was able to give them relief so they could sleep, but they were back at it within a few hours. My parents and I rode back to Port-au-Prince and went to their house. Street after street was filled with debris and bodies. Some died at the time of the quake, others died afterward because their homes were demolished, and they hadn't been able to get a tent (priority going to the elderly and families with young children) and so were sleeping literally in the streets. Dangerous.

Back to my parents, they refused to stay in Port-au-Prince. They said they would not leave the village permanently until other medical personnel relieved them or they treated every person. I had no choice but to stay with them. I am now back in Port-au-Prince. I came into the city to get medical supplies and food. I did not see evidence of efforts to clean up where buildings were destroyed. I have heard that large front end loaders and dump trucks are coming by ship from the U.S.

I was given the name Pierre Frere as having Internet service in his home. He has made donations to ICC many times. He said it was an honor for him to help people who were treating the injured. An honor and $50.

I do not know when I will return to Los Angeles. The need here is so great. This is where I have to be. I could not sit in your beautiful home with all the food and electrical power available and know the need here. I do not want to sit on the phone all day soliciting money. Being here is my small contribution. I am going back in-country to serve the people too ill, old, and poor to come into Port-au-Prince to be treated. Also, people in the hills are afraid someone will steal their meager belongings while they are gone.

I miss you. Did I already say that? I think about you no matter what I am doing. When I walk for five miles in the hills and jungle to find injured people, I think of you. When I treat a person with multiple cuts and abrasions that have been untreated for over two weeks, I want to tell you what I have seen, and I think about you. I think about your telling me the dissolution is waiting for the clock to run out. You cannot respond to this email because I will not be returning to Pierre's home. I do not want to overstay my welcome.

Royce, I promise that I will call or email you as soon as I find another Internet provider or find an operable phone.

As soon as I can...
Nichol
Royce's hands trembled.

The second email from Pierre Frere read:

Hello, my darling beauties and Royce:

First, thank you for the thoughtful gifts you gave me. Tru, I love the whistle. I am wearing it around my neck on a chain. The babies I am treating like to blow it and make ear-piercing "whoos." Teddy, thank you for the photo book. I show my patients my beautiful family. Sophie, thank you for the journal. Sometimes there is no paper to write chart notes. I have been using my journal. Plus, it gives me a way to remember what is happening here. My days are so busy, I might forget.

I miss you. I hope you know I would not spend time away from you if it were not important. People are dying here from lack of food, water, and shelter. They exist in the streets or outer edges of crop fields. Medical personnel are flying into the country every day, but the need is still great. But, Sophie, stay at school. I will tell you when I think it's safe for you to be here. If you girls could make an announcement or put up flyers at school that Haiti needs doctors, nurses, technicians, medical supplies and money, that would be helpful. People should not give to a charity they have never heard of before. Pirates crop up overnight taking money that only goes to themselves. If you want an organization to support, there is International Child Care, which has a hospital in Port-au-Prince, Haiti, and clinics in Haiti and the Dominican Republic. ICC has been in Haiti about 40 years. If you need more information, call ICC-USA. I think it's in Michigan.

I hope you are being nice to Emaline and Kristina. Give them a chance. They are in a new environment and taking care of new people. Be on your best behavior, because if you're not, I will hear about it. And love your brother while he is there.

A man allowed me some time on the Internet, and I need to leave now.

I will call or email again when I have access to a phone or Internet. Do not reply to this email, because I will not be here to get any messages.

Girls, I love you. Please take care of your father.
Nic

Royce looked at his watch. The girls were in school. He forwarded the second email to Sophie. He planned to call when Teddy and Tru got home and read the second email to them. He decided not to tell them about the first email.

Three weeks later on a Saturday afternoon, Royce was in the study, reviewing Phelan's latest letter concerning the proposed settlement to Tamra. It seemed that finally by giving her a sum of money with a lot of zeros she would be gone. Except that she was unable to make decisions while she was in the hospital. Except that she could not take care of Morgan.

The telephone rang, and in some cavern of the 31,500 square foot dwelling Lindy got the phone. She buzzed Royce. "Nichol for you, Mr. Kallas."

"Oh, right, got it. Teddy, Tru," he called on the intercom.

"Hello?" Royce's voice sounded like it had gone on a long hike.

"Royce, can you hear me?" Nichol asked.

Royce put the phone on speaker. "Yes, we can hear you. Teddy and Tru are here with me."

The three of them stood leaning toward the phone speaker.

"You guys should see the telephone equipment. It looks like a combination of space age and ancient history. I think Alexander Graham Bell would be proud. Enough of that. How are you? What have you been doing?" Nichol said.

"We're here missing you," Teddy said. "Tell us where you are."

"I am at Hôpital Albert Schweitzer, about three hours north of Port-au-Prince, that is, if you have four good tires, which no one has." She could not stop talking. "I have been here since I left the hills. All the doctors and nurses who are coming to Haiti go to Port-au-Prince, but there are needs all over this country. This hospital is operating on patients eighteen hours a day. A lot of amputations. I'm sorry. I start talking and cannot stop. I miss you all so much. You are so dear to me."

"We can hardly function without you here. Emaline and Kristina are doing their best, but they cannot replace you," Royce said. "When are you coming home?" *Please say you are coming home.*

Nichol did not speak for a moment. They thought they had lost the call. "Nichol, are you there?" Royce asked.

"Yes, I am here. You cannot imagine what it is like here. People walk for ten-twelve hours to get here. They have the stump of an arm or leg covered in a dirty towel. They lost limbs after a cement block wall caved in during or after the earthquake. Haiti isn't known for building according to code. Women are giving birth in the dirt. They need us. I cannot leave. I love you so much, and I cannot come home yet."

Teddy and Tru had started crying as soon as they heard Nichol's voice quiver. Tru put her hands over her mouth and squeezed her eyes shut. Royce's eyes filled with tears when Nichol said she could not leave. He wanted her home, and it was physically painful that they were apart.

"How about if we come to you?" Royce said.

"Where would you stay? What would you do here? There isn't a Motel 6 up the road to stay in. No Hiltons. No malls," Nichol said with an edge in her voice.

Royce wondered if she was getting in a couple of digs, as if what she was doing mattered, and the way Royce and his children lived was irrelevant. No, his loneliness was getting to him.

"I know you are right, Nic. We just miss you so much," he said.

"And I miss you, too. I will be able to call you every week—or so—for a few minutes. Royce, you have not told me about your acquisition of the railroad in Honduras. Did you buy it?" Nichol said.

"Yes, yes, we did. I have almost forgotten about work."

"Nichol?" Tru said. "Do you get to hold the new babies? Do they get sick because they were born in the dirt?"

"Yes, I do get to hold the babies. There is an obstetric—that is for babies—department at the hospital. Guys, I have got to end this call. Royce, I have a big favor to ask you."

"Sure, what is it?"

"Do you think you could pay for the phone calls? It is a great expense for the hospital for me to make these calls," Nichol said.

"Yes, how would I do that? Do you want a credit card number?"

"No. Call the Pittsburgh office of the hospital and get the details. Look up the hospital on the Internet. It is hospital without the "s," Hôpital Albert Schweitzer. Look, I love you and want to be home with you."

"We love you, too," Teddy said.

"Me, too," said Tru.

———

"Me, too," said Royce.

When the call ended, the three of them looked at each other, like "Now what?"

The girls had paid attention when Royce said he loved Nichol.

On Monday Royce gave instructions to Tiffany to find the hospital on the Internet and find out how to make a donation. He asked that the donation be in Nichol's name and that a portion of the donation compensate the hospital for phone calls to the U.S. Tiffany handled the wire transfer with Royce's bank. The woman in Pittsburgh said that the cost of the calls was about thirty dollars. He said he was fine with the amount.

According to Royce's instructions Tiffany handled the transfer of $1,000,000 to the hospital.

Chapter Forty-Four

Life proceeded whether Royce was prepared or not. Tru expressed to Royce that they needed a larger swimming pool. She wanted to be on the synchronized swimming team at the 2016 Olympic games. According to Tru, the "old" pool, while fine for her home practice with the Los Angeles Synchronized Swim Club, was not large enough to train for the Olympics. The new pool measured eighty-two feet by 164 feet, truly Olympic sized.

Tru then cajoled her father into hiring Marina Kazlosovich as her personal coach. Marina was on the Soviet Union's 1992 Olympic synchronized swimming team. In 1993, Marina, while traveling to California to attend a wedding, told the customs officials at San Francisco Airport she wanted to defect to the United States. Apparently the United States had a shortage of swimmers because Marina and her swim fins were admitted. She missed the 1996 games because she was waiting to receive U.S. citizenship. She was a member of the 2000 and 2004 U.S. teams, where she won bronze medals. She might turn Tru into a Communist Olympic synchronized swimmer, because, although she fled the USSR, she found Communism in theory to be more stable for the masses than whatever it was the United States called its political system.

The next time Nichol called, Royce talked to her before telling the girls she was calling. "The divorce settlement—the financial part—we are making progress. Right now it is a matter of who blinks first. Tamra gave me power over her finances, which puts me in a weird position. I am petitioning the court to have a conservator appointed, someone to be responsible for her finances, so there is not a

———

conflict of interest. Tamra is still in the hospital, and Morgan is still here. According to Laramie, the doctors aren't giving her a discharge date yet. I gather Tamra has more issues than just the baby. I talked to Phelan about that power of attorney naming me guardian over Morgan. He said I can petition the court to be relieved of my duties as guardian, but he doesn't think I would prevail because, short of putting Morgan into the foster care system, there is no one else to take him. Since I have the resources to care for him, a judge would say, 'you are doing a great job. Keep it up.'" Royce realized he hadn't taken a breath.

"I am sorry you are going through that," Nichol said. "Please keep Morgan until Tamra can take him back. Please, for me."

"How are you faring?" Royce said.

"I am overly tired because of being in-country and coming back to the hospital, and then going back in. I still send people to the hospital with crushed limbs that need to be amputated."

"I am going to call the girls now. I love you and hope to have good news next week."

As Teddy and Tru told Nichol about their week, Royce noticed they were telling her things they had not mentioned to him. He thought he had been making big improvements in communicating with them and being on top of their school and social lives. There was still so much to learn.

Nichol called two weeks later. They spent Saturday at home waiting for her to call. The first thing she did, in a tired, scratchy voice, was to thank Royce. "When I asked if you would pay for the phone calls, I did not realize you were going to go over the top."

"Well, I am an overachiever."

"The donation—in my name no less—has been the talk of the hospital for a couple of days. That donation is going to make a significant difference to people here."

"What else do you need, besides a return ticket to Los Angeles or a plane?" Royce asked.

"Oh no, I am not going to ask for anything for a long time," Nichol said.

"Please ask for a return ticket," he said.

"Nic, Nic, I got a part in *West Side Story*. I'm going to be Maria," Teddy said.

"A blonde Maria! Congratulations."

"I have a Russian swimming coach, and she said I have real potential," Tru said.

"That's my girl," Nichol said. "Okay, Royce. What have you done that was especially good this week?"

"I, I, showed up," he said. "How is that?"

"A little lame, I think. The girls beat you. How is Sophie?"

"She calls every day wanting news about you. We read everything on the Internet. Haiti certainly has a volatile history," Royce said.

"Nic, how many babies were born this week?" Tru asked.

"Five, honey. Four in the hospital and one in the field."

"There was a baby born in a field?" asked Tru.

"In field means that it was at the woman's home or village clinic. The baby was born at the woman's house. It was a baby girl."

"Nic, we need you here." It was Teddy.

"Oh, Teddy. You do not know how torn I am between wanting to be home with all of you and wanting to make a small contribution at the hospital. I have arguments with myself all the time."

They traded stories from the past two weeks, and then Royce said, "I would like to talk to Nichol for a moment alone. Is that okay with you girls?"

Teddy gave Tru a "be quiet" glare. "That's cool," Teddy said. "Good bye, Nic. We'll talk to you next week. We love you."

"Love you, Nic," said Tru.

"Love you both back. Tell Sophie I love her."

Teddy grabbed Tru's hand, led her into her room, closed the door, and put one finger up to her lips. She smoothly and swiftly picked up the handset and pushed the button for the extension of Nichol's call. They sat together with the phone between their heads.

"…what I am doing in the office half the time," Royce said. "I swear, if you do not come home pretty soon, I am coming there and picking you up myself."

"I have been thinking that I should set a definite date. That way, you and I will know what to expect in the meantime. I was thinking Christmas," Nichol said.

"Christmas?" Royce said. "Christmas? It is not even Easter yet. Please tell me you are not being serious!"

"I'm going to end the call now," Nichol said. "I have been feeling a little out of it for the past couple of days."

"You can't stay until the end of the year. Are you okay?" Royce asked.

"Yes, just a little upset stomach. I will be fine."

"I love you."

"I love you best."

Teddy mouthed "I love you" to Tru, who put both hands over her mouth and then put them on her heart and cocked her head to one side.

Nichol laughed. "Ah, a competition for loving. Please kiss the girls for me. I will talk to you soon." She ended the call.

The girls touched their lips together ever so slightly.

The calls from Haiti were erratic. Nichol sometimes was in-country and did not come back to the hospital for two weeks. Teddy became convinced Nichol was not coming home. During each call, Royce and Nichol talked about their loneliness.

Both Tru and Teddy were showing how the separation from Nichol affected them. They had difficulty in subjects in school they generally sailed through. Royce asked Emaline to hire tutors for them. The girls were short with each other and sometimes would not help Emaline find something or, when she asked them to straighten up their rooms, they ignored her, a Teddy-like behavior inherited by Tru.

Royce told Teddy he had to go out of town on business, which was not unusual, except that one of the days was also Emaline's day off. Emaline said she could not switch the day, since she was helping her daughter who had a high-risk pregnancy. Royce asked Teddy to take care of her sister and said Kristina and at least one of the housekeepers would be in the house at all times.

"Sure," Teddy said, "I'll watch out for Tru." She raced to her bedroom and her cellphone to start planning a party. She whispered conversations full of giggles and "Oh my God!" On a three-way call with her friends Marcy and Xandy, Teddy said, "My dad's gonna to be away for like five days, and the nanny's gonna be gone, too. We're going to have a party to celebrate my birthday."

"No way," said Xandy.

"Way," Teddy said.

It started out with several of Teddy's girlfriends from Harvard-Westlake and the boys they hung with. Then someone told friends from local high schools who had friends in college, who told a bunch of fraternity brothers and little sisters. Word got out about the party, and it was on.

Marcy and Xandy went to Teddy's early in the afternoon to make the tennis court look festive with birthday decorations.

"You know, nobody's going to care about decorations. They're going to want to get wasted and listen to tunes," Xandy said.

"I hope your dad has good homeowner's insurance," Marcy said.

"Why would you even like think about that, you know?" Teddy said, while she removed the net.

Xandy giggled. She ran around the court retrieving random tennis balls.

"Because there are people coming to this house tonight, who will see how big it is, and who might get funny ideas, not ha-ha funny, about making some easy money," Marcy said, making significant eye contact with Teddy.

"Are you planning to go to law school after college?" Xandy said.

"Probably. I dunno. Maybe. But, anyway, okay?" Marcy said. She shrugged her shoulders up toward her ears.

The girls agreed they didn't want to do any cooking and settled on simple munchies. Xandy said, "You better get salty and sweet."

Using Teddy's dad's credit card they called Trader Joes and ordered bags of popcorn, cans of assorted nuts, bags of tortilla chips, fresh salsa from the deli, limes, lemons, bags of assorted candy bars and a birthday cake. They asked some of their friends to bring beer (and to include 64 calorie beer because all the girls would be on diets). The girls' cellphones were beeping like a roomful of bookies during the Super Bowl. They shrieked from time to time, reading text messages.

"Teddy, do you have any idea how many people are going to be here tonight?" Marcy said.

"No, why?" Teddy said.

"Aren't you worried about people we don't know trashing the place?" Marcy said.

"We aren't going to be in the house. I will lock all the doors, so no one can get in. Same with the pool house," Teddy said.

"Garage, Teddy," said Marcy. "Cars, expensive cars."

"And the horses," Xandy said, twirling in circles around the tennis court.

"We'll have the music and booze out on the tennis court, so they will like follow their noses and land where we want them to be," said Teddy.

After the food was delivered, they sat down on the patio to smoke a joint. It was a beautiful spring day, temperature in the seventies, sun on their faces.

"Teddy, this party is a little out of character for you. Why are you doing it?" said Marcy, handing the roach clip to Xandy.

"Because everyone needs to par-tay!" said Teddy, throwing her arms into the air. "And it's my birthday! My family isn't even here for my birthday. Like so obvious."

"Yeah. What else?" Marcy said, waving her hand to move the smoke out of her face. "Bathrooms, we need bathrooms."

"Look. I just want to let loose, you know. My dad won't be here. My nanny won't be here. Nichol won't—" Teddy stopped and passed the clip to Marcy without taking a hit.

"When is Nichol coming home?" Xandy said.

"We don't know. She said she doesn't know. I guess things are pretty bad there. I don't know, man. The whole thing like freaks me out, you know," Teddy said.

"A lot of celebrities are doing special shows to raise money for Haiti." Marcy said. "That's it! We should charge admission to come to this party, and we'll use the money we get for Haiti."

"How cool would that be?" Xandy said, stretching.

"Yeah, okay, that's a good idea," Teddy said. "We won't set an amount. We'll ask people to give whatever they can."

Surreptitiously, so they weren't on Kristina or Lindy's radar, the girls changed clothes three or four times, sometime trading outfits with each other. They were excited and squealed like fans in a mosh pit. Tru followed them around—even though Teddy told her to bug off—and studied their demeanor for future reference. The party girls had dinner with Tru to make it look like a regular night. Tru said she was going to tell, but they swore her to silence on penalty of totally embarrassing her at school.

The night was blue black, no wind and no rain. A perfect night for a party. About 8:00 p.m. some of their friends, who brought their friends, started showing up. The girls stopped squealing and put out snobby cool private girls' school vibes, which they had perfected. As more people arrived, when the girls were in close proximity to each other, they made funny faces, like *look what we did.*

"Teddy, some people are doing mescaline buttons

and acid. I hope no one melts," Marcy said, talking in Teddy's ear so she could be heard over the music.

"Yeah, I don't want anyone thinking Velvet and Shampoo are unicorns with wings, you know," said Teddy. The three girls giggled. Teddy had already put the horses in the barn and padlocked the door.

The music was good. Someone decided to be DJ. He just went through CD after CD, plugging them into the dual CD player. People danced. Teddy danced with everyone and anyone, latching onto a couple of random guys. She danced by herself and looked up at the sliver of a moon, sharp enough to cut, as she turned around and around with her arms above her head as though she were going to pull down the sky. One guy was really old, like over 30. "So why did you come tonight?" Teddy asked the guy. He said his name, but the music was too loud to hear what he said. It sounded like "Morgan." She said her brother's name was Morgan. She introduced herself as Theodora.

"I was following the trail of the mescaline," Morgan said. "I hadn't done that in a long time. There's a semi-famous book *The Teachings of Don Juan* about this guy's experiences with mescaline. It's a cult favorite," the guy said in between songs. He said other stuff that Teddy couldn't hear, something about a man doing mescaline buttons and turning into a crow. He asked her to go for a walk, and she declined, with a smile.

Teddy thought they were pulling off the party with no one in the house aware of what was going on in the tennis court, but at about 10:00 Kristina found Teddy standing on the perimeter of the tennis court.

"Teddy, what are you doing? There are cars parked three and four deep out on the street. Does your father know about this? He didn't say anything to me about it."

"Oh, he's like cool with it."

"You're just lucky there's no neighbor at the end of the cul-de-sac. I think you should have your guests leave."

Xandy walked up to them. "Hey, Kristina. How's the baby?" She held her beer bottle behind her back.

"The baby is fine." Kristina showed Xandy the baby monitor. "Of course, I probably can't hear it out here."

"We're fine," Teddy said. "Why don't you go back in the house in case Morgan wakes up."

"Thanks for checking on us," Xandy said. "That's awesome."

Teddy and Xandy watched Kristina leave the tennis court and walk toward the house.

"Do you think she'll snitch on us?" Xandy said, taking a sip of her beer.

"I dunno. There's no one to tell now. Like what's she going to do, call the police?" Teddy said.

"Who's calling the police?" Marcy said as she joined them. She had a small bag of popcorn.

"No one. Morgan's nurse came out here checking on us," Teddy said. "I think she was more worried about all the cars on the street than all the people here." She stuck her hand in Marcy's bag of popcorn.

For reasons that no one could explain, there were no incidents at the party, no one fell into the hole where the pool used to be, and the party broke up by 2:00 a.m., more or less, not because they ran out of booze, but because most of them were in school and had classes later that day. When the crowd was reduced to a couple dozen people, Marcy turned the music off and said "good night" to the stragglers. When the three girls were alone, they looked at all the beer bottles and cans and pizza boxes littering every surface on the tennis court and the tables on the patio. Teddy said she would get a gardener to clean up everything in the morning.

"Guys, it felt so good to not care about everything for a few hours. So good," said Teddy.

"I'm glad it helped you," Marcy said, sitting on a swivel chair at a glass top table, nursing a soda.

"Yeah, way cool," Xandy said.

"I'll go back to being Miss Responsible tomorrow," Teddy said.

Teddy did ask the gardener to clean up the mess before she left for school that morning, and then she basically forgot about how it looked. Friends and kids she didn't even know came up to her at school and told her how awesome the party was.

That afternoon she was in the house helping Tru with her homework—and almost nodding off because of lack of sleep—when Lindy told her she had a call from her father.

"I wanna talk to him, too," Tru said, running after Teddy as she walked toward the game room.

"Hi, Dad," Teddy said.

"Hello, Theodora," Royce said. Oh Oh. He called her Theodora.

"How are you?" she said.

"I'm fine. How are you today?" he said.

"Okay." She was not going to give him an opening. He was going to have to do it on his own.

"Tell me about the party." It was a demand, not a request.

"I had a party in the tennis court with some of my friends," Teddy said, "to celebrate my birthday. You weren't here for my birthday."

"You must have a lot of friends. I understand there were over two hundred people at our house. Please explain,"

Royce said.

"I think maybe some of my friends brought some people."

"And who supplied the alcohol?" he said.

Wow! Who ratted me out? she thought. She glared at Tru. "Some guys brought beer."

"And you were drinking?"

OMG! "Well, I had a taste of a beer," she said meekly, somewhat honestly. "And it was only lite beer."

"What have Nichol and I instructed you about drinking and letting your friends drink at our house? You are fourteen years old, Theodora!"

"You've told me that I can't. But what does it matter what Nichol said? She's not here anymore," Teddy cried, not dramatic tears to get her way, but honest tears.

"Oh Teddy. She is not going to be gone forever. She will be back," Royce said.

"When? When will she come home?" Teddy cried, all the fun of the past night dissipated, like vapor.

"Honey, I do not know when she will be home. We have to talk about the party. I know that the only people who came in the house were Marcy and Xandy. You used good sense there. What was not good sense was having the party at all. You purposely chose to do it when Emaline and I were both gone. I had specifically asked you to take care of your sister."

"I did take care of her!" she gulped. "I helped her with her homework a little bit, and we had dinner together." She looked at Tru as if to confirm what she had said. Tru started to walk away, and Teddy grabbed her by the arm. Teddy was going to find out if Tru was the snitch.

"You are only fourteen," he repeated. "You cannot go to a party unless Nichol and I approve, much less have a party at home with alcohol."

"I checked on Tru a couple of times during the night. She was zoned out," Teddy said in her defense. "And Kristina was here."

"Teddy, please. Own up to this. I would like to get past this, but not until you take responsibility for having the party without my permission, serving alcohol to minors and without adult supervision—"

"There were some adults there." She regretted saying that as soon as the words came out of her mouth. "I didn't give alcohol to minors. It was just there. People got their own drinks. And my friends from school went home early because we all had school today. Dad, do you want to hear something good? At the party we charged for people to come in, and we collected $2,348. We're going to donate it to a charity in Haiti. We asked people to kick in whatever they could. I'm going to tell Nichol, and I hope it will make her happy."

"Teddy, you are infuriating. You make good decisions and bad decisions at the same time. Since you are not volunteering to be responsible, I will do it for you. You are grounded and no cell phone for a month—"

"Dad, you can't take my cellphone. No, please. Ground me longer, but don't take my phone. I'll die."

If Royce was able to analyze his tight throat, rocks in his chest, pain in his jaw, and slight tremors in his hands, he would have concluded that he was having a heart attack or his feelings of anger, frustration, concern, confusion and love had him by the gonads. Royce, though, was not having a heart attack, and he was unable to assess his feelings. Because Tamra was still in the hospital, the settlement portion of the divorce had ground to a halt, and Nichol was

4,000 miles and 180 days away. Although he continued to run and work every day, his only respite was daydreaming. He remembered scenes from years past and attempted to resuscitate them to the present day, especially the days on the yacht and the desert and Telluride houses.

Royce remembered conversations with Nichol that were precious moments.

At the end of May Tamra was still in the hospital, and Morgan was still in the nursery. The girls loved playing with him, walking him in Tru's buggy, feeding him.

Royce left his office one morning at 11:00 to meet Teddy's teachers at Harvard-Westlake. He had four half-hour appointments set up. He always got good reports about Teddy. He wanted to see how she was handling school with Emaline tutoring her and to get information about her classes beyond her "it's cool" response to any questions. Her teachers confirmed that her grades had fallen in all her classes except dance and musical theatre.

The only questionable remarks came from teachers about Teddy's apparent efforts to modify her school uniform.

"Mr. Kallas, there is one issue of which you need to be aware," Teddy's social science teacher Mrs. Skinner said. "Teddy has been warned three times by me that she wasn't conforming to the rules related to uniforms. Specifically, about wearing her skirts too short or wearing high heels instead of her loafers."

"I can't imagine she's the only girl to test the rules about appearance," Royce said.

"Oh, yes. There is a particular group of girls." She stopped, thought about saying more.

"And?" he asked and looked at his watch.

Mrs. Skinner continued. "Teddy is a card-carrying member of a group that flaunts the rules."

"There, you see. Teddy probably just wants to conform to her friends' short skirts."

"Mr. Kallas. Teddy is the ringleader."

"Teddy? At home I notice her wearing too much makeup. She is allowed to wear lip, what is it, the shiny stuff. Not lipstick."

"Do you mean lip gloss? That's the only makeup we allow the girls to wear," Mrs. Skinner said.

"Yes, that is it. Lip gloss. Well, I have seen her with eye shadow. We tell her she is not allowed, and she says 'Dad, all my friends wear eye shadow.' So, I think she is just copying her friends. I do not think she is the instigator."

"However it happens, she must follow the rules."

Royce agreed and left. One of the other teachers had a similar complaint, and he decided with as much enthusiasm as a quarterback running toward defensive ends that he would talk to Teddy. He was convinced, though, that Teddy was following someone else and was not, what did Mrs. Skinner call her, the "ringleader." And he decided he had to get on her about her grades.

Later that day, Royce, staring out the windows with a view of multi-story buildings and the mountains in the background under a vibrant blue sky as though it had been painted with fluorescent colors, decided he would have the conversation with Teddy about her school uniform over the phone, instead of in person. Although he wished it were not true, he was a sucker for Teddy and Tru, and his stern in control visage deserted him in their presence.

"Hi, Dad. How come you're calling me?" Teddy was watching a movie in the theatre.

Oh, Teddy, he thought. *How do I ever make it up to you?* "Hello, Theodora."

"Boy, I must be in some trouble still if you're like calling me Theodora. What did I do this time? Did you talk to my teachers?"

"Yes, I had the meetings, *Teddy*. Your teachers were very complimentary about your participation in the classroom, the assignments you complete, but your test scores and your oral presentations are not measuring up to your past performance."

"I'm glad you had like good meetings. Bye." Teddy was conditioned to having only brief conversations with her father.

"Not so fast, Teddy. Did you hear me about your grades? They are lower than what I know you are capable of, aren't they? Also, evidently you have been modifying your school uniforms. I heard two complaints today. You know I pay a lot of money to send you to that school." Royce was always in steady waters when he injected money into the conversation.

"What do you mean? I wear my uniform to school every day. I don't like it, but I wear it."

"Apparently, you have been wearing heels rather than your required shoes," Royce knew with certitude she was not supposed to be wearing heels. "Those uniforms were not cheap, Teddy. Why are you deliberately violating the rules?"

"One day I wore heels because they were brand new, and I had to like show them off. It was just one day. And I don't shorten my skirts. I like kind of roll them up. You know. That's all."

"Teddy, as your teachers confirmed to me today, you are an intelligent, resourceful, and an *imaginative* girl.

Please do not be disrespectful to me pretending that you aren't shortening your skirts, however you are accomplishing it. And your grades. You haven't answered my question."

"I like don't know, okay. I'm just doing what I can," Teddy said, sullenly.

"Thank you." Thinking he knew the reason for part of Teddy's distress, he said, "I know how sad you are that Nichol isn't home yet."

"Are you sure she's coming back? I like really miss her."

"Yes, I am sure. I am sure it will be soon." He put his elbow on his desk and rested his head in his hand. "Soon, sweetheart. And, Teddy, do you think you could stop saying like all the time?" It reminded him too much of Tamra inserting that word into every sentence.

At the beginning of June, Nichol called after a silence of several weeks. Tru and Teddy joined Royce.

Royce said, "You have been there five months."

Nichol told Royce that Haiti was in the middle of its rainy season.

"I thought it was ninety degrees and dry year-round," Royce said.

"No, our rains begin in May and lead to floods and landslides until July. Rivers of mud flow down denuded hills like lava. You should see it."

Royce was not interested in her recitation of the weather. She did not seem to zone in on the impatience in his voice.

"We get rains at night. Torrents of rock and gray mud sweep away tents and people's possessions. I saw one man who sifted through clay mud one morning, and the only thing he found was one of his daughter's shoes."

Teddy had been quiet. It seemed she was drifting further and further away.

Nichol continued to talk about the rain. "Mud is everywhere. It fills every drainage ditch, every walking path, every crevice in the concrete rubble. That breeds mosquitos."

"I ask you this question every time you call, and I am going to ask it again," Royce said. "When are you coming home?"

"The mosquitos lead to malaria. The number of patients increases exponentially. I am Haitian. This is my responsibility."

"But—" he said.

"No, 'but,' Royce. You would not leave one of your companies in distress. You would not leave the girls uncared for. In the same way, I must minister to my people's broken, twisted, weakened bodies."

Nichol sensed anger and frustration, especially from Teddy, even though—or because—she did not speak.

"I am going to end the call now," Nichol said. "I haven't been feeling well."

"Are you okay?" Teddy finally spoke.

"Yes, my darling girl. Just a small problem in my lower region. I will be fine," she said.

"What's 'the lower region'?" Tru asked.

"I'll tell you later, Tru," Teddy said.

Chapter Forty-Five

Evelyn's caregiver Jason wanted her money. Pure and simple. He needed an attorney to prepare an amendment to Evelyn's trust or to write a new one. He didn't know any attorneys. He had kind of asked around with his associates with no luck. One day he was stopped at a signal and saw an ad on a park bench for Luis Hernandez, Jr., Esq. He liked the slogan: "We Won't Stop Until They Beg for Mercy!" He memorized the phone number.

One day while Evelyn was taking a bath—she had started taking decapitated Barbies into the bath with her, probably stolen from Tru—Jason called Hernandez' number. A receptionist answered and put him through to Hernandez' assistant, Karleen.

"What can we do for you today, Mr. Gerard?"

"I'd like…I have a friend who needs a lawyer."

"And what are your friend's legal needs?"

To hand over all her money to me, Jason thought to himself. "She needs to have her trust redone."

"We do trusts and wills. Would you like an appointment with me? I handle all of the first-time meetings," said Karleen.

"That would be okay, I guess. When is your earliest appointment?"

Karleen looked into space for a moment. She had her calendar memorized, but if she gave him an answer too quickly, it would appear that she or Mr. Hernandez were desperate for clients. They were in fact desperate for that very thing: a real paying client.

"I have a cancellation in the morning. How about tomorrow at 9:00?"

"No, I work during the day. I get off at 4:00 in the afternoon."

"Yes, I have tomorrow at 5:00."

Jason had found the trust documents in the bottom of Evelyn's pajama drawer one day when he was snooping. He put them in the red, white, and blue gym bag he carried into the Kallas home every day.

On the day of his meeting with Karleen, he looked through the trust, most of it was gibberish to him except the Revocation section where Evelyn had the power to change her half of the trust created with her husband. She received $50,000 a month for incidentals from his portion of the trust. In the Trustee section Evelyn and Royce were co-trustees, and that was about to be changed.

For the appointment Jason wore a suit, a not-too-expensive suit, navy blue, clean, pressed, fit properly, white shirt, blue and green rep tie. He could have been going door-to-door preaching millenarian restoration Christian domination and handing out *The Watchtower*, could have been the principal of a private day school, a federal tax auditor, or could have been going to an appointment with an attorney, a crook hiding in plain sight.

Karleen came out to the reception area exactly at 5:00 p.m. They sat in her office, with faux wood paneling on the walls, ubiquitous posters of hot air balloons ascending in the desert sky, a whale rising out of the water to meet the Sun, and redwoods in northern California. A goldfish bowl with a ceramic Neptune sitting on turquoise rocks, plastic algae hanging vertically, but no goldfish, sat on Karleen's desk. He thought it would be fun to know whether she was being ironic or simply too lazy to replace the goldfish.

"What happened to your fish?" Jason asked.

"They both died, first Petey and then Elvira. I'm

evidently not a fit ichthyologist." Without trying to be covert, Jason checked out Karleen. She had golden brown skin, the color light-skinned people strived to get, playing chicken with skin cancer, but hers was natural, deep black eyes, and shoulder length straight black hair. She was wearing a pale coral suit—a color that was hers, as though she had ordered the color custom made—with a long-sleeved jacket and pencil skirt, into which she fit with architectural precision. *Boobs, butt, it is all there. And classy,* thought Jason.

"Did *you* name the fish?" Jason was having too much fun and was not getting down to business.

"No, my seven-year-old son named them. He decided what sex they were and named them. I don't blame him, though, for their deaths. Now, what can I do for you today? You spoke about a friend with a trust." So much for the fish.

"I am the friend of a ninety-year-old widowed woman. She is quite wealthy, although I am not privy to exact numbers. She has a trust, here's a copy." Jason took a thick document out of a binder he had carried to the appointment. "She would like to amend, or whatever it's called, her trust. Since she is frail, I thought I would help her out." Oh, yes, Jason wanted to help Evelyn in whatever way facilitated the money getting to him.

"Why doesn't your friend come herself? I know that you said she is frail, but if she can't leave her house or nursing home, whatever, we're more than happy to go to her," Karleen said, and she was speaking the gospel truth. Karleen and Hernandez would be ecstatic to go to Evelyn.

"I don't know. I think it might be too taxing on her even if you visit her at home. She lives with her son, daughter-in-law, and granddaughters. Can't I give you all the pertinent information?" *Can't we have a transfusion right here in the office*, Jason thought.

"If your friend gives you and us written permission to share information about her financial and legal matters, yes, you can give us information. However, she would need to sign the new trust or amendment. I'm wondering, though, uh, how are you her friend, how did you get this copy?"

"I'm her caregiver, and she gave me this copy. Her son is very controlling. He has his hands in all of her affairs. I think it scares her sometimes. I don't think she will want to meet with you, but I'll ask her and let you know. I'll call you, hopefully by tomorrow."

Karleen didn't want him to leave the office, but there was no reason to keep him any longer.

"How much would it cost for you to do an amendment?"

"I can't answer that until I know the extent of the changes your friend wants to make to her trust. An average restatement is $3,000. Could be higher or lower. You said that she is well to do. You said she is quite wealthy."

"Yes, she is."

"Can I call you tomorrow so that we can set up another visit, we hope in the lady's home?"

"No, let me call you. I'll be at work all day and will have to call you when I have a break." What Jason really wanted was Royce and Tamra out of the house before he made a call. He left Hernandez' office.

At the end of the day, Luis Hernandez, Jr., Esq. asked Karleen if there had been anything interesting in the office.

"I had a whale—no, correction, caregiver to a whale—in this afternoon," Karleen said. "He wants us to go forward without having met the woman. What do you think of that?"

"Baby, we're dying here. We've got to get some new business in the door. I've got property taxes coming due on my hog of a house. I can't unload it. My wife doesn't want me to sell it, and if I did, I wouldn't get what I put into it. And, on a *lighter* note—" Hernandez was being sarcastic, which came through in stereo, in his voice. The sound was like a cow whose udder was pulled by an amateur. His febrile face had an expression that was a close cousin to a smirk, as though he couldn't part his lips, and in trying to pull them apart, his eyes started to bug out, as though he were an owl cuckoo clock.

Upon Evelyn's death, the trust assets were bequeathed to Royce, except for personal items, such as jewelry, that was gifted to seven females, including Tamra, Sophie, Theodora, and Truesdale. In the event of Royce's death before Evelyn, the trust went to Sophie, Theodora and Truesdale, equally, to be managed by institutional trustees until their twenty-fifth birthdays.

The only time Evelyn left the house with Jason was for shopping trips and when he accompanied her to doctors' appointments.

Jason wrote on a yellow legal pad the names of each of her doctors, with a column for the doctors' specialties. He also had a column which was a "yes" or "no," whether Royce kept in touch with the doctors. Cardiologist, endocrinologist, podiatrist, ear/nose/throat, primary care, physical therapist. *There*, Jason thought, *is the answer*. Royce had never, to Jason's knowledge, called or received calls from the physical therapist. Jason made an appointment with the physical therapist, on the chance Royce checked up on him.

The next call went to Hernandez' office.

———

419

"Hello, this is Jason Gerard, Karleen."

"Nice to hear from you, Jason." Karleen keeping the enthusiasm in her voice to a minimum.

"I'd like to make an appointment with Mr. Hernandez. I'll be bringing Mrs. Kallas into the office with me. Is next Tuesday available?" Jason asked.

"Let me check." Pause. "Yes, it is. I'm going to block out two hours with Mr. Hernandez," Karleen said.

Perfecto.

Jason told Evelyn the night before her appointment with Hernandez, "We have an appointment tomorrow, so let's pick out a nice outfit (as if they all weren't nice)."

"Why am I going to the doctor?"

"Because he wants to make sure you're healthy," Jason said.

"I am healthy, and I don't have anything to wear." She stuck a naked, headless Barbie in front of her face. "Tell Barbie why I need to go to the doctor."

Jason drew a line in the sand. He would not talk to a headless doll.

For Evelyn's visits to doctors, Royce allowed Jason to use the Cadillac SUV. Jason felt it was a hedonist pleasure sitting in that car. Evelyn squawked the entire time they drove to Hernandez' office.

"Mrs. Kallas, dear. We are going to be seeing a new doctor today. All you have to do is talk to him a little bit. That would be okay, right?"

"I don't want to go to a doctor, don't want to talk to a doctor."

Jason was counting on Evelyn telling Royce that she had gone to see a doctor who only talked about money.

Royce would accept that Evelyn misinterpreted the appointment.

Evelyn walked into Hernandez' office with a pout on her face, but with the carriage of a well-bred lady.

"Hello, Mrs. Kallas. My name is Karleen," speaking as though Evelyn was hard of hearing and as though English wasn't Evelyn's native language.

As she shook hands with Karleen, Evelyn said, "You have pretty hair. Are you my doctor?"

Not understanding, Karleen shot a look at Jason to see if he might have a clue. "No, ma'am. I'm an assistant to Luis Hernandez. He's an attorney."

"So where is the doctor?" Evelyn asked, looking at Jason.

"This is my surprise to you. You like surprises, right?" Jason asked.

"Surprise." That was the sum total of Evelyn's opinion about being in an attorney's office.

"I'll take you to Mr. Hernandez now," Karleen said.

Hernandez rose from behind his desk and walked around the side. He put out his hand, having rubbed it on his pant leg, because it was sweaty. "Mrs. Kallas, I am so happy to meet you."

"Are you my doctor?" Evelyn asked.

Not being privy to the conversation in the reception area, Hernandez was confused. He looked to Karleen for help. She simply smiled, beamed actually. She thought this appointment was going to be a wild one. "No, ma'am. I'm not your doctor. I'm an attorney. I hope you will allow me to help you."

"What do I need an attorney for?" It was a fair question, one to which she would not get an answer from any of the three other people in the room. "Why do I need you?"

"Because you expressed to Jason that you wanted to make changes to your trust," Hernandez said.

Evelyn looked at Jason and then at Karleen. "You two would make a cute couple," she said, pointing first at Jason and then at Karleen, "except Jason is gay."

Jason reddened, not because she was wrong, but because he had never told a soul. His father would have beaten him senseless if he knew.

As for the other man, the man who was not a doctor, searching in her well of experience, she did not know where Mr. Hernandez, attorney, fit. Therefore, she would do the only thing appropriate: check out. Evelyn sat back straight, legs crossed neatly at the ankles, hands resting in her lap, a smile on her face, hair neatly brushed, faint bit of lip gloss (Teddy's suggestion). She looked the part, the rest was gravy.

"Mrs. Kallas, I've told Mr. Hernandez' assistant Karleen that you want to make changes to your trust," Jason said.

"Uh huh," Evelyn said.

"I wrote down the changes you told me you want to make. May I give the changes to Mr. Hernandez?" Jason asked.

"Uh huh."

Jason did indeed have a list of changes. He read them:

"Jason Gerard replaces Evelyn Royce Kallas and Royce Hamilton Kallas as trustee. Jason Gerard shall receive $10,000,000.00 (ten million dollars) annually for services rendered to Evelyn Royce Kallas Trust. The payments are due, beginning the date the changes to the trust are signed by Evelyn Royce Kallas, and annually thereafter. The rest of the trust is to remain in effect as originally signed by Evelyn

Royce Kallas." Jason realistically knew he would only have one shot at getting the money.

Hernandez said he could make the changes that Jason proposed. "Mrs. Kallas, do you want these changes to your trust?"

Another question. "Uh huh."

"I understand that it is difficult for you to get out. If you would prefer taking care of this now, rather than coming back, Karleen can have the changes made in less than an hour. There's a Denny's about a half block away if you want to stretch your legs and get a cup of coffee, or—" At that point, Hernandez' voice wandered off somewhere south of Anaheim. He was already spending his enlarged, engorged fee for this case.

Jason took Evelyn by the hand, and they walked to Denny's. He ordered a piece of cherry pie for her and coconut with whipped cream for him. And two hot teas. They had a conversation the way they had conversations every day at home, to wit, Jason told Evelyn a fact about something in the universe, and she responded, of sorts:

"A woman claims her 16-month old son can do the times table, read and write in English, and speak Thai," Jason said, smearing whipped cream over the entire surface of his pie and putting a spoonful of the whipped cream into his tea.

"It's probably not true," Evelyn said, eating her pie in ladylike proportions with her fork.

"Which part of it?" Jason asked.

"It's probably not true that she has a 16-month old son." Evelyn's word for the day was "probably."

After receiving a call from Karleen that the document was ready for Evelyn's signature, they left Denny's and returned to Hernandez' office. They were ushered into

Hernandez' office as soon as they arrived in the reception area.

"Mrs. Kallas, when you change your trust, the process is called 'restatement,' so the document we prepared for you is a Restatement of the Kallas Family Trust. You have the ability to change your half of the trust. Reginald's portion of the trust is irrevocable. It cannot be changed. Simply put, you have the ability to do whatever you want to…as long as it's legal," Hernandez cackled.

I wonder if the plants on the shelf are real or fake, Evelyn thought.

"Do you have any questions, Mrs. Kallas?" asked Karleen.

"Are those plants fake?" she asked.

The three of them were stymied as to how to proceed, because this puppy was starting to widdle on the floor.

"Mrs. Kallas, do you have any questions about what Mr. Hernandez is doing for you?" Jason asked.

"What is he doing for me? I don't want to talk to a doctor."

"Mrs. Kallas. If you could sign this Restatement here, and I will notarize it. Okay?" Karleen asked. She put a pen in Evelyn's hand and put her finger on the space for Mrs. Kallas's signature. Evelyn put the pen tip on Karleen's nail attached to the finger that was on the space for the signature. She scribbled in little circles.

Karleen was undaunted. "Evelyn, put the pen right here," as she moved Evelyn's hand to the place to sign. "How do you sign your name? Jason, help me out here. Does Mrs. Kallas have a driver's license or identification card? She does, okay. How does she sign?"

Jason took her identification card out of her wallet and handed it to Karleen.

Karleen, still holding onto Evelyn's hand over the place to sign, said, "Okay, sign Evelyn Royce Kallas. Evelyn that's right, keep going." The three of them had stopped breathing, and the universe did not exist outside of Hernandez's office. They watched the pen move oh so slowly. Like watching the birth of a baby, coming out bit by bit with each contraction, exhilaration and terror. "Okay, now Royce. Yes, like that. Good girl. Now Kallas."

Evelyn stopped writing. "Is this pen real or is it fake?" she asked.

"It's real, honey," Karleen said. "Come on, you're almost finished. And then you can go home and—"

"—take a hot bath with your Barbies," Jason finished.

"With your Barbies. Right. Okay, you've got K-A-L-L. Come on, we're on the home stretch," Karleen said, with hope in her heart. "You did it. Doesn't it feel good to have that out of the way?"

"Jason, here is an invoice for our services," Hernandez said.

"Twenty-five thousand dollars?" Jason asked.

"For expedited service and a measure of difficulty in the execution of the Restatement."

If it had been Jason's money that was paying, he would have put his fist through Hernandez' face and then tipped over the fish bowl on his way out.

They left the office in the Cadillac to ride home.

"Did you like that doctor? Jason asked.

"She didn't answer me about the pen. It might not have been real," Evelyn said.

"She told you it was real."

"But she was lying."

Jason was a nervous wreck. Evelyn had signed the Restatement of her trust. He needed to take a breather before he executed the next part of his plan. About 8:00 that night he went to a sex shop he frequented, Slap and Tickle, on a street a block from Hollywood Boulevard. The front window was adorned with a full-size (in every aspect) blow-up male doll, rabbit vibrators in purple, cobalt blue, sunny yellow, and silver, and penis sleeves. Fortunately, for the timid and weak of heart, the window was blacked out and so one had to be inside the store to appreciate the decor.

Excited at what new toy he might find, Jason walked up and down aisles as though he were shopping for groceries, picking up a random toy and putting it back on the shelf. Tourists filled the store, especially girls in their early twenties (the clerk checked ID at the door; 18 and older admitted) who giggled and surreptitiously—photography was prohibited—texted their friends after taking photos with their phones of vibrating dildos and artificial vaginas.

Jason went to the video section of the store. "Donny Does Dallas," "Henry Humps in Hollywood," and "Rochelle Rocks Rocky." As he read the description of the "plot" on the back of "Anthony and Austin, Part 5" a voice over his left shoulder asked, "A little light reading?" Jason had never been approached in that store before, and he felt embarrassed. He turned around and looked into beautiful brown eyes.

"Hello, my name is Ramon."

Jason debated whether to tell Ramon his real name. He decided to take a chance. "Hi, I'm Jason."

"Why are you looking at that trash?" Ramon asked.

"Well, I, I—," Jason stuttered, completely flummoxed.

Ramon reached by Jason, brushing his shoulder with a muscular arm and picked up another video, "Ramon Rides Richie" and handed it to Jason. "Now this is a video worth watching."

Jason looked at the cover and turned to look at Ramon. "You made this video." He wasn't sure if he was disgusted or in love.

"Would you like to watch this and maybe learn something? It's very educational."

"Uh, yeah, maybe I would."

Ramon put the video back on the shelf. "Well, then follow me. I happen to have a copy at home." He started to walk toward the front of the store and looked back to see if Jason was following.

Jason, in fact, was stuck to the spot. He knew how to be the aggressor. He was unfamiliar with this role. "Sure, I'm right behind you."

Chapter Forty-Six

Jason left Ramon late that night, leaving his head in a whirl.

On Thursday instead of going to work, Jason stood in front of Evelyn's bank First State Bank and Trust in Beverly Hills with his new trust account checks in his hand. He had $9,500,000 wired to an account in New York that dumped into an account in Grand Cayman. He got a cashier's check for $193,800 made payable to Ferrari Beverly Hills and a second one for $300,000 made payable to him. He took $6,200 in cash.

He then went to the safe deposit box desk. He changed the signature card after showing the clerk the trust named him trustee. When the clerk pulled out the box, Jason felt weak in his lower limbs. He had only seen boxes that large on TV. The box was at least a foot high. The clerk put Evelyn's safe deposit box into one of the tiny rooms where Jason could look at the contents of the box in private. Jason lifted the lid off the box and found 17 jewelry boxes filled with diamond, ruby, and emerald necklaces, earrings and rings. *Wow, I've hit the mother lode,* he said to himself. He put on one of the ruby and 18 carat gold rings on his pinkie. In a velvet pouch he found a diamond encrusted cuff. Jason had brought his gym bag, and he put all of Evelyn's jewelry into the bag. The safe deposit box was as empty as his heart.

He knew Royce would learn about the withdrawal that day and would attempt to have the wire transfer voided because of Evelyn's diminished mental capacity. Jason was prepared. He would continue to play dirty by moving the money into more accounts.

He drove out of the bank in his Hyundai Accent (the

last time he drove that car) and went to his bank. At his bank he deposited the $300,000 cashier's check and asked the manager to contact First State to verify the authenticity of the account and funds adequate to cover the transaction. He didn't want the money held by the bank for seven days or some bullshit like that. The bank manager admired the ring on Jason's hand.

His next stop was a Ferrari dealership.

Jason holed up in the Beverly Wilshire Hotel. No one knew he was there. He was going to live on the $300,000 and the money he would get for Evelyn's jewelry, knowing he couldn't go into a jewelry store and sell it. To avoid law enforcement, he would have to use a fence, probably out of the country. He didn't have plans to stick around Los Angeles or even the United States. He was going somewhere that required a passport. In the meantime, he hung around the hotel, lying in bed.

Chapter Forty-Seven

One morning, Evelyn waited in her room for Jason to come to work. She sat in one of the plum velvet chairs in her suite. Alma had given her a bath and helped her dress. Evelyn was wearing a turquoise St. John Santana wool matching sweater and pants. She wore leopard print Ferragamo flats. Her hair in its boyish cut, was neatly combed. Her manicure was perfection, and, if one could see her toes, her pedicure was superb, too. It was her mind that was unraveling, thread by thread.

Alma waited an hour into Jason's 8:00 a.m. shift for him to show up. He was usually punctual. Alma told Evelyn she didn't want to leave, but she had to get home to relieve her babysitter. She asked Emaline to check on Evelyn.

Evelyn was hungry, and she hoped Jason would come soon for breakfast. She sat with her hands in her lap. She waited. Did Royce say something to Jason to upset him? Royce could be that way. Abrasive. She hoped they had not had a difficult moment between them. Jason was a sensitive boy. When Jason did not come in time for breakfast, she found her way to the breakfast nook and was served a cheese omelet. She then walked through the house.

Royce took a call from Dwight Gregson, manager of the trust department at First State Bank and Trust.

"I need to confirm a transaction involving your mother's trust account, a withdrawal for a total of ten million dollars," Gregson said.

"What? Of course not. I have not made withdrawals in any amount close to ten million. There has been a mistake of accounts."

"No, sir. I am certain this withdrawal was from your

mother's account. It was made by the new trustee. That's why I have a question about the transaction."

"There is no new trustee. Since my father's death, I have been trustee. What are you talking about?"

"I'm looking at the transaction paperwork. It was signed by Jason Gerard, trustee. I saw the restatement of trust."

Royce put the call on speaker and began to pace. "Why did you not call me sooner? This is negligence on the part of the bank thirteen different ways, Dwight. The damage has been done and now you call me." Royce's righteousness propelled his venom. "The bank will make my mother's account whole. Calling me after fraud was committed is unconscionable." He had to think for a minute who Jason Gerard was and then remembered he was the caregiver his mother had told him was so trustworthy.

Royce ordered Gregson to put a hold on the account, and Gregson gave him the account number for the New York account to which the wire transfer had been made.

Royce called the house to talk to Evelyn, something he had never done before. He attempted to explain to her that Jason had changed her trust document and had written himself a check for $10,000,000 and had possibly taken her jewelry. Evelyn touched her ears to see if her earrings were still in place. She didn't believe Jason would cheat her. She assumed Royce had said something to him to offend him. He asked her if she had changed her trust.

"Now why on earth would I do that?" She had not thought about her trust in months, was sure Royce was hallucinating or drinking too much. "You must be mistaken."

After talking to Royce she took a nap. She slept

curled up on the loveseat in her suite.

After her nap, she decided she had to find Jason. She walked outside looking for him. Standing on the front lawn, she looked at the desert plantings. Those ugly things from the fields. She still didn't understand why she wasn't supposed to dig them up, but remembered how angry Royce had been, holding a plant in each hand and turning red as he told her she was not under any circumstances supposed to pull them out of the ground.

She stood in the driveway looking for Jason and then went to the pool house, which was locked. She looked into the hole that was going to be Truesdale's new pool. She remembered when Jason took her to the original pool and had her do water exercises. As he lounged while she paddled in the water, he had said, "This is where it's at." She decided to wait for him in the pool since that was where it's at, whatever "it" was. The pool was six feet seven inches deep. She walked around the pool until she saw a construction ladder at the shallow end. It was still in position as the workmen had left it.

Should I go down the ladder? I might get my SJ dirty, but if I go down there I can surprise Jason. She put her trembling right foot on the first rung and grabbed hard onto the sides of the ladder, then put her left foot on the same rung. In this way, she stepped down one rung at a time, stepping, holding fast, stepping. About half way down, she placed her foot on a rung, and her Ferragamo flat slid off. As she grabbed tighter onto the sides of the ladder, it tilted. She panicked. She didn't know how to correct it. The ladder tilted too far to the left, and it dropped with Evelyn still holding on. She fell onto the gray gunite. She felt and heard a crack that was not ladder fatigue. Two sawhorses fell over on top of Evelyn when the ladder fell.

She lay crumpled on the floor of the pool construction on her left side with her left leg and arm under her. The ladder and sawhorses lay on top of her. It took some time for her to understand what had happened. It may have been a few seconds. It may have been an hour. She realized she was lying in the hole. She did not know how she had gotten there. Starting to sit up, she felt a hot pain in her left hip, leg and arm and cried out, "Awk! I don't—" The ladder-sawhorse pile was too heavy to push off her with only one arm. She called out in a voice shaky from fear, from pain, from age. "Help! Help me! Truesdale. Teddy, Tru, Teddy, Reginald. Someone find Reginald."

They were in school or at dance, piano, soccer, swimming, cheerleader practice. Or dead. The housekeepers and chef would not have a reason to go into the back of the property. The gardeners were not working at the back of the mansion that day. The nanny would be out chauffeuring the girls about. The air conditioner was on, which meant that all the windows and doors were shut tight.

Evelyn tried to get up on her right elbow without sending that searing pain through her body again. She moved the left arm and screamed. She laid her head on the gunite, breathing through her mouth, and then she cried, tears running in rivulets across her scraped nose. "Help me, Reginald. Come find me. I don't know where I am."

Rain clouds moved in dark and malevolent. Royce made the long drive home from Wilshire to Calabasas that night. First a drizzle, then quickly a soft wet shower made specks on his windshield. His tired eyes were slits. Uncharacteristically, Royce left his suit jacket crumpled on the passenger seat, and he took his tie off and undid the top button of his shirt.

So that he could have a little peace he turned off his cell. He couldn't remember the last time he had done that. He just wanted to drive for a short distance with no other sound than Bob Dylan filling the interior of the car. He listened to each word of the songs and turned up the volume when he heard a lyric that mirrored his life. *Ain't talkin', just walkin'* particularly resonated with him. He nodded and hit the steering wheel with the heel of his hand when Dylan sang *"They will crush you."*

Royce drove home by rote with his head buzzing. There seemed to be more cars in the driveway than usual for a weekday evening. He did not want to go inside, see anyone, or deal with problems. His mother's change of trust was enough of a problem.

He parked the Mercedes in the garage and got a soft cloth from a linen closet built into one wall with shelves of cleaners, degreasers, waxes, and leather treatments. The garage lit up the other cars, glistening expensive metals, rubber, and leather: Silver Porsche GT2, ivory BMW Z8, infrared Cadillac SRX, gold tint Jaguar XKR convertible (Reginald's car Teddy wanted to drive), robin's egg blue with white soft top 1962 Pontiac Bonneville convertible (the car Teddy wouldn't be seen dead in), coral red with white top 1954 Pontiac Starchief, black Maserati Spyder convertible, and Nichol's red Maserati GranSport Coupe. He wiped down the Mercedes, using a protectant on the tires. He enjoyed cleaning the cars, talking to knowledgeable people about the cars, a holdover from his boyhood.

Reginald showed Royce how to properly wipe down a car, how to clean white wall tires, and later he taught his son how to oversee people to maintain his cars. Royce learned to appreciate taking care of things hardworking (and inherited) dollars bought. He learned to appreciate the beauty of an inanimate object. He learned to love that which could not hurt him.

Royce was so deep in not thinking that he dropped the cloth when Lindy called to him. "Mr. Kallas. Oh, Mr. Kallas. We couldn't get ahold of you. It's Mrs. Kallas." Lindy was hysterical. She was gasping for breath and had one hand, fingers splayed, on her chest.

"What's wrong?" Royce said. He had been crouched down cleaning the wheels and stood up as though he were placing himself in front of an Argentinian firing squad. He thought he might not want to know the answer to his question. *Is Tamra out of the hospital? Has she come back to get her son?* he wondered. "Is Mrs. Kallas here?"

"No, she's gone," Lindy said.

"Where did she go?" Royce said. Or more to the point, was Morgan gone from the house? He grabbed his jacket and tie.

"No one can find her."

"Why does someone want to find her?" Royce said.

Well, that stumped Lindy. She looked up at Mr. Kallas's eyes with a frown on her face. "Mrs. Kallas. Is. Missing. Your mother is missing."

"Mother is missing?" he said.

Lindy said something in Spanish he did not understand, and she shook her head.

They began to walk into the kitchen, except Lindy stopped when he asked her questions and faced him, out of respect for his position.

"Yes, Mr. Kallas. John-J came to work at four o'clock. He not find Mrs. Kallas, your mother. We looked in the house. All over. Tru and Teddy came home from school, and they walked up and down the street, and they not find her."

"Why did you not call me?" Royce said.

"We did call your office and cell. Your receptionist said you had already left the office, and you didn't pick up on your cell. We thought, we hoped we could find her on our own."

He walked into the house and was met by a group of people who had universal looks of panic on their faces: Teddy, Tru, Emaline, Kristina, John-J, Angel and Noel.

Royce put up his hand as though stopping traffic. "Give me a moment." He walked into his study and breathed. He walked back out and met the group outside his door. He walked to the foyer, with the mob following him. "John-J, where have you looked?"

"I looked in every room of this house at least once, and a few a second time, looked in closets."

"Has anyone looked outside?" Royce asked.

"Nana didn't go outside. Not after the Plant Fiasco," Teddy said, giggling, and then realizing her *faux pas*, she replaced her smile with an appropriate frown.

"Has anyone looked outside?" Royce asked—again.

"We looked in the front, and we went up and down Prado Del Grandioso," Tru said.

"What about the back?" Royce asked.

"I searched through your garage. I went through *every* car, Mr. Kallas," Lindy said.

"This evening I went out to the pool house," Teddy said. "It was empty. Locked. I went to the barn and the tennis court."

"All right, thank you." Royce said. He walked back into his study. He dialed 9-1-1.

"9-1-1. What's your emergency?"

"My mother, my ninety-year-old mother is missing."

"Does she have any physical or mental impairments?"

"Well, she is ninety years old. What do you mean?"

"Any physical impairments, does she walk with a walker? Mental impairments: is she a wanderer?" the operator asked.

"Yes, she is a wanderer." Royce would agree to any question that got the police to his house.

"Sir, the squad car should be pulling up to your address in approximately five minutes."

Royce touched his neck and realized he was not wearing a tie. He looked around his study and then remembered he had left it on a kitchen counter where he was accosted by his family and staff. He decided not to retrieve it. A minute later, he walked out of the study to greet two uniformed officers with the Los Angeles County Sheriff's Department, both in olive green shirts, pants, black boots, and equipment on the duty belt: gun, handcuffs, baton, pepper spray, flashlights, radio, Taser. The leather gave the odor of authority and squeaked as they moved.

"I'm Deputy Henderson, and this is Deputy Cooper. Your mother is missing?" Henderson carried a clipboard box and was filling out the Incident Report.

"Yes, perhaps since about two this afternoon."

Lindy, John-J, Noel, Emaline, Angel, Kristina and his daughters stood in a semi-circle, watching the officers.

"Your mother is a wanderer?"

"Yes, well, no, she does not wander anymore, now that we have round-the-clock caregivers," Royce said.

"If she has round-the-clock care, why didn't anyone notice she was missing?" Henderson asked. Fair question.

"Her day shift caregiver Jason Gerard did not come in today." *I'm going to kill the son-of-a-bitch,* Royce thought. He wanted to pace, but knew he would appear rude. He settled for crossing his arms.

"When was the last time you saw her?"

"I saw her at home when I left for the office at seven this morning. I talked to her about ten o'clock. She did not tell me her caregiver had not come in. Emaline," he pointed, "saw her at ten forty-five walking through the house. Noel made her an omelet. Emaline checked on her again at two and she was asleep in her suite. The first person who noticed she was gone was the second shift caregiver. He came in at four o'clock."

"What did Jason and Evelyn do during a normal day?" Henderson asked.

"They sometimes went for walks down the street, sometimes they walked back to the horses, but not since the construction," Lindy said. "She swam in the old pool. Usually they stayed in the house in her room."

"What construction is that?" Cooper asked, looking around the foyer, taking in the size of the room and the chandeliers overhead.

"We are building a pool," Royce said, rubbing his hands together for warmth.

"The biggest pool in the world," Tru said in what she thought was a grown-up voice and got an elbow from Teddy.

"Who lives here?" Henderson said.

"I do," Royce said, putting his hand on his chest, "two of my daughters Teddy and Tru," pointing to them (Tru smiling and giving a curtsey), "my mother, my nanny, the house manager Lindy, and Noel, our chef. Oh, and a baby nurse. And a baby."

"Let's go look at this construction." The entire group walked as one onto the patio. Henderson turned toward them. "Why don't the rest of you hang back here." Everyone

———

except Royce stopped walking.

The rain continued, and the evening sky was the color of a Brillo pad. At that moment, two additional cruisers pulled up to the house, lighting up the undeveloped fields red and blue. Henderson and four new officers spoke at the driveway for a moment. Royce followed them. He did not interrupt as Henderson briefed the officers, although he thought he could have summarized the situation more succinctly. Royce watched three of them go to the street and the fields. Then Henderson and one new officer, Deputy Glifford—dogged by vigilant Royce—turned on their flashlights, looked under the tables, looked into dark spaces on the exterior of the house, further and further into the back where the pool house was lighted.

Royce, Henderson, and Glifford got to the construction area. Henderson's flashlight moved from one end to the other. Just sawhorses and a ladder. They walked out to the barn and looked through the stalls.

"Your mother could have walked out on that trail," Glifford said. Over the radio he gave instructions to officers who were on the street to come back to the horse trail.

"I do not think she even knows this trail is here," Royce said. He registered it was raining for the first time that evening and wiped his face.

They checked out the tennis court and then walked back to the hole. Henderson stopped and jumped down into the pool. He methodically ran his flashlight from side to side as he moved further into the pool. The light hit on the upended sawhorses and on Evelyn. The deputies moved the sawhorses and ladder. Her beautiful turquoise sweater and pants and hair were soaked. Her left arm and leg were tucked under her at odd angles. She looked like a Barbie doll abused by a toddler. One shoe lay by the ladder. She did not move.

Evelyn would have been embarrassed by her appearance if she were awake. Henderson put his fingers to her jugular and then called into the radio on his shoulder for EMT.

"Is she alive? Oh, please," Royce half cried.

"Yes, sir, she's alive. We've called for paramedic service," Glifford said.

Royce, who had followed the deputies into the pool without invitation, moved toward his mother.

"No, Mr. Kallas, don't touch her. We don't know what injuries she has. Please wait, sir. Do you have any idea why she would be in the bottom of this unfinished pool?" asked Henderson, motioning for a deputy to take Royce out of the pool area.

"No, I, no, no idea. Oh, Mother." He stared for a couple of minutes. A deputy touched his arm, and he shrugged it off. Why would she have fallen in? Did someone push her? Did she use that ladder to get down here? Why? Royce's wet shirt hung on his chest, saturated with what was becoming a deluge. He ran a hand through his hair. The waiting deputy was not on Royce's radar.

Everyone who had been in the house, who had been asked to stay in the house, overpowered Cooper and rushed off the patio as soon as they saw Royce run into the pool. Henderson used his baton as a pointer (with promise of something else more menacing?) and told each of them to step back onto the patio. He pointed to the area where tables were grouped. Cooper and one of the other officers who had been called in from their search of the fields, stood facing the group as though they were a rabid pack of twelve-year-old fans waiting for Justin Bieber.

"Paramedics are going to be here in a moment, and they need for all of you to stay back so they can take care of Mrs. Kallas," Henderson said.

Teddy held Tru's hand, which was shaking. Their cheeks were covered in red blotches the color of watermelon. Their hair was plastered to their faces. Uncharacteristically, they did not care what their hair looked like. John-J stood with his hand over his mouth. Lindy, Angel, and Noel looked ill at ease with no furniture to dust or people to feed. Kristina went back into the house when the baby monitor went off. Light from every room inside the house illuminated the steady rain.

A moment later, an EMT ambulance came down the driveway "whoop-whoop-whoop," with blue and red lights flying off the garage doors. The two EMTs were out of the truck, almost before it stopped moving. Henderson met them. "Max. You pulled this shift again, huh? Hey, Caso."

"What do we have?" Max asked.

Caso took out a gurney from the back of the rig while Max and Henderson talked.

"Ninety-year-old woman, wanderer, fell or was pushed into the pool. It's about eight feet deep. She is unconscious."

The EMTs jumped down into the pool and an officer maneuvered the gurney down to them. Two police officers were relegated to holding flashlights on Evelyn. Caso put a blood pressure cuff around her right arm, a nose clip for oxygen, and pulse oximeter on her finger. He felt around under her left leg and arm. Out of her state of unconsciousness, Evelyn screamed, and Tru then screamed, and Teddy put her hands over her own nose and mouth.

"Can we have a flashlight down here?" Max said.

Glifford, who had moved up to the deck to give a wider arc of light, jumped down into the hole and held the flashlight on Evelyn, who made no sound as long as they did not touch her left leg and arm. "Let's see if we can get her turned over," Max said.

"Let me get ten of morphine ready," Caso said. It took him less than a minute. "Okay, on three we turn her over and put her onto the backboard." Evelyn's clothes hung over her. "One-two-three."

Another scream from Evelyn. They put the backboard on the gurney. Caso started an IV and gave her morphine.

Caso and Max picked up the gurney and, with the assistance of two officers, lifted the gurney up onto the deck, where four officers eased it up and over the lip of the pool. That was a sign for everyone on the patio to run over to her. The officers stopped them. "Now, you have to let the EMTs do their job."

"Deputy, I'd like to ride in the ambulance with my mother to the hospital," Royce said.

"No can do," Henderson said. "You can either drive over in your own car or wait and drive over with us. But we have more to write in the report before we leave here."

"I will drive my own car, officer. I cannot believe she was in the pool. I do not understand why she was out here." His shame was greater than his regret. He looked around at the assembled group, seeking someone to give orders to, but feared that if he opened his mouth, he would also scream.

"We'll see if we can make some sense of it, sir."

During this brief flurry of activity, Teddy and Tru hung by him, begged for his attention. "Dad, Dad, please." "We want to come, too. Please, Daddy."

"You cannot come with me to the hospital. I know you are worried. I know you are scared." Did he know that, or was he speaking about himself? "But let me go to the hospital by myself, and I will call you."

Tru burst into tears. She had held them in as long as

she could. She whimpered, "Daddy, is this all my fault?" Sobbing. She put one hand up to her eyes, and her little body shook as she sobbed. "Did Nana get hurt because I wanted a bigger swimming pool?"

Royce sat in a brown hard plastic chair connected by rods to identical brown hard plastic chairs in the waiting room of the Holy Charity Emergency Room. So many people had scratched their moments of existentialism into the surface of the chairs that they looked like Sanskrit. People in varying degrees of ill health sat in the other brown chairs. A toddler coughed and was comforted by a woman. The fluorescent lights did nothing for people who already looked sick. It had been two hours since the ambulance arrived at the hospital with Evelyn. Royce had been told nothing, except to wait until a doctor was available to speak to him.

Royce called Sophie and told her to wait until he had some news before heading home. He had not stopped to change shirts, and his slim fit spread collar Italian cotton dress shirt stuck to him. His $3,200 bespoke suit pants were ruined, but he did not know they were. He stared at his Edward Green $1,585 loafers, but did not see the discolorations in the leather, because his head was not focused there.

"If you don't send a helicopter, Dad, I'm going to drive up," Sophie said.

He sent a helicopter.

It was ten thirty p.m.

At eleven ten, the emergency room receptionist told Royce that he could go in to see his mother. Royce pocketed his phone and for the second time that evening attempted to straighten the tie that he was not wearing. Medical equipment was pushed back against the walls on two sides of the room. Royce heard a reassuring steady beeping noise and saw his mother lying on her back on a gurney. She was connected to the usual medical paraphernalia. In addition, her left arm was in a sling. Her face was red and covered with a clear glistening cream. A white sheet covered her to her neck.

A woman walked into the room wearing a white suit. For half a second Royce wondered why she wasn't wet like the rest of his world. "Hello, I'm Dr. Sweet. I've been working with your mother for a while now. As you can see, your mother is in a sling for a break at the radius. She is in a cast, which will immobilize her. Your mother scraped the left side of her face, and we're treating that with topical and IV antibiotics. Her left hip is fractured, and x-rays also show osteoporosis. We won't know the full extent of the damage until we get her opened up, but we anticipate she will need a hip replacement. We'd like to get her prepped now. Dr. Olmquist will perform the surgery, Dr. Bartlett will be the anesthesiologist. He specializes in elderly patients. They will be here in a moment. We need your consent to operate.

"She's sleeping now. She came to when we were putting her arm in the sling, and we gave her ten milligrams of morphine. She'd already gotten ten in the field. With elderly patients, we have to be especially careful administering narcotics. We've called in a consult with Dr. Ryland who is a geriatric internist. We've catheterized Evelyn since she can't walk right now. We'll take good care of her."

A man came into the room in blue scrubs and booties. "Hello, I'm Dr. Bartlett. I will be your mother's anesthesiologist. I need to ask you some questions regarding your mother's health."

A third doctor in scrubs walked into what was becoming an overcrowded room. "I'm Dr. Olmquist, and I will be performing surgery on your mother's left hip. The hip is fractured at the femoral neck." He whipped x-rays up on his iPad. "The risks of the surgery are dislocation, loosening, impingement, infection, osteolysis, metal sensitivity, nerve palsy, pain and death. If you need to acquaint yourself with the surgical procedure or the risks I've told you about, you can look on the Internet or get a second opinion and we will postpone the surgery for a while, taking into consideration that the sooner we get your mother into surgery, the sooner her recovery will start. Dr. Bartlett and I team up on all hip surgeries."

"Do you have VIP suites?" Royce asked as though he were calling for a reservation at a five star hotel. He was beyond asking relevant medical questions.

Dr. Olmquist looked at Dr. Sweet. "Umm, yes, we do. I'll tell Admitting to look for an available suite. But, initially she will be in ICU."

"I want her to have the best care."

"Is your mother lucid?" Dr. Olmquist said.

"From time to time. She has periods where she seems to blank out and will say or do something that does not make sense. I have not had her tested, but I believe she is suffering from dementia. But, of course, that is your area of expertise."

"We need to know what to expect when she is fully awake," Dr. Olmquist said. "You can pull up a chair on her right side now. Any questions?"

"I am hoping she will sleep through the night after the surgery," Dr. Sweet said. "Rather than your waiting through the surgery, I recommend you go home, get some sleep, and come back tomorrow to see her. Leave us contact numbers, and we'll call you as soon as surgery is finished."

"What if she wakes up and no one is here with her?"

"In ICU she will be monitored constantly," Dr. Sweet said.

Royce waited until his mother was taken to surgery, and then he walked back through the waiting room and out the automatic doors. He felt the air, cold and wet on his face. He breathed real air for the first time in hours. He watched rain puddling the parking lot.

He thought how difficult the last year had been. He controlled his emotions only by acknowledging those memories that were palatable. *I have to notify Nichol. She will come home now*, he thought.

Royce dragged himself down the long hall into his bedroom. The room was lit with golden flutes from table lamps. He sat down on his king-sized bed in his damp clothes and sagged into the mattress. He forced himself to stand up, rather than what he wanted to do which was to lie down and never get up. Someone had thoughtfully put his mail on his nightstand instead of on his study desk. He mechanically looked through the mail while he simultaneously worried about his mother and thought of solutions for Jason's conduct.

Included in the stack was an envelope from the Superior Court of Los Angeles County. He looked at the enclosed documents. Royce held the Order on Dissolution of Marriage. He stood and stared at the page he held in his right hand. Fifteen years of marriage. What didn't Tamra get from it? What did Tamra want that she didn't get from him? He walked into the bathroom and threw up into the toilet.

The rain was steady. Royce took the girls to see Evelyn in the ICU the next morning. A nurse named Elaine came into the room. She wore green scrubs and had the air of a squared away marine.

"Mrs. Kallas did very well in surgery," Elaine said. "As you know she did have a hip replacement. She will be having an EEG and brain scan this morning. She will be in the hospital for a few days longer than usual because of her age. We want to make sure she remains stable. After she leaves the hospital, she will go to a rehabilitation facility to help her recover with that new hip. In fact they will get her up to walk today."

"This news about her rehabilitation sounds like it will be difficult. But whatever needs to be done, we will get done," Royce said. "We will hire our own physical therapist and nurse so she can recover at home." When he said "nurse," he really meant Nichol.

"Can we sit with Nana and hold her hands?" Tru said.

"Yes, you can," Elaine said. "Gently, okay?"

"Be careful, girls. Do not hurt her," Royce said. He knew he had a stick up his butt, but he didn't care.

Teddy looked at him, hard. "Can she wake up?"

"Yes, she is just asleep, she's not in a coma," Elaine said. "She's been given a lot of medication that makes her sleepy, and it also makes her talk like, well, like she's had a couple of glasses of wine. When the nurses came in at six this morning she woke up. She looked puzzled, I guess because she was seeing strange faces. She has been awake a little since I've been here. I told her she has a new hip, and she won't have arthritis in it anymore. She seemed to track what I was saying. The only question she asked me was where she was."

Tru wasn't sure she knew what Elaine meant, but she nodded her head in a way that she hoped conveyed that she knew the medication was a serious matter.

Teddy and Tru pushed chairs to the right side of Evelyn's bed.

"Nana," said Tru. "We're here, Nana. Me, Teddy, and Daddy."

Evelyn opened her eyes, just a slit, as though a bright light were being shone in her face. In a thin, scratchy voice, she said, "Tru."

"Yes, Nana. And look over here. It's Teddy," Teddy said.

Evelyn turned her head as though her neck weren't working at full speed. Then she opened her eyes wider and saw Royce standing behind Teddy's chair. "Everyone's here," she said. Then she furrowed her brow and asked, "Where's Sophie?"

"She will be here soon," Royce said, his voice shaky. He noticed she appeared lucid.

"Why am I here? Can I go home now?"

"No, Nana. Not yet. You hurt your hip," Teddy said. "Doctors and nurses are taking care of you. And look! You have a cast."

"May I have a glass of water, please?" Evelyn said. "I'm so tired." She began to move her left arm. "Ow! That hurts."

"Go back to sleep, Mother. We will come back and see you later."

As Evelyn drifted off into a drug-dream, she called out, "Good night, Reginald dear. Is it nighttime? I'm so tired. I'm going to take a little nap."

Royce thought, *What if we hadn't found her? What damage was inflicted when her head hit the bottom of the pool?* He could not wait to get home and get a call from Nichol.

Royce felt reassured with Sophie by his side. He checked up on Evelyn throughout Sunday. She had indeed been given a VIP suite, which looked more like a one-bedroom luxe apartment or hotel suite than a hospital room. Hardwood flooring the color of a pecan snugged up against dark wainscoting that covered the bottom half of the walls, while cranberry and tan paisley wallpaper covered the upper half. Two large windows looked onto a tropical garden. Tan shutters were turned to let in light, creating stripes of white on the floor and bed. Tan linen barrel guest chairs sat near the bed. A wine bar with beveled glasses on the bar back sat in one corner. Recessed lighting gave the room a serene, quiet look.

"Look, Daddy. A big screen TV," Tru said in a bad attempt at a whisper.

"Dad, Nana's room has ambience, like a nice restaurant. You know what I mean?" Teddy said.

"We are not in the hospital to discuss the design features of the room, girls." He spoke as though it was Teddy's and Tru's doing that got Evelyn in the hospital or that they were not showing good manners. Royce was holding it together in a fierce, asshole kind of way. He got tears in his eyes.

Teddy turned away from him, and Tru full on pouted. Sophie shook her head at him. Royce ignored them.

Chapter Forty-Eight

At the time of Evelyn's accident, Royce had not heard from Nichol in weeks. He was at the mercy of her calls. In frustration and not a little bit of anger, he looked at the Hôpital Albert Schweitzer website and called the number. It was midnight in Haiti.

After fifteen rings, a man answered the phone. "Oui."

Royce did not speak French well. He did not speak Creole. "Yes, I am looking for Nichol Laurent, a nurse."

"Oui, Nichol," the man said.

"Is she there. At your hospital?"

"Oui, Nichol a l'hôpital."

"That is excellent news. I would like to speak to her."

"Non. Nichol pas de téléphone."

"There must be—"

"Au revoir." The man hung up.

On Monday, late morning, the rainstorm continued to drown Los Angeles. Rain gutters overflowed, and water reached to the curbs. The Los Angeles River surged through its concrete walls and swallowed two men who had walked to the edge playing chicken with the swollen water. *The Los Angeles Times* printed the annual photo of cars hydroplaning through the streets. Tourists were interviewed by the local Fox station, asking them how they were enjoying their vacations, to which they answered, "If we wanted crappy weather, we could have stayed home in Pittsburgh." The same declaration was made about Ames, Iowa, and Glasgow, Scotland.

Royce visited Evelyn, whose tests for injuries to the brain came back with news. A nurse gave him the written report of the CT scan of the head. "Evidence of bruising.

Moderate changes consistent with frontal temporal dementia." Royce was not surprised, but having a definitive diagnosis for her behavior saddened him. A physical therapist got Evelyn out of bed, which was an effort with the new hip. She walked toward the nurses' station with a cane and the physical therapist holding onto her by a canvas rope wrapped around her waist. The exercise was compromised, of course, because Evelyn's left arm was broken. She continued to be treated like a visiting celebrity, which lessened her demands to go home.

Royce went to his office and hung up his navy pin-striped jacket in the closet in his private bathroom. He looked the part of a major player, but decidedly did not feel the part. He attempted to keep his eyes open. He had lain awake for the past four nights obsessing about his mother, Nichol, Sophie, Teddy, baby Morgan, Tamra. The women in his universe gave him an ulcer and sleep disorder. The only person in his life who gave him pure happiness was Tru. He came to a decision, and he was angry he had not reached it earlier.

Royce left his mother in the care of the hospital staff and his children in the care of Emaline. One of his assistants was assigned the task of finding Jason, who had not surfaced.

Royce flew to Haiti. The airport was, once again, accommodating private planes. After he was spit out of the sweating throng of people in baggage claims and customs, he stood on the street in front of the airport. The hospital said a driver would meet him at the airport, but this was not the type of airport where people stood holding up signs with the name of the person they were there to meet. No, not that kind of place.

Women wore flowing dresses in beautiful blues,

greens, and purples and carried baskets on their heads with live chickens, with their legs tied together. The women approached him with outstretched hands and spoke Creole. When he did not respond, the women got angry with him and flicked at his arms with their hands, shouting "Fou blan, fou blan." "New Yawk Yanquis." "You New Yawk?" Royce let the wave of people push him back toward the entrance to the airport.

One man separated from the others. He grabbed onto Royce's arm and took another step forward and put his face in Royce's. His teeth were the color of Indian corn. His nose was broad, his eyes were black. His face was smooth and did not reflect the sadness, misery, and exhilaration of his country. He smelled of sweat and something sweet. As he spoke, spit flew off his lips onto Royce's face. He said in English, "We hear big man flying on his plane. We hear who is coming. Coming for Nichol Laurent."

Royce was puzzled.

"You want to know. You on the radio. The radio tell us big man's plane coming." The man slapped the top of one of his hands with the other, back and forth and laughed, a dry cynical laugh. He pointed at Royce and walked to a dirt area where cars and trucks of every state of disrepair were parked at odd angles from each other. Soldiers walked through the area pushing beggars out of their paths. The man turned back toward Royce. "My name René." He slapped his chest as if to confirm he indeed was René.

The man called René nodded his head toward a Toyota truck that once might have been white.

"People back there," Royce pointed over his shoulder, "were saying something to me. It sounded like 'foo blank.'"

"'Fou Blan?'" The man called René laughed, a sharp

sound, a sound to cut one's heart. "They are calling you 'crazy white.'"

"Umm. Where is Nichol?" Royce asked.

"Hôpital Albert Schweitzer, where we are going." They drove out of the lot and maneuvered down the dusty road. "We need gas." René stopped at a dirt lot with a tin shack the size of a closet in Royce's house that announced "Banc" and a single gas pump. The truck shuddered as René turned off the engine. He held his hand out to Royce.

"You need money? I only have American currency," Royce said.

"American dollars buy gas."

René watched while Royce took money from his wallet. His head was too close to Royce for the American's comfort. Royce handed him a ten dollar bill, but René shook his head, so Royce gave him another ten. René continued to look at the wallet, but Royce said, "No. That's enough."

People surrounded the truck as René pumped gas. Three men had what sounded to Royce like an argument with René. Royce wondered if he should call the police, but realized he did not know if the city even had a police department. When René got back in the truck, and the door closed with creaks from a lifetime in a tropical country, he said, "Haitians like to look at big American." René laughed, again with a tone that sounded as though he did not think it was funny at all.

"Banc," Royce asked, pointing to the sign. "That's a bank?"

"Not your bank. Haitian banc. For lottery. Every day lottery."

Royce nodded his head and wished he had worn cooler clothes. He had traveled to the Caribbean throughout his career. He should have known better. He needed relief from the intense smothering heat and the inside of the truck, with its cracked vinyl seats and dusty dashboard. Of course, the truck did not have air conditioning. He left his jacket on.

They made the long drive to the hospital. They rumbled over roads, with René honking his horn and shifting gears that, to Royce, seemed shot. The road was congested with vehicles of every description: large trucks carrying car parts, Mercedes with fur-clad women wearing oversized sunglasses and pursed lips, buses with people hanging out of windows or sitting on top, rusted bicycles. With no room for error, René passed Toyota trucks with armed men wearing blue uniforms sitting in the truck beds.

"Who are those men?" Royce said.

"Huh, those are police. Bad people. Stay away from them. They shoot you." René laughed again, a sound Royce was getting used to.

"What are those called?" Royce said, pointing to multi-colored mini-buses, from which music blared.

"Those are tap taps. All over city."

Motor scooters navigated dirty roads full of potholes and long fissures. Crumbled cement blocks that had once been someone's home filled a plot of land along the road where donkeys carrying torn burlap bags of charcoal were led by stooped men pulling on frayed ropes, and René swerved around them with expertise.

Royce had never before felt such a potent emotional and physical connection to the present moment. He sweated from the tropical heat and anticipation of seeing Nichol. He pulled out his handkerchief and dabbed at his face and neck. The Caribbean sun produced light he had only seen on his cruise with Tamra years and years ago. Vibrant green banana leaves, yellow and blue tap taps, and red searing hibiscus. The sea was a turquoise blue and clear. In the face of obvious devastation, he felt hopeful. He could make a difference, too. But then Rene said, "Don't go into the ocean here. It is poison. It looks pretty, huh. Waste goes into that water."

Crayola in a garbage can.

"How is Nichol?" Royce said.

"Nichol sick for a few days. We see this sick in more people. At the hospital. She went back in-country. She sick very much." He looked back up at Royce. "A doctor, a nurse took a jeep into valley. She lie all down on the dirt floor in a home there."

Royce kept his eyes on the road—one of them should—with one elbow on the door.

"Doctor says Nichol stay in hospital," René said.

"I didn't know she was ill. I thought she was working in the hospital. Is she all right now?" He turned toward René and, when René did not immediately respond to his question, reached out an arm, possibly to shake him. He spoke louder, "What has happened to her?"

"You ask doctor."

"But have you seen her?"

"Some days ago."

Royce pounded one of his fists on the cracked dashboard. "Tell me how she is. Is she very sick?"

René merely shook his head.

When it became clear to Royce that he could not extract any further information from René about Nichol, he asked René to tell him what they were seeing as they traveled on Highway 1 toward the Artibonite Valley. They passed yellow and green and blue houses made of cinder blocks with tin roofs sitting in large dirt yards with wooden slat fences. Goats and cows foraged for patches of grass in otherwise parched fields.

They arrived at Hôpital Albert Schweitzer in

Deschapelles six and a half hours after leaving the airport. Royce felt as though he had ridden a donkey the entire way. He was uncharacteristically sweaty. He could feel that his shirt was wet.

The grounds of the hospital were covered with trees that provided relief from the sun. But not the heat. Gravel walkways led to several buildings, including the hospital, a two-story cinder block affair.

René turned Royce over to Dr. Indore LaFontaine. She was impeccably dressed, about Tamra's height, wore at least four-inch heels and a floral silk dress. She wore diamond stud earrings and a thin diamond tennis bracelet. Her black hair was in a bun. She looked like she had just come out of an air-conditioned office, which Royce doubted considering the look of the hospital.

Dr. LaFontaine told Royce that Nichol suffered from cholera. "We're in the midst of a country-wide epidemic. She was so dehydrated that if we hadn't gotten to her when we did, she might have died." The doctor spoke with the same accent as Nichol, English over French.

"Died?" Despite the heat, Royce felt a chill run down his back.

"She is dehydrated, is vomiting, and has diarrhea," the doctor continued. Royce didn't understand why he didn't fall down, because nothing was holding him up.

"She had a rapid heart rate, leg cramps, and low blood pressure. We were afraid she was going to go into shock, but she was found in time and our personnel in the field started treatment. We have her blood pressure and heart rate under control now."

"Is she safe now? She won't die, will she?" Royce said. His voice sounded as though he was being strangled. *Might have died*, he thought. Why had he let Nichol go to

Haiti? The country was obviously too dangerous for her to be there. He was going to get her on his plane and get her out of the god-forsaken country.

"She is responding well to IV fluids and antibiotics. I expect that she will recover, but she has a severe case, so needs to remain in the hospital. She has been working tirelessly for months. She has no reserves to fight the disease. She needs to rest now."

"How did she contract cholera?" he said, in a tone that suggested it was someone's fault Nichol was sick.

"Clean drinking water is not always available in the field. She might have eaten food prepared with contaminated water or drunk bad water. Come. Walk with me. I will take you to Nichol's ward."

Dr. LaFontaine handed Royce a mask to wear over his nose and mouth. He cleared his throat as though he were swallowing dirt. He felt helpless. Royce thought he controlled his universe, but Nichol made a lie of his mastery. He commanded the intricate operations of his company, but could not—similar to his life with Tamra—manage Nichol.

The hot, heavy air hung from the low ceiling with fluorescent lighting. Pale blue cinderblock walls, some with long cracks, separated the wards. Royce registered smells like a strong disinfectant and something metallic. There were no distinct voices, only a general hum. The doctor's heels clicked on the gray linoleum-covered floor. She led him to Nichol's bed.

Royce was nervous and anxious. Nichol lay on her back in a bed in a ten-bed ward. Royce stood at the foot of her cast iron bed, and he rested his hands on the cool white metal with patches of rust. He barely recognized her. She had grown out her hair into a wild Afro. Her skin had a gray pallor. A thin tube that was attached to a clear plastic bag on a pole went into one of her arms.

In the niches of his brain he remembered a visit to a hospital years before where he stood at the foot of a young woman's bed. Tamra's hospital was pristine and held state-of-the-art equipment. This hospital ward did not have machines measuring vitals. It was clean, but the beds were obviously old.

Royce called Nichol's name in a soft voice so he wouldn't disturb the other patients. Most of them were missing limbs or had badly scarred faces. Women wearing flowered blouses and black skirts, whom he assumed were nurses, walked in and out of the room as they tended to patients.

"She don't wake up. She only sleep," said one of the patients, who was sitting up in her bed. She had only a stump of her left arm, which was heavily bandaged.

Dr. LaFontaine said something to the woman in Haitian Creole. She gestured for Royce to sit on Nichol's bed. Royce sat on the bed and could feel the thinness of the mattress. He looked back at the doctor, who nodded to him. Royce gave Nichol's shoulder a slight shake. She moaned and then opened her eyes, closed them, and opened them again.

Royce said, "Oh." His cosmos was again righted. "I have missed you. Oh, God, I have missed you. I love you, darling." He pushed the mask down to his chin, leaned down and hugged her.

She did not smell like Nichol. She had an institutional smell, like layers of sickness.

She grunted slightly and attempted to pull away from his embrace. "You're squeezing too tight." Her voice was slight, yet brittle. "Royce. You're here? How did you get here? Oh, Royce. You shouldn't have come."

He interpreted her statement to mean she did not want him in Haiti, but he forged ahead. "I could no longer wait for you to come home, so I flew down." His petulance returned. "Are you not happy to see me? Nichol, I have come to bring you home where you can recover and our family can be whole again. Dr. LaFontaine says you need to convalesce here for a few days since you require constant rehydration. And the trip would be difficult for you right now." Royce thought he was being entirely reasonable as he sat perched on the side of the bed, holding her lifeless right hand in his hands. Her skin felt like crepe paper.

In the pregnant silence, Royce thought the ward had the texture of a steam room. Even though Dr. LaFontaine was present, Royce took off his jacket and loosened his tie. He looked down at his suit pants. They were wrinkled. He saw light from the sun through slatted windows, heard the murmurs of disease, of tragedy.

With effort Nichol pushed herself into a sitting position. Her voice was thin and distant. Her demeanor unreadable. She didn't smile, was not affectionate. "I don't know, Royce, if I'm going back. I should stay here." She looked at the doctor.

He reminded himself that she was very ill. "You cannot say this. I love you. I am bringing you home."

"Where is my home?"

He wondered if she was delirious from a fever.

"Of course your home is with me. And the children."

Dr. LaFontaine excused herself, invited Royce to look at the rest of the hospital after his visit with Nichol and to have a conversation about the possible uses of Royce's $1,000,000 gift. She left the ward.

"I am needed here. I don't want the life I had in Calabasas. There I created an entitled Nichol. I have a renewed perspective being here."

Royce stood up. His face held great sorrow, but not resignation. "Why are you saying this? Has someone said something to you about your life with us? Or about the $1,000,000 donation? Did I make a mistake making it in your name?" His eyes were clouded and he set his jaw, determined to argue successfully in his favor. He looked at his fingers. How could one be prepared to hear and respond to a dispassionate rejection of one's life? "Nichol," he whispered, "my divorce is final. I brought the paperwork with me to show you." He began to reach inside his jacket.

Nichol weakly held out her right arm. Her hand shook. "No, don't. Please. Royce, I have broken my heart ten times over with my decision." Tears fell onto her cheeks, and she made no attempt to wipe them away.

Royce looked for a tissue box that did not exist. He retrieved his suit jacket handkerchief and blotted her cheeks. "Decision? How can you reach a decision that affects our entire family without talking to me about your intentions?" Royce stopped using his inside voice. "Nichol, I love you. Teddy, Sophie, Tru, we all love you. My mother is in the hospital. She needs you. She was in an accident. We have been existing since you left, not living. I thought you were waiting for my divorce to be final. Do you not love me?"

She cried harder, taking in gulps of fetid air. "I waited for you."

He felt the weight of her words. A lifetime in those four words. Their unhappiness created its own climate. They were silent for a couple of minutes.

"And then the earthquake," she said. "Here I think I save lives, instead of living in—" She stopped crying and looked at him as though she wanted him to fill in the blank.

"In what? Living in decadence? Sin, hell, disgusting materialism?"

Nichol patted the bed next to her. "Come, sit with me again." And when he did not move, she said, "Please." Sighing, a sigh full of meaning, but he could not conjure up that meaning.

Royce hesitated and then sat down and took her hand. So thin, so weak. He had been in too many hospitals in the past year: his father, his mother, and now Nichol.

"Instead of living in a constant state of limbo," she said.

What she said was true, and he was responsible for the truth. It was on his watch. He knew she would stay in Haiti. It hit him that he should not have come. He patted her hand, consoling her, consoling himself, and reconciling her decision with what he wanted. The heat was giving him a headache.

Royce was allowed to take Nichol onto the hospital grounds in a wheelchair. When he helped her get from the bed to the wheelchair, he saw that under her blue knee-length cotton hospital gown, she had lost weight and muscle mass. He thought at least twenty pounds. He did not think she was the type of woman who would be happy she had lost that much weight. Why did he not know, after all those years?

A nurse attached the IV pole to the wheelchair. Royce walked the pale, wilted Nichol on a pathway around the hospital. Gravel crunched under the wheels, and Royce had to push with some effort to get traction. They walked from shade to sunlight to shade. The sun was brutal. He put on his sunglasses and looked up at the sky. There was just a veil of white-hot light.

Royce watched people navigate the pathways in various degrees of illness. Some stood on the walkways next to the pale blue and yellow cinderblock buildings or sat on the ground on small squares of cloth. A woman sat under a tree, nursing a baby. A hunched over elderly woman with a short broom swept the dirt that surrounded the walkway. Briefly, Royce wondered why the broom did not have a longer handle.

They were more comfortable tackling the conversation without looking at each other, him talking to the top of her head. The dialogue was more productive and garnered no tears from either of them. They talked and talked, back and forth, back and forth. He told her what had happened to his mother and to Tamra, told her he was reconciling himself to having the baby for the foreseeable future.

"She's never going to be gone, is she?" Nichol said.

He said nothing. She was probably correct.

"Please reconsider. Please come home."

She looked at him and then at the hospital grounds. Moments passed. "This is what I can promise you," she said and held up a finger for each of her points.

He thought she was better organized than he was, and she was sick.

"I will stay in the hospital here until the doctor says I can fly. Then I will go back to Calabasas until after the New Year. I do want to see my girls. I have to hold them."

He noticed that she did not refer to Calabasas as home. He thought, but did not say, that when she got to Calabasas, she would not want to leave. There he would have home court advantage.

"I will return here in January, and I am staying for an indefinite period," she said.

He breathed in through his mouth and was beginning to speak. The smell of charcoal from someone's cooking nearby reminded him of the donkey carrying charcoal in burlap bags on the road.

"That is non-negotiable," she said, blocking whatever it was he was going to say. She delivered the laser-like words in a breathy voice.

"I admit I have no appreciation for the desolation Haiti experienced as a result of the quake, except on an intellectual level," he said. "I will educate myself about the myriad problems in the country." He knew he was back in asshole-speak.

"I want the girls to come here," she said. "Sophie would come right now if I told her it's okay. I want them to see my Haitian world."

"I do not know. Do you think it is safe for them?" He remembered Port-au-Prince earlier in the day. He could see Sophie here. Tru probably. She would go nuts for the children. Teddy. She would want to know where to shop.

"The country collectively is going through post-traumatic stress now, and people are wound tightly. But when the country gets back to 'normal,'" she made air quotes, "it is safe as long as they listen to me."

"All right, all right. We can talk about that when the country is—as you say—normal. I brought you something that belongs to you," he said.

"My—?"

"Your ring." He stopped the wheelchair and faced her. He reached for her left hand.

She moved her hand away from him. "I'm coming back here, Royce. You have to know that."

"I will stay here with you until you are well enough to fly," he said, putting the ring on the tip of his thumb.

"No, you won't stay here. You have businesses to run, and you just told me Evelyn is in the hospital. You can't stay here." She pointed to his thumb. "Put the ring in your pants pocket and do not take it out of that pocket until your plane leaves the ground."

"Will you wear it on your right hand now?"

"Are you paying attention to what is in front of you?" She looked over her shoulder. The movement made her wince. "Do you think I could wear what must be a multi-million dollar ring in this hospital?" She swept one arm out, taking in the grounds.

She successfully eviscerated him without even making a cut. All the clichés from all the heartbreak songs flooded Royce's brain.

He felt momentarily chagrined. "I do not understand how you choose to live in such obvious poverty instead of Los Angeles. I understand the desire to serve this country because of the great need following the earthquake, but to want to stay indefinitely, to want to *live here*. No, I cannot fathom that." He knew he had spoken harshly. But he had spoken honestly.

"Bend down so I can look at your face when I talk to you," she said.

He was surprised she could be so adamant while whispering. He parked the wheelchair in the shade of a walnut tree, swept leaves off a bench made of stones and sat down. He heard children's voices, looked around and saw them playing soccer. As they ran up and down the makeshift field, dust rose into the air, momentarily blurring them.

She leaned forward in the chair, putting her thin arms on her thighs. "There are different kinds of poverty, Royce. I don't understand how you can live in poverty in Los Angeles."

He sat and looked at her. There was no spark in her eyes, no dimple when she smiled, because she had not smiled since he got to the hospital. He stretched out his legs in front of him. His $2,500 shoes were covered in dust.

"You are not talking about skid row poverty, are you? What kind of poverty do I live in?" He was afraid of the answer. He dipped his head as if to prevent blows.

"Let's not do this," she said. "Haven't we done this enough?" She reached out her hand and put it on his knee.

"I do not know what you are referring to. Tell me."

The heat shimmered. He could see it, as it moved like a fog through the grounds of the hospital. He stood up and looked down at her. He crossed his arms.

She slumped down in the wheelchair, her shoulders hunched. "Please take me back to my bed."

The woman was still nursing her baby. Her shirt was bunched around her waist. A toddler, wearing shorts and a faded Harvard t-shirt that hung down to his knees, had his arms around her neck.

"Please. I need to know," he said.

She was quiet for a moment, and he wondered if she had stopped listening.

"All right. Poverty of the spirit. I know that is not a satisfactory answer, but that's what I feel. There is an absence in the house of joy and appreciation for the abundance of blessings you have. I know you work hard to protect your individual assets and the assets of your trust, and there is evidence in the house reflecting your success: the cars, the sheer size of the house, the yacht. Does ownership of these things make you happy?"

He was stumped. Does not one get joy from driving a Maserati?

"Do you love me, Nichol?"

"Yes," she said.

"Here, put your arms around my neck." He put his hands around her waist to sit her up straight in the chair. He felt her ribs under his hands. "Do you want to marry me?"

"Yes."

"*Will* you marry me?" He continued to hold her, their faces touching. He thought if he could get that ring out again, she would say yes.

"Can you be married to another woman who flies in and out of your life?" she said.

"I do not...I think...Dammit, Nichol. Cannot we work this out when you get home?"

She turned her face away from him.

"Oh, I have stuck my foot in it again. I am sorry, very sorry." He stopped. He was determined to understand what Nichol needed. "I have decided. I am not leaving."

She shook her head.

"No, do not dismiss me. I am staying here. I will wait until you are well enough to travel, and then I will take you home...uh, to Calabasas. I will abide by your decision to spend part of the year in Haiti." Capitulation was not in Royce's dictionary, yet he had agreed to follow this woman's mandate. He loved her, and, he was beginning to understand, that meant allowing, no, agreeing, to her terms.

"I think you should leave, but I hear you are determined to stay." She looked at him and held her arms up to him. He thought immediately of Tru when she was a toddler. "Here," Tru would say. "So," Nichol continued, "I will agree that you are staying until I can travel, and you agree I will be coming back to Haiti."

He took one of her hands and shook it, as though he was closing a deal. He smiled. "A gentleman's agreement."

He wheeled her back toward the hospital. The woman with the baby and toddler were gone, as was the woman sweeping the dirt. The children continued to play and kick up dust.

When they got to the ward, two of the patients were awake. They looked up as he wheeled Nichol into the room.

"Bon jou," one of the women said.

"Bon jou," Nichol said.

Royce nodded his head.

"Please take the ring," he whispered into her ear.

She shook her head "no."

"Will you ever wear it?" He helped her back into bed and figured out how to attach the IV pole onto Nichol's bed. She laid her head on the pillow.

"I hope so."

"We can get married when you come home. Recuperate for as long as you need to, and then we can have a wedding with us and the girls." He sat down on her bed and feeling the mattress wondered how she could lie on it comfortably.

"You've got it all planned out, don't you?" she said, without rancor.

He whispered in her ear, "I do not have anything figured out. I will accept any terms you list. Promise me you will marry me."

Nichol closed her eyes. She did not say anything for a moment. She lay so still he wondered if she had fallen asleep. In the silence he heard people talking. He was able to hear individual voices. Then she nodded her head slightly and opened her eyes.

"I am very tired. I can't talk anymore, but yes."

"I love you, Nic. We will get you well. We will take care of you." He leaned in and hugged her shoulders.

"Please, Royce. No more today."

"Oh, all right. All right." He did not know how to

stop talking. He wanted to keep the connection with her, was afraid of what could happen when he left her. "I am going to sit here with you. I will not talk. I will just sit here."

That is exactly what he did, in the blistering heat. He wiped the sweat from his face with his handkerchief. A nurse walked into the room. "Bring a cold washcloth for her head. And a bottle of water," Royce said. Pause. "Please."

"We have set out water for her in that pitcher. Her cup should be on the table there, next to her bed."

Royce watched Nichol drift off to sleep, her face, although wrecked with disease, was lovely. He wasn't sure he could get used to her hair, but, maybe when she got home, she would cut it. A wild, bohemian Afro didn't suit her. Looking at her plain cotton gown, he imagined her in classy Ralph Lauren and Michael Kors. When she got home.

Royce looked up at the windows high on the wall as the country fell into darkness, with a feeling of jealousy. Jealousy of thousands of strangers who had Nichol's heart and energy. He knit his fingers together as though he were going to pray. He brought his hands to his lips and blew into his fingers. He blinked fast to keep the tears at bay. Three weeks ago, he and the girls had talked to Nichol. She had talked about the seemingly impossible task of Haiti's recovery. She said there could not be renewal until all the 200,000 plus dead were buried and the injured healed and homes built for the newly homeless. Did she think she had to accomplish that all on her own?

She told him she loved him. He was able to contain himself with that thought. He looked at his phone and was pleased to see he was connected to the hospital's Wi-Fi. He read through hundreds of texts and then saw one from Lew that got his attention: "Got call from Det. Griswold, L.A. County Sheriff. Jason Gerard identified after being in car accident, driving Ferrari at high rate of speed. Crashed into Bentley. Dead at the scene." *That takes care of that*, he thought, and wondered for just a moment if Jason had acquired the Ferrari with his mother's money.

Nichol was asleep. Royce stood up to find Dr. LaFontaine. He needed somewhere to shower and sleep. One million dollars, he thought ungenerously, ought to get him a bed. He was instantly sorry he had thought that.

He walked slowly down a hallway, like an old man. His body could not handle the psychic punishment he had exacted on it. He found a secretary who told him the doctor was on the children's ward, but wanted to know if he would like to have dinner with her. She would be available in an hour. He walked outside. It was raining, and the wetness tamped down the dust. He stood under an overhang and watched people scurry through the weather.

He thought about the trappings of the world Nichol rejected. The trappings of *his* world. Poverty of the spirit. That's what Nichol said Royce was living with. He thought about what she was telling him and suddenly the truth of her words—poverty of the spirit—pierced his heart. He had so much: a garage filled with expensive cars, a mansion filled with rooms, grounds that would shortly include an Olympic-sized pool, closets filled with bespoke suits, a yacht with a staff. And he had so little: a mother who suffered from dementia and a broken arm and hip; a teenaged daughter who was rebellious despite, or because of, his wealth; an ex-wife whose desires could never be satisfied, who took advantage of him and his family. A child of another man living in his nursery. Poverty of the spirit.

He had to make changes, had to think differently. And he would. He would learn about the people of the world who suffered from the other kind of poverty. Of course he knew that poverty existed around the world, but he had to *feel* the suffering that Nichol served. He imagined sitting with her on the brick patio while they enjoyed a glass of California wine. He imagined her telling him about her experiences in the field and holding babies in the hospital. He had so much to learn so he could understand the world through Nichol's heart.

ABOUT THE AUTHOR

Kathleen is a former California attorney, with litigation experience and an elder law practice, where she represented victims of financial and physical abuse.

She has an MFA in creative writing from Antioch University Los Angeles and a certificate in fiction writing from UCLA/Extension. She has been writing for nine years. Her first novel *At Death's Door* has been published on Amazon. Her short stories, essays, and poetry have been published in *Emrys Journal, Lunch Ticket, Montreal Review, Lowestoft Chronicle, bird's thumb, Catapult, Bewildering Stories, The Poetry Jar, Rose Red Review* and *Arcadia*. She was a finalist in *Glimmer Train's* open fiction contest.

As a board member of International Child Care - USA, she has traveled to Haiti and the Dominican Republic. Kathleen volunteered as an attorney in Miami and Los Angeles, assisting Haitian refugees making asylum applications to the United States.

Made in United States
Orlando, FL
30 May 2024